THE **GIRLS** OF THE **GOLDEN WEST**

James Ward Lee

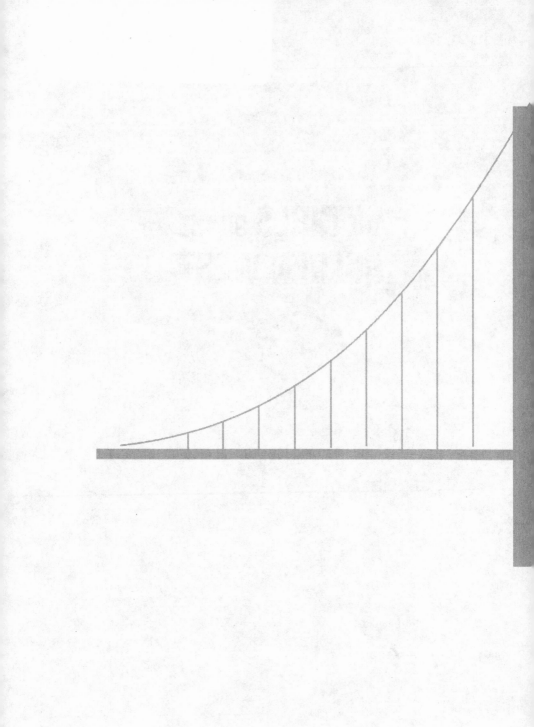

THE **GIRLS** OF THE **GOLDEN WEST**

A NOVEL

JAMES WARD LEE

Fort Worth, Texas

LIBRARY OF CONGRESS CATALOGING-IN-PUBLICATION DATA

Names: Lee, James Ward, 1931- author.

Title: The girls of the Golden West / James Ward Lee.

Description: Fort Worth, Texas : TCU Press, [2017] | Description based on print version record and CIP data provided by publisher; resource not viewed.

Identifiers: LCCN 2017017816 (print) | LCCN 2017018910 (ebook) | ISBN 9780875656779?(pbk. :?alk. paper) | ISBN 9780875656694?(cloth :?alk. paper) | ISBN 9780875656762

Subjects: LCSH: Retired teachers--Fiction.

Classification: LCC PS3612.E2238 (ebook) | LCC PS3612.E2238 G57 2017 (print)
 | DDC 813/.6—dc23

LC record available at https://urldefense.proofpoint.com/v2/url?u=https-3A__lccn. loc.gov_2017017816&d=DQIFAg&c=7Q-FWLBTAxn3T_E3HWrzGYJrC4RvUoWD rzTlitGRH_A&r=O2eiy819IcwTGuw-vrBGiVdmhQxMh2yxeggw9qlTUDE&m=fh me2LneOTxUb93MARtTMLrWhuLohPUa5tLjmy4DoyU&s=SYHt39HsKhyefp36m toxS13nVdVxvdBo701FaCLk-rM&e=

TCU Box 298300
Fort Worth, Texas 76129

817.257.7822
WWW.PRS.TCU.EDU

To order books: 1.800.826.8911

TEXT AND JACKET DESIGN BY ALLIGATOR TREE GRAPHICS

FOR JEFF GUINN, FRIEND AND MENTOR

PART I

BICENTENNIAL
FEVER

CHAPTER 1

I make it a point never to answer my door. Nothing good ever comes of it. It's nearly always somebody wanting to sell magazine subscriptions or paint my house number on the curb or get me signed up for one of the new off-brand churches that seem to be springing up all over Bodark Springs.

Last night about 7:30 the knocking became so insistent that I peeked out behind the curtains in the front room and saw three women who showed no signs of going away. The two I recognized were Ruby Lathem and Frances Bailey, old students of mine from long ago and now stalwarts of the Eastis County Historical Society. I didn't get a good look at the other woman, but I was pretty sure she was the graduate student from UT who wanted to interview me. Ruby had bored me for years. She was tedious back when she was a student at John Bell Hood High School. Now she droned on at every meeting of the local historical society. If a thing could be talked to death, Ruby was your woman.

I knew I was in for it, but I opened the door wide and said, "Evening, ladies, please come in."

Frances was widely known as Ruby's sidekick. Frances is Smiley Burnett to Ruby's Gene Autry. She probably sings about as well as old Smiley too.

Frances was very tall and built in such a way as to attract men of all ages. Her hair was an impossible shade of red—henna, I think they call it. She had burned through four husbands. Two died of natural causes, one was executed at the state prison in Huntsville, and one survived and lives here in town with his third wife.

Ruby was shorter than Frances and trim, not a bad looking woman for near sixty. Her hair was dark but flecked with gray, and she still had the figure I remembered from her days at the high school, though I wasn't supposed to notice back then. It was, even in those days of enforced modesty, hard not to notice a—oh, better leave it at that. Ruby never married, but she had a son that everybody in town thought was her little brother. People knew that she disappeared from town about twenty-five years ago and went off with her mother to French Lick, Indiana, for two years. They came back with little Donald, who was about a year and a half old. But most didn't tumble to the fact that the baby might be hers. Old Ida Lathem told everyone that the baby was hers and that she'd married and divorced in Indiana. My late wife knew better, knew that the baby belonged to Ruby. She even said she knew who the father was. I can't remember how she knew such a piece of desperate gossip. Most people believed Ida or said they did, at least when Ruby's "brother" Donald was around.

As the years passed, Donald began to look more and more like Buster Cooper, the man who'd squired Ruby around all through high school. Old Bert Little, the horse trader, always said, "Did you ever see a bastard that didn't look just like his daddy?" Even people who believed that Donald was Ida's son remarked at the resemblance between Buster Cooper and Donald Lathem.

But I'm wandering again. I've been doing more and more of that in recent years.

Back to the present. The other woman was much younger than Frances and Ruby. I judged her to be in her midtwenties. When I got a good look at her, my mind reeled. I can't ever remember a shock like this. I thought I was seeing Elizabeth Denney, a woman I'd loved forty years ago.

Ruby said, "Are you all right, Professor? You look like you've just seen a ghost."

4

I had, but I forced myself to come back to 1971. Now I didn't see Liz, who had to be at least sixty by now, or, damn, near seventy! But I saw an equally beautiful woman who could have passed for her sister or daughter. This young woman was no doubt what we used to call a real "looker." She was as tall as Frances and built the way Ruby was in her girlhood—and the way Liz Denney was. Her hair was red—not henna like Frances's, or like Liz's for that matter. The new woman's hair reminded me of the red in Virginia Johnston's hair. I was desperately in love with Ginny Johnston back before the turn of the century. But before I could get up my nerve to propose, she ran off with Adolph Hunsiker and was never seen in these parts again. I got over my broken heart before Easter and was off in serious love with Elva Brooks. And after Elva—

There I go, drifting off again, but this time it's a pleasant remembrance of things long past. Or not.

Ruby introduced us. She said, "Professor Adams—"

I stopped her and said, "Now, Ruby I'm not a professor and never was. I was a high school teacher forever, and then I had the misfortune to be made principal—again forever."

"But everybody used to call you Professor Adams."

"Yes, and they called old Emmett Jones 'Professor' and he taught shop and drove the school bus. I didn't answer to it then and I don't now. So go on with your introduction."

"Well, Mr. Adams, I'd like to have you meet Miss Annie Baxter from Austin. Miss Baxter, please meet Mr. John Quincy Adams the Second, our town's most distinguished resident."

I stopped her. "She means the oldest person in Bodark Springs, maybe in the county."

"No," Ruby said, "Mrs. Estell Bagley up near Cooks Springs is a hundred, so you aren't nearly the oldest."

And I said, "I guess you don't read the Bodark Springs *Weekly Star*. Mrs. Bagley died a week or two ago. It was all in that silly column that Mrs. Angell sends in to the paper."

"'Tidbits from the Springs,'" Frances pointed out.

Ruby Lathem brought things back to the subject at hand. "Professor Adams—sorry, Mr. Adams—Miss Baxter is here from Austin and—"

I interrupted, "Don't you mean Ms. Baxter? They don't say 'Miss' any more. They don't even say 'Mrs.' unless the person is ancient like the late Mrs. Bagley—and preferably dead."

"Sorry. Ms. Baxter's here from Austin on behalf of the Texas State Historical Society and the Texas Folklore Society helping us get ready to celebrate the Bicentennial in five years. Here it is 1971, and we haven't done a thing to get ready for the country's two hundredth birthday."

Actually, I knew what Annie Baxter was here for, but I preferred to keep my counsel, so I went on the defensive. "And you have come to threaten me that you want me to ride in a parade dressed as Benjamin Franklin. You hope I'll still be alive in 1976 when I'll be an even one hundred years old and can be paraded around as the oldest crock in town. It's no secret that I was born on the 4th of July in 1876, though I'm sure all of you are about to say that I don't look ninety-five years old."

Ruby and Frances said, in unison, "No, no, you don't. You could pass for—uh—"

Ms. Baxter stood silent, which I thought spoke well for her. Damn, everything about her was like Liz, even her unwillingness to flatter an old fool. "No, I couldn't pass for any age you are fumbling for to flatter me with. I'm ninety-five and look it and feel it and have the wrinkles to prove it. So go on with your story about the upcoming Bicentennial and my role in it if I'm still alive. And I plan to be. I wouldn't miss it for the world. So go ahead, Ruby."

"Well, Professor—oops—"

"Hey, let's stop right there. All of you please call me John Q. If you do that, you won't be tempted to stumble around for a title for me. And that includes you Ms. Baxter. Sorry to interrupt. You were about to make some point."

"Well, the long and short of it, John Q.—I'll never get used to that—is we want you to write a history of Eastis County."

"Oh, no! Not me. I may have taught history for two lifetimes, but that doesn't make me Samuel Eliot Morrison or W. J. Cash. It doesn't even make me Margaret Mitchell, whose *Gone with the Wind* passes in these parts as the real history of the South."

Ms. Baxter looked at the two other ladies. "Do you all think that book is true to Civil War times?"

"Oh, my, yes," said Frances.

6

"It is! I read the book and have seen the movie three times," Ruby burst out. "It really tells the story of the Old South."

"Did I pass either one of you in American history? Margaret Mitchell is about as true to the South as Frank Yerby."

"Who?" all three said in unison.

I said, "Never mind. It speaks well for you that you don't know Frank Yerby. He wrote *The Foxes of Harrow*, and it's as phony as *GWTW*. If I stumble around and try to write a history of Eastis County or even Bodark Springs, I'll make a bigger fool of myself than Mitchell or Yerby. No, thank you, ladies, I'm not in for such a project. Now, how about if I make us a cup of tea so we can get my proposed authorship out of everybody's head. I may even have some cake."

Frances said, "I don't suppose you have any sherry, do you?"

Ruby jumped in to save her friend from embarrassment and, of course, made it worse. "Oh, come on, Frances, you know Eastis County is dry. Professor—I mean John Q.—wouldn't break the law."

"What law's that Ruby? The statute of limitations has run out on anything I do. It comes with my great and decrepit age. Now let's see, Frances. Let me look in this hutch and see what might lurk there. Oh, yes, I have some Harvey's Bristol Cream and some amontillado. Which do you prefer?"

"The one with the long name."

"Amontillado. You must have read the Edgar Allan Poe story 'The Cask of Amontillado' when you took English. One man walls another up in a wine cellar after offering him some rare amontillado from Spain or somewhere. Remember?"

"Oh, sure," Frances said.

I knew she didn't remember, so I said, "Okay. Sherry for all—wet or dry county."

I got the glasses and the amontillado and began pouring the sherry into the tiny glasses my first wife thought so perfect for drinking sherry. Little glasses that won't hold more than a good thimble full. I had my own proper sherry glasses, but the tiny ones seemed right for these three. Nobody declined the illegal drink, so I toasted the trio and took a sip.

"Now, I'm not about to write a history of Eastis County or anywhere else. I have at least four good reasons. Maybe five if I put my mind to it. Anyway, I don't plan to waste five good years dredging up tawdry facts about farmers and bootleggers from this county when I could do something worthwhile in the ten or twenty or thirty years I have left. I mean to read all of Balzac and re-read Jane Austen for the sixth time."

"But John Q., who else is better for the task?" Frances asked.

I shook my head. "There must be fifty people in this town willing to scribble for the next five years going on and on about the hardy cotton farmers and drugstore owners who made Bodark Springs what it is. Whatever that is. No, I hate to be churlish, but no."

Ruby said, "Well, we were afraid that might be your answer, and that's why Miss—I mean Ms.—Baxter is with us. She's on a grant from the Texas State Historical Association and the Texas Folklore Society to produce an oral history of this part of the state. She's willing to spend whatever time it takes here in Eastis County to get our little patch of the world down on tape."

"On what?"

Ruby said, "Tape. You know, a tape recorder."

"Oh, I thought they used wire recorders for taking down what people say." I knew better. I'm not always the fogey I pretend to be. It keeps people like Ruby and her sidekick Frances on their toes.

Now that I reflected on the idea of Ms. Baxter being here who knows how long to remind me day after day of the lost love of Liz Denney, I wasn't sure whether that would be a joy or a heartbreak.

Frances said, "Everybody in the city says you're the smartest man in the county, and—"

I interrupted, "No, Frances, my old student, I'm not even the smartest man on this block. Old Doctor Lowry, the chiropractor, is smarter than I am. And then there are two doctors, a pharmacist, and old Earley Leonard the colored blacksmith—all of them smarter than I am."

Ruby jumped in, "Colored? Oh, Professor—I mean John Q.—you are behind the times. They don't say 'colored' for colored people—I mean black people—anymore."

"Have you forgotten what century I come from? I still say colored when I want to. And I belong to the NAACP, which, unless somebody has changed it since I got my last bill, is an association of colored people."

Ms. Baxter joined the fray, apparently hoping to deflect this sudden detour into what she feared might be rampant racism. "Well, I'm new to town, but everybody says you are super smart. May I ask you a question?"

"Of course. If I don't have to tell secrets or the whole truth."

She pushed a lock of red hair aside and said, "Are you a descendent of President John Adams?"

I laughed. "People new to town always ask that. The answer is no. My father, who hoped to add some glory to the family name and fool somebody into thinking we're of the 'quality,' named me John Quincy Adams II. It satisfied his plan for aggrandizement and may partly have been a cruel joke. Maybe he thought adding 'the Second' would fool somebody into thinking I was old John Quincy's nephew or something. I hated the name all through my early years and swore that I'd go to the courthouse and change it when the old man died. But then I went into the army while he was still alive and have been stuck as John Quincy Adams ever since."

Annie asked, "Was that during World War I?"

I said, "No, I was too old for WWI. I was in the army during the Spanish-American War. I was in Cuba from 1898 till 1900. Saw that fool Theodore Roosevelt—we always pronounced it 'Ruziefelt'—lead that silly charge up San Juan Hill. He was dressed up in the uniform made for him by Brooks Brothers in New York City. I didn't charge up that hill with the 'Rough Riders' as he called 'em. I was in the infantry. I got shot in the leg, and old Teddy didn't get a scratch."

"It sounds like you didn't think too highly of Teddy Roosevelt," Annie Baxter said.

"I always thought General Leonard Wood was the real hero of Cuba. He even signed up TR's 'Rough Rider' cowboys in the lobby of the Menger Hotel in San Antonio. Old Teddy got all the glory and landed in the White House. All Leonard Wood got was a fort named for him in Kansas or somewhere. After I got shot in the leg, I spent the last year of the war working in a field laundry. I was a real hero of the clean uniform brigade."

Frances asked, "Did they give you a Purple Heart?"

"No, I got some kind of purple ribbon. That and two bits will buy me

9

a cup of coffee at the Busy Bee Cafe. I might've got a Purple Heart if I'd waited seventeen or eighteen years to get shot. I hear the Purple Heart was invented during World War I.

"But Ms. Baxter, I can't imagine what you want to talk to me about. How do you know I know anything that will thrill the Folklore Society or my old pals in the Historical Association—if I still have any friends from that august body? Old Earley Leonard the blacksmith can tell you some Jim Crow stories that will get you a prize from the NAACP. And there's a bootlegger up in the north part of the county—way up on the Red River—who can give you the lowdown on the very most respectable citizens of this little county. All I'll do is ramble on like the doddering old fool that my sons suspect me of being."

Frances said, "John Q., nobody in this town thinks of you as 'doddering,' as you call it. If Ms. Baxter can get you to telling stories, she'll have to send to Austin for more tapes. You know every tale ever told in this county. Ain't that right, Ruby?"

Ruby jumped in. "Oh yes, Ms. Baxter, the Professor—John Q.—is a real raconteur, and he still remembers everything he ever heard. Why, I remember just the other week at the Society he told all about funeral customs he remembered from childhood."

I faked taking umbrage, "And so, since I have one foot in the grave, you think I'm the right person to talk about death and destruction? I don't find that flattering at all."

Ms. Baxter's eyes lighted up. "Those are the kinds of stories I want to get on tape, stories that capture the culture of the state—or this part of the state at least. Please let me spend as long as it takes to get a real human picture of Northeast Texas from a real person who remembers it all."

I still couldn't decide whether or not to submit to this reincarnation of Liz Denney and get my heart re-broke. Maybe I should just send her away, but then maybe I'd love having a Liz surrogate here to remind me of the year and the several summers I was so totally in love.

I decided.

"Well, as Frances and Ruby know, I do like to talk, so if you'll bring your tape machine around when you're ready, I'll tell some lies and some truths. How long, Ms. Baxter, do you plan to glean my teeming brain?"

She became businesslike. "First, if I'm to call you John Q., you're going to have to call me Annie. Second, I plan to stay in Bodark Springs as long as it takes to get you to really let go and tell me how it was in all the years you've lived here. Ninety-five, you say. And, third, what is that you said about your 'teeming brain'? I think I've read that somewhere."

"Oh, it's Keats. A sonnet. In the school books it's usually listed by the first line—'When I Have Fears that I May Cease to Be' and goes on with the part I quoted—"before my pen has gleaned my teeming brain.' I just butchered the line to see if you tumbled to it. Congratulations."

Since I was tired of Ruby and Frances and their twittering, I said, "Let's let the ladies you came with go away so we can set the ground rules for this inquisition. I noticed that you came in two cars, so I suppose Ruby and Frances came together and you drove that little bitty gray car I saw at the curb."

"Yes, that's my Toyota Corona, and it's big enough for me." She couldn't keep the touch of cattiness out of her voice when she said, "And it doesn't drink gas the way Ms. Lathem's Lincoln must."

Ruby said, "Gas is cheap. As long as it stays below fifty cents a gallon, I can afford my Lincoln, thank you."

She seemed a little snippy her own self when Annie—I've got to get used to calling her that if she is going to be haunting me this summer—mentioned the gas guzzler. I wonder what Annie will say when she sees my 1940 LaSalle and my new Buick Electra. They guzzle with the best—or worst—of them.

I ushered Ruby and Frances out the front door, "Ladies, thank you for coming and thank you for bringing Annie to sort out my memories or whatever she thinks is in this head of mine. This gray, unbowed head. Ruby, I'm sure you remember that—'Shoot if you must this old gray head, but spare your country's flag, she said.'" I had substituted in their English class for a semester.

"Well, I can't be sure. Is it from Robert Frost? He had gray hair."

I slapped my forehead. "Oh, Ruby, Ruby, where'd I go wrong with you?"

Frances broke in, "I remember, Professor. It was a poem called 'Barbara' Something, 'Barbara Fritchie.' Right?"

"You're right, but don't call me—"

Frances said, "Sorry, John Q."

I patted her on the back. "Anyway, I hope you made an A in my class. Now ladies, leave me with Annie so we can plot against you two and all the rest of Eastis County."

I was glad to send Ruby and Frances on their way. I'd had enough of them in four years of high school. I taught both of them history—American, Texas, English, and world civilizations. And I wrestled them through parts of several English classes. Once I was principal, I found myself teaching English when a teacher had a baby or ran away to get married or got fired for fooling with a student or just got sick. Even though I was trained to teach history, I often thought I did better in the scattered English classes I taught. I don't remember much about Ruby or Frances in English classes, but I sure remembered how dull they found my history classes, and how dull I found them.

I was off in some reverie again when Annie brought me back with a cough and a question.

"How long did you teach at the—what is it, John Something—High School?"

"John Bell Hood. You should know about him if you majored in history at—where was it?"

She said, "Baylor as an undergraduate. Then at the University of Texas for my master's. Now I'm in the dissertation stage for my PhD at Texas. And I perfectly well know who John Bell Hood was. I just didn't quite catch it before. Anyway, I don't always get everything when I'm this nervous, Mr.—I'm sorry, I mean John Q."

I tried to put her at ease. "Don't be nervous with me. Once we get to know each other a little, you will find, I hope, that I'm not an ogre. I have an act I do with people like Ruby and Frances. They expect it of me. So you plan to stay in Bodark Springs as long as it takes to do whatever it is that you plan to do with my aged carcass? Are you thinking of a jointly written memoir or something? If so, I'm not interested in dragging out my life for the public to jeer at. I was a school teacher and then a principal and not some kind of movie star."

Annie protested. "No, no, I just want you to tell me all you can think of about this county and maybe this part of the state. I don't mean to pry into your life."

I said, "Then why'd you wonder how long I'd taught at JBH High School? Isn't that a way to get me to tell you all about me and my possibly scandalous life?"

"Oh, my! No, sir, I just wondered since you apparently taught Ms. Lathem and Ms. Bailey back when they were girls that you must've been there a long time and knew hundreds and hundreds of students who make up the fabric of this part of Texas." She ran out of breath after her long sentence.

I laughed. "The 'fabric of this part of Texas' you say. You do have a way of putting things that I find refreshing. I think we'll get along well if we stay on the track of the region and not focus on the old resident who has lived here for an eon. Have you thought about the best place to stay while you waste your summer here?" Of course I knew all about where she planned to stay. You'd be surprised to learn how much intelligence I pick up in a day or two.

She frowned and said "Well, I have a small grant from the two associations; I'll stay at the Bidawee Motel out on the highway."

I acted as if I were appalled. "No, no, that'll never do. You must stay at the Cotton Exchange Hotel downtown. Then you can walk from there to my house. It's much nicer than that little rundown motel, and you won't need to drive to get anywhere in Bodark if you're at the hotel. When I heard that you were booked in at the Bidawee, I called my son and told him you needed to be moved to the hotel."

She was concerned. "Oh, I saw the hotel, and I fear it's far beyond the allowance TSHA and TFS have given me."

I was my old soothing self. "Don't worry about the cost. The Cotton Exchange will give you the same rate as the Bidawee Motel. And you'll be safer there. No telling who comes and goes along Highway 82 and haunts that old rundown motel. I work at the Cotton Exchange a few hours a week, and I can fix it for you to have a bedsit there."

She didn't know the term. "A bedsit?"

"It's what passes for a suite in a big hotel. You'll have a bedroom, a sitting room, a barely functioning kitchenette, and a pretty nice bathroom."

She was puzzled. "And you can fix this at the state rate? You must have some connections in this town. And you work there? I thought you were—what?—ninety-five years old. You must've retired some years ago."

"I *am* ninety-five, and I'm long retired. But my oldest son owns the Cotton Exchange, and I go in to relieve him a day or two a week. I don't have to change the linens or vacuum the floors. I just sit at the front desk or lounge in the manager's office. Even an ancient can do that. And it gives me a chance to see a few people who drift in to see if I'm still alive or ask me questions to test my senility. And I like eating at the hotel's restaurant, which you'll find to be as good as anything in Waco if not in Austin."

Annie was overcome. She said, "Prof—John Q.—that sounds wonderful, I don't know how to thank you. The room they assigned me looked pretty bad. It smelled of smoke even though it was labeled 'non-smoking.' And the noise of the highway was deafening. I'll go and get my things."

Reliable old John Q. again. "No need. When I called my son, he had Maybelline, a woman who works at the front desk, go over and get your suitcases from the motel. Since you hadn't unpacked, it was quick and easy. He is now installing you in Suite 307 at the Cotton Exchange. I called him when Frances told me you were staying at the motel and told him you needed a better place to stay if you were in town to pick my feeble brain."

She was amazed. "Oh, John Q. you knew all along what I was here for! You probably knew as soon as we rang your doorbell. You must have spies all over town." She patted me on the shoulder. "You *are* indeed a sly old fox. And a 'feeble brain'? I don't think so."

I liked her touching me. I was off on Liz again, but I caught myself. "Everybody has to have a hobby, and foxiness is mine I guess."

She still couldn't believe I had fixed her up in a nice hotel—and on the cheap. "And your son won't mind that I'm more or less freeloading at his hotel?"

"What can he say? I *am* his father, and besides, I own as much of the hotel as he does. Did Frances and Ruby tell you that I'm rich? Rich by Eastis County standards anyway."

She looked around the room and said, "I thought you might be when I saw this house. I can't believe teaching pays well enough to own a home like yours."

"It doesn't, but my father and his brother got rich on land they home-steaded just after the Civil War. My father homesteaded 160 acres south of town, and his brother landed down near Kilgore and—"

She interrupted. "His farm struck oil, right?"

"Exactly. When he died, my father inherited, and when my father was murdered, I inherited. It's a long and painful tale, and you promised that you're not here to winkle out my life story."

She blurted out "Murdered! Did you say murdered? Murdered? No, no, I promise not to pry, but I have to admit it sounds like a whole novel waiting to be told. Are you sure you don't want us to write your life story?"

I was adamant. "Absolutely sure. Now shall I walk you down to the Cotton Exchange, or do you want to drive the little Corona? You can either park it here or in the hotel lot. Either place will be safe."

She gathered her purse and said "No, I'll drive it to the hotel. Do you still drive?—Oh, there I go again insulting you. Of course you drive. I mean—oh shit. Since you offered to walk me, I thought—So I guess I *will* go now. Are you sure you ever want to see me again? After all, I—"

I wanted to hug her but didn't. "Yes, yes, yes. I'm startin' to like you. I can't wait for you to come back tomorrow so we can start my dissection of the denizens of Eastis County and environs."

Damn my time. Was it her I wanted back or was it the memory of another beautiful woman of a long time ago? A woman I never got over even though I married after she turned me down.

I could see her relief when I said I liked her. "Thank you. I was afraid I'd stepped in it with you."

"Not at all. I admire your spirit. A little anyway. Now, go in peace; the Lord hath put away thy sins."

After Miss Annie Baxter left (once in awhile I need to resurrect the old forms of address, and Annie seemed like a *miss* as she walked down the walk to her car), I was left with my thoughts. I had some worry about what I might let slip when Miss Annie and I got the tape going. She looked so damned much like Elizabeth Denney that I knew I had to be cautious. Even at ninety-five, I have secrets. Most of my sins are venal—certainly those involving Liz—but I've learned that the statute of limitations does not run out on some things. But then Annie has promised to stay off my life and spend her time dredging up the past of my part of Texas. I'll hold her to that.

I gathered up the tiny sherry glasses and took them into the kitchen. No more amontillado for me. After this "disturbance of women"—is that a collective noun like "murder of crows" or "covey of quail"? I guess I could look it up in my worn-out old Brewer's *Dictionary of Fable and Phrase.* In any case, I now needed some fortification of spirits, or succor of Scotch, or whatever collective applies to the liquor that stimulates but does not inebriate. See what happens to an old man's spring night? As Liz used to say when I talked too much, "Oh, Johnny, how you do run on!" Even today, when I hear Tony Bennett sing "I Left My Heart in San Francisco," I get a stupid mist in my eyes.

I really have to get hold of myself.

Before I could settle down with a drink or two, I had some phone calls to make. I knew people in Austin at the Historical Association and at the university who could tell me whether I should spend a lot of my non-valuable time working with Ms. Annie Baxter. I knew people who would give me straight answers to straight questions.

Finished with my spying—and feeling slightly guilty about my prying nature—I went to the breakfront where I stored my spirits and rummaged around among the blended Scotch whiskies. My two older sons like single malt, so I keep a supply of The Glenlivet or The Balvenie for them and for old ex-sheriff Joe Langdon when he comes by. I even have a bottle of Balvenie twenty-one-year-old stashed away to be opened in case of war—or in the unlikely event that a sudden breakout of peace with honor occurs. I'm happy with Johnnie Walker Black or even JW Red if my supplies are low. Since Eastis is a dry county, I have to make an occasional run to Centennial Liquors in Dallas to keep my spirits stocked—or maybe I should say to keep my spirits up. And, yes, if Miss Baxter asks, I do still drive. The state made me renew my license by taking a test when I turned ninety. I did and passed the written and the parallel parking, and I can take another one at a hundred if Texas keeps being nasty about such things. I don't suppose I'll mention to Ms. Baxter that the testing highway patrolman, Fred Hallmark, once made an A in my English history class.

I opened the cabinet above the breakfront and shifted the glasses around until I found a Baccarat rocks glass. I had to admit—reluctantly—that this was a special night no matter what came of it. I filled the glass with ice, scrabbled around till I sighted the JW Red and then the Black that I was looking for. I don't measure because shot glasses don't hold enough to drown a termite, so I let my two or three fingers "do the walking." Now I was ready to find my recliner and begin to worry about what was to befall me at the hands of Miss—no Ms.— Annie Baxter.

I didn't answer Annie Baxter about how many years I had been at JBH High School. I started in 1906 and was finally forced out in 1961. Count that on your fingers and you can see that it comes to fifty-five years, and no state in all the fifty will let anybody stay on till age eighty-five. If they know about it. But when I was born Texas didn't issue birth certificates. And since everyone on the school board had been a student of mine and nobody much hated me, I kept staying on long after I should've been cashiered. It took the Teachers Retirement System to figure out that I'd been feeding at the trough for more than half a century and send down word to the school board that I had to go. Austin figured that I'd been teaching and principalling for fifty-three years. Earlier, I said fifty-five, but I tend to forget the two years I took off.

I didn't stay on till age eighty-five because I needed the money. As I said, I'm embarrassingly rich for a schoolteacher. I kept the job because I didn't have anything better to do. And maybe because I thought I had something to atone for. But enough of those alien thoughts. I had buried three wives, raised three sons. I liked the school and the students and the teachers—those who didn't get tempted into some form of child molestation. There were four such felons in my thirty or more years as principal. Two women and two men, and I had some doubts about two or three cases that I couldn't prove.

I slipped into my recliner and sipped the Johnnie Walker. Now I could tell myself my life story. Late spring evenings and Scotch whisky free the memory a little. I was not lucky with my three wives, but I'm very fortunate with the three middle-aged men who call me Dad or Pop or Father—or the Old Man if I've behaved outrageously. After the Spanish War, I left my father's farm and started school at the Teachers

17

College in Commerce not far from here. That was, let me see, 1901. I got my teacher's certificate in 1904 and married Esther, who was a student at the college. She was a blond beauty of eighteen when I met her. She came from Honey Grove in the next county over and was majoring in art history. We had at least a little geography between us and a little history, though her brand of history was more rarified than my political and social kind. Edward was born in 1905, and I got the job here in Bodark Springs late that year and started teaching in the fall of 1906. Charles was born in 1908 and Homer in 1912. (Notice that there is not a John Q. among them. I'm not a mean man.) Esther died of the Spanish flu in 1918. I never had much luck with the Spanish either in Cuba or here in Bodark.

I don't know how I managed three little boys, but I got help from a woman I hired and from Esther's mother. In 1926 I married Jane Wayland, who taught in the grammar school here in town, but she was killed in a car wreck four years later. I wasn't driving, thank heaven. Her brother was on his way to take her up to Cooks Springs in the north of the county where her parents lived. He failed to stop at a railroad crossing. It wasn't even the T and P, but a little trunk-line railroad run by one of the lumber companies. Her family was having a party and I was to take the boys up the next day. Maybe if I'd been driving my new 1930 Model A, I would've seen or heard the train. I almost drove myself crazy feeling guilty for not driving her up that day. Now I don't suffer over it, but some nights as the clock strikes four, I see the car and the train and what the crash did to a good woman and her careless brother.

I didn't marry again till 1946, when I was seventy and Barbara, the woman I married, was sixty. She was not a teacher, but worked in the Eastis County Clerk's Office. We were married for four years when she came down with ovarian cancer and didn't survive the operation at the hospital in Sherman. That ended my marriage career. And high time, since I had such bad luck with wives. Maybe I'm a curse on women. I hope not, but I'm sure some people here in town think when a man buries three wives he's either careless or clearly under a dark cloud.

I don't plan to lay out this little sketch of life for Annie, but I have a feeling that Frances and Ruby have already told her at least the bare facts of my life. They can tell her that my sons turned out well. Edward is now sixty-six, Charles is sixty-three, and Homer is a lad of fifty-nine. Ed went to law school and made a world of money in Dallas suing corporations. He got so rich he retired in 1965 at sixty and came back to Bodark and bought the Cotton Exchange Hotel. I don't know why, but that's what he wanted to do, and I went in with him so we could spend a fortune in renovations to make it the finest hotel between Texarkana and Dallas—even if it's never very full and barely breaks even. It broke even about three years ago and shocked Eddie and me. But neither of us cares. We just like having the hotel in such good shape and the attached restaurant that's always being given stars by the rating agencies—not Michelin of course; we're not that good. Charles loved the farm that his grandfather homesteaded down close to the little town of Eden. That farm made a lot of money off cotton until the boll weevil came all the way from Mexico just a-looking for a home. In recent years, Charlie has given up cotton and turned the 160 acres into a dairy farm. He likes that, but I'd hate milking cows at four in the morning and the same cows again at four in the afternoon. Homer went to medical school and has been a thoracic surgeon in Fort Worth since—well, way back. Hey, I can't remember every single date. After all, I *am* within a month or so of ninety-five.

It's funny how you summon up the remembrance of things past when you tilt your recliner back and get soothed by Mr. John Walker of Kilmarnock, Ayshire. At least you don't have to worry about spilling secrets when he is your only auditor.

CHAPTER 2

I slept late after my encounter with the three women, not to mention my two encounters with Mr. John Walker. I'm usually up by six, but then I'm not often challenged by a trio of women desperately wishing me to bare my soul. Or spread scandal about my fellow townsmen—and women. Worrying about that will keep a fellow in bed.

As I looked at the bedside clock, I saw that I'd lain in bed till the number 8:15 flashed its green threat at me. I tried to remember the Housman line about lying abed till all hours. The best I could come up with as the numbers flashed 8:16 and then 8:17 were

> Up, lad: thews that lie and cumber
> Sunlit pallets never thrive;
> Morns abed and daylight slumber
> Were not meant for man alive.

That's all I can remember, but my failure to summon it up nags at me. Maybe I am failing the senile test that I'm always reading about in the *AARP Bulletin.* I can't make the poem come to me, but I can recall the title: "Reveille." And that at least is something. Maybe later today I can find my beat-up copy of *A Shropshire Lad* and see what else Housman says about slugabeds. Here I lay as the clock more or less screamed 8:21 at me. The birds were warring outside my window, and the sunlight was doing its best to blind me. So "up, lad, up, 'tis late for lying." Ah, there's another line. Now all I have to do is recall about twenty more. I can see the poem on the page, but it flees from me. I made my way to the bathroom, performed various morning ablutions, and went downstairs for a visit to my waiting coffeepot.

Here in my golden years—no, those were a couple of decades ago. What are these—my platinum years? Here, in whatever metal is assigned to nonagenarians, I always eat the same breakfast—a small bowl of Raisin Bran, a piece of dry whole wheat toast, and a cup of coffee with fake sugar and fake cream.

Then I dressed. I've made it a point now that I've become so aggressively aged to dress up with coat and tie and polished shoes and carefully combed hair when I present myself to the public. Somebody has to set a standard here in Bodark Springs, Texas, in the late spring in the year of our Lord one thousand nine hundred and seventy-one. Since I'm the oldest person still mobile, the duty to display a little sartorial elegance is up to me. I find my best lightweight tan pants, a medium-blue button-down shirt—Sea Island Cotton, of course, a red Countess Mara tie with a muted blue stripe, and my Brooks Brothers blazer with the gold buttons. If the brothers Brooks could outfit old Teddy for war, surely they could suit me up for peace. All dressed, I look at my hall mirror and, for what seems like the millionth time, find I can't believe what "Time's fell hand" has done in ninety-five short years. Oh, well. I put on my straw fedora with the colorful band, find one of my gold-headed sticks, and step onto the porch of what many in town call "The Adams Mansion."

My father bought this pile after he inherited his brother's oil holdings down at Kilgore and shortly before he himself was killed. The house dates to about 1880 and was built by a plantation owner when cotton was king in this part of the state. Bodark once had three cotton gins and the biggest cotton exchange between Memphis and Dallas. Its exchange didn't compare to Dallas or Waco, but for part of the late summer buyers from all over crowded the old Cotton Exchange Hotel and made the small town seem like a metropolis. And then came 1920, and the boll weevil happened. And then the depressed 1920s for farmers

21

of cotton, and everything else happened. And then the depressed 1930s for everybody happened. I remember those hard times and how Uncle Dave Macon on the Grand Ole Opry used to sing "Twenty-cent cotton and forty-cent meat,/How on earth can a pore man eat?" Now, Eastis County and those that border it are mostly dairy farms and wheat fields. Cotton is king somewhere, but not in my part of Texas. I think they even tore down the Cotton Palace in Waco. It was made of bales of cotton and was one of the wonders of the Texas world when I was a kid.

I stood on the front porch looking at the flowerbeds Mr. Metcalf and his crew kept up for me. I was never a yardman, even when I was younger. I hated farm work and remember chopping cotton and thinning corn on my father's farm when I was ten years old. I couldn't wait to get off the land. The Spanish-American War saved me from the kind of drudgery that my father endured all his life and that my middle son seems to like. My real life started when I went to the teachers' college and met Esther. I recall how she liked flowers and yard work in the small house we had when I got the job at John Bell Hood. She always had daffodils in the spring, and I'm delighted to see the beds and beds of daffodils that Mr. Metcalf makes each spring. I think of Wordsworth and the "ten thousand he saw at a glance." And then I recall one stanza from Housman that Esther made me memorize when we first met at Commerce and walked in the woods close to the college:

> The boys are up the woods with day
> To fetch the daffodils away,
> And home at noonday from the hills
> They bring no dearth of daffodils.

I don't remember any hills around Commerce, but the pastures scattered here and there in the woods produced "no dearth of daffodils." I hope it's not some reflection on my two other wives, but since Esther came first and bore my sons, I still think more fondly of her than of Jane and Barbara. Then there is Liz, the woman in California who was the love of my life when I decamped to the Golden State back in the early thirties. She still is, even after all these years. But I'd better not dwell on lost loves. I hope our sons remember their mother with the same devotion I still feel for that girl and woman I only knew for about ten years. Damn the Spaniards and their flu!

I was still gazing at my flowers when Bunny Davidson came up the walk with his leather mail sack slung across his shoulders. He was holding letters and junk mail meant for me I'm sure. Bunny is following in his father's footsteps. Old Tarp Davidson was the city mailman for many of my early years in town. When he retired, Bunny, whose real name is Buford, passed the civil service exam and got his father's old job.

Bunny said, "Hey, Professor, I hear you got a beautiful young ghost writer come to town to write your life story. I hope you keep me out of it."

I punched Bunny on the shoulder and said, "I can't believe how fast the gossip grapevine winds around this town and chokes the life out of it. How do you know the pretty woman everybody seems to be talking about is not a new girlfriend? Maybe you can pass that word around and help my sagging reputation. But I'll tell you this: It'll be a cold day in hell when I let somebody write my life story. First off, nobody would publish it and second, it'd bore the life out of anybody who read it. Maybe it'll help if you let out that I *have* fallen for a twenty-something."

"Well, maybe I will. Anything I can do to help. Say, I've been looking at these daffodils of yours for several days now. Remember how kids used to pick 'em and take 'em to school and put 'em in their inkwells? Then the flowers sucked up the ink and turned blue."

I suddenly saw all those inkwells with beautiful daffodils ruined by blue-black ink. "I remember. You must have gone to school forty years ago. I haven't seen an inkwell in nearly that long. And as far as I know kids don't have much interest in flowers like these. They now want roses and carnations and orchids for school dances. Nobody even looks at wildflowers except for the bluebonnets when they come in."

Bunny had put down his mail sack to look at the flowers, and I thought that spoke well for somebody I'd taught years ago. He said, "You're right as usual, Professor, about changing tastes in flowers, but I still remember that poem where the guy sees acres of daffodils, what? 'moving their heads in sprightly dance' or something."

"I'm glad you remember something from that class." I had taught Mrs. Sprayberry's English class while she was off having a baby. "The poem you almost remember is 'I Wandered Lonely as a Cloud,' and the line you are struggling with goes like this:

> Ten thousand saw I at a glance,
> Tossing their heads in sprightly dance."

"Boy, Professor, you must have some memory for a man your age. You must be nearly eighty now."

"Well, Bunny, all I can say is that your spy network has let you down. I'm ninety-five."

He pretended astonishment. "Damn! Ninety-five?"

"Yes, and I can finish that poem you barely remember:

> I gazed and gazed, but little thought
> What wealth to me this show had brought,
> For oft, when on my couch I lie
> In vacant or in pensive mood
> They flash upon that inward eye,
> Which is the bliss of solitude;
> And then my heart with pleasure fills,
> And dances with the daffodils."

Bunny was truly impressed. "Amazing!"

"Not really. Now off you go, Bunny. If we stay here reciting poetry all morning I'll never get downtown to meet my newest ladylove. Be sure to put the word out that an old man is about to do something foolish. Of course nobody'll believe you."

He shouldered his mailbag and said, very positively, "They will if I tell it right."

"Good man. See you, Buford."

I took the mail Bunny had brought and went in and threw it on the hall table. Maybe Rosie would put it on my desk when she came in to clean and make soup that will last most of the week. Rosie Mawbry was a fine soul food cook, but since I was almost a fanatic about not over-eating, I didn't often get to sample her neck bones and liver or collards and rape. Once in awhile, she would get in a pet and leave some of her cooking in the refrigerator to tempt me away from my spartan diet, and sometimes it worked, and then I had to fast for a day or two. I always ate at the hotel restaurant on Sunday night. That way I could see friends who made Sunday evening a night to dine out. I might point out, when Annie asks, that Rosie is a colored woman. Rosie would be insulted if I called her black or assigned her parentage to Africa. Rosie Mawbry is all American in more ways than one—and her four sons who served in the US Army bear witness to that.

I didn't shut the front door but closed the screen carefully to keep the flies out. Nobody much locks doors in Bodark Springs. Well, I hear that Ruby Lathem and several maiden ladies (I bet they don't use that term nowadays) lock up tight day and night. I can't prove that. I get much of my intelligence on such matters when Rosie and I visit on Tuesday afternoon.

I knew it would take me an hour to walk the five blocks from my house to the Cotton Exchange Hotel. Not that I'm crippled or even need this cane I carry for effect, but I was certain to meet a dozen people who know me and would want to chat. I was right. It took me forty-seven minutes, because I had to answer questions about my ghost writer, my new lady friend, my failure to answer my doorbell from at least two people, and more from three people who heard that I'd died. I made it safely to the hotel and made my way across the lobby when Edward came out of his office and saw me headed for the restaurant.

He cut me off. "Wait, Dad, I'll join you. Are you here for breakfast, or do you plan a rendezvous with your new sweetheart?"

"Oh, I see the word is out about my philanderings. Good. I'm glad people recognize that my age is no bar to my charms."

Edward said, "I have no idea what you might get up to with the alluring Miss Baxter. But congratulations I suppose. Glad to see some fire in the old man."

"Edward, it's 'Ms.' Join the twentieth century."

He nodded. "Right. I didn't know you had joined the language police."

"I'm just trying to keep up with the times. It's my way of staving off old age. Have your own gray hairs made you quit admiring a well-turned ankle? Now, don't start thinking like an old man. I don't."

25

He grinned and said, "Obviously. At least if what I hear is true. And I'm sure it's not. I'd bet money you're the one spreading rumors of your new romance with this stunning young woman. Red hair and blue eyes! I hate to think people'll be saying things like 'There's no fool like an old fool.'"

"That's good news, Edward. I'm glad you notice what Miss Baxter looks like."

He chided me now. "It's Ms., Dad."

"You always have to have the last word. I'm really here to see whether Ms. Baxter is ready to set some times for my quizzing."

He turned serious. "Before she comes down, I want to talk to you about what she might be trying to get you to admit."

"Admit? Admit? What're you talking about? I know. You're afraid she'll get me started on the time I spent in California."

He took my arm. "That's not it. We can't talk here in the lobby. Let's go into my office."

I knew what he was worried about, but I didn't want to talk to him or anyone else about why I took a sudden leave of absence back in 1932.

Now that Ms. Baxter was here, ready to start poking into my past, rattling those skeletons in my closet, Edward was on the alert, ready to worry that old bone again. But since he was doing me a favor by putting Ms. Baxter up in the hotel, I couldn't just tell him to shut up, so we went into his office. And he started in.

He sat in a chair in front of his desk like an executive trying to put a client at ease. He said, "Dad, I'm your lawyer. And anything you tell me will be confidential."

I shrugged. "You mean like the seal of the confessional?"

He was all business. "Well, sort of. It's called attorney-client privilege and my lips are as sealed as a priest's would be. You could tell me anything, *I mean anything*, and it'd never pass my lips. Revealing a client's secrets would get me disbarred. I just want to know why Grandpa was murdered and why you left your job and turned down Governor Stering's offer to head the state education department. I am totally in the dark about stuff your lawyer should know. I never knew the facts about Uncle Fred's murder and what that had to do with Granddad's murder. I know you know more than you ever let on.

"I never told you about the newspaper man from Texarkana who came to town a few months back trying to rake up some forty-year-old facts about two men thought to be behind Grandad's murder. One of them disappeared. The other one was murdered."

"No, I don't believe you did. But I don't keep up on Arkansas crime."

"But that newspaper man's visit is not what worries me. This morning about seven, my phone rang and a woman said, 'Ask your daddy what he was doing in the Arkansas mountains back in the thirties.'"

I tried not to look startled. "Wrong number?"

Eddie sighed. "I know you know something about all this, Pop. Don't you think it's time you confided in your lawyer? You're about to be interrogated by a twenty-something who looks just like Liz Denney and God knows what you'll blurt out. I *am* your son and your lawyer and I don't want to see you hurt or disgraced or worse."

I said, "Don't worry about 'your daddy,' as she called me. I made a few enemies back in my principal days, and maybe somebody has decided to stir things up. Remember when I expelled Ann Graves after she had a sex party with those six football players? I have had poison pen letters and a few calls about those expulsions and a good many suspensions. That must be what this is about."

Edward said, sounding a bit weary, "I hope so."

"I wrote you and your brothers letters from all over California when I was out there tending to Uncle Fred's oil business. And you know all about Liz Denney and our ten-year love affair. You even met her when she came to Texas in 1939 to tell me she wouldn't marry me."

"Oh, all right, I'll leave you alone. You always knew what you were doing. Well, mostly."

I was on the point of telling him again to stay out of my business when his phone began ringing and wouldn't stop. He finally quit staring at me and answered it. I could tell it was the front desk by the way he grumbled at the phone. He listened for a second and said, "Pop's in here now. He and I are finished with our business it looks like and we will meet Miss Baxter in the restaurant."

"I believe it's 'Ms.'" I said.

We got up with nothing resolved, thank heaven, and went to meet Annie in the restaurant.

"Morning, Annie, I think you must have met Edward last night."

She was all smiles. "Oh, indeed, and he was very kind to have my suitcase brought to this wonderful hotel. I have a feeling that Suite 307 rivals anything in the Driskill Hotel in Austin. Of course I've never seen the rooms at the Driskill, but I can't imagine they outdo accommodations at the Cotton Exchange."

I said, "I have seen the rooms there and they don't come close to Edward's famous hostelry."

Edward almost beamed. Almost. "You're very kind," he said to Annie. "I'm sure you're in need of breakfast, so I'll leave you and my father to plan your days here in Bodark Springs."

Edward left us, but I could tell he really wanted to join us at the table to take Annie's measure and determine whether she was a secret agent or a blackmailer or maybe a hit woman. I knew she was none of those things. Before I left home this morning, I called a friend at the Humanities Research Center at UT and found that Annie Baxter was exactly what she claimed to be. But, still, I imagined that in the course of our meetings she would like more of my life's story than I was eager to reveal. Historians always want the whole story.

She followed him out of the room with her eyes. "I don't think your son likes me."

I groaned. "Annie, my son is a retired—or partially retired—lawyer. Lawyers suspect everybody. Maybe he thinks you want to sign on as my future wife. Word around town already is that I have a sweetheart who's visiting. The fact that I'm at least seventy years older than my presumed new love doesn't seem to register. I met three or four people on my walk who wanted to know what my intentions were. I didn't tell them that you're safe with me. I like to fan any salacious rumors that're going around. But your virtue is in no danger."

She smiled that Liz Denney smile that always melted my heart. "I never thought it was, John Q. You're as open and correct as anyone I've met in years."

"I hope that's a compliment."

"Oh, it is."

Annie ordered bacon, eggs, grits, pancakes, and two biscuits. She drank a glass of orange juice and was on her second cup of coffee when her food arrived. It occurred to me that she probably hadn't eaten since leaving Austin yesterday. Or maybe she was trying to put on a few pounds.

No, it couldn't be that. I could tell with my practiced eye that all her pounds were arranged properly. Here I go wandering off again. At my age, I'm not supposed to be aware of female anatomy. I'm old and obsolete. But I often excuse my appreciation of all beauty by remembering the Thomas Hardy poem "Afterwards." I can't make the whole thing come to me, but it ends something like this:

> And will any say when my bell of quittance is heard in the gloom,
> "He hears it not now, but used to notice such things."

Maybe if Eddie and I are still on terms when my bell of quittance is heard, he could have Hardy's line carved on my stone—"He was a man who used to notice such things."

I noticed that Annie had finished with her substantial breakfast and was staring at me. I realized that I'd drifted off into a memory of forty years ago, and she was too polite to jerk me back to the moment.

I said, "Old people daydream, you know, and they do it at the oddest times. No reflection on your company or anything."

She dabbed her napkin to her lips and then carefully folded it and placed it next to her plate. "I wondered if your thoughts were troubled. You and your son seemed to be a little apart. I hope I'm not the cause of any rift in the Adams world."

"No, no, nothing like that. As you may have observed, children often want to be parents of their parents. Eddie is running true to type I fear."

Then I laughed and said, "Hell, Eddie is sixty-six and divorced, so maybe his three children already have him in their parenting sights. Would serve him right."

Before she could suggest anything about our conferences, I said, "Annie, I have a plan. How about I go home and get my car and we take a tour around the county so you can see what you have to deal with here? I suppose since you're working on a PhD in history, you know more about Texas than I do, but I know this county pretty well."

"Well, actually, John Q., I'm not majoring in *Texas* history. My field is early American. I got this grant because all the other history graduate students—the ones in Texas history—got the plum spots: they were assigned such historic places as Bexar County, the Hill Country, the Gulf Coast, the Rio Grande Valley, and El Paso and the Trans Pecos. Oh, and that tabletop they call the Panhandle. So please let's get started with a tour of my assigned patch—the neglected Northeast Texas. I have a car here in the hotel lot, so I can drive us and you can be the tour guide."

Then I remembered the tiny car parked at my house last night. "I saw your car last night as you left my house, and I doubt that I can fit in one that small. I have a veritable land yacht and it knows the roads already. Meet me in front of the hotel in an hour. It takes me that long to walk home and pass pleasantries with everyone I know, especially those that think you're a golddigger after my money or that you're my ghostwriter."

Since it was the middle of the morning, I knew it wouldn't take long to walk home. Honest folk were at work by now. But I suspected that Rosie was already at my house and would start her interrogations about the new woman in my life. I was right, but I managed to brush her off and get to the garage to get my classic 1940 LaSalle Series 50 ready for the excursion.

I love this car. It's the last year of the LaSalle, one of the finest cars GM ever made. The company at one time called it the Cadillac LaSalle since it ranked just slightly below the Cadillac and well above the Buick. Mine was a beautiful maroon with huge whitewall tires, two fog lights mounted just behind and above the front bumper, and a spotlight on the driver's side. It was a car to love, and since it required knowledge of a stick shift, I suspected that Ms. Annie Baxter wouldn't be after me to let her drive. Girls—sorry, women— her age often don't know how to shift. I bought this car new just before the war. It was late in 1940, and I learned that LaSalle wasn't making any 1941s. I drove it very little during WWII since I had an A sticker and only got four gallons of gas a week. Four gallons would hardly get this jewel of a car out of the garage and up to the courthouse square. When war broke out, I bought a 1941 Ford and kept it till 1949. I still don't drive the LaSalle much. It has about nine thousand miles on the odometer. Mint condition. I now have a 1970 Buick Electra, but here was an occasion when I thought the LaSalle with the suicide rear doors and the plush upholstery was the proper machine for taking a woman on a tour.

The look on Annie's face when she saw me pull into the oval in front of the hotel was worth the price of admission to this show. She couldn't believe anybody in Bodark Springs had a limousine like my maroon Series 50.

"Wow," she said.

I hate when women say "wow."

I got out like the gentleman I was pretending to be and opened the door for her. When I handed her into the front seat, she was still exclaiming over the car. "Gosh,"—and I hate that too—"Professor—sorry, John Q.—this is the most amazing car I've ever seen. I've seen some Cadillacs in Midland, but never one like this."

"Of course not. This isn't a Cadillac."

She was incredulous. "No? What is it? Some foreign car?"

"No, it's pure General Motors. It's a LaSalle, a 1940 LaSalle. The last year GM made LaSalles. And you may never see another one unless you go to a car museum."

I started the car and drove out onto Main Street while she was still looking at the interior appointments and being impressed. As I drove down the street, dozens of people hollered at me, "Hey, Professor, I see you have the yacht out." Or "Hey, Prof, I hear you got company!" Or "Professor Adams, what a beautiful—uh, uh, car." One of the women teachers from my days as principal saw us and said—as I feared she would—"Wow!"

I spent the rest of the day—with only two fill-ups at Texaco stations—driving Annie Baxter all over Eastis County. Since she was not as up on Texas history as I thought she might be, I explained that Eastis had been a part of Nacogdoches County in the early days of the Republic. Nacogdoches County in those years made up about a tenth of the state. After that, for a short time, all the northern border was Red River County. Then after 1845, we were a part of Fannin County, which stretched from Red River County almost to the edge of the Panhandle. There's still a much-reduced Red River County lying between Bowie County and Lamar. Sometime about 1870, the new counties on the Red River border were founded. And we had Fannin, Lamar, Eastis, Grayson, and counties on and on to the edge of the Panhandle. She didn't know why so many counties in the north of Texas and all through the Panhandle are square. And all about the same size. I explained that the counties were all about the same size and square for a reason: so the county seat could sit in the middle of the county, about fifteen miles from everywhere. That made it possible for farmers to ride into the county courthouse and pay their taxes and enrich the town merchants. Then they could get home in time to milk and feed. I did mention that those square counties on the Red were not square at the top but wrinkled by the Red River's wandering course. I was a real *Texas Almanac* on this day-long ride. I guess it's a good thing the LaSalle drinks gas. The stops gave Annie a chance to go to the dirty restrooms in the Texaco stations along our route. I shouldn't gripe about Texaco stations since much of my money comes from the Texaco stock that came to me after my uncle and my father were dead. I didn't mind the stops since my bladder is the same age as I am.

As we were pulling into town, a police car sounded its siren and signaled me to pull over. I did, and Sergeant Stowers, who once made a C+ in my junior history class, came up to the driver's side. I cranked the window down and said, "Was I speeding, Sergeant? I think I was going about fifteen miles an hour."

"No, no, nothing like that, Professor. Your son, Mr. Edward, reported you missing and asked us to look for you. Sheriff Daniels has deputies scouring the county. Your son thought something had happened to you."

Annie spoke up, "Does Mr. Edward, as you call him, think I'm a kidnapper? Or just a bad influence?"

"No ma'am, but we all know the Professor and try to look out for him in case he, uh, uh—"

I said, "Gets so senile that they have to put out some kind of APB for a Missing Elderly or Graybeard or something. No, Chester, I'm fine and Ms. Baxter has no evil designs on my person. Thanks for worrying about me. Can you get on your radio and call off the sheriff and the other posses? I'll report in to Edward if and when I return Ms. Baxter to the hotel."

"Right you are, Professor. I'll get on the horn. I'm glad you're all right."

"I know you are, Chester, and I truly appreciate it."

CHAPTER 3

When we got within a block of the hotel, I pulled the car into a space in front of the Ben Franklin store and cut the engine.

"Now, Annie, I'll bet you fifty cents that when we drive into the oval in front of the hotel Edward'll be standing there with his hands in his pockets jingling his change in the left hand pocket and his keys in the other one. I don't want you to fret about Edward and his ways. Everything's going to be fine. You're going to tape me if it takes all summer. Edward and Charles—you haven't met him yet—worry about me. I'm not sure whether they think I'll wake up some morning and won't know where I am, or whether they fear somebody will take advantage of my trusting nature. That's where you enter the picture, sadly. But I trust you completely and that's what's going to matter here.

"As usual, in the end I'll get my way, tho' hell itself should gape and bid me hold my peace."

"What did you say about hell? Oh, I know, probably Shakespeare, right?"

"Yes. You could tell by the language—'gape and bid me hold my peace.' It's *Hamlet*. I hate to be pedantic—no, I don't! In the play, young Hamlet's out on the battlements about to confront the ghost of his father. He plans to stand in the way as the ghost moves toward him and stand with outstretched arms to 'cross' the ghost. His friends warn him that the ghost might be an evil spirit and, as they put it, 'blast' him. Then Hamlet says he'll cross him 'tho hell itself should gape and bid me hold my peace.' I don't think it'll come to such drastic measures with my sons. They're really good men with my best interests at heart. But they don't know you, and I think I do."

She smiled that Liz Denney smile and said, "How can you be so sure of me?"

"I'm sort of sorry to admit this, but I've checked you out. I know people in the Historical Association and in the Folklore Society as well as the UT History Department and the Ransom Center. They tell me you're the pick of the PhD litter. Maybe they thought it would take their best when they decided to saddle you with hardscrabble Northeast Texas and somebody cantankerous like me. Somebody suggested that there was some favoritism at play when they passed out the plum assignments to the Hill Country and the Trans Pecos and such places. The powers wanted to let the Texas history majors get a jump on you since you're smarter and more likely to make lemonade if given lemons. My sources also say—and I talked to four people last night and three this morning—that you have more integrity than Mother Teresa."

She looked out the window and then turned to me. "Wow, John Q., you are on top of things."

"I am. And don't ever say 'wow' again if you want to stay on my good side."

She smiled and said, "I'll watch my language and mind my p's and q's from here on."

"Not necessary. Just be yourself and things'll be great—and don't say 'wow.'"

Then I laughed to let her know her "wows" didn't really count against her.

"Now when we get to the hotel, leave Edward to me. Go on up and rest after this exhausting ride in the LaSalle. Tomorrow, come to my house and we'll start the taping. How does 10:00 a.m. sound?"

"I'll be there, and I must say this ride in the 1940s limo was great, and the tour was informative, and even in your golden years you're a better driver than my fiancé."

35

"Justin Cole, right?"

Again she was startled. "Damn, John Q., do you know everything?"

I tried to look wise and said, "Just things that matter, and I've decided that you matter. Now, let me crank this fine Detroit machine and go into the jaws of Eddie."

As we drove into the oval in front of the hotel, I was only partly surprised to see Charles standing next to Eddie, who was jingling the keys in one pocket and his change in the other.

I stopped the car, killed the engine, and got around the car before Annie could get out and get her door closed. "Evening, Gents, are you two worthies waiting for Lady Bird or Lyndon or somebody famous to drive up?"

Charles was in his white milking coveralls, so it was clear that Edward had summoned him to an emergency meeting. I made it a point to shake hands with Charles and then with Edward. It pays to keep your children off balance. Then I introduced Charles to Annie and told him that she would be in town for the summer to perform an inquisition. He was polite but wary. He wasn't sure he should shake hands with her, but when she extended her hand, he took it, rather graciously, I thought, and said "pleased to meet you" or some formula phrase that I couldn't quite hear. I suggested that Annie was tired after an afternoon in the LaSalle and should be allowed to pass so she could go freshen up.

Edward kept jingling his change, and Charles said, "Pop, could I have a word?"

"Certainly, Son, get in the car."

Before he could suggest otherwise, I was around the hood of the old Series 50 and behind the wheel. He had no choice, so he climbed in on the passenger side. I started the car and was moving out of the entrance to the hotel as Edward was shaking his head and wondering, I suppose, what I was planning for my Number Two son.

I eased the LaSalle out onto Main Street and headed south. I glanced over at Charles and said, "When I pulled up at the hotel and saw you there with Edward, I thought Homer might jump out from behind one of the pillars and hit me with a tranquilizer dart or whatever doctors use to subdue out-of-control patients."

"Oh, come on, Pop, nobody wants to subdue you. And Homer's on your side anyway. Edward calls him every night and Homer says, 'Leave the old man alone. He sure as hell won't get some girl pregnant at his age. Besides, what if he does?' Then Edward says Homer cackles like he did when we were boys."

"Hell, maybe I should have named that boy John Q. III. He may be the chip off the old block that I need to shield me from you two."

"Dad, I always wondered why he was named Homer Winslow and Eddie and I got named for Mom's uncles. Homer Winslow seems an odd name for an Adams."

"That was your mother's doing. She did all the naming. We had a deal, and it was that none of you would be named John Quincy. She was an art history major if you remember and was quite taken with the paintings of Winslow Homer, but she thought Winslow would be a hard first name for a little boy, so she reversed the names."

Charles shook his head and said, "Damn good thing she wasn't devoted to Pablo Picasso. I would hate to have a brother named Picasso Pablo Adams. Hey, Pop, where are you taking me? I just wanted a quiet word."

"No, you wanted a whole paragraph if I know you, so I'm taking you back home to your dairy. You have two or three hundred cows to milk, and they won't milk themselves, even with all those fancy milking machines you have."

"Oh, Dad, I got a dozen men to tend the cows. And my truck is back at the hotel. How'll I get back?"

"Lucy can drive you back. Maybe she can talk some sense into you. I think your wife likes me better than you boys do and'll give me the benefit of the doubt. Or, better, Edward can drive your truck down to get you, and then on the way back to town the two of you'll have time to lay a snare for the old man."

"Dad, we're not trying to trap you or make your life miserable."

"I know. Y'all are just worried because you think there's no fool like an old fool and because Annie has red hair and blue eyes—and some other attributes—and that I'll try to swap my horse and dog for her. "

"What? You don't have a dog. That girl hasn't got you to buy a damn dog since the last time I saw you, has she?"

"It's a song. Don't you remember the words to 'Sioux City Sue?' Here, I'll sing it to you."

All three of my sons hate it when I try to sing, so I always manage a few bars when I'm with 'em, especially if we're in company. So I unlimbered my melodious voice and sang,

> Your hair is red, your eyes are blue
> I'd swap my dog and horse for you,
> Sioux City Sue, Sioux City—

"Enough! Enough! I remember the song. And you still can't sing a lick."

"Well, I like blue eyes and red hair and all that, and if I had a dog—"

Charlie was laughing now. "You're way too much to bear! Neither one of us is in the least worried that you'll start some love affair with Miss Annie Whatshername."

"It's Baxter, and it's Ms. Then what're you two guys worried about? You think she's a con woman after my money. Hell, Edward has my business so tied up in red tape that even the IRS can't get at me."

"Dad, we know you're too smart to lose your head over some skirt. And nobody thinks you're senile. Hell, even at ninety-five you're more on top of things than I am. But I do wish people would quit saying you're the smartest man in Eastis County. It'll give you the big head."

"So why are you and Edward and half the town so worried that I'm about to take up with a woman seventy years or so younger than I am? Hell, I've had three wives—and a few lady friends that you boys don't know about, but all that was a long, long time ago."

"Boy, I'd like to hear about the ones I never heard about. I hope it was when you were single? I hope you never ran around on Mom and Jane. Surely not Barbara. You must have been way over seventy when she died."

"You'll never know about anybody but Liz. I've kept the others deep and dark in my secret file."

"Maybe Homer can give you some truth serum and get those secrets out. Pop, we're not worried about Annie Baxter stealing your heart away. Or your money. What we're afraid of is, is—"

"Oh, out with it. Tell it."

"All right. When she starts spending hours and hours with you and

38

gettin' you to talk into her tape recorder we worry that she'll get you to tell some personal things that don't need to be aired. After all, you used to disappear, once for a couple of years, and then for I don't know how many summers. I still wonder what you did away from here."

I wanted to get off the subject of my missing years. "Well, I must say it's a relief to know that even you and Eddie don't know everything about me. And if I've kept you guys in the dark all these years, don't worry that I'll tell some stranger—with 'attributes'—what my own flesh and blood'll never find out. Now I'll turn this fine old LaSalle around and take you back to the hotel so you can tell your older brother that you didn't get anywhere with me. Do you hope to inherit the LaSalle when I croak? Don't worry, I may leave it to Lucy. Annie won't get it. She can't drive a stick."

He was quiet for a moment. "How about if I bring up something that has nothing to do with Eddie's worries or Ms. Baxter?"

"Go ahead. I can always stop the car and we can have a man-to-man talk. I hope you don't have any questions about sex. Didn't I explain that to you last year?"

"Dad," Charles said.

"Sorry, I seem to try to turn everything to a joke. Go on."

"I wonder if you have reservations about what I've done with my life. Eddie got rich suing corporations, Homer makes a fortune cutting chests, and I'm still down on the farm like your dad was. In other words, where do I stand in your ranking of sons? I heard you quote Hermes Nye that a man should have three sons—a doctor, a lawyer, and a body and fender man. I sometimes think I'm the body and fender man in this trio."

"Charlie, I knew that old lawyer and folklorist Hermes well, and I remember the line about three sons, but I've never for one second thought less of you for being a farmer.

"Look at me. I spent more than half a century as a schoolteacher, doing what oldtimers thought of as woman's work. You wanted to go to A&M and major in agriculture, and then you've made a great success as a dairyman. And not only that, you're more successful as a husband than Eddie was. You're not the family's 'body and fender man,' though I'd be proud of you if you were. Not only that, but I'm more likely to come to you for advice than I am to Homer or Eddie. Maybe living on that farm makes you embody some lines I memorized from Matthew Arnold:

> My special thanks, whose ever balanced soul,
> From first youth up to extreme old age,
> Business could not make dull, nor passion wild,
> Who saw life steadily and saw it whole."

Charles doesn't roll his eyes when I quote poetry, and I appreciate that about him. I said, "I know you are not what Hamlet calls 'passion's slave.' I admire you more than you imagine, and Lucy is too damned good for you. So there! If you were a little boy, I would kiss you the way I did sixty years ago."

Charlie seemed to be relieved and embarrassed. "I had no idea. I always thought I was a failure in your eyes and in the eyes of Homer and Eddie. Gee, Pop, I don't know what to say. I may start blubbering."

"You do and I'll throw your ass out of this car while it's still moving. Then I'll go back to the hotel and make a pass at Annie."

Charlie laughed. "You haven't slowed down a step."

"Oh, yes I have! If I hadn't I might really make a play for Annie. Ha! Now, when you get back to the hotel, tell Eddie if you guys keep on harassing me, I'll send Ms. Annie Baxter back to Austin."

He looked startled. "Really? Really?"

"Yes. But add if I do, I'll rent the Jim Hogg Suite at the Driskill Hotel— you know the one LBJ always stays in—and stay there all summer till the taping is done."

I left Charlie laughing as I pulled out of the oval of the Cotton Exchange Hotel. He didn't think I was serious. Edward was nowhere in sight. It was getting close to his cocktail hour. Mine too. I could already taste the Johnnie Walker on my tongue as I headed toward the garage to put the LaSalle away. I had to keep it clean and unbruised till 1976 when I'd drive it in the Bicentennial Day Parade. I'm sure Ruby Lathem'll have a banner on the car saying "The Country is 200 Years Old Today and John Quincy Adams the Second is 100." I'll still be driving the old bus that day. Maybe I'll let Ruby ride in the passenger seat.

I figured I had eased whatever worries Charles and Eddie had about me. In fact I felt nearly celebratory that evening, so I helped myself to a generous dram of Johnnie Walker before I headed for my recliner. That's when the phone rang.

I started not to answer it, but I thought maybe I hadn't eased Eddie's mind like I thought I had. If there is a worrywart-in-chief, that would be Eddie. If I didn't answer, he would come rushing over to see if I had fallen or suffered a stroke. He might even call the police again. So I picked up the phone and said, "Hello. Is that you, Eddie?"

A woman with a country-sounding voice said, "I know what you done back in Arkansas. You may be sure your sins will find you out."

I said, "Who is this?"

But I was talking to dead air. Stories all talk about a receiver being slammed down or a dial tone that buzzes, but in real life, you just find yourself talking to somebody who has hung up.

Even John Walker didn't send me off to sleep as I had hoped. I lay awake for what seemed like hours, but when you are ninety-five, sleep comes no matter what troubles your mind. And maybe I could rely on Macbeth, who noted that sleep knits up the ravelled sleeve of care. Maybe if I am lucky this call was a dream, and sleep will knit up the sleeve.

CHAPTER 4

I woke up at my usual 6:00 despite my restless night. After the coffee was made, I repaired to the front porch, mug in hand, to sit in my rocker and watch Bodark Springs come alive. It was a little early for much foot traffic on my street, and the cars all seemed to be creeping along Main Street, loath to park. Maybe the drivers were putting off the inevitable workday. In an hour or two, girls with book bags would skip toward Robert E. Lee Elementary School, and boys would drag their satchels on their reluctant ways to classrooms given over to readin', writin', and arithmetic.

I'd almost begun to doze when Estelle Stringer came creeping up my walk. She's tall and as stringy as her name might suggest. Her grizzled hair was in a bun at the back of her head, and her sharp, pointed nose always seemed to precede her like the figurehead on the prow of a ship. Here was a visitor I dreaded, and I don't say that about many of my fellow Bodarkians.

"Morning, Professor. I see you're sitting alone on your porch this morning. Is everything all right with you? I hear you have a visitor."

Now I was in my element. "Oh, I do, Estelle, but you know how young people are. After a night of unbridled passion, they want to sleep late. You can hardly get 'em out of bed once they're in it."

She both giggled and choked, "Oh, my! My, my, my. Are you saying?—You're embarrassing me, Professor. I don't know what to say. I never. I mean, at your—Oh my."

"Why are you blushing so, Estelle?"

Her sharp nose was beet red now, "Oh, my—I just never thought—Oh, my—You can be sure your secret is safe with me. You know I've never been one to gossip. No, no, mum's the word."

"I know, Estelle, you're the soul of discretion. I know you don't tell tales out of school unless they are necessary for the good of man- and woman-kind. As I remember, you told me about that divorced woman about a block down who'd been carrying on with the county judge? I can't remember for sure who told me. I think it may have been you. Wasn't it you?"

Now she stood tall and righteous. "It was me, all righty. I told you because I thought you might put a bee in the judge's ear. I'm not one to gossip, but a person can trust you since you're so, so—"

"Venerable?"

"Exactly. Venerable. You always know what to do in curious and embarrassing circumstances."

Then I decided to let her up. "Oh, Estelle, let's see"—and I looked at my watch—"let's see, in about three hours, the young redhead you've heard so much about will come down the street from the hotel where she's been staying—and will continue to stay—and bring her tape machine to get me to tell her all the gossip I know about life in this town and this county. And I *am*, unlike you, one to gossip. She'll be in town for most of the summer, so maybe I can get a little romance going if I play it right. What do you think?"

Now the redness was gone and Estelle was back to normal. "Oh, Professor, you've been puttin' me on. You *are* a caution, John Quincy Adams!"

"Why thank you, Estelle. Now I have to go in and get gussied up for my new sweetheart."

Cheered by my fun with Estelle, I made my way into the bathroom to shower, shave, and otherwise primp for the day ahead. I found a blue-striped shirt, some medium gray pants, a maroon tie with swallows on it, and my lightweight Hickey Freeman plaid sport coat. My final move, after knotting the tie carefully, was to find the black, well-polished loafers made to my last by M. L. Leddy's in Fort Worth. Leddy's is famous for western wear and handmade boots, but they make a fine dress shoe and a superb loafer. I'm one of their better customers. I always go by when I'm visiting my son Homer in Fort Worth. Rolando Hernandez, the bootmaker, and I are thick as thieves since I've been being shod by him for nigh on fifty years.

Exactly at ten, Annie Baxter came up the walk lugging her tape recorder. It seemed a heavy load for a woman, but I wasn't quick enough off the mark to help her. Besides, I'm not as strong as I once was.

"Morning, Annie, can you make it with all your equipment?"

She was bright and cheerful. "I'm fine, John. I'll have it all set up if you'll show me where we're going to talk the day away."

I finally managed to help her with her satchel, which I learned had enough reels of tape to record a session of parliament. We set up in my study, which, fortunately for both of us, was on the first floor. I put the tape machine on a library table, drew up two chairs, plugged her machine in and said, "Now for the gleaning of my teeming brain, right?"

She busied herself with her infernal machine. "Right. Let me get the machine going and you can clip that lavalier mike onto your jacket."

"That what mike?"

She was all business. "The little microphone lying on your end of the table. Now when you have it on, you need to say a few words so I can test the gain."

"The what?"

She was all for informing me of mechanical things. "The gain: the level of sound. Are you ready?"

I couldn't resist. "Can I just sing something?" I didn't wait but began

> Your hair is red, your eyes are blue
> I'd swap my horse and dog for you.

"Oh, John Q., as my Granny Baxter would say, 'you're a caution!'"

I laughed, "A caution? You're the second person who's said that to me this very morning. Do you know the song?"

She brushed a lock of red hair out her eyes and said, "Of course I know the song. You don't get this far in life with red hair and blue eyes without somebody singing 'Sioux City Sue' at you. By the way—or maybe not by the way—I hate the song. My father sang it until I thought I'd run away from home. Now, Mr. John Quincy Adams, tell me a story."

I didn't get it. "A story? What do you mean?"

She was now all business. "I *mean*, tell me a story. I don't plan to ask you a question and then get a one-sentence answer and then ask you a question and get a one-sentence answer and then ask you a question and get a one-sentence answer until the tape is full of stichomythia."

Now she was the "caution," and I hadn't heard anybody use stichomythia in fifty years. "Oh, Ms. Baxter, you warm my heart. I'll bet fifty cents we're the only two people in Eastis County who know what stichomythia is! Damn, what a start to a spring and summer. Now, what do you mean 'tell me a story'?"

"Just this. I want you to start talking about anything that interests you. You're a longtime member of the Texas Folklore Society, so you know all about the culture of a place and a people. Talk to me about anything that'll get us started on this place—Bodark Springs, Eastis County, all of Northeast Texas—where it lives and what it lives for."

I was more and more impressed. She knew many things a person of her age wouldn't. "No, wait, you can't be quoting *Walden*. I'll do the literary quotations if you please. You may want me to back life up into a corner and so forth and so forth the way old Henry David said he was up to at Walden Pond."

She busied herself with the machine for a minute or two and then looked up and said, "I'm gonna go to the library or maybe a bookstore when I get back to Austin so I can pin you to the wall with famous quotations the way you do me. All right, let's get to work. We can start anyplace. You can tell me stories about songs and ballads, about folktales or funeral customs or food or marriage rites or why the sea is boiling hot and whether pigs have wings. See, I got one on you. How about that? Maybe the best way to start is to tell me how life was when you were growing up here."

"Now you're thinking to out-quote me, but I had children and read 'The Walrus and the Carpenter' to all three of them a million times. So there. I'm still ahead. So you want to know how life was for me. I thought so. You want me to tell you my life story, all my secrets. Is that it?"

She quickly remembered my ground rules. "No, no. I promised not to pry into your life, but I didn't promise not to pry into the lives of the county. I just want to know how the people lived. The work they did, the religion they practiced, and the beliefs they had. I even want to know what they ate and how they dressed. How they amused themselves."

She was throwing subjects at me faster than I could process them, but I had to seem quick on my feet. "And you want me to make this into a story? All right, let me start with who they were and why they were here in the first place.

"People like my father came after the Civil War. They wanted to escape the destruction of a way of life they'd grown up with. They came into Eastis and the other counties along the Red River from the lower South—Alabama, Georgia, Mississippi, and maybe West Tennessee. Or they came from the Upper South down through Miller County, Arkansas, and into Red River County. Then some kept going until they ran out of wood and water. This country around here was a particularly good part of Texas for cotton farmers from the Deep South because the southern parts of all these counties lie in the 'Black Waxy Prairies.' Are you bored already?"

She looked up from her machine and said, "No, but much of this I know from my courses in history. I'm glad to hear a version from somebody whose relatives really came west back then. But I guess I should say my interest is mostly in the way the people interacted with their neighbors and with the land."

I have to twit her when I can or else she'll think I'm behind the times. "Interacted? I'll bet they use that word a lot at UT. So now who's being the pedant? But I get you. I'll keep boring away.

"I always remember how hard life was for the country people in these parts. There weren't many town people for a long time. Bodark is a metropolis compared to what it was when I was a boy. Nearly everybody lived in the country, growing cotton in the south parts of these counties and working timber and growing something to eat in the poorer, red-dirt north. People who don't know anything say, 'Hard work won't kill you,' but it will. People in town lived to be a lot older than people on farms. If you saw somebody of sixty, you were looking at an old, old person. Hell, even in town a person of sixty was old back when I was a boy. Plowing with mules, chopping and picking cotton, sawing down trees and hacking crossties'll wear you out. I'm sure picking citrus down in the Rio Grande Valley or roughnecking in the oil fields takes the same toll. Hard work is highly overrated as a tonic for longevity. Life was just as hard on women. Harder, I always thought. They worked alongside their husbands and fathers in the field and then had to cook on wood stoves, milk cows, churn butter, have babies, and build a fire in a washpot to get filthy overalls halfway clean. Then they ran the clothes through three Number 3 tubs full of water, and then, using a rub board and lye soap, finished off the wash. Next, they had to wring out the wash by hand and hang it on a clothesline. I've not seen the figures, but I bet life expectancy for farm women was fifty or so. Farm life killed my mother when I was a little boy. Is all this what you call 'interacting' with the land? They used to say that the West was fine for men and mules, but hell on women and horses. I suspect the saying would fit this part of the state better if it said it was hell on women and mules since the mules pulled all the plows and cultivators and wagons. And the women did the worst kind of work."

I was pleased that Annie looked impressed. Even nonagenarians have some vanity when they can inform the young. She said, "Exactly. And now you're telling me a story. I can't let you quit now. If farm life was that hard, how did they relieve the misery of the work? Did they sing or tell stories?"

I was in lecture mode for better or worse. "No, they mostly went to church. That was the entertainment. I've heard many a farmer go on and on about good preachin.' Not the kind of sermons you hear in the Presbyterian Church or even the Methodist Church today—or even back then. They liked to hear a Holy Roller preacher cut down on the Ten Commandments. Revivals were best. Then some serious hellfire could erupt. Revivals were always, or almost always, held in late summer after the crops were laid by. Do you know the term *laid by*?"

I could see that I had stumped her for once. "No, I'm sure I don't. I grew up in Midland, and I was always a city girl. My daddy was manager of a Safeway store and my mother was a nurse. I don't know why I'm using the past tense. They're both alive and still doing the same work. So, no, I don't know that term. What was it? Laid off?"

"No, laid by. It means the crop is finally planted and plowed and hoed and weeded and is now ready to grow unattended till time to harvest it. There are a few weeks when a farmer is not in the field from sunup till sundown. Revivals were best for damnation talk, but the best church of all was the 'all-day singing and dinner on the ground.' I'm not sure the Pentecostals and Holiness people had that custom, but the country Methodists and the Baptists sure did. Have you ever been to an all-day singing?"

She tried to remember and couldn't. "No, but I've heard my grand-father talk about 'em. He grew up in Macon County, Alabama, and he remembers some of the food women made up for those dinners on the ground. They didn't really eat on the ground, did they?"

This really took me back seventy years to a time I'd almost forgot. "I suppose they did way back in the country, but in civilized places like Eden, where I grew up, and at such sophisticated places as Cooks Springs—a little irony for the tape here—the churches had rough wooden tables that old boys nailed up from one tree to the next. I've seen those old tables groan under the weight of fine country cooking. There would be piles of fried chicken, stewers of chicken pie and ham pie, mountains of fried pies—apple and peach and pear. The poorest people would be embarrassed to bring pots of turnip greens and snap beans and hominy and corn on the cob, but their food went almost as fast as the meats. And then lots of the best cooks would make cobblers and plate pies with calf slobber that stood two inches above the filling."

She made a face. "Calf Slobber? Yuck."

"No yuck to it. It's what we all called meringue."

She giggled. "Why am I not surprised? But wait, I guess you're trying to indoctrinate me to what the folklorists call 'folk say.'"

She paused to change a reel on her recorder, and I said, "If you say so. Scholars always have to give a name to regular stuff. Like the way we talked back then."

I tried to remember what she wanted to hear about and said, "You suggested funeral customs a while ago. Was that because you think I may need one soon? If so, forget it. I have a five-year plan. When I turned ninety, I said, 'I'm giving it five more years and then I'll see.' Now, at ninety-five, I've decided to give it another five and take stock again. My prediction is that I'll float into the Bicentennial with all sails flying and satisfy Ruby and Frances by riding in their damned parade dressed as Benjamin Franklin."

She loved this silliness and said, "Not one of the Adamses—John or Samuel?"

"No, I've had a plenty of Adamses already. A father who named me my awful name, and three sons named by their mother, and one of them has a name nearly as bad as mine."

She wanted me back on the subject. "Besides church, wasn't there any other kind of entertainment? Games? Dances? That sort of thing?"

I got back on track. "There were square dances and play parties, but the Baptists were so strong in Eastis County that no hug dancing took place at all. I suppose you people out in West Texas call hug dancing 'round' dancing as opposed to square dancing."

She was now a step behind me I was glad to see, and I was pleased when she said, "No, I've never heard of round dancing or hug dancing, but I can imagine. Of course everybody knows about square dancing. I'm not sure what you mean by 'play parties.'"

Now I could really tell her some heady stuff for her report. "Well, in order to avoid the terrible sin of hug dancing, frontier people came up with the play party 'game,' which was a dance by another name. The play party game was like the schottisch or something. You sort of skipped and promenaded and held hands or danced apart. I'll bet you know some of the songs they played. There was 'Shoot the Buffalo,' 'Weevily Wheat,' and lots of others. My favorite is 'Skip to My Lou.' Remember that one from playgrounds?

Can't get a redbird, bluebird'll do
Can't get a redbird, bluebird'll do
Can't get a redbird, bluebird'll do
Skip to My Lou, My Darling.

Little red wagon painted blue
Little red wagon painted blue

49

Little red wagon painted blue
Skip to My Lou, My Darling.

And how about:

Find me another girl prettier'n you
Find me another girl prettier'n you
Find me another girl prettier'n you
Skip to My Lou, My Darling."

She clapped her hands. "Oh, yes, I know that song. And they just skipped around? Is that right? I appreciate your singing it to me, but you can't sing a lick, John Q."

Faking hurt feelings, I said, "I deny that. I thought I sang that well. You just don't appreciate a proper folk voice. Wait'll I sing you some ballads and songs. Okay, back to play parties if you're through making fun of me. And you're more or less right: they just skipped and hopped around. There's a whole book about play party games written by an old boy from over in Lamar County. I don't mean he lives over in Lamar now. He's a professor at Columbia up in New York, but he came from a tiny spot in the road called Pin Hook. I have a copy of the book here somewhere if you want to see it. It's called *Swing and Turn: Texas Play Party Games.* His name is William A. Owens, and if you want to know how hard life was early in this century, the kind of life I've been telling stories about, his memoir *This Stubborn Soil* will do a better job than I can about hard times in Northeast Texas. He had it harder than most people I ever heard of. He's about the same age as my son Edward, but their lives don't compare. Old Bill Owens made it by what my daddy called 'main strength and awkwardness.'"

Something went wrong with Annie's machine and tape began spilling out onto the floor. As she turned off the recorder and tried to restring the tape—or whatever you do to get the yards of tape back on the reels—I drifted off as I've been doing since we started talking at that damned machine. Old John Earl Cogburn said talking into one was like talking to a damned stump. Remembering that I was about to launch into some boring story about dancing took me back to the years in San

Francisco when Ms. Elizabeth Denney and I wore out the dance floors at the Fairmont Hotel and the Mark Hopkins up on Nob Hill. I'd learned to dance when Esther and I took a social dancing class in college, but I'd let my skills slide for years after Esther died. Jane was a Baptist and disapproved of dancing, so I grew rusty, but when I spent the year in California, Liz, who loved dancing, brought back my vaunted twinkle toes. I mean we really "danced the light fantastic" as the song says. When Paul Whiteman and his orchestra did a stint at the Mark Hopkins we never missed a night. We were San Francisco versions of Fred and Ginger when we got on the mahogany.

"John Q., have you left me again?"

I said, "Reveries, Annie, are an old man's curse. Where were we exactly, when your infernal machine turned on you?"

"I think you were going to tell me some stories about dancing and some girl named Tootsie Something."

I must have mentioned Tootsie Lines while I was off dreaming of dancing with Liz Denney. Now I was back and thought *Annie wants a tragedy.* I have one. "All right, Annie, let me tell you a square dance tale about the tragic death of Miss Tootsie Lines. Tootsie was a girl of about eighteen, and she loved to dance. This was a long time ago. I was just a yearling boy when Tootsie met her sad end. I wasn't around for this tale; I got it all from Edna Lawrence, who lived up in the north part of the county, up near Cooks Springs. That's where Tootsie lived. I'm pretty sure Tootsie wasn't her official name, but I never heard any other one for her. Back before the present century had barely got underway, back when people didn't have much entertainment outside of Holy Roller preaching, people all over Eastis County held play parties and square dances. They met in people's houses if they had a big enough living room or if there was a community center or a school house with room to push the desks aside to dance—or play a play-party game. Ross and Nobie Smith almost always provided the music for square dances, and old Bock DeShazo—everybody pronounced it *Deshazer*—was the caller. Ross played the fiddle and Nobie, his wife, picked the guitar. From time to time Ross would find Nobie off-key and say, '*G*, damnit, *G*.' You know about square dance callers, don't you?"

I had her here for sure, and she said, "No, I'm not sure I do. Tell me."

Ever the explainer, I said, "Well, the couples would pair off and do the dances the caller called. He would say, 'Now promenade,' and they would march around the room. Then he might say, 'Couple up the same old four,' and they'd get back in pairs and do-si-do. Old Bock had a real line of patter. Here's one I remember:

Ladies join your lily white hands,
Men join your browns and tans,
Ladies bow, and gents know how,
And if that ain't huggin' show me how."

I caught myself and said, "Hey, wait, this may've started as a story about dancing, and now I'm turning it into a tale of death and destruction. I'll tell you the sad tale of the night Tootsie Lines danced twenty-seven straight sets at the community center up at Cooks Springs and it killed her. Well, you can imagine that when all that dancing was done, Tootsie was wringing wet with sweat. All that do-si-do stuff is hard work. It was a cold night and Tootsie and her fellow walked about two hundred yards to the Lines's house. Tootsie went in, didn't dry her hair or take off her wet clothes. Just fell into bed. As Edna tells it, 'Tootsie slept with her head in the winder and caught the sinus and died.' I went up to the graveyard back about 1936 just to see if I could find Tootsie's grave. I did, and her tombstone was homemade out of concrete with the words spelled out with marbles pressed into the mortar when it was still wet. All it said was 'Tootsie'—no years, no RIP, no 'only daughter of' etc., etc. Just 'Tootsie.' I went hoping to find out her real name, but all in all, maybe Tootsie was enough. I guess she died and was buried just as she lived. Just plain Tootsie."

Annie was having to choke back her laughter.

I said, "Didn't you find that tragic? I can't believe you're laughing at the death of that young woman."

She said, sputtering, "'Caught the sinus and died.' I don't believe this. You made this whole saga of Tootsie up to make fun of me."

"No, I swear. It's the truth if I've ever told it. Well, maybe it's the truth. I got most of the story from Edna Lawrence, but I did go up to Cedar Grove Cemetery to look for the marker, and it was just as I said. Just plain Tootsie. But you're right; it's a funny story. A lot of the funeral stories I know end up being funny. Many stories about deaths and funerals turn out to be funny when they're told long after the events. At the time they're tragedy and heartache all the way, but the telling softens them. I guess it's a matter of laughing to ease the sadness. You probably don't have enough tapes to record all the funeral customs I've witnessed and pondered over in this absurdly long life—the funny and the sad."

Now she was fully in sync with her machine, or so she thought. When I worried that we'd use up all her tape in one day, she said, "I have enough tapes to record a session of the State Legislature next time they meet."

"All right, let me wrack my brain and see what I remember about old-timey funerals. For one thing, most people in this part of the world managed their own undertakings. They didn't embalm, but some women laid out the body and got it dressed. A carpenter then made a pine box, and that was that. If they could find a preacher, one came and spoke. If there was no preacher, somebody read a little Scripture and the body went into the ground. The favorite passage, Edna said, was from the Book of Job: 'Man that is born of woman hath but few days and is full of trouble, springeth forth like a flower and is cut down like a weed, fleeth when none pursueth.'

"Towns all had undertakers. Little towns didn't have mortuaries, which in the corrupted currents of this world are called 'funeral homes.' The local furniture dealer usually had a room far back in the store that held about three coffins, and way in back of that was the embalming room. And all undertakers had portable rigs that they could take to somebody's house if families insisted on staying with the body while it was embalmed."

Annie grimaced, "Why would anybody want to stay in the room for something so macabre?"

I grimaced along with her at the thought of undertakers, now "funeral directors," pumping out the blood and filling the body with embalming fluid. I almost gagged when I remembered that my three wives had undergone this indignity. I started drifting off again, but I caught myself and said, "I have no idea. Or maybe I do. Modesty or fear of necrophilia. I remember when Mrs. Eugenia Sprayberry died, and they called Thurman Whitmire, the undertaker, and told him to bring his equipment out to her house. Now, Mrs. Sprayberry didn't live but about a mile from the undertaker. Anybody else would've called Thurman and asked him to bring his hearse out to the house and pick up the body. But Mrs. Sprayberry's three grown daughters insisted on being with their ninety-year-old mother all through the embalming. Thurman told me that they wanted her covered up during the embalming so he wouldn't see their mother naked. They had washed her and covered her with a sheet, and they held onto the sheet while Thurman drained her and put in the embalming fluid. That's pretty serious modesty even for those days."

I hate funerals, maybe because I may be the main character at one in a few decades. I said, "I must have attended five hundred funerals in my long life, especially since nearly every graveyard in three counties is full of people I knew or taught or ran into on the street. Most funerals are sad affairs, but some are as funny as you find the story of poor Tootsie Lines."

"Sorry, John Q., I didn't mean to laugh, but it's pretty damned funny if you think about it, and I think you meant it to be funny."

I agreed, "Maybe I did at that. I'll tell you one more before we both get worn out by the sound of my voice. This is about one of Bodark Springs's dope fiends."

She reacted as I knew she would. "What? Dope fiends? I can't believe what you just said."

I feigned innocence. "What do you call them? Substance abusers?"

Miss Prim sat up straight and said, "Well, that's a lot better than 'dope fiends,' which sounds like something out of Fu Manchu or *Terry and the Pirates*."

"I can't believe you know about Fu Manchu. Anyway, I aim to tell my story. This woman, Marie Dale, had been a dope—sorry, a substance abuser—all her life. She didn't buy drugs off the street because there were no drugs on the street in Bodark Springs back when this happened. In fact, until 1915, you could buy any drug you wanted in the drugstore without a prescription. But all this happened way after 1915. Actually, it was in the 1950s.

"Back to my story, which I seem to keep interrupting. Marie had for years enjoyed terrible health and talked constantly about it. She always managed to find a sympathetic doctor—if not here, then in Paris or Sherman or Bonham or God knows where. But she always got her dilaudid or morphine or codeine or anything she asked for. If worse came to worst, she would fall back to heavy doses of Stanback Headache Powders. Well, at long last Marie proved her ill health was real, and though she was probably only about sixty, she died. Her daughter, Jackie, found her curled up dead in the bathroom where she had lain for two or three days. When Jackie called the undertaker, he saw all the drugs lined up in Marie's bathroom and called in the coroner—old Doctor Lawrence—who undertook to perform an autopsy. I doubt that he did any more than look at the body and make a cut or two for form's sake. Then he pronounced that poor Marie had died of a heart attack. Young Thurman Whitmire, old Thurman's son and heir, did the best he could with the body. You know a corpse swells up and turns dark if it lies around a few days before anybody finds it. Thurman painted her up and deemed her ready to be seen. At the funeral, people all gawked at the body, but hardly anybody said the required phrase, 'Don't she look natural?' She didn't. I can testify to that."

Annie was hating this recitation, but I couldn't stop now. "Now comes the funny part: Her cousin, Hattie Nichols, came up to the coffin, looked in, and said to Jackie in a voice that rang out all over the church, 'You ain't gonna bury your momma with that ruby ring on her fanger!' Jackie said Thurman couldn't get it off. Hattie said, 'I sure as hell can,' and she got a little stool that Preacher Maddox, a notably short man, kept up behind the pulpit and positioned it right in front of Marie's clasped hands. Hattie got on that stool and leaned in and leaned in and leaned in until she could get a grip on Marie's hand. I was in the congregation and almost choked when Hattie got so far up in that coffin that her dress rode up and you could see the tops of her stockings and the garter belt that held 'em up. Hattie came down off the stool and said, 'I God, I got that ring all right.' She said to Jackie, 'Your Ung Claude bought that when they got married back about 1923. It's probably worth a fortune now. You could buy a new car, which you surely need, with the money that ruby ring'll bring.'"

Annie was almost beside herself with the giggles at the thought of Hattie showing her substantial behind to the congregation. I went on when she had gained control of her tickle box. "There wasn't a reliable jeweler in Bodark, so Jackie, under Hattie's direction, took it to a gemologist in Dallas to have it appraised. Hattie said, 'Maybe he'll buy it and you can buy your car over in Dallas and drive back to Bodark in style.' The highly reputable gemologist in downtown Dallas said, 'This is very nice for a synthetic. If you put it in a $200 setting, it might bring $300.'"

I had worn myself out with jabber. "Now. Let's call it a day. You can turn off that machine and leave it here for another day, and I'll take you down to the Busy Bee Cafe for lunch."

Annie said, "That funny story is one of the saddest I've ever heard. Let's go. I could eat a horse."

I said, "And you might if you order meat at the Busy Bee."

CHAPTER 5

The walk downtown to the Busy Bee was just as I knew it'd be. Half the town seemed to be out hoping to get a glimpse of the *femme fatale* who had bewitched the old senior citizen—the seniorest of all Bodark citizens, I'm told. I didn't have to introduce her to more than twenty-five people. Another twenty-five or so said, "Hi, Professor. Hello, Miss Annie."

I said, when we were almost at the door of the Busy Bee, "I hope you can stand all this notoriety. Maybe I should've fixed you some lunch at home."

"No, no, I'm loving this. I don't think I've ever been the center of attention like this."

I paused at the door and asked, "Not even when you were Miss Waco?"

She stopped and grabbed my arm. "Oh, my God! How do you know about that? I've tried to live that down for years. Do you know everything there is to know about me?"

"No, just some of the high points. You know I've got history friends all over Texas. If you hang around as long as I have, you get to know everybody. And when I was on the phone checking you out, I found that *your* history friends love to gossip as much as mine do. Nearly as much as Mrs. Estelle Stringer, who lives down the block from me. She was sure you were staying with me and came up this morning when I was sitting on my porch to see what she could learn. I told her you were too tired to get out of bed after a night of passion."

Annie almost tore the sleeve of my Hickey Freeman coat off. She said, "You didn't! John Q. You didn't! You didn't!"

Now I had something to laugh about as I rescued my sleeve. "I did! I really did, but after seeing her nearly fall off my porch, I told her you'd soon be walking down from your room in the Cotton Exchange. I'm sure she peeked out her window until she saw you come up the walk to my house. Maybe spring puts the mischief in me."

She giggled again. I might have to break her of giggling. She said, "You *are* incorrigible. I knew that before I showed up in town. You're right: I have history friends who know you, and they tell as much gossip about you as they do about me."

So she knew me after all, but I said, "Well, I was never Miss Waco."

"But you probably dated 'Miss Somebody or Other' when you were between wives. You know E. Hudson Long, who taught English forever at Baylor? He said you, as he put it, 'cut a dash' back in the day. He didn't say what day."

Now I almost giggled. "Enough! Enough! Here we are at the door of the Busy Bee, and you can get ready to be the observed of all observers in this little eatery."

"*Macbeth*?"

"*Hamlet.*"

I've been a regular at the Busy Bee from the time old Bear Higgins opened it just after World War I. Bear has gone on to the greasy spoon in the sky, but his only son Harold has been running the place since just after World War II. He seemed to be waiting just inside the door, probably to get the cafe's first look at Annie.

I said, "Hello, Harold, what's good today?"

He looked past me at the beauty I was with and said, "Everything, Professor. Same answer I always give the question you always ask. Hello, Miss Annie, it's a thrill to have you grace our little establishment. I've put you and the prof at a table right in the front window. Your good looks should counteract his grumpiness. And when people see you looking like a goddess of spring, they'll flock in and make me a rich man."

She laughed and said, "Make you rich all in one day?"

He bowed. "Seeing you already makes me rich."

I said, "Go away, Harold, and send Becky over to take our order. We're here to eat, not to hear you practice your comedy routine for the Lions Club."

He stood tall and said, "I hope you'll be there next week, Prof. I have some killer one liners about you. You too, Miss Annie. Welcome! Welcome! Becky is on her way."

"'Is he always so, so, so—I don't know, so—?"

"No. But the whole town's probably ready to put on an act for you. I hope all this foolishness doesn't drive you back to Austin."

She smoothed her skirt and said, "No. I love it. Even with my fiancé, I'm pretty old news. Here I feel like a star."

"Like Carole Lombard?"

"Who?"

"Before your time. Hello, Becky, Meet Ms.—"

Becky had her pencil poised over the order pad, "Oh, I know, Professor. The beautiful Annie Baxter from Midland and Waco and Austin. Your son Charlie was in an hour ago and told me all about Miss Baxter."

I got her monologue stopped when I said, "It's Ms. Now then, Becky, are you recovered enough to take our order?"

She began writing. "Yes, sir. I know what you want—soup and salad with oil and vinegar on the side. What'll you have, Miss?"

"How about a cheeseburger and fries? And iced tea without sugar."

I said, "Becky, what's the soup today?"

She flipped her notebook closed and said, "Vegetable. The same soup Bear Higgins made when he ran this joint. You ask everytime you come in and always get the same answer. Do you want it or not?"

"Of course I want it. I always want it."

Annie said, "You must know everybody in this whole county, and all of 'em must track your every move. Did you ever think of running for office? You could probably win in a landslide. Have you ever thought about it?"

"No, never. Right now I don't have to do anything to disappoint anybody—anybody except my offspring and their offspring. And speaking of which, here comes my daughter-in-law. Lucy is Charlie's wife, and she's one of my favorite relatives."

I jumped to my feet. Or jumped as much as a ninety-five-year-old can jump. "Lucy! I can't imagine what you're doing in town in the middle of a workday down at the dairy. Don't you have to clean out the barn or something?"

She was all smiles. She was always all smiles. "Come on, Poppa, I haven't cleaned a barn in two decades, and I haven't cleaned the house in one. Charlie does all the work. All I do is eat bon bons and dream of inheriting the LaSalle."

I hugged her and said, "So Charlie told you about my threat to leave the car to you when I die?"

"He did, but I don't have any designs on your car—or your horse or your dog, or . . . "

I interrupted her dig. Obviously Charlie told her about swapping my horse and dog. I said, "Ah, Lucy, I take it that you want me to introduce you to Annie Baxter, who hates the song you are referring to. All right, Lucy, I'd like you to meet the new love of my life, Miss Annie Baxter."

Now Lucy was on the offensive. "It's Ms., Pop. Hello Ms. Annie. You've taken this town—this county—by storm just by visiting this old horse. He was growing dull till you hit town. Now he's like a young colt."

I feigned outrage. "From horse to colt in two short days. That makes me like a vampire with new blood. Is that what you're suggesting? Here, sit down and you can watch Annie eat a cheeseburger and me indulge myself in the old person's soup and salad."

Lucy looked disappointed and said, "I'd like to, Pop, but I don't want to be a third wheel. Besides, I'm not in town for fun. I have to go see Dr. Powers about a filling that's hurting like hell. Gotta go. Nice to meet your Ms. Annie, and you know I love you, Pop."

She was gone, and Becky brought the vegetable soup that had probably been simmering since Bear Higgins made the first pot.

After Annie had eaten half the burger and all the fries, and when I was partway through the soup and had one bite of the salad, she said, "You must know everybody in town. Do you?"

I didn't need long to answer this question. "Yes, I do. Well, all the grownups. I don't know the latest batch of children, but I fear they know me as some kind of comfortable old scarecrow. Bet I've stumped you with that reference."

"Yes, you did. You usually do. As I said, when I go back to Austin in a week or maybe before to meet with my adviser and spend some time with Justin, I'm gonna have to go to a bookstore and get some books of poetry so I can keep up with all your references. Or maybe Bartlett's book full of quotations."

I couldn't wait to show off. "It's from Yeats's 'Among School Children,' and he later says a line I like and that tells my story: 'old clothes upon old sticks to scare a bird.' That's me. I probably scare flocks of birds and schoolchildren of all races and creeds."

Ever the historian, she said, "Since you seem to know everybody we see in town, I wonder if you know as many blacks—I suppose you call them coloreds—as whites?"

"Probably not. I was principal when *Brown v. The Topeka, Kansas Board of Education* was handed down. And while some places in Texas had integration trouble, our school board made it an easy thing to obey the law. We integrated the high school first and the other grades soon after. I'd already known a good many colored people—blacks to you—from just being around, and after 1954, I began meeting students and parents regularly. It was a smooth transition here, though I'm not sure everybody feels the way I do. You still see a good bit of prejudice."

She seemed pleased. "It's good to know that most of it went well. I know Mansfield, somewhere in North Texas, had a real mess. KKK and all like that."

"That's true, but we're a little farther north, and you probably know that back in 1861, Eastis and several other northern counties voted against secession. They weren't abolitionists, but they weren't rabid anything, and hardly anybody in this part of the state had slaves. The election was a fairly close vote, about four hundred-plus against leaving the union and three hundred-plus for joining the Confederacy. That was a tough time. Old Sam Houston was against secession, and the vote in the state went against him heavily. Over in Cooke County, a bunch of people got hanged after secession. You probably know more about those hangings than I do. But we never were as fanatical as some parts of Texas were."

Annie was modest about her knowledge. "I'm sure I don't know more about those hangings than you do since you know everything and everybody, which just amazes the hell out of me, but we did study that when I was still at Baylor. A scandalous business."

I looked across the restaurant toward the jukebox and said, "Speaking of knowing everybody, look across at that table about halfway back. Don't stare! You see the pretty woman with the curly hair?"

She looked and said, "The woman wearing the twinset and the pearls?"

"The what set?"

Now she could teach me something. "Oh, John Q., I thought you'd know all about women's attire. A twinset is a pullover sweater with a matching cardigan."

I took the lesson with a grin. "Right. I always heard my various wives and sweethearts call it a sweater set. I need to get some lessons on feminine wear if I'm to keep up this new reputation as a lothario."

If truth were told, I probably knew more about fine women's clothes than Annie did, but no use to show off. Hell, Liz Denney was a fashion plate back in the best days of my life. I decided I might tell Annie about Liz before it was over. In many ways, Annie was Liz, the Liz I once knew. I thought of Yeats and his idea that there is always a beautiful woman who is "the Rose of the World." Her perfection passes from generation to generation. From Helen of Troy, "the most beautiful woman in the world" that the goddess promises to Paris, to Yeats's Maude Gonne. Yeats says, "Who dreams that beauty passes like a dream." Here I am sitting at a table in a small-town cafe with a woman whose beauty is passed like a dream from Helen to Liz to Annie. If I don't stop thinking things like this, I may have to be put in a home for senile old lovers. I haven't seen Liz Denney in over thirty years, but I still dream about her from time to time, and not a day passes that I don't think about her. After our love affair was over and she determined never to leave San Francisco, we both married again and were both widowed again. We exchanged Christmas cards and birthday greetings from time to time, but inertia took over and I haven't heard from her in more than a decade. I hope she is alive and well.

Annie brings me back to the little cafe on Main Street in Bodark Springs Texas, and I am no longer in Troy or Sligo or San Francisco when she says, "I'll teach you what I know about women's wear as the spring runs into summer. Then you'll be on your own. What *about* the woman in the pearls?"

Here I go again. "You say you want stories. This may turn out to be one of my better stories. Too bad you don't have your taping machine. The woman in question is Jo Ann Powell—or was once—and she was a child star here in Bodark. She could tap dance, sing, do cartwheels across the stage, and then end her tumbling act with the splits. You could see the matrons in the audience in their girdles gasping when little Jo Ann ran across the stage and landed with her legs completely, how do you say it? Well, 'split apart,' I guess. You know what I mean."

She squirmed and said, "I do, and I wince to think about it, but I have a question. Where did little Jo Ann put on her show? Was it at the movie house?"

"No, no, no. It was at the school auditorium. I said earlier that our only entertainment was church and square dancing. Well, that was way, way back. But in the thirties, we had stage shows at the high school every month or so. Some local group would rent the space—you know, the Civitan Club or the Rotary or the American Legion. And then once or twice a year, the schools would get together a talent show. That's when little Jo Ann was in her element."

I drifted off again and began remembering all the shows we put on. One group—this was before integration—would put on a minstrel show with some recognizable citizens in blackface. Somebody always did Al Jolson singing "Mammy, how I love you, how I love you," and—

"John Q., have you left me? I want to hear about the woman in the twinset."

I came back to the moment. "All right. Little Jo Ann was the apple of everybody's eye, and no one loved her more than her parents, Ralph and Marie Powell. Ralph owned the cafe about two blocks from here, the cafe where the Greyhound bus stops. I'll take you there one day, but it's not as good as the Busy Bee and not even to be compared with

Edward's restaurant at the Cotton Exchange. Anyway. Ralph had a good bit of money and Marie inherited some from her folks over in Fannin County, so when they read in the paper that Hollywood was looking for a little girl with talent to replace Shirley Temple—do I need to tell you who Shirley T—"

She interrupted, as she was doing more and more as I droned on too long. "No, do you want me to sing a few bars of 'On the Good Ship Lolllipop'?"

"Quit interrupting! All right, back to my story. Ralph and Marie knew they had the winning candidate in little Jo Ann. All she needed was some sausage curls and she could walk right into the set with W. C. Fields or Bing Crosby or anybody in Hollywood. Well, Ralph went down to Wood Chevrolet and bought a new 1938 Chevrolet Master Deluxe, the four-door model. As I recall it was brown, but that's neither here nor there. I heard that Ralph spent eight or nine hundred dollars for it. They loaded up little Jo Ann and set out for Hollywood.

"People all over town were pretty sure Jo Ann would soon be on the silver screen. Marie told everybody in the Ladies Auxiliary of the VFW that Jo Ann would make the town of Bodark Springs and all of Texas proud. Ralph didn't brag much, but you could see that he shared Marie's dream. So off they went out through West Texas and New Mexico and Arizona and—"

Here she was trying to get to the heart of the story. "Oh, come on, John Q. I know how you get from here to California. I've nearly worn out Route 66 going both ways. I may be a young thing, but I've made a few trips in my day, and—"

Now it was my turn to break in. "Were you going out to Hollywood to get in the movies? Didn't Gene Autry make *Sioux City Sue* back in the forties? You would have been perfect for—"

"No, I wasn't even going to Hollywood. I have two aunts in Bakers-field, and my family and I used to go out every two or three years to visit. We started when I was in elementary school, and my last trip was two years ago. Me in the movies! What a crazy idea!"

Not too crazy, I thought. "Well, after all your hair is red, your eyes—"

"Oh, hush up, John Q. Tell me what happened to Jo Ann."

"I'll get to that. You know the meaning of the word 'garrulous,' don't you? It's the old folks disease, practically an epidemic in these parts. So, Ralph and Marie loaded the car full of Jo Ann's spangled outfits, diaphanous dresses, and frilly pinafores. They hardly had room for Jo Ann and her little poodle. Ralph wanted to leave the dog at home, but Jo Ann threw a wall-eyed fit, what your generation probably calls a 'tantrum.' They set out and nobody heard a word for five or six weeks. That proved to the women at the VFW and the people who worked at Powell's Cafe that Jo Ann was being made a star. Then they came home. Ralph refused to talk about it, but Marie couldn't quit telling how they went from studio to studio, even managed to trap old Jack Warner in a restaurant, and tried to get the fools who make movies to see that if Jo Ann was not a replacement for Shirley, she could be the next Deanna Durbin."

Now she was stumped. "Who?"

I laughed. "Annie, you are impossible. Don't you ever watch television? You probably didn't know who W.C. Fields was, either.

"Okay, let me finish my tale. It's not the tale of woe that you might think. Well it was for Ralph and Marie, but Jo Ann was relieved. I had her in three classes, and she told me that once she got a look at all the 'crap'—her word—in Hollywood, she was glad to get back to Bodark Springs. When she was eighteen or nineteen, she married Ray Barber, who, strangely enough, is a barber. Owns his own shop and belongs to all the civic clubs."

Annie looked skeptical. "How did that turn out? Once she had years to think about it did she end up being sorry that she didn't make it big? And how did her marriage to this Barber the barber person work out?"

"See for yourself. Here comes Ray to join her for lunch."

When Ray came in, Jo Ann jumped up, as she always did, and met Ray halfway across the cafe. They hugged and she gave him a peck on the cheek. Then, hand in hand, they almost skipped their way across the room to their table.

"That's how it worked out," I said. "Jo Ann would've hated being famous. You could see a little of that when she was a child and Marie was pushing her to dance and sing and do the splits. And old Ray Barber would've died if Jo Ann had been made a star by her stage-struck momma. They have four children, and not a one of them can sing a note."

She couldn't resist. "Neither can you, John Q."

"Watch it! Mess with me and I'll give this cafe a stirring rendition of 'Sioux City Sue.'"

She laughed out loud. "You would, too. So Jo Ann was the only performer ever to come from Bodark Springs."

"Well, after the Beatles and Elvis and Buddy Holly and that bunch, you couldn't drive down the street without every passing garage door being open and full of teenagers bangin' on drums and abusin' guitars and screamin' 'Yeah, Yeah, Yeah,' or 'Peggy Sue.' Fortunately, there are only old people on my street, and so I wasn't noised to death night after night the way some people were."

She persisted. "But nobody made it big, I suppose."

I thought for a minute and tried to remember any stars from my little town. "No, old Royce Flatley's boy Rufus changed his name to Royal Crown and tried to make it as a hillbilly singer. He would've run his head in the fire to get on the Grand Ole Opry, but he never made it to Nashville. He started out in honky-tonks up in Oklahoma, played some at Legion halls and VFWs, and one time got on the Louisiana Hayride over in Shreveport for two or three sessions. Then he got drunk and was killed in a car wreck over near Honey Grove."

She persisted in trying to annoy me. "So Bodark is barren of talent?"

I took exception. "Except for me, and you'll have to admit I tell a fine tale. And I can sing better than you'll admit. Now that you've finished your burger and fries plus that delicious slice of coconut cream pie with calf slobber on it, I'll walk you back to the hotel so you can absorb these wonderful tales I've told you. Then I'll go home and take one of my many naps."

She protested. "You don't have to walk me back, I can—"

"No, I've seen how all the men in town look at you, and I'm afraid some masher will intercept you and—"

She obviously needed my instructions. "Some what? Masher?"

"You know. Some lout who'll try to take advantage of you, grope you or something like that."

She rose from her chair and said, "Don't worry, John, that's why I have a Derringer in my purse."

I was pleased to see that our Annie Oakley was armed. "Damn, Annie, don't shoot anybody on the streets of Bodark Springs. It'd take me an hour to get you out of jail. So you go your way if you're not scared, and I'll limp my way back to my recliner, my very best friend. At least till you came to town."

CHAPTER 6

I try never to take more than one nap in the afternoon. I can't say the same as the evening wears on and I'm watching television or reading a book. Some days I get three or four naps between 3:00 in the afternoon and 10:00, which is my usual bedtime. Some naps leave me refreshed and some scare me. After one of those that leaves me roiled and disturbed, I wake up lost and terrified. Often, I don't know where I am or what day it is. Those wakings are disconcerting for a few minutes, but then I get my bearings and am all right. Most of the time. But not when I dream of Uncle Fred and my dad. Those are nightmares even if they occur at three in the afternoon.

My father and Uncle Fred were identical twins, and, even as older men, looked exactly alike. That fact turned out not to be a good thing for Dad. They were so alike that there were times I mistook one for the other at first glance. Just thinking that I might dream of Fred and Dad kept me from the nap I anticipated when I sent Annie on her way. And even though I'm in the comfort of my recliner, I'm afraid to drift off because I might dream about murder and mayhem. The murder that scares me to this day.

It's no wonder these memories have resurfaced this week. It's an old man's habit to live in the past, but I'm not old. Ha! Well, not every day.

Some days I feel ninety-five and others I'm still a lad of eighteen with the world lying before me, as Matthew Arnold says, so various, so beautiful, so new. Ah, well. "Alack" and "well-a-day" and all that crap.

Psychiatrists and television psychologists and a dozen Dear Abbys say it's best to bring the hidden out into the open. I never really felt that way. If I start re-living those days back in the early thirties, I can't see how it'll help me struggle with the early seventies. In fact, I think I've been weathering the later years of my life pretty well without dredging up the ugly business of the thirties. But today. Today. Today. I can't submerge the memories of Uncle Fred's murder followed by my father's.

Here's the short version of what got things in a mess. Uncle Fred got crossways with some people named Scroggs from western Arkansas. Harry Scroggs followed the oil boom into East Texas when Uncle Fred was riding high, wide, and handsome on a sea of oil. Scroggs thought Uncle Fred was carrying on with Lula Mae Scroggs when Harry was working the night shift on one of Uncle Fred's rigs. Maybe he was and maybe he wasn't. I'll never know. Harry thought he was, so he got two of his brothers to lie in wait for Uncle Fred one night. They blocked his car with a battered old hay wagon somewhere between Kilgore and Gladewater, and when Uncle Fred got out, they beat him to death with one of those big pipe wrenches found on oil rigs. Before Fred went down, he managed to get off a shot and tore a chunk out of Lawrence Scroggs's side.

There wasn't much law in Gregg County back then, and though Fred Adams was rich and prominent, he wasn't popular with the law or the public. His death was put down to what the sheriff called "highway robbery by persons unknown." Lawrence Scroggs hightailed it back to Arkansas where he found a quack doctor to sew him up on the q.t. The other Scroggs boys went on as if nothing had happened. Harry went to Uncle Fred's funeral in Kilgore, and he made Lula Mae go with him. I suppose he thought seeing her presumed lover lying in a casket would make her cry out her guilt and fall to the floor weeping and keening. She seemed untouched by the funeral. On the other hand, maybe old Harry thought this would be an object lesson and keep her a faithful wife in the future. Maybe it did, and maybe it didn't. I never knew. I never knew whether Lula Mae was triflin' on Harry with Uncle Fred, but something tells me she wasn't. I was at the funeral and she didn't look very shocked to see Uncle Fred being laid to rest. But maybe she was a good actress.

But here is where, as Bert McGlothin used to say, the cheese got more bindin'. My father was at the funeral, and since he looked exactly like Uncle Fred, Harry decided that possibly he'd killed the wrong man. And what was he to do, he asked himself—at least as I reconstructed it later. He might as well kill Dad, just to be on the safe side. What if Lula Mae was unfaithful and thought she saw her lover still alive? The puzzle keeps me up nights even now.

Harry tracked Dad back to Eastis County and planned to lie in wait for him the way he had for Fred. He had to wait over a year, but he was a patient devil, and you know what they say, "Revenge is a dish best served cold." When he finally did get a chance to do his deed, he had two brothers and a pair of Arkansas cousins with him. This time, they planned to shoot Dad. I suppose they didn't want the murder of the two brothers to look alike. One was bludgeoned to death, so they'd shoot the other dead. They found Dad out in the field on the new Farmall tractor he'd just bought. As my father reached the end of the row he was plowing, Harry and his relatives jumped out of some johnson grass that hadn't yet been plowed and shot Dad out of the seat of the tractor. Since Dad knew in reason that the Scroggs boys had killed his brother, he went armed with a 1911 Colt Automatic that was the army's pistol of choice in World War I—and later in WWII and Korea. Dad, though badly wounded, managed to fire the whole clip into the weeds. He killed Harry and a cousin named Marsh and possibly one named Sam. Not only was Dad killed, but some of his assassins were dead or wounded, and then the fat was in the fire.

If anybody wonders how I know all this since I wasn't there (and I wasn't), I had a witness. There was a watcher, Roy Parsons, one of the field hands on Dad's farm. He saw the shooting from across the field, and then, as he crept closer, he saw the survivors drag their dead and wounded across two acres to an old pickup and get away.

When I heard that my father had been killed and that the sheriff had said almost the same words the sheriff of Gregg County had said about Fred's death—"person or persons unknown"—I doubted if I'd ever learn more. Then old Roy Parsons came to town one day and found me getting ready to bury my father. "Mr. John, I know what happened down in Eden the day your daddy got shot."

I was amazed. "You saw it, Roy?"

"Yessir, I did. I can't tell the sheriff or nobody but you. If I tell the law, they may think I done it, and a pore old nigger ain't got a chance if they can make it look like he killed a white man. If I tell you the whole story, you got to promise me that you won't tell a living soul. I mean cross your heart. Will you promise me that, sir?"

I promised him, and I've kept that promise. Old Roy's long dead. Hell, everybody connected with this sorry business is dead but me.

Not long after the funeral, word seeped out from Arkansas that this wasn't over. There was a blood feud that could only be ended when everybody named Adams in Northeast Texas was dead. The threat came in the form of a note to a local newspaper over in Bonham. It was written in pencil and mailed from Gillham, Arkansas. Unsigned of course. Joe Branson, the newspaper guy, didn't publish the poison pen—or pencil—note. He came over to Bodark Springs and gave it to me and told me to be alert. It turned out that I was the only Adams now living anywhere in the whole band of counties along the Red River. Uncle Fred never married, and I was an only child. My sons were safely away, and I deduced that I was the only Adams within gun range. I saw I had my work cut out for me. Well, now that I've busted out that gory memory, I can lean back in my recliner and nap peacefully, if Dear Abby and all those psychobabblers are right. Or maybe not.

CHAPTER 7

Annie showed up the next morning exactly at 10:00 with a mischie-vous glint in her eyes. She said, "I spent my whole evening being entertained by your three sons."

"You mean Homer has come to Bodark to rescue his old dad from the clutches of a redhead with blue eyes?"

She slapped me on the shoulder. "Don't be silly. No, Homer thinks I should fall in love with you and marry you and get my hands on that 1940 LaSalle and all that goes with it."

I grinned to think of Homer and his jokes. "Maybe being a chest sur-geon keeps more than his operating tools sharp. Maybe he's turned into a comedian."

She smiled at the memory of the evening. "Actually, I had a great evening. The food at the Cotton Exchange was out of this world, and the company of three smart and cultured gentlemen couldn't have been more refreshing. They love you and respect you and know that you're not going to go daft here in your golden years and 'swap your horse and dog' etc., etc."

I was puzzled. "Then what did they want?"

She was ahead of me as usual. "I guess you forgot that tomorrow is

Lucy's birthday, and Homer's brought his wife up to help everybody celebrate. The womenfolks are down at Eden, and the men were having a boys' night out."

Then my memory cleared and I said, "I remember about Lucy's birthday. Not only am I invited, but Lucy told me to bring a date. Guess who she meant? I didn't know Homer and Beth could make it, but I'm glad. I haven't seen either of them in a month or more. Homer is fun to be with, and Beth is almost as pretty as you. I guess this pre-birthday party was to plot against the old man."

She laughed. "No, not all. They're all three delighted that I'm here to, as they say, 'put a spring in the old coot's step.'"

I snarled, "Coot? Why the damn whippersnappers, Roy! I'll massacree them galoots."

She smiled and said, "I think I saw that movie too. You don't do a bad Gabby Hayes, but you still can't sing a lick."

But I wondered why she was at the boys' night out. "I thought girls were barred from stag events."

"Oh, I was going into the restaurant alone when Eddie saw me. He jumped up, and then Charlie and Homer were on their feet. Eddie called the waiter and had him set an extra place for me at the table. I resisted, modestly and coyly I'll admit, but I really couldn't wait to sit down with all the Adams sons. It was worth it—not just for the free five-course meal—but for the company."

I said, "Maybe if you agree to be my date tomorrow night, you can get your fill of the Adams mob. Maybe with the women there they can get you aside and persuade you to pump me for all my little secrets. Did they bring up Maureen Lasky?"

She became alert when I mentioned a female I might know. "Who?"

I didn't plan to get too involved in my various sweethearts, but I did wonder who knew what. "Never mind. What about Ernestine Brown or Elizabeth Denney?"

She laughed, "If those are old girlfriends, I bet they already know all they need to know about your various between-marriages courtships. They're pretty observant men if our talk was any indication."

I grumbled as old men are supposed to do. "I don't think anything is

73

sacred in this little corner of the world. If I lived in Dallas, I might not have to put up with so many prying eyes. Now, out with it, what did they want?"

She looked at the ceiling and said, "I'm not sure exactly, John Q., but I got a hint that they weren't worried that I'd enthrall you with my red hair. What I inferred, probably wrongly, was that they worried you would tell me things that wouldn't be, as Charlie put it, 'in Pop's best interest.'"

Here we go, I thought. "I have no idea what they think I'm likely to blurt out to you that'd send me to Huntsville."

Still worrying about my "lost years." I'm sure they hoped that my occulted guilt wouldn't unkennel itself as I got wound up on the tape machine. Oh, well.

I passed my worries off for the moment. "I'm glad the boys took to you and fed you well. I don't want you to go hungry here in Bodark. I hear for the party tonight they'll have *pate de foie gras* to start, then guinea hen under glass. So maybe today we can be less elegant and go to Powell's Cafe. There you can meet the former star Jo Ann and her brother. They inherited the place from Ralph and Marie and often work there together. What are we going to talk about today?"

She consulted her notebook. "Well, I thought marriages, and—"

Now I am the interrupter. It's not always Annie who breaks into our conversations. "Is this a proposal? If so, I accept. When do we set the date?"

She smiled and said, "I'm afraid Mr. Justin Cole would have a broken heart if I jilted him for a man with a 1940 LaSalle. I'm interested in the way marriages have changed over the years in this part of the world. Today, big city marriages average out to $10,000 a pop. I doubt if half that much changes hands today in Bodark Springs, and I know that old-time marriages were dirt cheap. So, Johnny, tell me a story—or stories."

I smiled my biggest smile and said, "Johnny? My, oh, my, how informal we're getting. Now it's Johnny and Eddie and Charlie. What will the women at the party tonight think?"

She thought for a second and said, "That I'm a friendly West Texas girl. What else? All right, *Professor*, tell me about old-timey weddings."

"All right. Let me see. Maybe not just weddings, but courtships, weddings, marriage tales, shivarees, honeymoons, and divorces. The whole romance world as it was once lived, or at least as I know about it. Will that satisfy your folks in Austin?"

She fired up the machine and said, "Whatever you tell me'll fill tape, and a full set of reels will tickle 'em plumb to death."

"'Plumb'? You're fittin' right in up here in the north country, aren't you? Keep talkin' like a country girl and not a PhD candidate and you can get all of Eastis County eatin' out of your hand. You won't need me. You can roam the county on your own and get songs and stories and superstitions and histories—real and fake—enough to fill a whole book of folklore."

She punched the button that said "record" and said, "So what is a shivaree?"

I was off and running. "Shivaree is what louts and hangers-on used to do to the bride and groom on the wedding night. Nowadays, all anybody seems to do is tie tin cans on the getaway car and paint tempera paint on the back window saying 'Just Married' or '1+1=3.' But in olden times things went much farther. I'll tell you all about shivarees when I decide to launch my boring tirade on love and marriage."

She grinned. "Why? You got something against marriage?"

"No, I've done it three times. And happily each time, so I should be a paid spokesman for wedded bliss by now. So far I'm unpaid, but I'm in the market for a sponsor. I guess *tirade* was the wrong word. I should've said *disquisition.*"

She checked to see that the red light on her machine was on. "All right, let me get the tape rolling for your dissertation on marital happiness. Tell me about when you were married the first time."

I held up a hand. "Wait. I thought we weren't doing my biography."

She was quick to say, "We aren't. No! No! I don't want to know any secrets about your married life or anything like that, but if you tell me what was customary when you got married—when was it?—early in the century?—I mean, uh, it'll give me a glimpse into what, uh—Oh, sorry, I'm fumbling for words again. Forget it, John Q."

I didn't mean to cause her consternation. "No, no. I didn't mean to climb up on my high horse. Or secrecy mare or, oh, hell, now I'm fumbling. Of course I'll tell you how it was back in 1903. That may be the best way to start out about the way courtships and weddings changed during my long and boring life. Let's see. Esther and I got engaged back when we were in college at Commerce. I had my mother's rings. I think I mentioned that she died when I was little. I gave the diamond one to Esther and kept the plain band for the actual wedding. My dad told me those rings came down from his parents. Good thing, too, since we didn't have much money at the time. Dad did, I guess, but I was set on being on my own. This is boring. Sorry."

"No, you tell it your way, and I'll decide if it's boring. So far it's not, but if it gets torpid, I'll yawn or something."

I dared her to yawn when I got rolling. "Okay. As soon as school was out, I went over to Honey Grove and asked her daddy if I could marry Esther. I may've even said, 'have her hand in marriage,' but I hope I didn't. That kind of talk would've been out of some English novel. Anyway, he said yes, and we found a preacher at the Methodist Church there and made a plan. Esther's mother took it from there, and it was all bridesmaids and flowers and ushers and best men and whatnot. I was nervous, couldn't see the bride for a day or two, and rode my horse back to Eden to wait."

I stared at her to see if she was about to yawn. "All right so far?"

She laughed and said, "It will be if you hurry up and tell me the good parts."

There were good parts to tell all right. "The wedding went off, rice was thrown, and Esther and I got in my buggy, which had tin cans tied to it in weak imitation of a proper shivaree, and we rode along behind my pacing mare back to Bodark. I put the horse and buggy up at the livery stable, and—oh, yes, we had livery stables—and caught the T and P to Fort Worth to barely make it in time to catch the Missouri Pacific to Houston and then the Frisco to Galveston. We honeymooned at the old Beach Hotel, which was the forerunner of the famous Galvez Hotel. And that is the end of the story. Honeymoons are secret. You'll see when you and Mr. Cole go to St. Kitts or Turks and Caicos or Martinique or someplace where they serve drinks with little umbrellas."

She seemed pleased at my honeymoon tale such as it was. "You do sound like a romantic, *Johnny*. And I did like hearing about your marriage."

I told her to hold on, the good part was yet to come. "Our story is nothing to compare to Dulcie Moore's when she married Floyd. They got married about 1935—long after Esther and I did, and only a few years after I married the second time. I think I told you that Esther died of the Spanish flu in 1918."

She nodded. "If you didn't, somebody did. Anyway, I knew it. She was the mother of your three sons, right?"

I had to think for a minute to get dates right. "Yes. Edward in 1905, Charles in 1908, and Homer in 1912. They didn't have a mother very long. I raised 'em with the help of Esther's mother, who moved from Honey Grove after her husband died. She lived in the house with me and the boys till she died in 1925. She was eighty. By then Eddie was at UT, and the other two were old enough to look after themselves. Oddly enough, they were never troublesome as teenagers. All right, I'm through talking about me and mine. Back to Dulcie and Floyd. Dulcie was from over at Savoy, and Floyd was from somewhere up across the Red in Bryan County, Oklahoma. Dulcie had been a housemaid here at the Cotton Exchange way before Eddie bought it. Floyd was a painter of barns all over three counties. As best I remember, both were orphans and led sort of rackety lives till they got to sparking pretty heavily. They courted and broke up, courted and broke up, courted and broke up until one day Floyd grabbed Dulcie and tied her up with a piece of plow line and told her he was gonna keep her locked up in a barn that was vacant down south of town. He said he was gonna damned marry her if he had to hogtie her and drag her ass to Oklahoma where they were not so particular about whether the bride was willin' or not. He said he'd seen grooms tied hand and foot and married to women who'd got in a family way back in Oklahoma. Well Dulcie died laughing and said, 'Hell, Floyd, I didn't think you was ever gonna ast me. Let's go to the courthouse rat now.'"

I was even amused as I was telling this tale. "Floyd had a 1929 Model A coupe, and he drove it up on the square with Dulcie still hogtied. He ran into the courthouse and got Judge Walters, whose barn Floyd painted the week before, and begged him to get his book and come out to the car and marry them. Well, the judge began to see the humor when he got to the car and saw Dulcie all tied up. He said, 'Floyd, if you'll untie her, I'll do the service right here.' He did. Married them in the front seat of Floyd's Model A. I know this is the truth because Dulcie told it all over the county for years and years. She was proud to be the only person in the world, she said, who got married in the front seat of a Model A Ford, and then she'd add, 'I ain't sayin' a word about what used to go on in the back seat.'"

I was on a roll, as the young people say. "Now, I'll tell you about Edna Lawrence and her wedding. Edna was from up in the north of the county east of Cooks Springs and lived on a farm where, as she used to put it, 'I done the work of a man.' She had two brothers, but they ran away rather than work like slaves for her daddy, old man Ingram, whose grandson described him as 'Satan. A pure and T devil if there ever was one.' Edna had been slipping out at night to meet Daniel Lawrence after old man Ingram and old lady Ingram went to sleep. After a month or so, Daniel—she always called him Dan'l—begged her to run away and get married."

Annie was not about to yawn now. She said. "I can't wait to see if anybody gets hogtied now."

I ignored her and went on. "As Edna tells it—or rather told it—since she's been gone for several years—'I waited till the clock struck eleven, then I got the grip I'd packed and slipped out the back door to go and meet Dan'l. I had to walk five miles in the pitch dark till I got to the Brushy Settlement where Dan'l was gonna meet me. He didn't dare come any closer to the farm because he knowed my daddy'd shoot him with that old twelve gauge he kept by the front door. Probably woulda shot me if he'd knowed that I was runnin' off. Well, I didn't get snake bit or eat by a wildcat, and Dan'l was waitin' for me. Then we walked another five miles to get to Harm's house.'"

I interrupted to point out that Harm had been named Hiram at birth.

Annie said, "Harm, you're saying, right?"

"Right. Harm Lawrence, born Hiram. Okay, back to Edna's tale as she told it. 'Harm had an old high-wheeled Dodge, about a 1928 model as I recollect it, and we set off for Oklahoma. At about four o'clock in the morning, we woke up a justice of the peace that Harm knowed. He got his wife up as a witness and we was married in the front room of their house. I don't know what we done about a marriage license. I think Dan'l got one later when he was haulin' a load of lumber up to Oklahoma. I can tell you I didn't have no honeymoon. I don't know any country people who did. Me and Dan'l moved in the log house that Harm and his wife, Maydell, lived in, and wouldn't you know it I was back to workin' like a man. But it was different then. I had a man of my own.'"

Annie saw the sadness of Edna's life and said, "I'm glad I live in a different time."

"You should be," I said, and went on, "She said old man Ingram got over being mad and made regular visits to Edna and Daniel, usually to borrow money. He never learned to drive a car. Never had one, Edna said, but he used to come the ten miles or so to where Edna and Daniel lived in a little shack on Harm's place they'd moved into. He drove over on his tractor. He had a made-up kind of wagon that he pulled behind it, and old lady Ingram would sit up in it surrounded by pillows and quilts. I knew Edna pretty well, but I never saw Dan'l. He got killed when he drove his truck up on what Edna called 'the Number 8 Highway,' and got hit by a logging truck. This was probably just before World War II."

Annie found this story funny and said, "Well, all I can say is that I ain't gonna slip off in the middle of the night to get married. I'd get snake bit for sure, or et up by a mountain lion. I ain't gonna walk no five miles. Me and old Justin's gonna drive to our wedding."

I laughed at her dialect and said, "Is Eastis County rubbing off on you or are you making fun of my people?"

She grinned. "I'm making fun of you. It's the least I can do to keep you talking. Seriously, this is stuff I've never heard before. I'm entertained. Really."

"All right, I'll tell you about shivarees and then we can make a plan about Lucy's birthday party. Back in what for you is ancient days when a couple got married the people in the neighborhood would try like hell to ruin the wedding night. They would bang washtubs and anything that would make noise right outside the bedroom window. They'd sing and holler and try to be sure the first honeymoon night would be one for the couple to remember and maybe later pass on to other newlyweds. In a few cases, the menfolks would kidnap the groom and take him way off in the country and leave him, especially if he was already dressed—or undressed—for bed. Of course they wouldn't leave him miles from home for very long. They knew—the single ones—that all this could come back at 'em. Where people were really mean, they might dunk the groom in a rain barrel. Bad as all that was, it doesn't compare to the Middle Ages when the lord of the manor got to take the bride to bed first. That was worse than another custom from days of yore—and this is pretty bad. The neighbors would gather outside the bridal chamber and wait for the groom to come out and show the bride's nightgown with blood on it. I don't need to explain the symbolism of that bit of barbarism to a PhD candidate, do I?"

She squirmed in her chair and said, "God no! Yuck. Maybe I'll never marry. Or maybe stay here in Bodark, marry you, learn to drive a car with 'three on the tree,' and drive you all over the place in the LaSalle."

I joined in the fun. "Done!" I said. "Now if you're through flirtin' with me, let's turn off the infernal machine so we can get ready for tonight's festivities. You go back to the hotel, rest after all these hair-raising stories, and then get dolled up for Lucy's party. I'll come to the hotel a little before seven, ring your room, and wait for you in Eddie's office. He'll be in the ballroom harassing the help and gettin' in the way. We can then prepare for a grand entrance to impress my children and grandchildren—and maybe a great-grandchild or two.

CHAPTER 8

O f course I have no idea how Annie spent her afternoon, but I made good use of the time by leaning way back in my recliner and taking two or three naps. When I woke I knew I could face as many relatives and well-wishers as Lucy's party might draw. I decided to go the whole hog, so I took a shower, re-shaved, and started working on my wardrobe for the evening. I found a blue shirt with a white collar and cuffs that I had made in London—cufflinks, of course. I usually get a dozen shirts a year from Bond Street. They have my measurements from a trip I made to England about three years ago, and I haven't varied an inch in any direction since then. Well, not much. I may be two or three inches shorter than the six-three I was when I was forty. I decided on a midnight blue suit that was semi-bespoke from Neiman-Marcus. Semi-bespoke meant that it wasn't fully created by a tailor. A person went into N-M, selected an Oxxford suit off the rack, then got completely measured before the suit was sent off somewhere, taken apart, and fitted perfectly to the measurements their tailor took in the store.

I know this sounds like I aspire to be the dandy of Bodark Springs. Well, hell, why not? Somebody has to keep up a little tone way out here in the provinces. I found a regimental striped tie that the haberdasher in Bond Street told me was the colors of the Coldstream Guards. Maybe it was and maybe it wasn't. Nobody in this county will know, and 99 percent of the denizens of Eastis never heard of the Coldstream Guards anyway. The shoes were cap-toed black leather made by my old friend Rolando at Leddy's. The long socks were a deep midnight blue with clocks on them—discreetly placed, of course. I wound and set my eighteen-carat gold Zenith pocket watch—hunter case, needless to say—and dropped it into that pocket of the suit some sissies use for pocket squares. Then I put the rosette on the end of my gold and platinum watch chain in the buttonhole on my left lapel. So here I was, if I may borrow a line from Raymond Chandler, clean, shaved, and sober, and I didn't care who knew it.

When I got to the hotel, Maybelline Mowry, one of Rosie's nieces, was on the desk. She saw me and said, "Lord, God, Mr. John, you done gussied yoself up like a Philadelphia lawyer. You dressed up for that young lady I hear you sweet on? She mighty fine lookin' with all that red hair and that body outen the *Playboy* magazine. Wooooee, y'all gonna be somethin' when you hit that ballroom. Mr. Eddie gonna die with the jealous when he see you two."

"You think Eddie is after my date?"

She laughed and said, "If he ain't, he plum' crazy."

I was tired of Maybelline's ragging. "All right, Maybelline, quit foolin' around and ring her room."

She wouldn't leave her joking alone. "Yeah, that Miss Annie's some-thin' all right."

"It's Ms. Annie."

She was incredulous. "Miz. Miz. You mean she married?"

"No, not Miz as in Missus. It's Miz as in Miz."

She kept up her act. "You foolin' with me now. If she ain't married, it gotta be Miss. I wadn't born yestiddy."

"All right. Have it your way and ring Miss Annie. And, by the way, you can drop the Aunt Jemima routine. I know you're in your third year at East Texas State."

She grew more serious. "Sorry, Professor, I guess I'm like everybody in town. All of us worry about you falling in love at your age. Who knows what harm might come of that."

"Well, Maybelline, men have died from time to time, and worms have eaten them. But not for love."

She must have struggled with the allusion. "I know that's from Shakespeare. Knowing you, I'll bet it's from *Hamlet*."

I laughed now. "No. But I'm glad you were close. Your years in Commerce haven't been wasted. It's from *As You Like It*."

She smiled. "You always have to have the last word, don't you, Prof?"

"Just sometimes. Ah, here comes the dangerously alluring Ms. Annie Baxter."

The phone rang and Maybelline dashed behind the counter and busied herself doing the business of the Cotton Exchange Hotel as I greeted Annie and suggested we go into Edward's office. "I'll help you prepare a face to meet the faces that you'll meet."

Annie frowned. "You never quit testing me, do you, John Q.? Who's it from?"

"It's T. S. Eliot. 'The Love Song of J. Alfred Prufrock.' Since you said you were interested in my little quotation quizzes, maybe I have an extra poetry book or two to tide you over till you get to Austin."

Before we got to Eddie's office, Annie handed me a note that read: "Ask the prof how many people he's killed."

"What do you think this means? Have you killed somebody? Like way, way back."

I felt my face flush hot. I could only hope Annie hadn't noticed. "Maybe," I said calmly. "You remember me telling you I was in the war with Spain, don't you? Well, we shot rifles across great stretches of ground. You could never tell if you hit anything. So maybe I did. Somebody shot me. I've still got the scars to prove it."

"Oh," Annie said, "I wonder why anybody would warn me about your war service."

"I wonder too. Maybe when you've taught as long as I did, you make a few people mad. This may be a way of getting back at a senile old man. Or maybe somebody is jealous of me being seen all over town with a beautiful woman whose hair is red and her eyes are blue. Want me to sing our song?"

"No, no, no, you can't sing a lick."

Now I was really worried. Somebody had slipped a note under

Annie's door. That meant my nemesis was not off in Arkansas, but here in Bodark Springs. I knew there was worse to come, and I needed to make preparations for the axe to fall.

When we were in Eddie's office and safe from intrusions, I gave Annie a brief rundown on all the grandchildren. Eddie has three offspring ranging in age from the early forties to the late thirties. I couldn't recall the ages exactly, but I named them off—George, the eldest; then Charles II, named for his uncle Charlie; then Louise. Charles and Lucy also had three—Robert, Ann, and Margie, all early thirties or late twenties. Oddly enough, all my children produced in threes. I'll have to ask Annie if the third time is always a charm. She's a budding folklorist and should have an idea about that old saw. Maybe it *is* a charm. I'm lucky with three boys—middle-aged men now—but not with my three wives. Homer and Beth's threes were Sally, Joan, and Sam. Sam was the youngest of the grandchildren; he's still in his teens. I told her there might be great-grandchildren and maybe a great-great or two. Even I have trouble keeping up with the newest unless I have a scorecard.

"Okay, Annie, I'll introduce you to Beth, the only daughter-in-law you haven't met, and then you're on your own. As we say out here in the sticks, 'It's root hog or die.'"

She frowned. "Why do you always use that pig image? I heard you say it before. Don't worry about me. I'll manage. I imagine they'll flock to me to see the evil woman out to steal Great-Grandpa's heart. And his 1940 LaSalle."

Now I was ready. "Let's make a grand entrance. Take my arm as we enter the ballroom and look adoringly at me."

We moved to the ballroom and one of Eddie's bellhops opened both doors and stood aside to let the notorious pair enter the crowded room. At that moment, as they say in novels and plays, "A hush fell on the room." Then three or four unidentified little urchins ran toward me shouting "Grandad John!" It should have been "Great-Grandad John," but those from the minor generation are as confused about identities as I am. Thus began what should have been one of the most disorienting nights of Ms. Annie Baxter's life. But it wasn't. She took the whole

Adams tribe in stride, talked as if she'd known the sons and daughters and assorted offspring and they'd all been friends from Midland or Waco or Austin. I more or less faded into the background and, as they say in legal circles, relied on the Fifth Amendment.

So the evening wore on and I wore out. I retreated to a comfortable couch that Eddie had thoughtfully sent in for me to sit on and hold court. Nobody joined me for what seemed like an hour until Homer came and sat down.

He was grinning from ear to ear. "Well, Pop, this was supposed to be a celebration for Lucy's turning, what, a Jack Benny thirty-nine? But it looks more like an occasion honoring your sweetie from Austin."

"Oh, come off it, Homer, you know I'm not the old fool that all my descendants seem to think I am. It'll be a cold day in Mozambique when I lose my head and heart to somebody seventy years younger than I am. I'm bulletproof, but you and Eddie—and maybe Charlie—might run off with a girl of twenty any day. "

He laughed and said, "I know you're safe, and so do all of them. They just want to give you some attention to get you out of the rut that goes with being Bodark Springs's oldest and most distinguished resident."

I refused the title. "Which I'm not. We have a congressman from here, and a district judge that may someday get appointed to the Supreme Court. Hell, old Early Leonard the blacksmith contributes more to life hereabouts than one tired old schoolteacher."

Homer turned serious, so I was alerted. "Anyway, I didn't come over here to chide you about your social life. I wanted to have a word or two about your health. You look good and you seem fit, but you *are* at an age where you might need more than luck to keep on being hale and hearty."

"And you're suggesting?"

The doctor in him took over. "How would you feel about a trip to Temple to Scott and White for a full workup? Or, hell, we can both afford it, so let's go up to Rochester and let the people at Mayo Clinic prove that you'll make it to and beyond the Bicentennial. That's what I hear some folks in town are trying to gear you up for."

I was in refusing mode. "Old Ruby Lathem just wants to ride in the front seat of the LaSalle. Thanks for coming over, Homer, but I'm not about to go to some fancy clinic. Those people always find a brain tumor or something dreadful. I'll just take my chances and hope to die here in Bodark with no fanfare and no chemo or whatever you call the stuff that makes your hair fall out. Edward's busy worrying about my legal life and you're on me about my physical life. Old Charlie is the only one to let me alone to rust unburnished, as Tennyson puts it. I'm doin' fine, but you look a little peaked tonight."

Homer laughed. "Hell, I'm a doctor, and we're supposed to look 'peaked,' as you country people put it. We know better than to seek medical advice or go to fancy clinics. And Eddie'll probably stay away from courts and judges and other lawyers now that he's made his pile. I still think you're lucky to have Eddie and me to cover those parts of your life. If you won't listen to us, let me give you one little piece of advice: Just don't wreck the LaSalle. I hear Lucy and Beth and Miss Annie are all hoping to fall heir to the old battleship someday."

I groaned. "Why do I have to keep saying this? It's Ms. Annie. And I'll be driving that car when all you sprouts are in a nursing home."

Homer wouldn't leave it. "I guess you've never thought of a retirement home for yourself, have you?"

I started to rant. "No! Not just no, but *hell no!* Don't go puttin' ideas about that in Edward's and Charlie's ears. I'm stayin' put out in the old house on Main."

Homer was almost winding down. "And driving all over hell and half of Georgia in that big Buick Electra. I hope you don't have a heart attack and kill somebody when you're going sixty on Highway 82. Ah, hell, Dad, I don't want to live long enough to go to your funeral. I'll bet nobody in this room is looking forward to seeing the last of you. I don't suppose you have a burial—"

I interrupted. "Damn it, Homer, just quit all this doomsday talk. Clinics, rest homes, burial plots. I don't care what they do when I croak. They can just sharpen my feet and drive me in the ground for all I care."

"All right, Pop, I'll go and leave you alone. Maybe I'll get Ms. Annie to dance with me."

As Homer waltzed off to dance with Annie, I couldn't help but laugh to myself. They all mean well, but they want to make me old before my time. I remember about ten years ago when the three of them turned the guest house—the old mother-in-law house—in my backyard into a gym for me. I go out every day and use the treadmill, the resistance machines, and the stair-stepper. Nowadays Lucy always wants to talk about my diet. I told her I follow the prescription of the old Chicago newspaper guy, Mike Royko. He said, "To lose weight, don't eat anything good." I told Lucy I exist on sprouts and kumquats. Actually, I eat mostly vegetables and fruits, and those sparingly. I wish they'd all leave me alone. I can't help but remember the Donne poem that starts "For god's sake hold your tongue and let me love/Chide my palsy or my gout,/my five grey hairs or ruined fortune flout"—and so on. I can't remember all the rest of it. Maybe I *am* gettin' senile after all.

A little boy of about five came over to stare at me. He said, "Are you my great-grandpa?"

I said, "Yes, sir, I guess I must be."

"Well, damn!" he said and skipped away.

What a perfect way to end my day! Now I could escape. I walked over and kissed Lucy and told her to have many more birthdays because I sure as hell planned to. Then I said, "I'm off. I've got thoughts to think and Scotch to drink. Tell everybody I had a rare time."

Annie caught me as I made for the door and asked if we were on for tomorrow for more taping. I said, "Yes, if the Lord spares us."

CHAPTER 9

Annie arrived at my house promptly at 10:00 a.m. ready to tackle another day with the town's ancient. She looked fresh, so I assumed she hadn't stayed at Lucy's party until the late hours.

She explained her freshness when I asked her what time it broke up. "I left about 11:00 and was in bed long before midnight. I got a good night's sleep and am ready for more tales of the Eastis County Woods. Did you enjoy the party?"

I remembered Homer's probing. "Not much. I thought we might've made a bigger splash when we made our grand entrance. When you and I walked into the ballroom, I started to go over to the bandleader and ask him to play 'Sioux City Sue' so I could sing about you to the assembled throng."

She made a gagging sound. "Oh, John Q., you can't sing a lick, but then that band couldn't play a lick either."

"I *can too sing*. But you're right about the band. I think they're kids from the high school that Eddie hired because he used to be sweet on the trombone player's mother. Eddie likes to keep old girlfriends friendly. Not a bad trait, I'd say."

She laughed. "I'll bet you keep your old girlfriends friendly too, John Q."

"Well, it's easy enough when they're all dead. I've outlived almost everybody I was ever sweet on—wives or sweethearts. But enough about my salad days."

"I'll bet you had some 'salad days.' Oh, you stole that phrase from Shakespeare. Wasn't that 'salad days' a reference to Cleopatra?"

I was pleased. "It was. Clever girl. You don't let an old man get away with anything do you? Not even a little plagiarism."

She liked being one up on me. "No, and I've started keeping a weather eye on you since you can be pretty tricky. Were you having a bad time with all those revelers and that passel of little kids?"

I thought hard for a second. "No, I didn't mind the kids, though one of the little 'uns took a look at me, said 'Well, damn!' and ran away. I didn't get a chance to talk to any of my many grandchildren since Homer cornered me on the couch and started in about my health. Wanted me to go to Mayo or somewhere and have some people of his persuasion poke and prod at me. Hey, that's some fine alliteration! Then he started in about putting me in a nursing home."

She laughed, "Surely not a nursing home. Did he really suggest that?"

"No, he said retirement home or assisted living warehouse or some such attempt at sugarcoating, but I figure they're all the same. And I say to hell with 'em. Did you get to meet everybody? I saw people crowding around you before I left. Did Eddie monopolize you? Maybelline said, 'Mr. Eddie fixin' to get sweet on Miss Annie.' I told her he was way too old for you, but she said, 'I don't know 'bout that. He see his daddy followin' aroun' after her like he's a little puppy dog. And you twice as old as Mr. Eddie.'"

She grinned and said, "And what did you say?"

"I said, 'It's Ms.'"

She started looking at the tapes in her bag. "Anyway, Eddie told me he has a ladylove over in Bonham. Have you met her?"

"No, and he's never talked about her to me. I know that I have to work a couple of nights a week at the hotel so he can be off somewhere. Needless to say, Maybelline keeps me current on his goings and comings and adds a lot of her own speculations, but his private life is not my concern. I don't ask him anything, and I sure as hell don't want him prying into my business, though none of my doin's have to do with women. Well, except for you of course."

She wasn't sure how to take my attitude toward privacy. "You never ask any of your sons or grandchildren about their lives? That makes you an oddity. Most parents snoop and quiz and sneak around to find out what their kids are doing. I know mine always did—and maybe still do."

"Not me. I follow the dictum of Mrs. Eddy."

She frowned, "Who?"

Now I was one up on her. "Mary Baker Eddy, the woman who founded Christian Science. She said, 'You've got to let everyone go to heaven or hell at his own speed.'"

She fumbled in her bag for a tape or something and said, "And you never interfere? You *are* a marvel, John Q."

I liked that characterization of me. "So they say. It's marvelous that I've been around this long. Boyd McGlothing used to say that he wanted to live to be ninety and get hung for rape. I've never been accused of rape, but having all the gossip going around about you and me here near the end of my ninety-fourth year is nearly as good. I don't suppose my grandchildren got on to you about hanging out with Grandpa."

She grinned. "No, not all. They said my presence put a spring in your step, and not a one of them really thinks you're sweet on me or that I'm after you and the LaSalle."

I laughed again. I seem to do that a lot nowadays. "Good. Though I'll have to admit I enjoyed the scandal. What do you want us to talk about today? You can crank up your machine, though I'm sort of like John Earl Cogburn about tape recorders. He said, 'It's sort of like talking to a damn stump.' Did I tell you that before?"

"Of course you have." Snippy.

She looked at her notes. "Have you exhausted the subject of marriage? If you haven't, I'd like more *real* scandal. Scandal that doesn't involve you and me."

I didn't have notes to consult and buy time with. "You know, I've been thinking a lot about the twists and turns of marriage as I've seen it in these parts. I have a few more stories if you can get that reel on and flick the record switch. I want to tell you about the Snead family and all the stuff they got mixed up in over two or three generations. Ready?"

She turned on the recorder. "Let 'er rip."

I cleared my throat ready to launch into a story or two. "Well, the story starts way back before I knew any of the Sneads. I know they had three sons—Boss, George, and Taft. Boss was the oldest by several years. For some reason, they never gave him a name, just called him 'Boss.' I have no idea why. The truth of this is that Boss went through life—he's now dead—without a name. He couldn't read or write, but when he got wealthy and had to deal with banks and contracts, somebody taught him to sign checks and bills and business papers 'J. B. Snead.' Maybe Boss's story shows that education is not for everybody. I don't believe that of course; after all, I *am* a school man."

She looked disbelieving. "You're not making this up, are you? There really was a man who never had a given name?"

"I swear. I knew Boss fairly well at one time. His brother George had a name, though I can't swear that he had a middle name. Now Taft, who was born about 1910, was named William Howard Taft Snead. They shorted Boss in the name area, but went full out on Taft.

"Sometime after Boss and George left home, old man Snead and his wife fell out. Notice I'm using the local parlance. They quit speaking, didn't speak for twenty years. They lived in the same house, slept in the same bed, and ate at the same table. But they never spoke. I know this because Taft told me all about it. He said they would sit at the supper table and old man Snead—I never knew his name, but he probably had one since most people, even Sneads, do—old man Snead would say, 'Taffy, tell your mama to pass them biscuits.' Mrs. Snead would appear not to hear the request till Taft would say, 'Mammy, Daddy says pass the biscuits.' Then she'd pass the biscuits. Taft swears they never spoke. Not a word for twenty years."

Annie frowned. "John Q., you don't really believe that two people lived and slept in the bed together for twenty years and never spoke."

"Annie, to quote A. E. Housman, 'I tell the tale I heard told.' Yes, I guess I do believe it. Taft Snead was not a liar, and I've heard other people say they had dinner at the Snead house and the old couple never said a word. Old lady Snead—I never knew her name either—died, and several people told me that old man Snead went off in the woods and stayed for three or four days. Everybody believed he went off to grieve for her. I guess I believe that too.

"Back to Boss. He had a few cows and ran a little, if you'll pardon the expression, half-assed dairy. He didn't have many cows, but he milked a few and sold the milk to a bigger dairy in Bonham. He had an old Model T that'd been cut down into a pickup. He would haul three milk cans from his little farm, but only two of the cans held milk. The third one held bootleg whiskey. He didn't make the whiskey as far as I know. He just bought it from moonshiners and sold it to bootleggers in Bonham. This was way back when the whole country was dry, and the woods along both sides of the Red were full of people making whiskey. I heard that even Taft had a little still made out of a Model T radiator and sold all he could make to his older brother. Boss got pretty well-to-do during the 1920s. He did so well that when Prohibition was over and the whiskey trade was not so lucrative, he invested his money in a bunch of land and a couple of hundred cows and became a legitimate dairy farmer. He got rich in the milk business and only half rich in the whiskey business."

She changed a reel and said, "And what happened to Taft?"

"Nothing much. He was the poor relation. George went to work for Boss once the dairy business succeeded, but Taft did a little of this and a little of that and ended up working in a grocery store. He was a pretty good-looking young man, so he married two or three times to not much avail. One of his wives got so mad at him that she threw a hammer at his 1933 Chevrolet as he was backing out of the driveway after he'd called her a sorry slut. 'Scuse the French. The hammer broke the windshield but stuck there in the middle of the driver's side. Taft drove the car to town. I saw it, and everybody who did said, 'Old Taft was lucky that woman didn't have a gun.' Taft thought the whole episode was funny and left the hammer stuck in the windshield till Jim Tom Pledger, the Chief of Police, made him get a new windshield."

Annie sighed. "That's a strange tale. You knew them pretty well I take it."

I was just gettin' underway. "I guess I did, but, wait, I'm not through.

92

Boss's dairy was not far off a crossroads that had a little country store off to one side. It was the only business for miles around. It was run by Hubert Farmer and his wife Ruth. It was the only store around that had electricity, and they got the juice from a Delco system that was housed in a little building next to the store. Hubert was connected to some other people named Farmer—cousins or something—who had a wholesale business over in Paris, so he was away a good bit doing work there while Ruth ran the store."

Annie got out a pencil and flipped the pages of her notebook. "Wait. What's a Delco system? I have to annotate everything you tell me and I've never heard of a Delco system."

"I'm no electrician, but as I understand the way it worked was to have a bunch of wet cell batteries connected together. Those batteries, as I remember seeing them, were made out of heavy glass, glass like you see in a building that has a wall of glass bricks. The batteries were full of acid and worked sort of like the dry cell battery in your car or your flashlight. Only a lot better. I guess if you're forced to do a full disquisition on Delco systems, you're gonna have to look 'em up."

"No, that's all I need. Go on about Ruth and Hubert. Tell me how this ties in to Boss Snead."

She must have guessed what I was about to tell her. "I'll bet you can guess what happens next since Boss is in walking distance of the store and Hubert's away several days a month. Do you want to guess at what comes next?"

I could see that she must have tumbled to where this story was going. "They had an affair, right?"

"Correct. Ruth had a little girl, but she rode the school bus in to Cooks Springs to grammar school. After the school bus ran and Boss had done the morning milking, he would hightail it down to the Farmers' store. They didn't have many customers until late in the day when farmers and wives were done working, so Boss and Ruth got to hanging up a 'Closed' sign on the door and heading into the bedroom just off the meat counter. After several months of this furtive love, Boss moved Ruth up to his little house next to the milking shed."

She was all ears, "And then?"

"Then nothing. Hubert had to run the store full time and raise the little girl. He may've been glad to get rid of Ruth because she was a nag if I ever saw one. But she may not've nagged Boss all the time since they had two daughters, and by the time Boss was really rich he bought each of the girls—all grown up now, of course—a Ford Thunderbird and sent one to A&M and one to East Texas State. Boss and Ruth are long dead, and I never heard what became of the Snead daughters or the daughter that Ruth and Hubert had. End of story. That's all I know about that family. Oh, Taft is dead too. I don't know about George. I hear he left for California back near the end of the Dust Bowl days."

Annie checked her tape reels. "You tell a good married-life story. Do you know more? I've got tape to last till Midsummer Night. Whenever that is."

I wondered myself but then offered, "I think it's June 21st, but we don't celebrate it in this country as far as I know. I hear it's still big in Europe. It was in Shakespeare's day. You know Pyramus and Thisbe and Snug the Joiner and all those forest folk and spells cast and so on."

She remembered something and chuckled. "Right. I do know that play. We did it in high school. I played Titania, and you can imagine how that went over in Midland. All right, I'm set up, so if you have another story, let's get it on tape."

"I'm ready when you are. I've got at least one more. I'll tell you the story of Maydell Brown and her three husbands. It's the strangest one that ever took place in these parts."

She looked as if she had me in mind. "Why? Didn't you have three wives?"

I now had her. "Yeah, but not at the same time."

"What? You mean she had three husbands *at the same time?* Was that here in Bodark Springs or way off in the country?"

"Nope, it was here in this very town. It was back during World War I and some years after. Maydell was married to Jordan Brown first. They got secretly married over in Red River County on the day he left after being drafted into the army. He got shipped up to Camp Pike, Arkansas, and then over to Europe. After a year living alone, she started messin' around with Robert Mason from over in Lamar County. Robert was determined to marry Maydell, but, as she kept telling him, she already had a husband. Finally, he talked her into going up to Hugo in Choctaw

County, Oklahoma, and getting married under the names Robert and Maydell Brown. Then, since nobody knew she'd married Jordan way over in Clarksville on the day he got drafted, everybody thought she and Robert were a legal husband and wife. They set up housekeeping over on Star Street. Maydell was writin' and gettin' letters from Jordan all through the war, but she told the postman that PFC Jordan Brown was her brother."

Annie was amazed as I hoped she would be. "It must have taken some juggling to keep that up till 1918 when the war got over?"

I was quick to get all this told. "Actually, no, it was 1919. Jordan got put in the Army of Occupation and had to stay in Germany another year. When he got home, he found the couple living in what you might call bigamous happiness. As he told it later on, he loved Maydell no matter what she'd done. So he moved in with Robert and Maydell on Star Street."

Annie said, "That's only two husbands."

I elaborated happily. "So far. Then in 1930 Maydell fell in love with a man named Roger Brown—same name as Jordan and Robert, though Robert's was an assumed name since he was really Robert Mason. You with me so far?"

Another frown. "So far I guess. Old Maydell must have been some woman."

"She was I guess, though I never saw the attraction when she was a student in my history class. Anyway, Maydell told Roger that she was already married, but he said he would just kill himself if he couldn't marry her. Well, she felt sorry for him—she was notably soft hearted, people said—and told him the whole story as it had developed so far. He told her he didn't care. He was willing to be a third husband. They could set up housekeeping somewhere on the edge of town and live together part time. So it worked out that Maydell told Robert and Jordan that she had to spend two or three nights a week working as a maid at the hospital. When people saw her going over to Roger's house and coming back in the morning, she told them that her other brother Roger was living with their bedrid mother and that she had to help out nights."

She hoped I wasn't makin' this up. "Then what happened? Did she and Roger really get married? You said she had three husbands. This sounds like two husbands and a lover."

"No, she and Roger simply went to Love County, Oklahoma, and got married in the county courthouse in Marietta. She told the other two husbands that she had to go to Sherman to see a cancer doctor because she was sure she had cancer of the liver. So she caught the bus and met Roger in Gainesville and they hooked 'em over across the Red to the courthouse. You got to remember that this was before social security numbers and all sorts of ways to track people down. Nowadays, with computers and such, all these marriages would've shown up."

She was eager to hear the end of this tale. "And then what happened? Did they live happily ever after?"

"No, Robert and Jordan found out about Roger after a year or so. They were furious. Jordan said, at the trial, 'Hell, judge, that woman was guilty of trigamy.'"

She was puzzled again I was glad to see. She said, "The trial? For what? Bigamy?"

"Murder. Robert and Jordan got mad and hung Maydell on a tree out behind the house on Star Street. When he heard that Maydell had been killed, Roger left the country and was never heard of again. The trial was a mess, and since it was so complicated, Robert and Jordan only got two years in the state pen because one juror said, 'That bitch got what she deserved.' Robert and Jordan were put to work on the Eastham Prison Farm down in Central Texas. One day Jordan got mad at Robert and beat him to death with a short-handled hoe while they were working in a sugar beet field. Then Robert got life without parole. End of story."

"John Quincy Adams the Second, I believe you just made that up."

I definitely had not. I said, "I may've taken a few liberties when I invented conversations, but in the main the story is true. Ask Edward. He knows as much about that as I do. If you aren't going to believe what I tell you, maybe I'll just shut up."

She started laughing. "No. No. I believe you. It's just that the things that happen are so strange that I'm afraid people who read my findings will think I'm making stuff up to impress the people who are paying for my research. Go on if there are more tales of love and marriage in your capacious memory."

She was resorting to big words now.

I said, "Capacious? I'd hardly call the ramblings of an old man the products of a capacious memory. But I'll drag up one more story from my collection of oddities. It's the story of Reevie Lee and Thelma Todd."

Again with pencil and paper. "Reevy? How do you spell that?"

"I think it's R-e-e-v-i-e. It must've been a nickname. In fact, if I remember right in this 'capacious' storehouse, his real name was Robert E. Lee like old Marse Robert."

She put down her pencil and said, "Marse?"

"Right. His slaves called General Lee 'Marse Robert.' You know 'Marse' for master. How am I gonna tell you Reevie's story if you keep asking for footnotes?"

Pencil at the ready again. "Sorry. Go on."

"Reevie, who worked in the coal mines north of here, married Thelma Todd, whose daddy sold popcorn from his little portable popcorn maker that he rolled around town. He usually set up in front of the movie house—but you don't need that for your report. Anyway, Reevie married Thelma and they had two girls—Maggie and Eleanor—and then Thelma decided that she didn't want to be married to Reevie any more. I don't know why. I never know why anybody decides to quit and get divorced. Life, as I've discovered, is pretty much a mystery."

She twisted a lock of hair and said, "Are you stalling just to devil me?"

"No, an old man has a right to his digressions. Besides, some of this background may be relevant. You never know. Where was I? Oh, Thelma decided to leave Reevie and take the girls back to her daddy's house. One Saturday, when old man Todd was manning his popcorn wagon down at the Pines Theater, Reevie decided to have it out with Thelma. He took a twelve-gauge Remington shotgun, leaned it up against a tree in the Todd yard, and began to holler for Thelma to come out on the front porch so he could talk to her."

Annie was again incredulous. "If he had a shotgun with him, he must have meant to do more than talk."

I wanted to drag out this tale. "I'm not sure what he would've done if Thelma had been meek and agreed to come back to him and bring the girls. Maybe he would've left the shotgun where it was. But Thelma said—and I'm not inventing dialog here because Gladys Lundy, the Avon lady, saw and heard it all—Thelma said, 'You go to hell you reprobated son of a bitch, I'll never set foot in that house with you again.' And

Reevie said, 'Well, you dirty whore, you ain't gonna set foot nowhere again,' and he pulled the shotgun out from behind the elm tree in the yard and shot Thelma right off that front porch. Then he turned the shotgun to his head and pulled the other trigger. I did mention that this was a double barrelled Remington, didn't I?"

Annie was making another note. "I guess. I don't remember. Go on. So Reevie killed himself and Thelma both?"

"No, Reevie didn't kill himself. He blew off his ear and scarred up the side of his face. He fell down on the ground, and Gladys ran to the phone at the barbershop down the block and called Jim Tom Pledger, the police chief. Reevie was hauled off to jail, tried for his crimes, and was sentenced to twenty years in the state pen in Huntsville. He got out after four years, got religion, and came back to Bodark as a Holy Roller preacher. Lots of people went to hear Reevie preach at little brush arbor meetings and off-brand country churches all over three counties. I hear that he could draw a crowd because he was a murderer and because he had just one ear, not to mention the scarred up face on that side of his head. He died a few years after he got religion and came back to the county."

"What killed him?"

I laughed at the memory. "He got an ear infection in the only ear he had left. That turned into pneumonia and he died in July. Death in the summer of pneumonia seemed strange to country people who always thought you died of pneumonia in the winter. I guess I'd say irony finally got to old Reevie—losing an ear in an attempted suicide, then getting the infection in the ear he had left, and then getting pneumonia in the summer. And that is the end of that story. The end of all my love and marital stories. I guess you know 'marital' can be turned into 'martial' by shifting two letters, and lots of the marital stories turn out to be martial and result in carnage."

She wanted more. "What happened to Reevie's girls? I should say Reevie and Thelma's girls?"

"They both got married and still live here in town, but don't go talk to them. They suffered as little girls and again as grown women because people keep telling the story of Reevie and Thelma to this day."

She promised not to ask the girls—women, now. "No, I won't. I'm going to Austin for a few days when I leave here. Maybe for a week. Justin is missing me, he says. I hope it's all right for me to leave the tape recorder here in your study while I'm gone. I have my room all cleaned out at the hotel if Edward wants to rent it while I'm gone."

"Oh, he won't rent it. You could've left your stuff there. I'll be manning the hotel for a few days so Eddie can go off and do whatever he does."

Curious about what I did at the hotel, she asked "What exactly do you do when you are 'manning' the hotel?"

"Not very much. I go in in the late afternoon and park myself at Eddie's desk or sit out in the lobby looking old and interesting until the restaurant closes. Then I check all the receipts and lock up the money in the safe in Edward's office. Then I stroll home in the cool, cool, cool of the evening."

Now she worried about an old man doing something she thought might be dangerous. "Aren't you afraid somebody'll rob you when you're taking the money from the restaurant to the office?"

"No, most people hereabouts know I'm armed and dangerous. I always take my 1911 Colt Automatic with me from the cash register to the office."

I'm not sure she believed me. "And you know how to use it?"

"Of course. Didn't I once defeat the Spanish army? And I've practiced some in the years since the war in Cuba. I think you worry too much about me. Go home and spend some time with Justin. Then come back and I'll see if I can make up some more tales to surprise you with. Call me when you get back and I'll see that Suite 307 is cleaned and ready for you."

PART II

ANCIENT HISTORY

CHAPTER 10

With Annie gone for a few days, I have time to reflect on things that have been surfacing—at least in Eddie's mind and in the poison pen calls and notes under doors. Maybe it's time. Maybe I should write down a part of my life that I've kept hidden for four decades. I can always put my confessions in a safe deposit box down at the bank so Eddie can read them when I'm gone from this earth in about ten years. Yes, I'm planning to get past one hundred. I read in the paper that over thirteen thousand people in the USA are over the century mark. I plan to be among that number when the saints go marching in. Why do I always revert to poems and songs when I get in a vacant or pensive mood, as Wordsworth would say?

Annie wondered if I could use the 1911 Colt Automatic, .45 ACP. Damn right! You'll see if I decide to go on with my story. Let an old man sleep on it. Maybe tomorrow I'll feel like putting pen to paper and reliving those years after my father was murdered.

The next day, before the day was far advanced, I went downtown and bought a ream of good lined paper and a bottle of ink and a new fountain pen. I couldn't type with any efficiency, and I was pretty sure I couldn't think and type at the same time. When I was a boy in school we spent a certain amount of time on penmanship. I learned the Spencerian system, but later, when I was teaching and my boys were in grammar school, everybody used the Palmer Method of penmanship. I used to practice that when I made the boys fill pages and pages of cursive script. So if I was going to put my lost years on paper, it would have to be with pen and ink—and written clearly. I still had a steady hand and what I wrote looked better than the dubious penmanship of most eighty-year-olds and any of the students at JBH High School. At least I don't shake. Old Early Leonard, the blacksmith, says his daddy's got the palsy so bad that "he couldn't stick his finger in his ass with both hands." Early never says why his daddy'd want to.

I took all my paper and pen and ink upstairs to a desk that was in one of the bedrooms that Barbara used for a study during the four short years we had together. I didn't want to write downstairs where anybody might come in and see my papers. Annie'd be back in a few days and I sure didn't want her to see what I was putting down. And then Eddie or Charlie or Lucy might show up at any time to see whether I had lapsed into senility and needed to be sent to the home for incompetents.

Just as I was coming downstairs after stowing my writing materials, the doorbell rang and rang. I, of course, had no intention of answering it, but then the phone started in. I picked up the receiver and found Lucy on the other end. "Let us in, Poppa. We know you're in there." I hadn't remembered that Lucy had some kind of portable phone in her car to cloud an already-overcrowded ether. I wasn't sorry to have some company if it'd put off my having to face my earlier life. When I went to the door, I found Lucy *and* Charlie standing on my welcome mat. I'd have to get rid of that irritating invitation to my house someday. Maybe put down a mat that said "Go Away."

"Come in, come in. This is an unexpected pleasure since I haven't seen you in ages."

They weren't fooled of course. "We were with you just last night," Charlie said. "Are you going to play the forgetful old coot with us? It won't work. We're onto all your tricks."

I snorted. "I doubt that. Who knows, I might go into total senility at any moment. Of course I remember last night. Lucy was resplendent in green satin and you were in that drab medium gray suit that I've tried for years to tell you to get rid of. Shall I tell you what Homer and Beth wore? And all the grandchildren?"

Charlie said, "Not necessary, Poppa. We just came over to see why you left the party before it got underway good."

"Maybe it was because Homer was in a mood to ship off the old man to Mayo Clinic, or maybe it was because those so-called musicians that Eddie brought in were fouling the airwaves with raucous flats and sharps. Or did it ever occur to anybody that I might have a late date with a lady or ladies unknown? Since it's too early for a drink, maybe I can make you coffee or tea. I have some Darjeeling I ordered from Messers Fortnum and Mason in London."

To make things hard for me, Lucy ordered tea and Charles coffee. I busied myself in the kitchen while Charlie studied Annie's tape recorder and even made as if to play a tape before I ordered hands off. Lucy stood in the kitchen door and watched me to see whether my palsied hands might need a sudden rescue from the boiling water. All my ministrations complete, we settled in the living room—or parlor as Jane always called it—and had a nice conversation about grandchildren and the dairy business and my health and whether Rosie was preparing satisfactory meals for me. In other words, they were checking to see that I was alive and well and more or less in my right mind. A man of almost ninety-five needs those checkups from time to time, and I didn't resent the visit or the pointed observations. And then they got down to what had really brought them to town. Lucy had got a letter in the mail that said, "Your father-in-law needs to repent of his sins and get right with God. I know what he did years ago in Arkansas and God will punish him for sure. He needs to repent, repent, REPENT!"

"What does that mean, Pop?"

"How should I know? I haven't been in Arkansas in years, and as to repentance, I guess everybody needs to—what does it say, 'Get right with God.'"

"But this letter says you did something years ago. In Arkansas. Can't you remember anything whoever wrote this means?"

"All I can tell you is that this must be the work of somebody I failed in school way back. You say the letter came in the mail? Where was it sent from?"

Lucy pulled the letter out of her purse and read the cancellation and said, "It says it was mailed from here in town—I mean Bodark, not Eden."

I said, "Well, that makes me think it's somebody here in town with a grudge. Don't worry about it. The statute of limitations has run out on anything I might have done when I was a youngster."

I knew better.

In most ways their visit had started out to be soothing. Now it was anything but. I'd had a turbulent night. Dreams that made no sense. In one dream, I could see Uncle Fred, but he kept dissolving into some woman, some harridan. I guess this is what they mean when they say a dream is hag ridden. I was awake by 4:30 after tossing and turning for at least two hours. There was nothing for it but to get up. I had coffee made by 5:00 and was sitting on the front porch getting a good look at the sunrise. As I rocked and sipped, I tried to sort out all that had happened back in the thirties. Father was dead, murdered by those damned Scroggses, and my second wife dead two years before. Poppa had inherited all of Fred's wealth, and after Poppa died, I inherited both estates. When the dust settled I thought I had enough money to buy Dallas. And I was famous in some quarters. Governor Sterling had big plans for me to be in Austin and help shape educational policy for the state. I might have done that if it hadn't been for the threat made by the Scroggs tribe and all that it led to. Old Sam Rayburn, the congressman from Bonham, had me up to testify before the House Subcommittee on Education. He then suggested that I might be offered a job in Washington. If I'd taken a job in state government or certainly the federal government, I might've been subjected to serious probing of my goings and comings, and everything I'd done might come out. And, maybe in my subconscious mind, I thought I ought to suffer some penance by staying at John Bell Hood. But going back to teaching was not an expiation. It was what I trained for and who I was. Now, after all these years, I know I did the right thing to stay at JBH. See, I'm already confusing the timelines. I guess I'll have to start writing to get everything straight.

Once I was alone, I trudged back upstairs to start putting pen to paper. Here, for better or worse, is what happened. All written in my clear and sometimes remorseful hand.

Once I learned about the threat on all the Adamses, I went to the school board and asked for a year's leave of absence. I told them I had to go to Kilgore and settle my Uncle Fred's business, though I had sold his holdings to Texaco a month or two before. My first lie. Then I said I'd have to go to California because Fred had business out there. He had done business in Southern California, but I didn't need to do more than cash the checks that came in. That was the second almost-lie. I felt bad about telling both of them, but I had no idea how long it would take to do what I had to do.

It took me a while to get myself organized. It was a month or so after I got my leave in June that I was ready to work my plan. I had to go down to Dad's farm and put somebody in charge. Even though the farm wasn't making much back in 1932, there were some hired hands and sharecroppers trying to get by and I couldn't abandon 'em. One of the most industrious farmers was a man named Bill Helton, and I made him the best deal of his life. I said, "If you'll be the manager of this farm till I can do something with it, I'll pay you whatever you ask and give you a free hand." You can imagine he jumped at that, especially when I told him he could move his family into Dad's house. The amount he asked for was embarrassingly low, so I doubled it and made him feel like the richest man in Eastis County.

Once the farm business was settled, I went through Dad's house and found his 1911 Colt, some worn overalls and work shirts, a pair or two of almost worn-out Levis, a heavy Carhartt jacket, and one of his old felt hats. Fortunately, my father and I were the same size, just as my sons are all the same build as I am. Not that they'll ever need any of my clothes. I quit shaving, though I hated the idea of growing a beard. They are itchy damned things, but necessary for what I had in mind. I didn't see a barber for a year after I made my plan, so you can imagine what I looked like after a few months. But I was long gone from Bodark before I started looking like a Mountain Man.

I made a trip to Kilgore and several trips to the bank in town and put together $10,000 in cash. Nobody worried about my withdrawing such sums, because it was customary to pay workers in cash. I took Bill Helton to the Bonham First State Bank and established an account for him with sufficient funds for him to pay his hands for a year or two. I didn't tell him why I was using a bank in Bonham, and he didn't ask. You may wonder why I didn't worry that Helton would take the money and run. I thought he was trustworthy, but if it turned out that I was wrong, so what? I was made of money from the estates of Dad and Uncle Fred. Most of that money was in banks in Dallas and Fort Worth and Tyler and Kilgore and Gladewater. And a scary amount in Bodark Springs. There was even a large sum in the Bank of California in San Francisco. Fred did have interests in California, even though I lied about the need for me to go out there.

Since I was between housekeepers—this was long before Rosie—I shut the house up completely. I nailed up boards over all the doors and painted the words "CONDEMNED" on them. Let people think what they would. It was better than taking some caretaker into my confidence. I got Helton to go up and mow the grass from time to time and paid him a nice stipend in addition to the wages I had set aside in the Bonham bank for him and his workers.

I put my cash in a small steel box I had Burl Leonard, Early's daddy, make for me in his blacksmith shop. It was flat and thin enough not to look like some kind of strongbox. I had an old navy sea bag that I hid the box in along with clothes, the .45, soap and washing accessories, and some ordinary pants and shirts. I wore the overalls and work clothes and thumbed a ride to Paris to catch the train for Texarkana. Once in Paris, I visited a gunsmith and had the .45 cleaned and oiled. I ordered some shells and three ammunition clips. Once that was done, I caught the train—dressed as I was—and made my way to the Texas side of Texarkana.

Edward, if I'm gone to glory or somewhere and you're reading this, let me say I'm sorry for all the details. I guess I want the record to be complete. I don't plan to hold anything back. That will satisfy you and your brothers if you are all still alive when you crack open my safe deposit box at the State Bank.

When I found a copy of the *Texarkana Gazette* I searched the ads for houses for rent on the Arkansas side. I found a three-room house not far off State Line Avenue for $20 a month. I dragged my sea bag across into Arkansas and took a year's lease on the house. Since I paid the whole year in cash, my by-now disreputable appearance didn't cause the owner any concern. Then I went up and down State Line looking for a used car to buy. I wanted a sedan so I could haul whatever I needed for my stay in western Arkansas. A 1929 Ford set me back $185. It had seen some rough use, but seemed to run pretty well. Arkansas is full of mechanics, and I was able to get it in good running shape before I left Texarkana. I had to register it and get an Arkansas driver's license. That took some doing and some moderately serious lying. I was John Barker, and I had lived up in Polk County till a few weeks ago when my house was burned to the ground in that wildfire in the Ouachitas that I read about in the *Gazette*.

I had to take—and pass—the driver's test and register the car in Miller County, Arkansas. Then I was ready to spend a week or two in my little shack of a house on Chestnut Street. It didn't have electricity or running water, but there was a pump in the kitchen connected to the well. I went to a used furniture store and bought a bed and a straight chair. When the old man who owned the store grudgingly delivered the bed and chair, I was happy enough to give him three dollars extra.

Once established as John Barker of 132 Chestnut Street, Texarkana, Arkansas, a white male aged 55, I could begin in earnest. I drove my rattletrap back across the Texas line and made my way to DeKalb where I bought a used twelve-gauge double-barrelled shotgun and two boxes of buckshot. I went to a hardware store and bought a hacksaw. Back in Texarkana, Texas, I bought a Winchester .30-30 rifle and three boxes of shells, a Leupold scope, and a pair of Leupold 10X50 binoculars. In my little house, I took the hacksaw and sawed off the barrel of the shotgun to about eight-and-a half inches. I sawed off the stock to about eight inches behind the trigger housing. Now it would fit in my seabag. Of course it would be illegal as hell in Miller County or in any Arkansas County where I planned to set up next. I went into town after my amateur gunsmithing and bought the biggest and best first aid kit I could find. Then I went to a drugstore and bought more bandages and various ointments. You never knew what you might need. On the way back to the house I bought a five-gallon gas can to put in the back seat of the Ford. Then to a hardware store and bought a short-handled shovel, a trenching tool, I think they're called.

I spent a few days in Texarkana getting the Model A looked at by two different mechanics. I never trust one. I spent almost as much getting the valves ground, a new set of brakes, five new heavy-duty tires, plus belts and fresh oil as the car cost to start with. I had learned on the trip to DeKalb that the car could use some real attention if I didn't want to get stuck in the middle of the Ouachita Mountains.

I didn't know for sure where the Scroggses lived, so I made my way north, stopping at courthouses to look at land plats. I found nobody named Scroggs in the Little River County Courthouse in Ashdown, nor were there any property owners named Scroggs in Sevier County according to what I could find in the courthouse in DeQueen. Then I hit paydirt in the Polk County Courthouse in Mena. The only Scroggses who owned property in the county were way back in the sticks out past the little settlement of Shady. Now all I had to do was start prospecting around the Shady community till I got wind of anybody named Scroggs. It wouldn't do to go out there and start asking. I had to more or less establish myself somewhere in the vicinity. I found a rundown farmhouse—again no electricity or running water—near the Brushy settlement about five miles from the Shady Schoolhouse. Since I didn't plan to be here a year, I rented the shack by the month at a cost of $7.50. Remember this was 1932, and times were hard. I went back into Mena and bought a hunting guide's license. That would let me be in the woods with a gun. I couldn't hunt, but the theory was that I could guide hunters. I didn't plant to hunt game. Only people.

Dear Eddie and anyone else who reads this:

I meant to hunt down the two surviving Scroggs men who had killed my dad and kill them in cold blood. I know how that sounds. I'm not a killer by nature, though I may've dispatched a Spaniard or two back in 1899. Any killing I proposed was to keep the damned Scroggses from killing you and me and your brothers. You may recall, a note was sent to the newspaperman that all the Adamses in Eastis were marked for death. Since the Scroggs family had a record of murders, I took 'em seriously. When somebody is determined to kill you, you can call the police or you can solve the matter yourself. Calling the police is only good after you're dead and somebody else makes the call. All right. I just want this on the record. I planned to commit murder, and, by God, I would bury the bodies if I got away with the killings.

Is this the father that you thought you knew for all your sixty-six years? You got letters from me during the time I was away, but they were all from California. Until you read this, you won't know for sure what I was doing, but maybe you suspected that I was not out in the Golden State getting over my father's murder and Jane's death and being a self-indulgent crybaby. Your questioning me last week made me think you had an idea that I was up to some crime. If you wonder how you got those few letters from California while I was in Arkansas, let me tell you. I would write the three of you letters, put them in an envelope addressed to the postmaster in Compton or Mojave or Indian Springs and ask the postmaster to mail the stamped, addressed letters to you guys. Simple? It must have worked since you couldn't prove that I wasn't out in California soaking up the sun or drinking orange juice right off the trees.

In Mena, I got my guide license in the name of Jon Schneider. Notice the different spelling of John. I needed to keep the first name John or Jon for all my aliases since I didn't want to be surprised if someone used a different first name I had made up. I might not answer to Bill or Sam or something, and that, in rare cases, could cause suspicion. With the license in hand, I began roaming the woods. I located the two shacks the Scroggses lived in, and I watched the two surviving males—my targets—going and coming. It wouldn't do just to walk up and shoot 'em dead. The two or three women I saw around the place would see me and know that a tall man with a beard and unruly hair had killed their men. And that description would fit the Jon Schneider that people in and around Polk County knew. Or thought they did. I had to wait until I found Estes and Jeremy—I learned the names from the plats in the courthouse—out in the woods. When I did, I would use the 30-30 from long range, or for short range the shotgun, which I wore in a shoulder sling I devised to give me quick access. I wouldn't trust myself with the .45 unless I was really close.

I spent two months or more using the binoculars to spy on the

Scroggs men and women. The men didn't stray far from the little patch they were tending up near the house. But I knew that sooner or later they would need to go out for meat, and even if deer season was a month or so off, they were pretty notorious poachers. I had learned that from a game warden or two who stopped me to check my guide license. And, of course, the game wardens who checked my credentials had a good description of the guide Jon Schneider. I had to strike as quickly as possible when I did strike and then get the hell out of the Ouachita Mountains.

The Civilian Conservation Corps, which did a lot of work in this region, hadn't yet been established, but there was a good deal of locally funded road work going on out in the area around Shady. If I could find and kill the Scroggs brothers near some of that work, I might be able to bury the bodies long enough to get clear of Polk County. Much depended on luck. Too much.

One day when the weather was dreary and I was slinking in the woods about three miles from the Scroggs cabin, looking for places where they might hide and poach a deer or a turkey or anything edible, I heard a noise close by. I suspected it was a bear since Arkansas used to be known as "The Bear State," and bears were often spotted in the woods. That's why I carried the sawed-off shotgun in a sling. When I turned to look, I saw Jeremy Scroggs aiming his rifle at me. He pulled the trigger and missed. Then his brother fired a shot that hit me in the shoulder. Fortunately, it was the left shoulder and, as you know, I'm right handed. I pulled up the shotgun and fired both barrels at Jeremy. He erupted in a fury of blood and brains and fell back into a pile of dirt made by the road crews. Estes was reloading his single-shot rifle when I stupidly dropped my Winchester and pulled the .45 out of the pocket of the Carhartt jacket that once belonged to Dad. I emptied the clip in his direction and figured I'd probably missed. I hadn't. Five or six of the eleven shots in the magazine hit him in the chest and did as much damage to him as the shotgun had to Jeremy.

My shoulder hurt a little, but I was pretty sure the bullet had just grazed me. I didn't take time to look. I could do first aid later unless somebody heard all the shooting and came after me. My car was a mile away, but I had the trenching tool in my knapsack. I'd use it to bury these two villains. I have no idea why Jeremy shot at me. Maybe they were just bloodthirsty or maybe they had seen me lurking in the woods around their shack. While I was using the trenching tool to dig a hole, a real bear came out of the woods and dragged Jeremy off into a creek bed. I have no idea where his body ended up. If the bear didn't eat him, some other animals did. I buried the other Scroggs in a shallow grave and made for my Model A. I checked my shoulder and applied some of the ointment and a bandage to it. It hurt like hell, and I hoped the adrenalin would kick in and take some of the pain away before I left the woods. I chewed and swallowed four aspirin tablets, fired up the car and made my getaway, expecting to find the sheriff and two or three deputies headed toward me on the old logging road that led back to my shack near Shady. Once again I was lucky. When I got back to my shack, I got my gas can out and liberally spread gas around, grabbed the few belongings I had in the house—I kept almost everything in the car no matter where I was—and set the cabin ablaze. Then I headed for Mena, expecting to find my way blocked by lawmen. Again, I was in luck. I made my way to Mena, then turned south toward DeQueen.

Once in DeQueen, I went to a dime store, bought some scissors and a razor, filled the car and the gas can, and headed south. Somewhere before I got to Ashdown, I pulled well off the road and cut on the beard till I had it down almost to the skin. Then, using cold water and soap, I managed to nearly kill myself shaving off the beard. If you don't believe it's hard to dispatch a beard with cold water and a cheap razor, try it!

I seemed to be committing crime after crime, and I wasn't through. Back in Texarkana, I slipped into the house I'd rented and poured gasoline all over the floor and set it ablaze. I jumped in the Ford and headed for Texas. When I got to Hooks, I went into the barbershop and got my hair cut. The barber was amazed that my hair was such a mess. The shop was one of those that back in the day offered a hot bath in their bathhouse for fifty cents. I availed myself of the service, changed into clothes that looked almost respectable, ones I'd kept in my seabag all along, and started driving west. I was not going home, but I was getting as far away from Polk County, Arkansas, as I could. I still had over $5,000 in cash, so I was up for some travel. A few miles east of Clarksville in Red River County, I went well off the highway and committed one of my last crimes. I took the license tags off the Ford, soaked a pair of Levis in gasoline from my can, stuffed the jeans in the gas tank's filler spout, and lighted the homemade wick. I ran as far as I could before the car exploded—burning, I hoped, the shotgun and rifle, all the clothes I was not wearing, my sea bag, and every remnant of Jon Schneider, murderer, and John Barker, arsonist. There was a stock pond not a mile from the car, and I threw my dad's .45 in that. I kept the license plates under my shirt till I found a bunch of trashcans alongside the road waiting for the county to collect trash. I put one of them in one can and one in the other one and hoped they'd end in a landfill in Red River County. I kept walking till I reached Highway 82, where I flagged a Greyhound bound for Dallas.

Once in Dallas, I checked into a small hotel for a few days while I went to E. M. Kahn and outfitted myself with three suits, two sport coats, some shirts, ties, underwear, and shoes. When the store had the clothes altered, I checked out of the little hotel and into the Adolphus. I had been a bum for months, and now I wanted to eat in the French Room, go to the movies at the Majestic, and live like the rich guy I was. I spent a month in Dallas, and then I caught the train for San Francisco. The letters you guys got from California had real return addresses once I rented a house at 70 Hancock Street in the Mission District not far from Mission Dolores. Since I had claimed to be in California to so many people, including you, I decided to be a Californian for a while. I love being in the city that the columnist Herb Caen calls "Baghdad by the Bay," but I knew that after a year, I had to come back to Bodark Springs to live out the rest of my life. I wrote the school board and asked for my old job at John Bell Hood. But I requested a second year. That was because I had met Liz Denney and planned to court and marry her if she would have me.

The school board rehired me and gave me another year's leave. Before I left California, I got a letter from Governor Miriam "Ma" Ferguson offering me a job in Austin working at restructuring Texas education. I would've liked that, I think, but if I'd accepted, I would likely be in such a fishbowl that old Jon Schneider or John Barker might have surfaced. I'm sure I'm wanted by the state of Arkansas, for there is no statute of limitations on murder. Of course the fact that I'm not guilty of murder might be hard to prove. I meant to murder the men who killed my father and my uncle, but things turned out in such a way that I acted in self-defense. I'd defy you, Edward, with all your lawyerly skills, to have got me acquitted of murder. I was too much around west Arkansas burning houses and cars and shooting up the countryside to look as innocent as I was. And, needless to say, I was guilty of at least three counts of arson. By the way, I made the two burned houses right for their owners. I sent anonymous money orders to each owner for a thousand dollars—all this for houses that wouldn't have brought two hundred dollars for the pair. As my daddy used to say, "Money won't spend itself."

I'm not sure why I'm baring my soul in such a lurid manner, but since you seem interested in my life and since you're my firstborn, maybe I'll fill you in on some of the less criminal aspects of my ninety-five years. What I have written so far only takes me up to my mid-fifties, and I've had forty more years of less exuberant life. You may think it is destructive to a person's mental health to have done my deeds in western Arkansas. It hasn't had that effect on me. It wasn't pleasant to kill two men, but if I hadn't I wouldn't be writing this and you probably wouldn't be reading it. That is, if the threats of the Scroggs brothers were ever carried out, and I have no doubt that they would've been. I looked into their faces on that hill in Polk County and I saw evil. As Hamlet says of Rosencrantz and Guildenstern, two people as dreadful as Estes and Jeremy Scroggs, "They are not near my conscience." The thing that I reflect on most is all the twists and turns of the first year of my two-year sabbatical. The whole incident in Arkansas took a toll. Not for the killings, but for what Shakespeare calls "the posthaste and romage in the land." It was not easy for me to be Jon and John and burn houses and a car and evade capture. It took San Francisco and a woman I met there to, as they say, cleanse my palate. After my California sojourn, I could come back to Bodark Springs with some semblance of good cheer. The only regret was that I couldn't persuade Elizabeth Denney to come back with me. She would have been an acceptable stepmother for you three guys, though all of you were too old by then to benefit from a woman in the House of Adams.

Maybe I'll say more about Elizabeth as I scratch away at this narrative. And maybe not. I guess nobody but me would be interested. Well, Annie'll like to hear the romantic details of those California days, if I tell her when she gets back from Austin.

As you know, when I left for parts unknown, Homer was still in college and just about ready for medical school, and Charles was already out of A&M. I sent Homer $100,000 to pay his tuition. That would see him well into an internship and a residency if I never came back. You were already doing well in Dallas, but I sent you $100,000 so you could buy a house in Highland Park—the one you got over a million for when you retired to unpretentious little Bodark. I deeded the farm to Charles and gave him enough to start his dairy herd. If I'd died in the woods of Arkansas, you three would have come into three fortunes—thanks to Uncle Fred and Dad. Hell, you know my earnings as a schoolteacher wouldn't have paid for a small house in Eastis County, much less a mansion in Highland Park.

I started to tell you about Elizabeth Denney but then decided not to. Oh, what the hell! I rented a house on Hancock Street and began decompressing, as the deep-sea divers say. I started going to the public library to read the newspapers and see if my crimes had made the national wire. Then I got interested in California Gold Rush days and spent many hours in the reading room. There I met Liz Denney, who was a widow of about thirty. She taught English in one of the high schools and was spending part of her summer reading up on Bret Hart and Mark Twain, both writers about the Gold Rush. One day, I got a good look at her for the first time and—ah, hell, this is too stupid even for a total fool like me to say. Well. I'll say it. It was love at first sight. I don't believe in love at first sight any more than you or Charlie or Homer must. But there it is. Believe it or not. I'm not good at describing people, but since you have seen Annie, all you have to do is visualize her and you have a description of Liz Denney as I knew her then. Liz's hair was not as red as Annie's, but was a rich auburn, so not so far off from Annie's glowing red. All three of you met Liz in 1939 when I dragged her back to Bodark Springs hoping she would finally break down and marry me. She didn't, and I have not seen her since. We corresponded a few times, and sometime during World War II, she married a banker named Lancaster. I married Barbara, pretty much on the rebound, in 1946, when I learned that Liz was married and living happily ever after with one of the richest men in San Francisco.

I spent a year madly in love with Liz. That was 1933. I found that she lived two doors down on Hancock Street, and so we spent nights alternating from my place to hers. I have nothing to add about that! I bought a 1934 Ford, and we explored California. I proposed over and over again, but I knew she would never leave San Francisco no matter how hard I tried to get her to come to Texas. We spent that year and every summer between then and 1939 together in San Francisco. Since I was a teacher, everybody assumed I was off working on a doctorate or attending conferences. I'd bought the house on Hancock Street so I had a place to stay if Liz was off for any length of time. She had aged parents in Salinas and felt she had to spend a few days a month with them. Each fall, I sold the car I'd bought and bought another one as soon as I got back in the summer. It was an ideal life, except that Liz wouldn't break down and marry me. After the trip to Texas in 1939 when you guys met her, she decided that since I couldn't or wouldn't leave Texas, we had to end it. By the way, the engagement ring I bought for her is still in my safe deposit box, as you'll see when you read this confession. Now that I reflect on it again, maybe I *will* tell Annie the California love story—or a little of it—since she seems so interested in an old man whose life she thinks couldn't have had any spice. But maybe I won't tell her that she is Liz to a T.

I hope you and your brothers are alive to read this drivel,

Your loving father

I put my confessions in an envelope and sealed it. I wish I had some red sealing wax like English documents used to have, but I'll have to rely on saliva and a gummed envelope. Now I'll walk it down to the Eastis County State Bank and put it in my safe deposit box. I began worrying that I'd fall and break a hip on the way downtown, and then somebody at the hospital would pass the document on to Edward before I was ready for him to read it. I don't know much law, but if he learned that I was wanted in Arkansas, he would've had to turn me in or be guilty of aiding and abetting a felon. I really needed to be careful so I could hide it away among my souvenirs down at the bank. Not many of those really. The only things in my box are three sets of rings from my wives and an engagement ring Elizabeth Denney returned when she realized she couldn't leave California for Texas and I couldn't break away from my life here. I guess *amor vinci omnia* only works if you're a Roman. And then I have $100,000 in cash, just in case I get a telegram like the one Mark Twain claims to have sent to a dozen of his friends. It said, "Flee at once, all is discovered." His friends fled, he claimed. There is clearly a chance I'll get such a message. It never hurts to have a stash. I sure needed the one I had when I went off to Arkansas. Fortunately, I made the bank safely, and I can now rest knowing that someday Edward or some other heirs will know my ignominy—or my resolute nature as a revenger. I can only hope whoever reads it will give me the benefit of the doubt. I don't know why I care, since I'll be dead. That is unless we have an earthquake and the bank's contents are scattered all over town before I shuffle off this mortal etc.

I leave the bank after greeting my ex-students who work in the cages or staff the New Accounts desk. As I make my way down Main Street, I'm struggling to see how much of a Shakespeare sonnet I can remember. It begins,

When to the sessions of sweet, silent thought
I summon up the remembrance of things past,
I sigh the lack of many a thing I sought . . .

I guess it'll come to me or it won't. I can always resort to an old text-book to read the whole sonnet.

The thoughts that I'm summoning up today are not, mercifully, about what I call "The Arkansas Incident." I'm remembering the year in California with Elizabeth and the years we had before she jilted me and I married Barbara more or less on the rebound. I suppose I should name one memory "The Arkansas Incident" and the other "The California Idyll," or maybe "The Summers of Love." Isn't that what the hippies called San Francisco in 1967—"The Summer of Love"? Well, I had several summers of love in California between 1933 and 1939, when Liz finally sent me packing.

CHAPTER 11

I doubt that I'll follow up on my threat to Edward in my sealed letter and tell Annie about the years between 1933 and 1939. I was back teaching after 1934, but most summers I spent in California trying to persuade Liz to marry me or going on vacations with her. One summer we took the SS *Lurline* from San Francisco to Honolulu and spent an idyllic summer staying at the Royal Hawaiian Hotel on Waikiki Beach. We swam and failed at surfing and went to the Banyan Lounge of the Moana Hotel to listen to Harry Owens and the Royal Hawaiians play his "Sweet Lelani" and other lovely songs of the islands. We went to a luau, drove across the Nu'uanu Pali to the other side of island, and swam naked in the waters off the north shore. We mostly made love at the Royal Hawaiian, but once we took our pleasure in a secluded spot on Diamond Head and once in the sand near Hanauma Bay. I was in my fifties, but being with Liz, almost twenty-five years younger, made me feel the way I did when I was first courting Esther. Hawaii still calls to me. Even today, on most Saturdays, I tune my radio in to *Hawaii Calls*, a program from the Moana Hotel on Waikiki. Announcer Webley Edwards and musician Harry Owens still take me back to the islands.

And then when I hear Tony Bennett sing about those little cable cars that reach almost to the stars, I lament the fact that I'd left my heart in San Francisco. Mostly Liz and I would spend the summers in our Mission District houses near the school where she taught English. One or two times we took road trips up the coast to Puget Sound or down to San Diego. We were lucky to both be schoolteachers since we had summers off. I didn't have to explain much to my sons or anybody, since teachers were all supposed to be off in workshops or attending conferences. Back in those days, my sons were not so worried about my activities, since I was living what seemed to them to be a normal life and all three were busy with their own careers. I saw them from time to time during the school year, but when summer came, I was off like a shot, singing "California, Here I Come." Liz and I ate seafood on the Fisherman's Wharf, giant prawns in Chinatown, roast beef at Ernie's, and drank martinis at the Top of The Mark, once the hotel converted a floor into the famous bar and grill with its panoramic view of the city. The summer of the World's Fair in 1939, we spent much of our time on Treasure Island in the middle of the bay between San Francisco and Oakland.

"*Ou sont les neiges d'antan?*" Villon was right in his poem about lost ladies. Elizabeth Denney is a lost lady. Lost to me, at any rate. I don't guess the snows of yesteryear apply to our time together. We didn't have any snows in those summers. California, in my memory at least, always seemed to be bathed in sunshine. I can almost forget the fogs that used to shroud the Bay.

After all this maudlin and murderous reflection, I'm ready for Annie to return and get me telling more tales of other days gone by. Not days of my secret life, but stories about olden times in Northeast Texas. If she still wants marriage stories, maybe I'll tell her about the wedding I attended at what we used to call "The Quarters."

CHAPTER 12

After a week away, Annie came back with her fiancé Justin in tow. She said somebody had stolen her car from in front of Justin's apartment, and he had to interrupt his dissertation to bring her back to keep gleaning my probably failing brain. Justin Cole was a nice young man. He seems to be the kind of person I would have picked for one of my granddaughters, and I approved of him as the future husband of someone who was fast becoming my best friend. That seems a silly thing for an ancient like me to say, but Annie had endeared herself to me in the short time we had spent together. She was Liz come back to life. I wasn't an old fool in love with a girl the way some in town thought I was. She was comfortable—and, what the hell?—she did remind me of Liz Denney. They were of a similar temperament, and oh, did they look and act alike! Sweet natures and sharp minds.

Justin said, when we were introduced, "Mr. Adams, I think I might get jealous of you. Annie may be in love with you."

"No, Mr. Cole, Annie has better sense than to get taken in by an old fool of an ex-schoolteacher. She talks about you too much. I was getting tired of 'Justin this, and Justin that,' all the time she's been here, but now that I see you and the way she looks at you, I know for sure where her heart is."

We were all kidding around, but I was happy to see that Mr. Justin Cole, PhD candidate in political science, was somebody worthy of the girl who had begun to be an avatar of Liz Denney, even though I had no romantic inclinations toward her. Hell, I am ninety-five, and as Hamlet tells his mother, who is probably about forty, when he his berating her middle-aged sexuality, "The heyday in the blood is tame and waits upon the judgment." Mine sure as hell's tame.

They had arrived in Bodark about 5:30, so I invited them to stroll down to the Cotton Exchange Hotel for dinner. Justin had to be back in Austin even if he had to drive his worn-out old Dodge half the night. A little sustenance and two or three cups of coffee would help him stay awake. When I saw his old car, I despaired of this couple's future transport. Annie's Toyota gone for good and Justin's Dodge on its apparent last legs. I thought I might have to do something about this sad state of affairs. But in due time.

I ushered the couple into the restaurant just as Maybelline came after me. She said, in a stage whisper, "Mr. John, I need to have a word with you before you leave." I assumed another poison pen note had surfaced. If not that, then maybe something mundane. Maybe Eddie was off to Bonham and I'd have to show up a day or two early to be a lobby ornament and a money securer, but I was never more wrong.

The dinner with Annie and Justin amazed me. Annie ate a T-bone steak, a baked potato, broccoli, a large salad, rolls, and a piece of coconut cream pie for dessert. Justin ate a piece of broiled halibut, some asparagus, and no dessert at all. I ate a cup of French onion soup, a green salad with oil and vinegar, and a side of Brussels sprouts. Annie seemed to be eating for three—her, Justin, and me. I hoped her large appetite was not just for two, since Annie didn't need to be pregnant if she was to finish her PhD. And then I thought: remember Mrs. Eddy and don't start trying to run everybody's life. I left them with her dessert and Justin's coffee and went out to see what Maybelline thought so important to tell me.

Maybelline was twitching with excitement when I came to the desk. "Mr. John, I 'spec you fixin' to be in trouble womanwise. Pretty soon you gon' have more women than a Greyhound bus can tote. Ooo, weee!"

"All right, Maybelline, cut the dialect and try and tell me what you're rambling on about. Oh, and if you're trying to quote the old Jimmie Rodgers song, it's 'got more women than a passenger train can haul.' Do you have a message from Edward?"

"Okay, Professor, back to standard English. About an hour ago I took a reservation from a Mrs. Lancaster from California, and she said—"

I almost fainted. "*Oh, my God.*" Surely this wasn't the Mrs. Lancaster I knew. "A reservation here? Did this Mrs. Lancaster mention me?"

"Yes sir, she did indeed. She asked me if I'd send you a message that she would be at Love Field a week from tomorrow at 9:15 p.m. The flight—here let me look it up—the flight, she said, is American 2435. She asked if you would meet her plane."

I was having trouble thinking now.

May went on, "Oh, she said tell you, in case you forgot, that she was once Elizabeth Denney. Does that name ring a bell?"

I don't know what to say about this. Did the intensity of my recent reveries create this sudden incarnation—Liz Denney, in the flesh, here in Bodark? I don't know how long I stood in front of Maybelline, no doubt with a plainly stupefied look on my face.

"It sets off all the chimes of Big Ben. Did she say how long she planned to stay here at the Cotton Exchange?"

I had not heard from Liz Denney in almost twenty years, and I had no idea why she was coming to a place she obviously didn't like to see a man she had dumped more than thirty years ago.

I had left Maybelline, and I guess she was afraid I had had a stroke. And I almost did. When Maybelline saw me come back to myself, she looked at her notes and said, "She said she would be here for a week. From Friday to Friday."

Now more or less recovered, I said, "Well, Maybelline, you can cancel her reservation."

It seemed that now Maybelline was as startled as I had been. "What? What? You gonna send that poor woman back to wherever she came from with no hotel to stay in? You just want me to call her up and say, 'Stay the hell away'? I don't know as I can do that. Mr. Eddie might fire me if I—"

"No, I don't mean to send her away. She'll stay at my house. Do you have to know every detail of everybody's life? You don't need to call her or worry Edward with this. When I pick her up at the airport, I'll explain her change of venue."

Maybelline was having trouble with all these new developments. "Venue? Venue? You done talkin' worse dialect than I does. Who is—ah, hell, ain't none of my business. I swear, Mr. John Quincy Adams, you a plumb caution."

"That's the third time somebody has called me a 'caution' this month. Thanks, Maybelline, I'm sure you'll get to see Mrs. Lancaster while she's here in Bodark Springs."

She cracked her knuckles nervously and said, "I hope I do. I sure hope I do."

I thought if it ain't one thing, it's a whole bunch of them. Wait. I need a quotation about trouble here. *Hamlet* of course—"They come not in single spies, but in battalions." I don't need Liz coming back into my life just when Annie is probing into my mind and Eddie is worrying about my legal soul and Homer is planning my descent into a nursing home. And then there's Lucy, who has her eye on the LaSalle. I know she doesn't really, but it furnishes me metaphors for poetry to say that she does.

Who or what was behind this sudden visit? I hate mysteries—at least real life ones. I love Chandler and Rex Strout and Dashiell Hammett, but I don't like my life messed with. I'm not a character in some novel plot. Hell, maybe I *am* in the middle of a plot here. Maybe the fine and meddlesome hand of Edward Adams, Esq, is behind this. Has he heard from the mysterious caller and wants to find out what Liz knows about those missing years? No, he wouldn't want to bring in somebody from outside the family to air dirty Adams laundry. Aha, I think I have it. He wants to save me from Annie.

As I made my way back to the Adams mansion. I decided that when Annie came at 10:00 in the morning, I'd tell her about Liz Lancaster *nee* Denney. I was going to have to ask her to drive me to Love Field to meet that plane, and I might as well let her know something about the woman I was meeting. Not everything, but enough to assuage her curiosity. I wouldn't go into the incident at Diamond Head forty years ago or the nude swimming on the north shore. If a man ever needed two or three drinks of Johnnie Walker after this news, I was that man.

After the soothing of the Walker family of Scotland, I sought my bed and tried to remember the ending of an Edna St.Vincent Millay sonnet that had a lot to do with my California idyll. I finally got out of bed and found the poem that begins "What lips my lips have kissed" and so on. The last line says it all about those years by the Bay: "I only know that summer sang in me/A little while, that in me sings no more." Damn and blast! Oh, to be seventy again.

When Annie showed up exactly at 10:00, she was full of thanks for the wonderful meal and the chance for me to meet Justin. She was effusive, and I hate effusive, so I got her stopped and said, "I hope I can ask a great favor of you."

Still bright as usual, she said, "Of course. Whatever you need—within reason!"

"Next Saturday, do you think you could drive me to Love Field in Dallas late in the day?"

Now she was truly puzzled. "I'm sure I can. In the LaSalle. I hope, I hope."

"No, I was thinking more of the Buick. It's newer—a 1970 model—and doesn't require a person to use a standard transmission."

She bristled. "I can drive a stick. I drove one all through high school. Did you think just because I'm only twenty-five that all I can manage is an automatic?"

"No, no I just didn't—" and then my mind played one of its tricks when I remember that Liz was not much more than twenty-five when I met her.

Annie seemed somehow amazed and said, "Who is this Liz person?"

Now I was the puzzled one. "What? What do you mean?"

"Well, you sort of drifted off and were saying 'Liz was not more than twenty-five when I met her.'"

"I said that out loud?"

She looked funny and said, "Well, sort of *sotto voce*, but clear enough for me to hear it."

"Sorry, I thought I was thinking to myself. But I'm glad I said it out loud—or sotto voce, as you put it. You're going to meet Liz next week if you'll drive me to Love Field. It's her plane from San Francisco that I'm meeting. We agreed, as you recall, that our talks were not to lead to autobiography or memoir or whatever, but since Mrs. Elizabeth Lancaster is suddenly to descend from the skies, you may be in for some personal stuff if you can stand to hear an old man's misspent middle years."

She was all ears. "I'm dying, I mean *dying* to hear anything about you. I mean *dying!*"

"All right! All right! Enough gushing! I can't imagine why you want to know an old man's innermost secrets."

Now she grew unaccountably solemn. "Let me explain. I never knew my grandfather. My mother told me stories about him from the time I was knee high to a, to a, oh—you know, little. I heard so many stories that I used to dream about him and tried to imagine what he looked like and how he talked and what he would've thought of me and—sorry to gush. After I'd been here and spent time with you, I suddenly knew I'd found the grandfather my mother told me so much about. I'm sorry, John Q., I don't mean to take some advantage of you and prod you for secrets, but anything you tell me'll be a light into my grandfather's life. Does that make sense?"

It made a little sense. Maybe or maybe not. "No. I don't think you can create me as your mother's father. No. Well, maybe you can. How the hell do I know what goes on in anybody else's head? But I'm perfectly happy to play grandpa if it helps solve some longstanding desire for a generation you missed. I never knew my grandfather, but I don't ever remember wanting to know him. But then people are different. What is it Ray Charles says, 'different strokes for different folks'? Anything I tell you about old John Q. and his transactions with Mrs. Liz Denney has to be with the tape recorder off, all right?"

She jumped to agree. "Perfectly all right. We will have two separate conversations while I'm here with you. One public and one so secret that I won't tell anybody unless you say I can. Not even Justin."

"I believe you mean that, but I can remember the days when I did some pillow talk. Anyway, I'm sure we can work out the two John Q.'s and the two Annies. By the way, I never have heard whether you have a middle name. Do you?"

She blushed. "I do, but I don't want to tell you. You'll laugh."

"No, I promise."

She ducked her head and said, "It's Sue."

I couldn't help myself. I roared with laughter and sputtered out "Your hair is red, your eyes are blue/ I'd swap my horse and dog for you."

She stamped her foot the way Liz used to. "Now, you old creep, you see why I didn't want to tell you."

"It'll never come up again, either in prose or in song. I really do promise. Now I'm ready to tell you about Liz Denney. I need to go back a little to 1932 when for several reasons I took a year's leave of absence from school. My father had been killed and I had estate matters to settle and some other things to take care of. My father's only brother got rich in the oil fields around Kilgore, and when he died my father inherited, and then all that money came to me. That's why I'm so filthy rich today."

I wasn't about to go into the murders of my father and uncle and the "some other things" I'd had to do, even though she might have surmised I'd done something more than shoot off my rifle during the Spanish American War. If Annie wanted me to play grandpa, she wouldn't want one who gunned down two people and covered it up. She'd want a kindly old ancestor. Even one slightly soiled by his love life. Wait a minute, you old fool, nothing in your love life shows any sign of soiling.

"Where was I?"

She smiled. "I think you were drifting off into some kind of reverie."

"I hope so. You know the little Emily Dickinson poem about reverie, don't you?"

She smiled, "No, but I'm sure you're going to quote it for me."

"I am, so prepare yourself. At least I'm not singing:

To make a prairie it takes a clover and one bee,
One clover, and a bee,
And revery.
The revery alone will do,
If bees are few."

Then I said, "I suppose I should quote some unknown person who said a man who relies on the words of others, has none of his own worth hearing."

She was eager to hear more. "No, I'm hanging on your every word, but I would like for you to get back to the story of your, what, sabbatical?"

"Sorry. I had some business east of the Rockies before I set out for California to see to some of Uncle Fred's other business. I went to several parts of the state but wound up in San Francisco. And while looking up some reading material in the public library, I met a beautiful young widow who was working in the library on some project connected with her job teaching English at Mission High School. She helped me find some Mark Twain California stuff—I can't remember why I was looking for his days in the West. Anyway, she was very helpful, and for several days I invented more reasons to need her help. One thing led to another, and I found out she was a widow, was twenty-five or so years younger than I, and wouldn't be loath to have dinner with me."

Now Annie was into it. "Oh, I'll bet you were a devil with the woman with your Texas accent and your impressive wardrobe. Were you the clotheshorse then that you are now?"

"I guess I've always put a premium on grooming. Is that a bad thing? Some writer I once read—here I go citing sources again—said there is a danger in being too well dressed. At least I've never worn spats."

Puzzlement again. "What are spats?"

"I'm gonna let you look that up. I can't be responsible for your total education. Just let me say that I think Clark Gable wore spats in *Gone With the Wind*.

"Mrs. Denney and I started keeping steady company. I guess your generation would call it 'dating.' Oh, and she was Mrs. There was no Ms. back in those days. One interesting thing about Liz was that she kept her maiden—oops—birth name. At least she did till she married Mr. Lancaster. Don't press me for details on that. Do I have to go into intimate details for you to see the way lovers progressed back then?"

She giggled. "I wish you could, but I know it would embarrass you. Just let me imagine that you and Liz did more than hold hands and go to the movies."

Now I was a little embarrassed. "We did. Her late husband was from Seattle, her folks lived down near Salinas, so there was no bar to keep the two of us from practically living together. I bought a small house two doors down from hers in the Mission District near where she taught at Mission High School. We alternated between her house and mine. I kept the house for years. Until the romance was over in 1939."

Annie looked sad. She said, "So for a long time, you were like a true married pair, I assume."

I said, "Now are you quoting Kipling's 'The Ladies'?

> We lived on the square like a true married pair,
> And I learned about women from her."

She looked bleak. "Nope. I don't know that poem. I don't know much about Kipling."

"All right, I can't quote the whole thing from memory, but the first part tells my story. Wanna hear it?"

> I've taken my fun where I found it,
> I've rogued and I've ranged in my time,
> I've 'ad my pickin' of sweethearts,
> And four of the lot was prime.

"All four of my serious loves were prime, and when Liz comes, you can meet the only one that got away. So yes and no, we lived on the square, but I begged and pleaded with her to marry me. She wouldn't, for several reasons, she said. Her husband hadn't been dead long enough, and my second wife hadn't been dead long enough. I argued that Jane's death was three years in the past, but Liz was traditional about some things."

Annie smiled and said, "Except for a little cohabitation? Sorry. That was crude."

"Apology accepted. I thought the same thing about the cohabitation at the time, but I couldn't kidnap her and drag her to the altar like old Floyd did with Delsie. Fall came, and I went back to Bodark and resumed teaching at John Bell Hood. We wrote passionately and planned to spend the following summer together. We did, and I kept up my suit about the marriage business. This rocked on for years. Summer in San Francisco or travelling together—Hawaii, once to London, up and down the coast. One Christmas vacation I persuaded her to come to Texas. She did, took one look at Bodark Springs, and, reluctantly it seemed, decided that we should end the summer romances. And that was that. I got the engagement ring back that I'd persuaded her to accept the summer before, and, years after, in 1946, I married Barbara and she married Mr. Lancaster, whoever he was. Some resident of 'Baghdad by the Bay,' I suppose."

Annie said, "And you never saw her again after 1939?"

"No, I came back to Texas and bought the LaSalle to help ease my pain. That's a joke. At least, I think that's a joke. Anyway, we exchanged Christmas cards and the occasional letter. And that all ended a few years ago. I haven't seen her, but I guess I will next Friday, if you'll drive me to the airport."

She almost jumped for joy. "I wouldn't miss this reunion for all the tea in China. So I guess the famous LaSalle is some kind of love substitute. Some kind of symbol. I get it now. Maybe that's why everybody has her eye on the maroon chariot."

"Probably. You mentioned all the tea in China. Shall I brew a pot of Darjeeling for us now?"

She sighed and said, "I thought you'd never ast. Is that Dulcie's word—'ast'?"

The tea ceremony over, my tale about Liz over, at least until she arrived at Love Field, Annie turned on the tape recorder and I started in about the wedding I'd seen years before in "the Quarters."

"As you can imagine, I must've attended hundreds of weddings here in Eastis County. Most of my students married and shamed me into attending their weddings. Some are still marrying—maybe for the second or third time—and they want me to come and watch it happen. Over and over, I sometimes think. Most are in churches, but a few are at the little wedding chapel and reception hall just off the square. It's a commercial enterprise owned by Abe Dugan, and I suppose it's for unbelievers if there are any in Bodark Springs, or possibly lapsed Catholics prevented from marrying after a divorce. Or maybe for the Reformed Jews in the county who don't stand in good stead with the Sherman synagogue."

Then I remembered a ritual I'd heard of but never seen. "I guess you know about couples 'jumping the broom.'"

She hit the pause button. "Doing what? Jumping the broom? No I don't guess I do."

"That was pretty common a long time ago. When a couple decided to marry and didn't have money for a preacher, they got some friends together and jumped over a broom handle. And that took care of the marriage, and everybody in the community then accepted them as wed. All that was mostly confined to the Negro—er, black—community. But not always. If people lived way out of town, they'd sometimes jump the broom. I've read that out in West Texas jumping the broom was a stopgap measure. A couple would jump over a broom handle if they couldn't wait for a circuit-riding preacher. Then when the clergyman arrived, they'd have a regular ceremony. Once in awhile a wedding out there would be performed in front of a couple and the two or three children they had after the broom ritual. Nobody thought less of them for not waiting sometimes years for a preacher to show up.

"The most memorable ceremony I ever attended was of a Negro—oh, right, black—couple who were members of the family of one of my housekeepers. Not Rosie. That was before her time. I think this was about 1934. The first remarkable and wonderful thing was that the wedding was held on the porch of the bride's house. The couple stood on the front porch facing out into the yard where all the friends and relatives were standing. The preacher, Reverend Samuel Coats, stood down two steps so everybody could get a good look at the bride and groom. There was no music, no bridesmaids, no flower girls. It was a simple but sensible ceremony that couldn't have cost Ben and Sally Jackson much money—that's their married name even though the marriage lasted hardly a minute. What happened was that when Reverend Coats said, 'I pronounce you man and wife' and the pair started down the steps, a figure rushed out of the crowd with a butcher knife and stabbed Ben Jackson in the stomach. He ripped the knife—one about eight inches long—upward into the chest cavity. Ben was dead before he hit the ground. The killer rushed out of the yard and down the unpaved street. We were all too stunned to move, so nobody thought to chase the killer, one Rosco Bascomb. In a minute or two I heard a car start, so I figured Rosco had a confederate waiting for him to kill Ben and escape. After a few minutes, I decided to go downtown and tell the sheriff what I'd seen. When I got to where my car was parked, I found it gone. It was my car that Rosco jumped in and drove away. Back in those days I never took the keys out of my car. Nobody stole cars here in the county. I learned to pocket my keys after that.

"I had to walk a mile into town to see the sheriff. Since it was Sunday, the sheriff's office was closed. I went to see the chief of police, who was parked on the corner outside Ralph Powell's cafe, waiting, I suppose, for some whiskey runner to come tearing through town with a load of moonshine. Rob Roy Pledger, Jim Tom's daddy, was chief then. When I told him what had happened, he said, 'Hell, Mr. Adams, that's in the county and not in my jurisdiction. Besides, niggers cut each other all the time. When Sheriff Joe Langdon comes back from Honeygrove, you can tell him.'

"Law enforcement wasn't integrated back in 1934. Nobody much cared what colored people—you are gonna have to get used to my terminology so I don't have to interrupt myself all the time—did to one another. But when I told Rob Roy that Rosco Bascomb had stolen my car, that changed things. The chief said, 'Come on, get in the car, and we'll see what that nigger's done with it.' We drove out of town toward Savoy and saw my 1933 Ford V8 down in a ditch. Rosco had run off the road and couldn't get the car out of the bar ditch. I guess he fled on foot. In any case, he was never seen again in the town or the county."

She wanted more. Obviously. "Is that the end of this story? Did the policeman get a wrecker out to rescue your car?"

"No, Rob Roy said I'd have to get the car out some other way since it was Sunday and Louie Ryan's garage was closed. Everybody knew that nobody drove Louie's wrecker but him. The chief said Louie was up in Cooks Springs visiting his in-laws."

She wanted me to go on. "So you had to leave the car in the ditch for the rest of the weekend?"

"No, I saw a farmer in the field plowing with a span of mules. He was obviously dishonoring the Sabbath Day and not keeping it holy. I went over and offered him five dollars to unhitch his mules from the disc harrow and go hook his doubletree to the back bumper of my Ford and pull it up on the road."

She griped. "Oh, John Q., why do I have to drag everything out of you? So you got your car and drove away? Then what? What is a doubletree and a disc harrow? By the way, did this farmer use the old biblical dictum about getting your ox out of the ditch on the Sabbath?"

"No. He took the five dollars and never said a word. I'll bet that old farmer—his name if you care was B. T. Mosley—hadn't seen a five-dollar bill since before Coolidge was president. You're gonna have to look up farm implements if you're gonna get the lie of this land. I think I have a farm implement catalog somewhere in this study that has pictures of disc harrows and doubletrees and horse collars and trace chains and nearly anything you'd find on a farm. Anyway, I did drive the car away. It had a smashed up left front fender and a busted headlight but was otherwise unhurt. Oh, and Rosco left the butcher knife on the floorboard. I rescued it since neither the sheriff nor the police chief wanted it as evidence. It's in the kitchen if you want to see it."

She groaned. "No thanks. Is there much crime now in Bodark Springs or out in the county?"

"Just the usual. Once in awhile, somebody will get drunk and shoot or stab somebody he knows. Those cases are simple and are usually either white on white or col—oops, black on black. The law doesn't worry much about the black-on-black shootings and stabbings. The whites who take to gun or knife are usually quickly arrested. Years ago, we had a lot of bootlegging and whiskey running all over northeast Texas."

Notebook in hand, she asked, "What's the difference between bootlegging and whiskey running?"

"Bootleggers make the whiskey in stills way out in the woods and usually leave the hauling of it to some old boys who have fast cars. You can always tell a runner if his car passes through unloaded. They used to drive 1932 Ford V8s with super heavy-duty rear springs. Unloaded, the back part of the car would sit way higher than the front. Loaded, of course, the car sat on an even keel. I don't know what they drive now. For a while the 1933 Ford V8 was the car of choice, and the last one I ever saw was a 1940 Ford Tudor. The time I'm talking about was when the whole country was dry—Prohibition, you know."

She was interested in our dry county. "And so now you don't have bootleggers and whiskey runners?"

"Oh, we do. Lots of people got used to cheap homemade liquor and wouldn't have any of that bottled-in-bond stuff you can get in the liquor stores in Dallas or up in Oklahoma. There must a hundred stills up along the Red, and I'm sure somebody has to haul it to people who sell it in small lots. There must be a dozen 'shot houses' in the Quarters where a person can get a small glass of whiskey for a pretty reasonable price. And then there are some trailers out on the edge of town where a person can get bonded whiskey or white lightnin'."

She wondered about my drinking. "But your Johnnie Walker is all legal."

"No. It's against the law to bring whiskey into the county. If I got caught with some half gallons of JW Red or Black, I could be fined. If I'm caught, I hope it's by Sergeant Stowers or somebody who made good grades back in the day. Maybe when we go in to Love Field to pick up Mrs. Lancaster, I'll have you stop at Centennial so I can get some material to make Manhattans for her—and for you, if you've any interest in lady drinks."

She seemed to miss something here. "Didn't I see somebody drinking in the restaurant the other night? Was that bootleg hooch?"

"No. That was all legal. The restaurant has a private club license and can serve members drinks. And the local American Legion Hall and the VFW can serve drinks. Here's a funny story. Back during the war, there was a prisoner of war camp over in Cooke County, and lots of the POWs got out to work on farms in the area. After the war, a few of the German ex-soldiers came back here and married local women they'd met when they were POWs. One old boy, Helmut Schmidt, came back, got married to a girl from Gainesville, and found himself a job in a machine shop here in Bodark. One day he was complaining that you couldn't get a drink 'in dis whole dom county.' Somebody at the shop told him you could at the VFW or American Legion if you were a veteran. One night he showed up at the VFW and asked whether he could join. Charlie Smart asked if he was a veteran of a foreign war and Helmut said he was. Old man Smart signed Helmut up without asking him what outfit he was with and where he served overseas. Helmut indeed had served overseas, but he didn't mention that he was in the Sixth Panzer Division of the Wehrmacht. He may still be a member for all I know."

She was interested in crime it seemed. "And there are no deep, dark unsolved mysteries like you see in the movies?"

"No, I don't think so. Most shootin's and cuttin's are in hot blood and the killer is caught right away—most of the time almost in the act. A few crimes are hard to prove. There used to be a spate of arson back in the Depression. Sometimes a person would burn down a house or business for the insurance. An old slumlord named Mike Sharp had rundown shacks all over town and way out in the Quarters. He'd rent 'em out for about ten dollars a month, but when times really got hard and some of his houses stood empty, one was likely to go up in flames—almost always on Saturday night when the volunteer firemen were out at the American Legion drinking. As soon as the main fire siren sounded, people up on the square would say, 'Which one of old man Sharp's houses is afire?'"

"Did they ever catch him?"

"Never. I suppose nowadays with most towns having fire marshals and ways to detect flammable substances, he might get caught. But all his fires were early in the 1930s."

"So that sums up the crime waves of Bodark and Eastis County?"

"Pretty much, except for the time that Mamie Dell shot her brother.

"Here's that story as everybody knew it, even within a week of the time. Mamie herself used to tell it, but her brother, Shorty, never mentioned it. Mamie had inherited a little old .32 caliber revolver from her uncle Isham. Shorty thought he should have fallen heir to the cheap little 'owl head' pistol. I think it was an Ivor Johnson make, the kind they now call 'Saturday night specials.' It wouldn't have brought two dollars. (I guess you never heard the expression 'hotter'n a two dollar pistol.') But Shorty thought he should have this worthless gun. Sentimentality, I suppose it was. One night, when Shorty knew Grady Dell would be at an American Legion meeting in town, he and Julius Bagby went up to the house that Mamie and Grady were renting about two miles out of town. About midnight, Shorty saw all the lights out and Grady's car gone, so he and Julius stood out in the road trying to figure out how to break in. You have to remember—no you don't since you didn't know Shorty—that Shorty Earnest was a moron. Doctor Farley said he had the mind of a ten-year-old. Anyway, while Shorty and Julius stood in the road plotting, Mamie got Grady's .32 Savage automatic, leaned out over little Tommy Earl, and shot Shorty in the foot. Shorty and Julius took off running. Even though Shorty had a couple of broken bones and was hurtin' like hell, he managed to run about a hundred yards down the road before he stopped. Mamie heard the running and then the stopping. She went to the back door and fired a shot up in the air. Shorty started hobblin' away. Everytime he slowed down, Mamie pulled off another shot in the air. All in all, she said she fired five times."

She couldn't believe this tale. "Did Shorty call the sheriff?"

"No. He never mentioned it. Mamie said she used to see him up town on Saturdays. He would be on crutches. I hear he went on crutches for nearly a month. She would say, 'Howdy, Shorty,' and he'd say, 'Hey, Mamie Doodle' and limp off."

Another puzzler for Annie Baxter. "Mamie Doodle?"

"I guess that's what he called her when they were little. They're both dead now, and I may be the only person who remembers that silly story. Or maybe not silly if you were Shorty."

She asked, "Who told you?"

"Oh, Mamie. She told everybody. She said she was a crack shot and hit him exactly where she aimed. It's a good thing she had Grady's Savage automatic 'cause that pistol she inherited wouldn't have carried to the road. She also said that her little boy slept through the gun's being fired right over his head."

She wasn't satisfied with the little crimes I had told her, and she said, "I guess there are other kinds of crimes to worry about. What about drug problems? We have 'em in the worst way in Austin now. People smoking weed and taking pills. Then there's all that heroin coming across from Mexico."

"As far as I know, there's not much of that here. There used to be a hot tamale salesman with a little oven-like thing on the front of his bicycle. Somebody told me that he'd sell you a marijuana cigarette for a dollar. This was back in the thirties, and he—they called him Half-Moon Hinojosa—disappeared from town years ago."

I went on. "I heard that Clio Richardson and some of her friends bought those hand-rolled cigarettes from Half-Moon and went over to Paris and got in a tourist court and smoked them. They claimed they didn't get any kick and didn't feel any hangover after it. Maybe Half-Moon was selling oregano or something."

She hoped for some scandals in our little town. "So no meth, no crack cocaine, nothing like that?"

"I don't know. I'm so old nobody would cut me in on the drugs if there were any. We always had a few dope fiends here in town. Probably still do, but I can't swear to it."

Again eager for more low life, she said, "Dope fiends? Is that what you call all users of illegal substances? Oh, wait, you did tell me about the woman who took dope and got the ring wrenched off her finger. You called her a dope fiend if I remember."

"I did, but she wasn't in the same league with a couple of dope fiends we have had. I know you hate for me to use the words 'dope fiend,' but it's what people used to call folks like Snowbird Smith and Lorene Lawrence. And old John Carlisle from back in the late twenties. Do you want me to tell you about them for your tape?"

She checked the reel to see if she still had space. "Sure. Snowbird? What kind of name is that?"

"I'll tell you in a minute, but first I ought to point out that lots of people who got addicted were doctors and nurses and pharmacists and people who had a lot of pain and got started taking serious dope. Snowbird was a pharmacist here in town, and he must've been sneaking drugs out of his cabinet and maybe diluting the narcotics when he filled a prescription. People who take drugs for a long time lose all the pigment in their skins—well, not all of it—but enough that they get extraordinarily pale. Old 'Snowbird' got whiter and whiter as the years wore on, till finally he looked like some movie actor in whiteface. You know, for a horror movie. Then one day, he took too much morphine and died behind the counter of his drugstore. Somebody said he was frothing at the mouth. I wasn't there and can't testify to the foaming and frothing.

"Another fellow, John Carlisle, was a victim of kidney stones. He had one after another for several years and had to get relief by taking morphine. He had some so bad that Dr. Clayton started giving him shots in the main vein, 'mainlinin,' they call it in the movies. John was a nice fellow, a family man who owned the Chevrolet agency here in town. His parents were rich, and once John got fully addicted and lost the dealership, his parents kept him in a hotel in Dallas and paid for him to go from doctor to doctor to get drugs. People from here used to see him sitting in the lobby of the hotel—not the Adolphus, mind you, but a lesser hostelry—and looking pale. I think he died, but I never got the full story.

"All right, one last sad tale. Lorene Lawrence was first Dr. Lawrence's nurse and then his wife. How she got addicted, I never heard. But she did, and that caused Dr. Lawrence a lot of grief. One day, in July of 1938, Dr. Lawrence drove to Dallas, bought enough drugs to last Lorene for six months, and came back to his house about three doors down the street from me. While Lorene was down at Eden visiting her mother, Dr. Lawrence took a hypodermic syringe, filled it with air, and shot it into his arm. The air bubble hit his heart, and he died with the needle still sticking out of his arm. Lorene was left with a house, a 1938 Dodge doctor's coupe, and enough drugs to last her till Christmas. Morphine, I think it was."

"And then what?"

"Well, this is a story that turns out pretty well. She used the drugs to taper off, and early in 1939 was clean and sober, as the AA people now say. She lived for seven or eight more years and died of a heart attack. End of story. End of dope fiend stories. I'm through jabbering for this day. How about if we take tomorrow off? I have a few things to do in town, and I'm sure you can spend time writing letters to Justin and your folks in Midland."

She seemed to be relieved from all the taping. "I like that plan. Besides, Lucy has been wanting me to come down to the dairy and have lunch with her. She's gonna show me how they milk cows and cool the milk and send it to Paris or Bonham or somewhere to be put in bottles and sold in the stores. I've never seen a milking machine, and I think I can work something I learn into my story."

CHAPTER 13

The minute my grandfather clock struck ten, Annie knocked on my door. I opened it, but she stood outside looking around the driveway. "I see you have company," she said. I told her I was alone and to come in the house. She said, "When I saw that silver car in the drive, I thought you must have a visitor."

"Just come in and close the door. I'm here alone ready to get goin' on your tape machine."

She kept looking around. "Oh, I just thought I might be intruding. Maybe Mrs. Lancaster had got here early or some other old girlfriend had surfaced. I never know what to expect from you, John Q. Did somebody park that car with the temporary paper license plates in your drive by mistake?"

"No. If you'll look at these papers, you'll see that the car is registered to one Annie Baxter of—"

She screamed. "What? What do you mean!"

I tried to calm her. "Settle down. It's an early wedding present for you and Justin. You'd never be able to visit him now that your old car disappeared. And his old Dodge wouldn't make many trips up to see you. And I sure as hell wasn't about to let you take the LaSalle to Austin."

She was in tears. "John Q., you are the sweetest grandpa in the world, but I can't take that car. My God! What would my parents think? No, you'll have to take it back to the Chevrolet place and get your money. What is it, an Impala? My God! I am shocked at you, and no telling what my daddy would say if he knew a man had bought me a new Impala. Oh, John Q.!"

"I called your parents last night and told 'em that I'm a rich ninety-five-year-old with no designs on their daughter. I told 'em it was an early wedding gift. They started in on the same 'Oh my God she can't take such an expensive present' as you just did.

I said, "'Too late. What's done is done. They don't take returns at Wood Chevrolet in Bodark Springs, Texas'. They oohed and ahhed some, but saw that I was a stubborn old fool and finally wound up thanking me and agreeing to the present. So say no more about it. The metal plates will be here tomorrow, and the car will be registered to you at my address. When you get new plates next year, you can change the registration to Austin. It's full of gas, so if you want to take it on the road, we can go to Texarkana and eat lunch at Bryce's, the best cafeteria in all of Texas."

Annie cried and sniffled and finally hugged me. She said, "You are the grandpa I always wanted, but I never wanted a rich grandpa. Just a good grandpa was all I ever hoped for. Just old Johnny. Damn, there I go blubbering again. Hell, let's get that Impala limbered up." Then she cried again.

When we got in the car and headed east on Highway 82, I was glad to see that she was a careful and skillful driver. I hadn't thought about her driving skills when I asked her to take me to Love Field to meet Liz. I didn't want to ask Eddie to drive me to Dallas and then spring Liz on him. But since Eddie was probably behind Liz's visit, I wouldn't exactly be springing it on him. In any event I sure as hell didn't want him to see me with Liz when she got off the plane. I might faint or have a stroke when I saw her after all these years. I didn't want to give him the satisfaction. I still drive as well as I ever did, I think and hope, but I'm not keen on night driving, especially to a big city like Dallas, so I enlisted Annie, my new best friend.

When we were nearly to Bonham, I thought to tell her about Justin's call. After I talked to her parents in Midland, I called old Clarence

Maxon in the political science department at UT and asked him to track down Justin Cole and ask him to call me collect as soon as he could find him. Justin called shortly after 9:00 all worked up with worry that something had happened to Annie. I calmed him down and told him about the car. He did the same rigamarole as Annie and the parents, but I prevailed as I knew I would. I told him I'd send Annie off to Austin on Saturday and let her stay there for a week. Told him not to wreck Annie's car. I figured I'd need that week to get used to Liz Denney all over again. If I could.

We ate a wonderful lunch at my favorite cafeteria in the whole world. Bryce's is so good I always order stuff I don't like because I know they'll surprise me with how good it can taste if they make it. I hate creamed spinach, but I always order it there—and love it till I try it somewhere else. After lunch, I had her drive us all over Texarkana as I told her about what the boosters called "The Arklatex." We crossed State Line Avenue so she could say she'd been to Arkansas. I exhausted my knowledge of stories about the Arklatex, which I explained should be the ArkOklaTex since Oklahoma was closer to Texarkana than Louisiana was. By mid-afternoon, it was time to head west so I could find my recliner and maybe sip a little Johnnie Walker before bedtime.

Then I remembered that we had never talked about the strange curses some people put on their enemies and how they often worked. I said, "You don't have your tape machine in the car, but we can pass some time if I tell you about the local voodoo hereabouts. You can either remember it or we can go through it all again when Liz has gone and you're back from Austin."

She kept her eyes on the road I was pleased to see. "Tell me. If it's good, I'll remember it. What brought that up today?"

"Well, as we were passing through Bowie County, I remembered some stories that went the rounds back in the fifties. The gypsies used to come through on a kind of circuit, and scads of people used to line up outside the gypsy trailers to get their fortunes told. Of course, nearly everybody really believed that the gypsies were out to steal children and that the fortune telling was a ruse. No children ever disappeared when gypsies were around, but you can't get ideas out of folks' heads. Anyway, gypsies all told women they would meet a dark, handsome stranger and

142

fall in love—even the married women got the same story. The few men that got their fortunes told were promised that money would somehow appear to them."

Annie put on her puzzled face. "Why were the customers mostly women? Are you saying men are less gullible than women? That would hurt my feelings if you're making that assertion."

"No, I'm not asserting any such thing. I'm sure men were as eager as the women to look into the future, but it seemed sissy to most of them to get a fortune told. Woman's foolishness, old Burt Little would say."

Annie laughed, "So you never went?"

"No. That's sissy!" Now we were both vindicated and laughed sheepishly.

I said, "When the gypsies came through they also sold love potions and High John the Conquerer Root and little bottles of something or other that would let you cast a spell on your enemies, and—"

She didn't have a pencil or paper to get answers. "Wait. What is High John the Conquerer Root?"

"Oh, High John the Conquerer would give you power over your enemies. I think it is also called St. John's Wort, but nobody I ever knew called it that. You could use it to cast a spell over your enemy, and if the person you hated heard about it, he might die or have warts pop out all over his or her face. I knew a couple of girls who got together way back before 1900 to wish a wart on some other girl's face. They claimed it worked and the wart appeared on the end of the popular girl's nose and she died an old maid."

She almost ran off the road thinking about voodoo. "You can't possibly believe all that kind of witchcraft. Are you superstitious, John Q.?"

"No, but I never walk under a ladder, and if a black cat crosses my path, I turn around and go some other way. Better to be safe, right?"

She asked, "Okay, so let's say somebody way back got a spell put on him or her. Could they use High John to counteract it?"

"Possibly. I never knew anybody to make a spell go away, but I did hear of a surefire remedy that the police down in Carthage or somewhere used when a person came to the station claiming a spell had been put on her—or maybe him. They took 'em over to the Xerox machine and had 'em lay a hand on the glass. Then they ran the machine and said

'The spell is gone.'"

She laughed. "Did that work?"

"Of course it worked. People who believe in spells and curses will fall for anything. But the guy that told me this said the station was overrun with people—mostly colored they said, racist or not—so they devised a better plan than taking up all that time on the copier. Once they got radar guns in Carthage or wherever it was, they simply pointed the gun at them and when it made a buzzing noise, they said the spell had been removed."

She kept her eyes on the road now. "I can remember all those stories, so you don't have to be taped for me to write them up. Any more?"

"Well, one other thing that I love to think about is the removal of warts. People claim if you rub a wart with a dishrag and bury the rag outside the back door, when the rag rots, the wart will go away. Of course the best thing is never to pick up a frog since that's what causes warts."

She laughed, "Oh, come on, you don't believe warts come that way. I hear they're caused by a virus or something."

"So I've heard. Old Grady Dell, the rural mail carrier hereabouts, was famous for curing warts. If somebody went to him for a cure, he asked them to count the warts and tell him the number. Then he would rub his hand over the warts, and, in a month or two, they'd go away. People swore to that. I wonder if a young girl—or an old woman for that matter—had warts in awkward places, Grady got to put his hand no telling where. A person could get arrested if too much touching took place. Or maybe not."

She drove and we lapsed into silence, and I worried about Liz's coming. By the time we got back to Lamar County to the outskirts of Paris, I still couldn't figure what to expect from Liz. I couldn't imagine what had moved her to come halfway across the country, after all these years. Was this just like the old song, a "sentimental journey to renew old memories," or had she come to accept the proposal of marriage I made forty years ago? I still had the ring in the safe deposit box, but if she was thinking to accept the old proposal, I might have to grab that $100,000 and make for Paris—not Texas this time, but Paris, France.

I had been silent for so long that Annie feared I'd decided I hated her company. She said, "Why so quiet, John Q.? Have I done something wrong or said some awkward thing?"

"No, no. You're the perfect travelling companion, and I am a great admirer of your driving. Maybe one day I'll put you behind the wheel of the LaSalle."

She squirmed with delight. "Oh, goody! Do you think we'll take it to Dallas?"

"No, we'll go in the Electra. I figure Liz will have a steamer trunk or something, and it might scratch the LaSalle. I guess I'll tell you why I'm so silent. I've been sitting here puzzling out what Liz Denney—now Lancaster—is coming to Bodark Springs for. I once proposed marriage and she turned me down when I made it clear that we'd have to live in Bodark Springs. Stupid me! I could've moved to San Francisco, but I was young—mid-fifties—and foolish. Oh, hell, here one comes."

She was startled. "Here comes what? I don't see anything."

"No, I mean here comes one of my interminable and boring sashays into some poem. I was thinking of Yeats's 'Down By the Salley Gardens.' Do you know it?"

She joked, "No, I don't think so, but if you hum a few lines—"

"Smarty. Here comes some of it, all I can remember:

Down by the salley gardens
my love and I did meet;
She passed the salley gardens
with little snow-white feet.
She bid me take love easy,
as the leaves grow on the tree;
But I, being young and foolish,
with her would not agree.

And some I forgot and then:

She bid me take life easy,
as the grass grows on the weirs;
But I was young and foolish,
and now am full of tears.

145

"I think that's right. There may be more, but I can't recall exactly. I know you think I'm a foolish old man to go on like this, but I was in love in a bad way back then. Maybe she was, but the way things turned out, maybe she wasn't. Now I'm worrying about this visit. She's only about seventy, and she may have forgot that I'm not the youthful fifty-something I was then. What if she's come back to take me up on marriage, ready to settle down in Bodark Springs?"

Annie was aglow. "If she's here for marriage, I'll dance and sing at the wedding and call her Grandma Liz. She'd be getting the best old grandpa in the western hemisphere. If she's up to anything else, I'll scratch her eyes out before we make it out of Dallas."

"You'll be driving, so don't go for her eyeballs. You might wreck the Buick."

"Ha. But I'm sure she's not up to anything nefarious. She damned well better not be."

"Okay, *que sera, sera.*"

She helped me not to worry. She said, "Just be patient. And try to get at least one song right. And don't start singing that Doris Day song or I'll run my new car in the bar ditch."

I mostly had a good time on this trip, at least until I started worrying about Liz. I was glad when we eased into Bodark Springs. I was ready to rest for about a week. Annie let me out and drove the car to the Cotton Exchange garage. I figured if Maybelline or Eddie saw the new Impala, I'd be getting a phone call. Maybe I'd just leave the damned thing off the hook. But what if Liz calls and explains herself or decides not to come? I was too dispirited even to crack open the Johnnie Walker. I stumbled off to bed and had the most restless night I've had since Barbara was dying of cancer back in 1950.

The next morning Annie was staying in her room to work on her notes, and I was cumbering a sunlit pallet till nine and feeling guilty for not rising at 5:00. The phone didn't ring, so I supposed Edward hadn't heard about Liz coming to town or was biding his time before unveiling his schemes, whatever they were. Unless he was up to something cunning, he'd certainly have been calling or coming by to offer me advice or to criticize me for still keeping up some kind of relationship with the woman he used to call my "California Sweetie." By noon I had not heard a peep from anybody, so I went down to the Busy Bee for soup and salad.

Annie came to the house in the afternoon, and I asked her if she'd seen Eddie and if he'd mentioned anything about my visitor. She said, "I saw him two or three times—when I went down for breakfast and later to get my mail. Oh, and when I was leaving."

"He didn't give you the third degree?"

She said, "No, he was, to use one of your ickier expressions, as friendly as a whipped puppy. Where do you get those strange locutions?"

"Locutions? You're thinking to intimidate me. To answer your question, it is some of what we call 'folk say,' a term you introduced me to last week, as if I had never heard of it."

By now, Annie and I were able to kid around as if we'd known each other forever, and I was feeling more and more like her grandpa. She had definitely grown on me. Maybe Eddie would think she'd grown on me too much when he discovered the Impala. If he'd seen or heard about the car, he sure wouldn't have kept it to himself for this long. Maybe he was gathering strength to call in the men with little white coats and a stretcher. If—or when—he did bring it up, I'd say, "So what if I bought Annie a little Impala; when Liz Denney, my California Sweetie, gets to town I'll go down to Statewide Motors and buy her a damned Cadillac if I want to."

While I was mumbling to myself, Annie was telling me about her letter from Justin. She said he wondered if I'd let her tape me talking about politics in this part of Texas. I tried to tell her that Eastis County did all the same things the state did—Democrats all the way till 1928 and then till Eisenhower took Texas in 1952, but she still wanted to hear more about what I'd observed in all the years since I had first been a voter in 1892. That was the year I proudly cast my vote for Grover Cleveland, who won a second term after one term out of office—the only president to have two non-consecutive terms. I voted for William Jennings Bryan a couple of times, but I didn't have a second winner till Woodrow Wilson. Then a spate of Republicans till FDR won for the first time in 1932.

I could see that this was boring her—and me—and suggested that we wait till Justin had some specific questions about politics in Eastis County. She read on and said, "He wants to know how Eastis County voted in 1928."

I said, "Eastis County did the same foolish thing as the rest of the country. Eastis voted Republican for the first time, and Herbert Hoover presided over the Great Depression, though it really wasn't his fault. He could've done better than he did when the worst started. It took Franklin D. to start some workable things to slow the worst of it down. Of course, as you know, it took the war to really put a stop to hard times. You should've heard the silly rumors that went 'round about Al Smith, a New York Catholic. They were building the Holland Tunnel from New Jersey to Manhattan about then, and some Smith haters spread the rumor that the tunnel was being built to Rome so the Pope's men could stroll over and tell Al Smith what to do. I heard that kind of talk all over town. Some ignorant asses must have thought Rome was just across the East River and not way the hell over in Europe."

She read some more from the letter. "Justin wants to know whether the Ku Klux Klan was a force in this part of Texas."

"Yes and no. There were always, here and there in northeast Texas, a few half-assed Klaverns that held the occasional cross burning. The Klan hoped to be a real factor in state elections, but in 1932 Ma Ferguson took on the Klan and won. That sort of ended them as a political factor, though they'd never been one here in the county. In some of the counties around here, they did things like tying some poor Negro to a tree and whipping him, but they never lynched anybody that I ever heard of. There was one case over in Fannin County that went the rounds: a mother/daughter team had a house of ill repute—just the two of them doin' the work—and that got the Klan all riled up. Maybe the Klan wives put 'em up to it, but one night, as I heard it told, some guys in sheets went over and whipped mother and daughter and told 'em they'd have to move out of Fannin. Somebody told me they pulled up stakes and moved to Red River County down between Bogota and Rugby. I hope they flourished. But I haven't heard much of the Klan in years. I hope Justin wasn't counting on anything of importance from my feeble old mind."

She put the letter away and said, "If you're fishing for a compliment about your feeble mind, forget it."

"Why don't we end it for the day? We can go eat at the restaurant, and maybe Eddie will come over to the table and inject his jolly self into our table talk. You go ahead and primp or whatever young women of your vintage do. I'll make myself presentable and join you about 6:00. Old people eat early. I suppose the fashionable hour for dinner in Austin is 9:00."

She said, "Not for me. I'm always hungry by 6:00. I look forward to seeing how you dress for the occasion."

She left, and I guessed I'd been challenged about the dress code for the evening, so I decided, after my nap of almost an hour, that I would change clothes and look like somebody from the back pages of *Esquire*. After a quick shower, I re-shaved, splashed on some aftershave, stared at my face long enough to decide I didn't look a day over eighty-five, and started rummaging through my closet to find proper attire for a date with a beauty from Austin. I put on a sport coat she hadn't seen, a fresh shirt, a tie that I hadn't worn in months, and some medium-gray pants. I slicked down my hair, found a narrow-brim straw hat, and set out for the Cotton Exchange on foot.

Once Annie and I got settled in the restaurant, Edward came over and drew up a chair. I suspected that I was in for a grilling about the car and the woman from California. But no. He was all affability and charm. He complimented Annie on the pants suit she was wearing and said, "Dad, that's a beautiful tie. Is it Countess Mara?" I explained it was a handmade silk that I got in Rome several years back.

He seemed in a puckish mood. "Oh, by the way, Pop, do you think you could work tomorrow while I'm out of town?"

I said, "Gosh, Eddie, I'm afraid I have some business to attend to out of town myself. Can you find somebody else?"

"Oh, that's not a problem. I can probably get Lucy to come in. She'd probably like a few days away from Charlie and the grandkids. She can eat somebody else's cooking and sleep late in the morning. Even get room service in bed. No, you go on and do what you have to do."

This was so un-Edward that I knew he was up to something. He didn't ask where I was going or try to persuade me to change my plans. Now I knew for certain he was behind Liz Denney's sudden visit. I hate it when my children get cunning on me.

When the deceptive smiling Eddie went away, I suggested to Annie that she come for me at about two tomorrow. We could go into Dallas to the Centennial so I could stock up on strong drink, and then we could eat at Chiquita, the best Mexican restaurant I knew of. There was no Mexican food to be had in Bodark unless you got chili and tamales in cans and chips in bags.

PART III

THE GIRL OF THE GOLDEN WEST

CHAPTER 14

Friday morning saw me up early, and I took the Buick down to Roy Roberts's filling station to get the oil and filter changed, the car greased, and the belts and spark plugs checked and cleaned if necessary. I doubted that the car really needed servicing, but I wanted perfection on this day of days. I had the car washed and waxed and detailed inside and out. While Roy was working his magic, I went home, ate my usual breakfast of Raisin Bran, toast, and coffee, and planned my wardrobe for meeting Liz Denney. I selected my best Savile Row suit in navy with a tiny maroon stripe—so tiny it was almost invisible. I got a white shirt off a hanger that I knew Bill Cop Cleaners and Laundry had cared for as if it had been a new baby. The tie was a mauve silk from Bond Street, and the shoes were cordovan wingtips from my old friend Rolando at Leddy's. About eleven-thirty I took a shower and shaved very carefully. I worried that I might wear out my face with all this careful shaving, but I had to look just right if I was to win Liz's heart again. I didn't dress in my finery until I'd rescued my car from Roy's place. When I saw it, I knew he'd given it his best wash and wax. It gleamed. All this was foolishness on my part, since Liz would only see it in the dark. But as my friend Tanner always says, "Err on the side of generosity."

Annie arrived precisely at two o'clock as I knew she would. I was dressed and ready to set out on what I hoped would not be some dreadful fool's errand. I almost felt like Odysseus on his way back to Ithaca to confront Penelope after ten years on the ringing plains of windy Troy and all those years at sea. Annie got in the car after remarking on its beauty, though she said she hoped I'd had a change of heart and would take the LaSalle. I promised that she could drive it one day soon. That is, if the whole ordeal with Liz didn't kill me.

Annie got behind the wheel, adjusted the seat to her five-foot-seven, and fired up the Electra. It took her a block or two to get the feel of the car, but we reached the western edge of the town and hit Highway 82 toward Bonham. When we got well into Fannin County, we would head south toward Dallas. Annie knew the route to Dallas as well as I did, since she had made the trip to Austin and back a few times since we'd started our project. I thought "our" instead of "her" project since I'd thrown myself into her work as readily as she had.

Once in Dallas, I directed her to the Centennial Liquor Store so I could load the car with what would be contraband once we left Dallas County and headed north. I bought two half gallons of Johnnie Walker Black—of course Annie couldn't forbear telling me that these weren't half gallons but 1.75 centimeters or grams or kilometers of whatever the hell Europeans were using to confuse honest buyers. I ordered a half gallon of Jack Daniels, one of Beefeater gin in case Liz had graduated from Manhattans and Old Fashioneds to martinis, a pint of vermouth, some bitters, and a jar of those expensive maraschino cherries the Centennial is so proud of. Annie suggested some Drambuie and some Grand Marnier in case somebody wanted an after-dinner dram or two. And she noted that I hadn't added any olives stuffed with pimento or garlic some other foreign matter. I did as she suggested. We almost filled the trunk with boxes of spirits, which made me hope Liz hadn't brought her whole wardrobe with her. It's a good thing the Electra has a capacious trunk. If we'd brought Annie's Impala, we might've had to put some boxes on the back seat.

I directed Annie over toward Cedar Springs Avenue and onto the street that housed Chiquita, the best Mexican food in North Texas. It serves Mexico City-style food instead of the usual Tex-Mex seen almost everywhere in Texas. Annie averred—one of her fine words

I'm sure—that her favorite place in Austin was Matt's El Rancho and her favorite dish was *chili rellenos con shrimp Mexicana*. I agreed that Matt's and the relleno suited my palate when I was in Austin, but I encouraged her to try some of Chiquita's broiled and roasted dishes. I had what I always ordered, *carnitas tampequinas*, slices of pork in a rich brown gravy. Annie had the relleno, which I could see was not much like Matt's. Since Annie was driving, I had two margaritas just in case. I didn't know just in case of what, but if a man was about to meet the woman he'd once loved almost to distraction and hadn't seen in three decades, two margaritas seemed little enough to work with. Just in case.

When we got to the entrance to Love Field, I had Annie drive to the Earl Hayes lot so we could stow the car there and take their shuttle to the main building. I didn't know what gate, but I knew we could figure it out when we saw all those TV screens with arrivals and departures. We had almost an hour to wait. I didn't know what might happen, but I told Annie we should both meet Liz at the gate, get the introduction over, and then she could go get the car and meet us at the baggage claim area. I felt like I was instructing a servant, but Annie knew I was nervous and eagerly complied. She said, "I may be almost as nervous as you are waiting for Ms. Lancaster to appear out of the blue."

"I doubt that."

We waited until the gates opened and the plane from San Francisco began disgorging its passengers. Annie said, "She must've missed her flight. I don't see anybody that looks like a seventy-year-old woman."

I didn't answer because I thought I might faint. I had to sit down, or at least lean against a stanchion. The first sight of the woman I had loved for so long was almost more than I could take in. Annie might have missed the beautiful woman dressed in the best West Coast style, but I saw Liz as soon as the first-class section emptied. She was dressed in what I would've bet was a dress from I. Magnin, a stylish hat, and shoes that must have run $250. Each. She was as slim as she was thirty or forty years ago, and her hair, now a discreet auburn—tinted, for sure—curling around the still beautiful face I remembered from 1939. I knew I was about to faint and crash on Love Field's marble floor.

Annie said, "Damn, John Q., she must have changed her mind or missed the plane. I guess we'll have to go back to Bodark Springs empty handed. At least we stocked up on plenty of—"

Then Liz grabbed me and said, "Oh, Johnny, you look better than I imagined. You—"

"Are you Liz?" Annie stared at the stunning woman and shook her head. "Are you Mrs. Liz Lancaster? Really?"

Liz smiled and said, "Yes, Annie, I'm Liz, but several years ago I began calling myself Liz Denney again. I haven't changed my driver's license, so I go by two names now. How do you do, and please don't look like you're about to faint."

Annie did look ashen, "I, I, I expected some other—How do you know I'm named Annie?"

Liz looked puckish and said, "You'd be surprised what I know. Now, let me look at Johnny, who looks better than he did when I saw him the last time. Johnny, you could pass for—"

"No, I couldn't, and you must be able to see that. Hell, Liz, my face looks like it's worn out two bodies. But you, my God, Liz, you didn't age. I feel like a man in the presence of two girls instead of two women. Damn!"

Annie knew when to leave. "Okay, *Johnny*, I guess it's time for me to get the car. I'll see you two in fifteen or twenty minutes if I don't faint from all these shocks that are flying about the air of Love Field."

Annie left, and I asked Liz the question Annie had but didn't get an answer to—"How do you know Annie's name?"

Liz laughed the laugh I used to die to hear. "Why Edward told me all about her. I'm here to rescue you from the clutches of that beauty with the real red hair and the figure that men have had sword fights over."

I knew it! "Edward? What the hell? Edward? How did he track you down? He didn't even know your married name. And as I recall, he was not too enthralled when you came to Texas years ago. Damn his time!"

Liz laughed out loud. "Why are you damning his time? Aren't you glad to see me, John?"

"I think I'm so glad to see you that I might keel over in a dead faint here in this terminal. But I still don't see how Edward found you, and I can't believe he still thinks that I'm interested in a romance with Annie Baxter. He worried that I was at first, but he got over it a week or more ago."

Liz said, "Edward called me more than two weeks ago. He got my address from the school district. They keep good records of their retirees. Edward couldn't have gotten information from them about me, but his private detective did. I mean your loving son had a private eye look for me. I felt like Mary Astor in *The Maltese Falcon* with someone turning San Francisco upside down looking for me."

"I don't believe Sam Spade had to turn the town on its head to find Bridgit O'Shaunessy or whatever Mary Astor's name was in the movie."

Liz went on. "I was flattered in any case. Now that I'm here and assuming that the nervous and excited Miss Annie doesn't wreck the car getting us out of Dallas, I take it that Edward will have a nice room waiting for me in his plush hotel."

"It's Ms. Annie. Try to keep up, Liz, and we won't be taking you to the hotel."

She grinned, "What? You're packing me off to San Francisco on the next plane?"

"No. I cancelled your reservation. You're staying at my house."

Liz giggled. "Oh, it gets better and better. Should I be flattered?"

"Maybe. Or maybe I was afraid you'd still be beautiful—and God knows you are!—and Eddie would work his wiles on you. I heard he has an eye on Annie, but everybody tells him he's way too old for her. She's not romantically inclined to him or me or anybody in Bodark Springs. She's engaged to a PhD candidate in political science at the University of Texas where she's working on a PhD in history. So your trip is wasted if the only purpose was to detach me from a girl seventy years younger than I am."

Liz looked shy and said, "I wouldn't have come here just for that. I wanted to see you and see how Time's Winged Chariot had treated you. And I really am delighted to see that you are little changed in all these years. Is there some fountain in Bodark Springs that men like you drink from? The fountain that Ponce de Leon was looking for? If there is, I want to taste its waters before I go back to Baghdad by the Bay."

When Annie got back with the car, Liz's bag had arrived. All she seemed to have was a carryon and a moderate-size suitcase. I was glad to see that it would all fit in the trunk. This seemed unlike Liz, who always burdened us with huge cases back in the days of my California sojourn. She explained it. "I had the rest of my clothes shipped to the Cotton Palace or whatever Edward called it."

"The Cotton Exchange Hotel. The Cotton Palace is something that burned years ago. I hope Eddie didn't have your stuff shipped somewhere else. Then we'd have to go to Neiman-Marcus to outfit you. There is no I. Magnin in Dallas, and all we have in Bodark Springs is a J.C. Penney catalog store."

Annie and I loaded Liz's stuff in with all the whiskey, and I handed Liz into the back seat. I climbed into the passenger seat next to Annie. We rode to the outskirts of Dallas that way, but I grew weary of talking across the seat to Liz and got Annie to stop at a Texaco in Plano ostensibly to buy gas. Then I got in the back seat with Liz. By the time we were halfway to Eastis County, Liz and I were holding hands and I thought maybe *amor* does *vincit omnia* after all. I was back in the thirties hearing the foghorns on San Francisco Bay. How did I get so damned old?

When we were back at my house, Annie and I got Liz's bags out of the trunk and into the house. I showed Liz up to the bedroom Rosie had gotten ready for her and told her that I was going to walk Annie back to the hotel to be sure some masher didn't assault her on the way. Liz didn't need *masher* explained the way Annie had. I said I would be back in twenty minutes, showed her the bottle of California pinot grigio I had for her in the refrigerator, pointed out the corkscrew, and told her to look around the house.

Annie and I walked half a block in silence and then I said, "What do you think?"

Annie practically gushed. "About Liz? I think she's perfect. If not for you, for somebody. I hope to hell I look that good in fifty years. I wonder what I'll tell Edward when he quizzes me back at the hotel. Do you think he's going to get on your case when he hears about Liz coming to Texas? And staying at your house?"

"No. You missed some of the conversation when you went to get the car. Eddie is the one who summoned Liz to keep you from getting your clutches on the LaSalle and all my stuff. He hired a private dick out in California to track Liz down. Then he called her and told her how much in danger I was in from your red hair and blue eyes. That was two weeks ago. Then he realized that you and I weren't an item and that your interest in me was neither romantic nor fiduciary. When he learned that, it was too late to call her off. I'm going to be as eager to see how he takes things when I start driving Liz around in the LaSalle and holding her hand in public. I can't wait to see what he'll do next. I never thought life could get this exciting. I owe you, Girl. If you hadn't come to town, I might be sitting around waiting for the Bicentennial and anticipating playing Aaron Burr or somebody in one of Ruby Lathem's skits.

"Here's a thought: you don't suppose Liz tinted her hair auburn to counteract one of your attributes? Maybe I'll swap my horse and dog for *her*."

We didn't see Eddie at the hotel, so we went our separate ways in peace and quiet. When I got back home, I found Liz sipping the pinot grigio and wandering around the house. I came in and we hugged for a long time. I was back to 1933. I hoped it wouldn't be the last hug. She had already put on pajamas and a large, heavy robe she found in my bathroom. She was standing at the foot of the staircase and looking at the full-length portrait of my first wife, Esther. She said, "Is that your last duchess painted on the wall, looking as if alive?"

"No, that's my first duchess, and Fra Pandolph's hands didn't work busily a day. I said that just to let you know I spotted your Browning reference. She's the mother of my sons, and that painting was in storage from the time Esther—that's her name—died until well after the death of my third wife. It would have been thoughtless to have her on the wall during those years. After Barbara died, I waited a year or two and brought out the painting, had it cleaned, and put it on the wall. My sons like the idea of their mother gracing the stairway."

She kept looking at the painting. "You always were a thoughtful man, Johnny."

"Apparently not. I let you get away. I always thought if I'd moved to San Francisco way back, I could've married you and lived happily ever after. But I had reasons. I don't regret teaching and being principal all those years, but I do regret losing you. I still have the engagement ring I tried to give you, but it's pretty clear I'm too old to put it on your finger now. But it would look good there even if we just treated it as a friend-ship ring."

Liz looked again at the painting and then at me and said, "I wonder how many people in this world wish they'd taken a different path at some time in the past."

"I do. Now I'm worn out from all the travel, and I'm sure you are too. We can summon up the remembrance of things past after a night's rest. I hope the room upstairs suits you. I sleep downstairs as a hedge against the day when I'm old and can't manage the stairs. I still subscribe to the old Dorothy Parker line, 'If I'm in bed each night by ten, I may get back my looks again.' And it's way past ten."

We hugged goodnight and I watched that beautiful woman go up past Ethel and make her way to the bedroom Rosie had ready for her. I was not lying when I pled exhaustion. I made it to my bedroom, shucked off the gay apparel of the day, and put on my silk pajamas. I was asleep within fifteen minutes.

Sometime in the night I felt the bed sink on one side and sensed that someone—I hoped Liz—had crept into my bed. Neither of us spoke, but after a few twists and turns, I found myself spooned, as they say, with the woman who had come two thousand miles to rescue me. We slept like that till mid-morning. Then there was a great scream. Rosie opened my door and saw two people welded together in my bed.

She screamed again. "Lord do have mercy knows," she screamed once again and ran from the room.

"It looks like we've been discovered and disgraced," I said. "I think I'm glad. What about you?"

"Me too. Who was that whirling dervish?"

"Rosie Mawbry. She's my housekeeper, but she's not supposed to come on Sunday. God, I wonder if Edward sent her?"

I slipped out of bed, put on the robe Liz had appropriated the night before, and eased into the kitchen to hear Rosie on the phone. She was saying in a whisper you could hear almost to the courthouse, "Lord do have mercy, May! I seen them two old people a-layin' in that bed. Do you reckon there was some fortification going on? I always thought that old man was too old to fortify."

I knew 'May' was short for her niece Maybelline and that the story would spread to the Quarters and then to the whole town. It wouldn't take till churchtime on Sunday for everyone in Bodark Springs and most of the county to think Liz and I had "fortified" in my bed. I hadn't been happier since Lyndon skunked Goldwater. My reputation was made.

"Well, Elizabeth Denney, you're a fallen woman for sure now. Rosie's been on the phone to her niece, who works at the hotel and has a better intelligence network than the CIA. Maybe you'll be hauled up before Judge Roy Johnson and forced to marry me. Eddie'll hold the shotgun."

Liz was still laughing from the Rosie event. "Works for me. Do they use white shotguns in this part of the world?" she said and laughed the laugh I hadn't heard in over thirty years until today.

I suggested that we not go to the hotel for breakfast. We could have Rosie, who shouldn't have been here at all today, rustle up some grub. Or, better still, we could get dressed and walk down to the Busy Bee so the natives could see the fallen woman and her seducer.

We took almost an hour getting ready. Liz came out in a pants suit in dark navy and some Chanel flats she must've had in her one suitcase. There was a carefully knotted Hermes scarf around her neck in a multitude of colors—blue, pink, mauve, gold, and some colors not found in nature. Her purse was from Bottega Veneta and must have cost more than a pair of handmade boots from Leddy's. I think the fragrance, delicately applied, was Chanel No. 5. If Annie had been here and had wondered how I knew so much about women's clothing and accessories, I could have told her of the many hours I'd spent in Neiman-Marcus in Dallas with Lucy and Beth when they were attiring themselves and I was buying Oxxford suits.

I sent Rosie home so she could tell anybody Maybelline had missed, and Liz and I strolled down on a fine spring morning to the Busy Bee Cafe. We got there at ten, just in time to catch the church crowd getting stoked up for morning services. When we walked in, all conversation came to an end. It reminded me of a stage direction I once saw in a printed copy of a play, "A flat, wet silence follows."

Back near the kitchen I saw Charlie and Lucy. When they saw me with the most beautiful seventy-year-old in the world, they jumped up and ran toward us. Lucy hugged Liz and said, "You're Liz!"

Liz admitted it, and Charlie, beaming, said, "Dad, you're a sight for sore eyes."

"What the hell's that supposed to mean? You just saw me the other day. I'm only about four days older."

Charlie laughed. "I know, but—you know—Oh, I have to be introduced to the famous Liz Lancaster."

"I think she goes by Liz Denney again. If Lucy ever turns her loose, I'll tell her who you are."

Lucy and Liz walked over and the unnecessary introductions were made. Everybody seemed to know Liz already. I'm sure all the patrons of the Busy Bee knew all about Liz and even whose bed she slept in last night. Lucy said, "I think I'm gonna have to give up my claim to the LaSalle. It's all yours, Liz."

Liz furrowed her brow. "The LaSalle? What is *this*? What's a LaSalle? It's not that car they used to make, is it?"

I said, "I own a 1940 LaSalle, which has become a symbol of something in the Adams clan. I think Lucy is saying you'll do to ride the fence with, as the old cowboys say. The word is that I'll die and leave it to my favorite. For a while, when rumors were hot and heavy, Annie was thought to be the heir, and then I threatened to give it to Lucy, and now you're supposed to be first in line. It's a fine car with few miles on it, but I'd hate for you to try to traverse those San Francisco hills with it. Are we gonna be allowed to eat?"

Charlie said, "Sure, Pop, we're at a table for four, so you and Liz can join us."

"All the tables in here are for four, Charles, but we'll be glad to eat with you two if Liz hasn't had enough of your fawning by now."

I was startled to see that Liz has the same kind of appetite Annie does. She ordered eggs, pancakes, bacon *and* sausage, and coffee as fast as they could bring it. I figured if I married Liz, I'd have to change my diet away from cereal and salads and three kinds of soup. Then I would gain fifty pounds and croak before Ruby Lathem got a chance to ride in the LaSalle in the parade.

While Lucy and Charlie were arguing over something to do with the cooking of bacon, I said quietly to Liz. "You haven't added a pound since I saw you years ago."

She said, also quietly, "I don't have anything I didn't have then. It's just lower."

Lucy said, "I heard that, and I'm in that same boat. But Charlie doesn't care, do you, Hon?"

Charlie groaned and said, "Leave me out of this discussion. I heard what you two are saying, and I know Liz stole the line from Gypsy Rose Lee."

Lucy, who once taught English, said, "T. S. Eliot said 'bad poets imitate; great poets steal,' so I guess Liz is a great poet."

I said, "I can testify to Eliot's assertion since I've been quoting lines from poets and novelists for years. Lucy probably thinks I'm just a parrot."

"Well, a myna bird at least." But she said it with a smile.

I ate one poached egg on a piece of wheat toast. I was the only person in the Busy Bee showing any restraint. Seeing Liz tuck into the huge breakfast made me long for ham and eggs and biscuits with butter and jelly, the exact meal Lucy and Charlie were eating. But I pride myself on being abstemious. It keeps me trim and erect when I see men and women of eighty all bent over. I shouldn't be so judgmental, I suppose. After all, the Scripture says, "Pride goeth before destruction and a haughty spirit before a fall." I hate it when half the town—hell, half the county—can't get that right and say "Pride goeth before a fall." Annie has pointed out more than once that I am a language snob and a pedant. Well, I didn't teach for half a century for nothing.

We said our goodbyes to Lucy and Charlie and absorbed the admiration of a cafe full of Bodarkians who thought I had retired from the sexual wars fifty years ago. It hadn't been quite that long, but close. But when they saw Liz and me holding hands as we exited, some of them must have wondered, "Where can I get whatever that old devil's taking?"

We stepped out the door and ran into Edward, who looked flustered and anxious. "Hello, Pop. Hello Liz. Hello, hello."

I said, "What're you stammering about, Edward? I know you sent for Liz to put me on some path to righteousness, but I'll bet you didn't count on her being such a beauty, did you? Now look what you've done. I take it Maybelline is spreading the good news."

Liz was laughing now. She said, "So you're Edward? I think I remember you from thirty years ago when I was here. I hope you don't think you created a Frankenstein when you invited me here. I'm almost harmless, but I can't speak for your handsome and delectable father."

Eddie recovered enough to tell us that the boxes Liz had sent were now at the hotel and would be delivered to the house as soon as one of the bellhops showed up for his afternoon shift. Then he said, "Pop is right. You *are* a beauty and must be a charmer to have kept him in California for two years back in '32 and '33."

"Two years? Johnny and I were only—"

I broke in and said, "We'll be on our way before somebody here in town suffers a neck injury from straining to stare at us. I'm sure we'll be at the restaurant tonight. Lucy and Charlie are inside if you want to see your brother and sister-in-law."

I hustled Liz away, but she was still puzzled. "What did he mean that you and I were together for two years? You were only in San Francisco for a little less than a year in 1933. I hope you weren't spending a whole year carrying on with some floozie in the Mission District or somewhere before you met me."

"No, I was doing something less interesting than carrying on with a floozie. I had business I had to take care of that year you think is missing. Well, it's missing in a way, but it was just a matter of business. I think I told you that my uncle had some holdings in Southern California that I had to dispose of."

Liz was moving on. "You never told me that, but it doesn't matter. We met and fell in love and I don't regret a minute. Do you?"

"Yes, I regret that you said no. But our year together changed my life. Remember Diamond Head and the Banyan Court and the north shore of Oahu? Maybe now that we're more settled in our ways, we can go back to those faraway places with the strange-sounding names, as the song says."

She laughed again. I could never get enough of her laugh. "Good! Just don't sing to me. You can't carry a tune."

"Annie always says, 'You can't sing a lick.' I don't know which criticism wounds me worse."

When Liz and I got back to the house, I said, "When your things come, do you want them taken upstairs to the room Rosie got ready for you, or did you like the sleeping arrangements from last night?"

"Oh, I'm afraid the stairs will wear me out, and your nice queen bed just seems to fit our bodies."

I didn't jump for joy but only because I can't jump anymore. But this was the first time since Barbara died that I've had a bed companion. I started to sing "Seems Like Old Times," but there are a few who don't appreciate my nice tenor voice. If Liz had liked my singing, I might've given her my finest rendition of "Happy Days Are Here Again." I hadn't been happy in a long time. I hadn't been miserable all those years after Barbara, but there hadn't been pure joy in my life. Annie was a great pleasure to me, but, despite the rumors, she was not someone I was in love with. Liz was. And is. What kind of old fool am I becoming? If she goes back to California in a week as she planned, I might just have to go west myself. I guess that answers the question about what kind of old fool I am.

That night Liz showered and dressed in some of the pajamas that had come to the hotel in her boxes, and I showered and dressed in some paisley pajamas and a matching robe I found in my walk-in closet.

We climbed into the bed that Rosie had made before she left. I'm sure she washed the sheets she was sure we soiled with all that fortifying. I said, "I'm sure you know what ninety-five-year-old men are not capable of. Sex is no longer a part of my vocabulary, and—"

She sighed. "That *is* a relief to me. I had some female problems and then a botched operation rendered my vocabulary, as you put it, void of sex. Hey, remember the song that goes if you'll forgive me, then I'll forgive you, and we'll be sweethearts again? We can be the kind of sweethearts that we thought teenagers were supposed to be when we were all naïve—and before the pill."

I laughed now, but not one as sweet as hers. "Count on me for hand holding and cuddling and spooning under the covers. What a relief! For a large part of my adult life, I was sort of sex crazed, but once the years took their merciless toll, I found myself greatly relieved. I will say this, though. I wouldn't have believed this sense of relief when we were young—or at least you were—back in those San Francisco days, back in what I sometimes call our 'summer of love.' Isn't what the hippies called the sixties out in your home state?"

So we went to bed unfortified and held hands and talked about the Royal Hawaiian and Diamond Head and the Top of the Mark and Ernie's and Fisherman's Wharf and the World's Fair of 1939, our last summer together. I thought, I may live to be the hundred that I'm always threatening, but if I die tonight, it'll be as a happy man.

We lay in the dark, holding hands, and after awhile I realized that I was the only one talking. Liz was asleep and, I hoped, dreaming of the days that are no more. I didn't know her whole life story and hadn't ever asked for details. Even back when I first met her I tried to mind my own business, especially since I had a serious blot on my "scutcheon" and didn't invite scrutiny. I knew she was near thirty and had been widowed a couple of years before we met at the public library. I learned that her married name had been O'Connor, but she had reverted to Denney a year or so after her husband's death. Both her degrees were granted to Elizabeth Denney, and she'd never changed the names on her diplomas or other documents. She must have liked her maiden name (I'll bet they don't call it that anymore). She told me that she married Herbert Lancaster and changed her name to his surname till he died. It was not the fashion back in the 1940s when she married for the second time, to keep your maiden—oh, yeah, it's birth—name. She was Mrs. Lancaster for some years after Herb died, but in anticipation of her trip to Bodark had begun signing herself Elizabeth Denney again.

I didn't know much about her marriages, but I knew Herbert Lancaster was president of one of the big California banks, Crocker or Wells Fargo or something. That accounted for the Hermes scarves and Chanel bags and fashionable frocks from I. Magnin. Since she'd never had children and apparently neither had Herb, I suspected she was richer than I am. I'd never ask of course. But I did note that she flew in on American in the first-class cabin.

I remembered the many times I'd tried to get her to marry me. I even got down on my knees twice to make my entreaties. I suppose I was jealous when she wrote me that she was marrying Herb. I looked him up and found that he was rich, but I never thought she was marrying for money. She could have married me if money was her quest. Hell, I was richer in 1933 and '34 than I am now, and I can still buy girls Impalas out of my money clip.

I knew she taught until she married Herb, and when he keeled over with a heart attack on the marble floor of the Crocker National or Bank of America or wherever he was president, she went back to teaching and stayed till she reached retirement at sixty-five. I had no clue what she had done between retirement in 1966 and now. Maybe she visited all those faraway places with the strange-sounding names that we used to talk about. I suppose she'll fill me in on details as we lie talking away evenings, now that talk would be our only evening pastimes. After all, we agreed that we were too old to cut the mustard. I think that's a Little Jimmie Dickens song, and I'll bet Liz the sophisticate never heard of Little Jimmie. I can see why she might have said no all those years ago since I listened to Ernest Tubb and Bob Wills and she had season tickets to the San Francisco Symphony and had met Dimitri Mitropoulos and Pierre Monteux in person more than once. Bodark had no opera or symphony when she came east in 1939 and refused me for the last time. Here we are in 1971, and the only opera anyone in this part of the world knows is the Grand Ole Opry. But maybe I'm too harsh on my fellow Bodarkians. The music teachers at the school and Mrs. Carlisle, widow of the late John the dope fiend, all go to Dallas for the opera and the symphony. I sometimes make fun of Mrs. Carlisle for her pretensions, but she's a sincere woman who runs the school library and tries to live down John's misfortune. Still she reminds me of the old *New Yorker* cartoon where someone says, "She is so refined that she never uses the objective case." And Lucinda Carlisle always pronounces "biography" as "bee-ography."

I drifted off to sleep running down the people I had lived among and loved for nearly a century. Damned old fool.

CHAPTER 15

Now that Annie was off to Austin for a week, Liz and I were left to our own devices. I was pretty sure a trip to Texarkana with side trips to Paris and Clarksville and Bonham wouldn't be the kind of entertainment that Liz Denney would find intriguing. Annie ate that trip up, but Annie, educated as she was, came from Midland. Maybe Liz and I could go to Dallas to Neiman-Marcus and see what wealthy Highland Park women were wearing this year. That didn't sound like something that would occupy more than half a day. We could always go to Fort Worth and visit the stockyards; after all, San Francisco had something called "The Cow Palace." I'm not sure what takes place in the Cow Palace, but I seem to remember that some national political conventions had been held in that very venue. (There I go again, using Annie words like *venue*.)

Maybe I'm the snob, not Liz. She might like what I could show her in my part of the world. We had sure spent months and months and months in hers. How about a trip to the Stockyards and a visit to M. L. Leddy's for Rolando Hernandez to fit Liz with some cowboy boots? Every San Franciscan needs some western wear, and that would be a way to introduce her to the real Texas. Rolando knows I can't wear cowboy boots, but I'd bet money that Liz could. Noting the appetite that

Liz exhibited at the Busy Bee and at Eddie's restaurant a couple of times since she'd been in town, I thought she might love The Cattleman's in the dead center and heart of the Stockyards. Another attraction in Cowtown would be that I could introduce her to Homer and Beth. They're sophisticated but not snobbish or upwardly mobile in high Cowtown society, even though they have climbed all the way to a gated community on the far west side of Fort Worth.

I proposed the trip and said, "I suppose, since you've always lived in San Francisco, that you don't drive. I know you didn't own a car when I was out there."

Liz was aghast. "Don't drive! Of course I drive! I haven't always lived in San Francisco. I was born on a farm in Salinas in the heart of Steinbeck country. I drove tractors and pickups and even a rickety school bus when I was a senior in high school. When I was in college at UC Santa Cruz, I drove a taxi in the summers. I have a Class A California chauffeur's license. I'll bet I can drive better than you. You sure don't know much about me, John Quincy Adams the Second."

"Then I assume that this trip you've made to Bodark is my introduction to the secret and inner life of Elizabeth Denney."

She laughed the laugh I loved. "Not in a million years, *Hoss*. You people in Texas do call one another 'Hoss,' don't you? I'll tell you what you need to know and not a syllable more. A woman must have some mysterious cloud floating about her."

"I won't pry. I know the real Liz Denney, the one I loved to distraction for a year and seven glorious summers. The one I never got over. The one I married someone else for because I couldn't have Liz. My sons' suspicions are confirmed: I'm a sentimental old fool."

Liz grew serious. "You may be sentimental, but you're not a fool. I probably am, though. I'm a slow, slow learner. I know now and knew then that I would never love anybody the way I loved you—and still do. I kicked myself for saying 'no' so many times. It may be because I knew you were holding something back, some secret that I would never learn. On the other hand, it may be because I was just a total fool. Now it's too late and—No, no, don't interrupt me! We can't go back."

She went on. "I married Dennis O'Connor when I was a green girl and he was just a boy. We thought we were in love, and I guess we were if you can love at such an early age—remember the song that goes, 'Young love, first love, filled with true emotion'? I guess that was us. Now I'm quoting songs like you always do, but at least I don't try to sing 'em. Dennis killed himself on a skiing trip to Tahoe. He was so damned adventurous! He slammed into a pine tree on the California side and died instantly, we think and hope. He started an avalanche and was buried in snow for a week or more."

Liz had tears in her eyes. "I wish you hadn't got me started looking at my sorry, misspent life. Let me tell you the epiphany that occurs to me *this very minute*: I don't think I trust happiness. That may be why I kept refusing you. After Dennis died, I didn't want to be disappointed again. I didn't want to take a chance. When I married Herb it wasn't for love. I was forty-three and decided that I didn't want to spend the rest of my days living alone. He'd been widowed and I'd refused the man I loved best. So Herb and I made the best of two damaged lives.

"I sound like a damned soap opera, don't I?"

"No, I don't think you sound mawkish or maudlin at all. I may be a fool, but I *do* trust happiness. At least I think I do. That may seem strange to come from an old man who has buried three wives and done no telling what-all else. No, you sound like someone on the verge of a discovery."

Liz was insistent on explaining something, I'm not sure what. "Maybe I'm on the verge of a discovery. By the way, in case you're wondering, I didn't marry Herbert Lancaster for money. Long after I made the mistake of turning you away, I inherited the family farm and orchard. I didn't have the money that Herb did, but I was more or less rich."

She paused a moment and then said, "I'm ready to shut up. So let's unlimber that Buick or maybe that famous LaSalle I keep hearing about and take a road trip somewhere."

"All right, I'll call Annie and tell her to stay in Austin for another week or two, and I'll let Rosie know I'll be off with 'the new girl' since Rosie thinks there may have been some shenanigans when Annie was around taping me. She probably thinks you're just another notch in my belt. What do you say we swing through Fort Worth for a day or two so you can get some boots made and—"

Liz croaked—if beautiful women croak. "Boots? What the hell! You thinkin' I'm about to become a cowgirl?"

"I hoped. And then we can spend a little time with my son Homer and his wife Beth. You met Homer once, but that was a lifetime ago, and now they'll have to certify that you're not some brazen hussy out to steal my youth. Homer trusts me more than my other two sons, and Beth, whom you haven't met, is on the list to get the LaSalle if you turn it down. After that, I'll take you down into the Hill Country."

Liz asked, "The Hill Country?"

"The famous Texas Hill Country. It's west of Austin and north of San Antonio and stretches out toward the desert for a couple of hundred miles. It's LBJ country. It's sometimes called 'The German Hill Country' since so many Germans settled there after the European revolutions of 1848. There are names like New Braunfels and Fredericksburg (named for Frederick of Prussia) and Luckenbach and Bandera and Gruene. New Braunfels published a newspaper in German until ten or twelve years ago. Some writer called the Hill Country 'The beer and sausage belt.' The land is not much good, but it's what the Germans managed to get when they fled Europe. But you'll think it the best land in the world when you see the countryside bathed in bluebonnets."

Liz didn't know our famous flower. "And they are?"

"The state flower, and if we go south right away, they'll be at their peak."

She didn't care about my state flower, but said, "All right, Hoss, I'm ready when you are."

"Do you have any jeans in all those boxes?"

"Of course I do, but I fear they're some Gloria Vanderbilts, not the product of Herr Levi Strauss, our California German. He outfitted gold rushers in denim and now covers the butts of every teenager in the Golden State."

I said, "And Texas rear ends too. And me if I decide to tog out in cowboy attire, which I haven't done in forty years or more."

Then I remembered the last time I'd worn Levis. It was precisely thirty-nine years ago, and I used a pair as a wick to burn a car in Red River County.

I shook that thought off. But I was pretty sure I wouldn't try to break in a new pair of Levis. The best I could do was to unearth some khakis I wear when I feel lazy. But Liz would have to make some serious sartorial adjustments. Maybe Beth could help her when we got to Fort Worth. You wouldn't see many outfits from I. Magnin at the dance hall in Gruene or the Broken Spoke in Austin, and I hoped we'd have the stamina to dance at both places.

I made the phone calls a man of my age has to make when he leaves town. I called Edward and set him to worrying that I wouldn't survive the trip. Lucy got stirred up that I was off on the dangerous highways of Texas. She offered to go along to see that the two seniors stayed out of trouble, but I staved her off. Rosie was told she could come in to work or not. She would be paid in any case. I guessed she would come in and get the mail, wash the sheets, look around for telltale signs of fortification, and report any suspicions to Maybelline. Rosie was almost my best friend and had been for years, so if snooping into my suspected sex life would give her pleasure, I didn't want to disappoint. I called Annie and told her to take an extra week in Austin. Then I called the Driskill Hotel and made sure I could have the Jim Hogg Suite for two nights. That done, I called the St. Anthony in San Antonio and booked a double room there for two nights. Since Liz and I were sharing the same bed, I didn't need a suite at the St. Anthony. But at the Driskill I absolutely had to have the suite that Lyndon Johnson used in Austin to twist arms and impress donors. Annie was happy to gather up Justin for dinner with us at the Driskill and then make a trip to the Broken Spoke if we could find which night Aubrey "Blue" Lowden would be playing.

It takes nearly an Act of Congress for a ninety-five-year-old to get out of town. I used to go and come as I pleased, but now I seem to be a ward of the city. Damn wonder the mayor doesn't have to sign a permission slip. Any minute I expected old Dr. Elgin to show up at my house to check my blood pressure and listen to my heartbeat. And maybe give Liz a quick eyeballing for signs of stress and sexual overexertion if he'd heard Rosie's speculations.

But leave we did. But only after Liz took many of her California clothes—all neatly packed. She almost filled the trunk of the Buick. I stuffed a garment bag with shirts on hangers, three sport coats, some pants, and some of what my Aunt Rene used to call *unmentionables*. I put Liz behind the wheel of the Electra as far as Gainesville, and then I took over to drive us down 77 into Fort Worth, the "Queen City of the Prairies." Our first stop was to be at Homer and Beth's so I could persuade Beth to take us to the Stockyards and help outfit Liz for a long stay in the deep heart of Texas.

Homer wasn't operating today, so the four of us made it to the Cattleman's in time for Liz to sample the rolls and fall to on the medium-rare porterhouse. Homer doesn't eat meat. He claims he's opened too many chests clogged with animal fat to jam up his coronary gates and alleys with red meat. He ate a baked potato, a salad, and some steamed vegetables. Beth had a ladies' filet, and I had my usual soup and salad. And a few rolls since Cattleman's is famous for them. Homer is an admirer of my diet and hopes he can imitate me and live to be a hundred. I hope he can. I hope all my heirs and assigns live at least as long as I have.

Then we walked across Main Street to Leddy's so Beth could indoctrinate Liz into western wear for the modern Texas woman. Before Beth could perform her duties as a fashion coordinator, I dragged Liz down the two or three steps to where my friend Rolando holds sway. Before long, he'd measured and probed her feet and massaged them to get the exact feel of both feet. Then he had her stand on papers so he could draw outlines for the boots I thought Liz needed. He sent off the plans to San Angelo so Liz would ultimately get a pair of simple black boots with a modest bluebonnet design on the sides. They'd be ready in a month, he told her. She said, "You can ship 'em to John Q.'s house. I'm sure you know the address."

I liked the sound of that. It meant, I hoped, that Liz was in no hurry to retreat to California. Beth found a few voluminous skirts, some blouses with floral designs on the shoulders, some jeans not made by Gloria Vanderbilt, and a lovely turquoise necklace. And a cowgirl hat which I feared Liz would never wear. Since I was forcing all these issues in one way or another, I insisted on paying. The whole shebang was cheap at a little over $1,000. Beth knows how to shop. She is a true daughter-in-law to old John Q.

We retreated to the Crestline Avenue mansion of Homer and Beth and had one of the most pleasurable evenings I've ever spent with an offspring. Homer never mentioned Scott and White or Mayo. He never remarked on Liz's porterhouse. And no mention was made of assisted living places where old men could be sequestered. As bedtime neared,

Beth attempted to show Liz to the room she'd occupy, but Liz was having none of that. She said, "Johnny and I are accustomed to using the same bed, and I doubt if either of us would sleep a wink if kept apart." That tickled Homer, who likes to think his old man still has something going on. And the way he'd sized Liz up from the moment he saw her, he couldn't but admire his pop's taste. I knew I should've named that boy John Quincy Adams III.

The next morning we set out for Austin. Liz started driving, and I directed her west to Highway 281 and then south toward some better scenery than was to be had going through Hillsboro and Waco. I took over at Hamilton and piloted us into Austin the back way so Liz could feast her eyes on fields and fields of bluebonnets. She was as impressed by the Texas state flower as I'd always been by the California golden poppies that she and I used to drive through. I'd bought a 1933 Ford a few days after I got to San Francisco. It hadn't occurred to me that a car in that city was more hindrance than help. But after I met Liz, the car worked out after all. It turned out to be good for road trips down to Santa Cruz and over into the Central Valley. I did all the driving back then, but if I'd known Liz was an experienced taxi driver, I might've let her drive so I could look. Oh well.

I had made so many trips to Austin during my days as a school principal that I knew the city well and could go the quickest way to Sixth Street and the Driskill Hotel, the oldest fine hotel in Austin. A valet parked the car and hid it in the recesses of the hotel parking lot, three bellmen took Liz's clothes and my simple garment bag up to the Jim Hogg Suite, and we admired the rococo lobby as we made our way to the elevator. Liz was impressed by the round settee that was in the middle of the Jim Hogg Parlor. I could picture Lyndon Johnson leaning in to coerce senators and governors and congressmen.

At exactly 6:00 Annie and Justin met us in the lobby so we could have dinner in the famous Driskill Grill. After Liz was introduced to Justin, Annie hugged me for as long as it took to make me blush. She and Justin both now called me "Grandpa John," which made me feel all of my ninety-five years. I don't know why I keep saying that. I'm only ninety-four, but old John Johnson once told me that when you get half way round the year, you are officially in the next one. I'll officially turn ninety-five on July Fourth. I don't know who started calling me Grandpa John first, almost certainly Annie since I'd bought her the Impala and had begun treating her like a granddaughter.

The dinner was just as I knew it would be. Annie ordered enough food to keep me going for a sennight; Justin was more cautious since he knew I was paying and only ordered broiled swordfish and a baked potato. Liz tried to match Annie in quantity, and I had soup, salad, and some steamed vegetables. I started to fear that if Annie and Liz ate like lumberjacks for the rest of the year, some new clothes would be required all around. But as Mrs. Eddy said . . .

Liz and I lay in bed holding hands and talking about the trip, the two young people, and what we might do the next day. Liz said, "You *were* in love with that young girl, weren't you? Don't deny it. And now I've come and spoiled it for you. Edward knew what he was about when he tracked me down."

"No, I was *not* in love with Annie Baxter."

She laughed and said, "Don't lie to me, Johnny."

"I'm not. Maybe I was—in a strange way. But wait before the 'I told you sos' start flying. See if you can understand. From the moment Annie and I started going about together and taping my mumblings, I fell in love."

Now triumphant, Liz said, "See?"

"The person I fell in love with was the *you* I saw in Annie. When we met all those years ago, you were just a little older than Annie is now. When I looked at her, I guess I saw you all over again. She moved like you, talked like you, thought like you. For a few weeks, she *was* you. And then when the door of the plane opened and I saw you, you may remember that I suddenly sat down for a minute while Annie was exclaiming that you must've missed the plane. I thought I was going to faint when I saw you. You were back! You were the young woman I'd dreamed about for years and years and years. Annie had been the *you* I first saw in San Francisco, and now the real you was standing in front of me, just as you were in 1933. And, by God, you are still here."

I stopped long enough to take a breath. "I guess everybody is right when they say I'm an old fool."

Liz hid her face. "Oh, John, you've made me cry. Oh. God, I never loved anybody but you, and I hope Dennis and Herb can forgive me wherever they are. I'm glad Annie stood in for me and made Eddie see how I was needed here. You're not an old fool, you old fool!"

We awoke in the morning, and I suddenly realized that I'd slept the only dreamless night since Arkansas. After the usual primping, Liz and I made our way to the grill, and I ate the kind of breakfast that Liz and Annie always did. I had steak, two sunny-side eggs, grits, biscuits, and jam. Liz was amazed at my sudden turn of appetite. I explained, "You can't be in love on Post Toasties." She didn't know that was the punch line to an old dirty joke, and I didn't tell her. After all, she is a refined Daughter of the Golden West.

Now that we were fuelled up for the day ahead, I proposed that we take a drive west into the LBJ Country around Johnson City and Blanco and Stonewall. Then we would go into Fredericksburg and see some "Sunday houses" if we had time. I wanted her to see Enchanted Rock near Fredericksburg, but I didn't plan to climb it as I once did on an icy day when I was about sixty.

LBJ was no longer in office, so I told her he might be at his ranch on the Pedernales River and we might get a glimpse of him if we could get close to his house on Ranch Road 1. I explained that Pedernales was always pronounced Per-duh-nales in this part of the world. She asked if I knew the former president.

I said, "Yes and no. I saw him a few times when he was a senator. He always knew my name. But it was the old politician's trick: some aide would whisper my name in his ear, and then he'd grasp my hand and shoulder and act as if I were an intimate friend."

Liz said, "I know about a dozen California pols who have LBJ's act down pat. I never knew any of 'em of course, but Herb, being a banker, knew most of them. I remember Governor Pat Brown hugging me and calling me by name. Then he asked me how my children were. I didn't say that I had none. I just said, 'Fine, Governor, thanks for asking.' As Holden Caulfield would say, 'Bunch of goddam phonies.'"

We drove close to the LBJ Ranch, but there was no sign of life except for some trophy longhorn cattle grazing on the lawn. We drove by the LBJ birthplace and then into Fredericksburg for lunch. At least Liz had lunch. I had soup and salad, which I barely touched since I promised myself after breakfast that I would never eat again. On our way out to Enchanted Rock, Liz asked about the Sunday Houses I had pointed out in Fredericksburg.

I explained as best I could since I only knew about them from books. "As you know, this is German country, full of frugal farmers who worked hard. As they prospered, they were able to build simple houses in town, usually about two rooms, so they could come in on Saturday, buy supplies, and stay in town for Sunday services. In case of illness, the houses were handy for someone to stay in town to get medical attention. "

Liz wondered whether all this was in the past. "And those houses are still there? Are they used now?"

"In recent years they've become popular, but not so much for the farmers who used them for church visits. Many, I hear, are refurbished and used for parties or something. There's a whole row of them somewhere in town, but I'm not sure what street they're on. These houses were popular in Fredericksburg, New Braunfels, and Castroville, and probably other places that I don't know about."

Since we were in Fredericksburg, it was a short drive to Enchanted Rock, which I explained was the second biggest outcropping of granite in the state. I was a fount of half-digested information. I told her about the time when I was between wives, and a lady friend of athletic pretensions dragged me to the top of Enchanted Rock in the dead of winter and how I slipped on the ice and was lucky not to break something.

As we parked and looked at the rock, she said, "What about now? You want to scale it to the top?"

"No, you go ahead. I'll wait below to catch you in case you fall."

Liz chuckled, "Sissy!"

"Damn right. All I'd need is a broken hip out here away from civilization. You'd have to tote me back to the car, and then I'd die in the hospital in Fredericksburg far, far from home."

Liz tried to shame me. "You really are a pessimist. I guess I won't climb it either. What if I broke a hip? Do you think you could carry me to the car?"

"I'm not answering that. If I said, yes, you'd know I was lying, and if I said no you'd think I was commenting on your size. I'm not biting."

We were about Hill-Countried out, so I turned us back to Austin

177

to rest up for our trip to the Broken Spoke with Annie and Justin. I explained to Liz as we drove back to Austin that the Spoke is the finest honky-tonk in Texas. It's a rundown shack of a building that seems to be made of two old army barracks slammed together. The floor is cement and has to be sprinkled with some kind of wax from time to time as the dancers waltz and two-step the evening away. The dance floor is in the middle of the room and the patrons sit at tables on both sides of the floor. The band is at one end and the tavern part is at the other. I mentioned that the smoke is sometimes as thick as the fog she is used to in San Francisco—or Frisco, the name sailors all called it and San Franciscans hated.

Back at the Jim Hogg we napped for two hours and then Liz donned one of the voluminous skirts from Leddy's and a ladies shirt with snap buttons and flowers on the shoulders. I, alas, was not Spoke-worthy: I had only some khaki pants and a regular shirt—a Brooks Brothers buttondown. We had arranged for Annie and Justin to pick us up on the Sixth Street side of the Driskill at 7:00. Knowing Annie as I did, I knew we wouldn't be standing in front of the hotel for more than three minutes. I was right. Promptness is one of Annie's many virtues. I do love her, but only as one of my nearest and dearest relatives. I hope Liz sees that.

I'd suggested that we go out on Sixth Street to Caruso's for seafood. It was a place I always managed to get one meal at when I was in Austin in the old days. Not ancient days, but in my last years as a schoolman, back when I was in my early eighties and before the Teachers Retirement System caught up with me.

The place was as I remembered it. It wasn't as fancy as some of the places Liz and I used to go to on Fisherman's Wharf when we were serious lovers in California. I doubted that any of those places still existed, but you never know about restaurant longevity in California. Or Texas, for that matter. Caruso's focus is on food, not ambiance. They serve the best seafood north of Galveston; they have everything that swims or crawls on the sea floor, but I satisfied myself with a dozen oysters on the half shell, while my companions made short work of trout almondine, baked halibut, grouper, and orange roughy. (I didn't mention that orange roughy was originally called "New Zealand slimehead.") They had salads, bread, potatoes both baked and fried, and dessert. How they were going to dance at the Spoke after all that food was a mystery to me. But many things are mysterious when it comes to the young and semi-young.

We rolled into the Broken Spoke at about 8:30 while Aubrey "Blue" Lowden had the crowd dancing a waltz. I made sure that Blue was playing because he's my favorite Austin musician. He's not Ernest Tubb or Ray Price or George Jones, but he's exactly what I like in a country band. He and his merry men don't write their own songs and assault the audience with 'em the way some hillbilly bands do. They're never going to make the Hayride in Shreveport or the Opry in Nashville. They mostly played the old-time standards and probably didn't know a single rockabilly song. I looked up Blue one time and found that he ran a backhoe operation by day and played honky-tonks a few nights a week. He and his men didn't wear fancy western suits or have so much amplification that you couldn't hear to dance.

James White, the owner, saw us to a table on the left side of the dance floor about halfway between the bandstand and the barmaid's station near the front door. Since Justin or Annie would be driving, I ordered a pitcher of Lone Star and three glasses. Then I remembered Liz didn't drink beer and Annie was the driver, so Justin and I had our work cut out for us. But I feared I might be alone with the beer since Justin and Annie hit the dance floor immediately,

I told Liz, "They make a fine-looking couple. She is, I think she said, five seven, and Justin must be six feet. Her red hair makes a nice contrast with his streaked blond. He could pass for a Southern California surfer."

Liz watched for a while and said, "They dance well together, but probably not as well as we used to at the Mark Hopkins or at that ballroom out in the Fillmore district. Do you remember its name?"

"Of course I do. It's the Starlight. Or was back in the mid-thirties. It's probably some hippie disco or something by now."

Liz looked at all the couples moving in the patented Spoke counterclockwise pattern and said, "Do you still dance? If you do, are you going to ask me?"

"I am, but I'm waiting for the song I asked James White to get Blue to play for me—for us."

Liz could hardly wait to hear what I had asked for "And that is?"

"You'll see. You probably won't recognize the tune, but when that old cross-eyed boy who does the singing starts, you'll see. Just wait."

Justin and Annie only passed by the table for Justin to take a sip of the Lone Star before two-stepping away. Blue had played several Ernest Tubb standards like "Walking the Floor Over You," "Blue-eyed Elaine," and "Thanks a Lot," and I was getting eager to hear the song I requested. It came after two or three Hank Williams songs, and I grabbed Liz's hand as the band came in fine and strong with the Old Bob Wills favorite, "Faded Love."

She said, "That line about missing you 'as heaven would miss the stars above' is gonna make me cry right out here on this damned floor in front of Justin and Annie and all these cowboys and hippies."

"Go ahead. You won't be the first person to cry in this joint, and I may join you when he gets to 'And remember our faded love.'"

Liz did cry a little. Quietly. "Oh, Johnny, you old fool, our love may have faded out, but it has sure as hell's faded back in. It has for me. I'm back, really back. And if you're not, I'll run over you in the damned LaSalle I still haven't seen."

"You're right about its fadin' back in. Oh, hell, look at Justin and Annie. They're staring at us. I wonder if they saw your tears or mine first. They must think us the worst fools to have let ourselves get separated for all these years. I hope they do better than we did. I'm ready to sit down before old Blue plays something sad."

Liz dabbed away a tear with a dainty handkerchief she had tucked into her skirt. "Sadder than 'Faded Love'? If there's one any sadder, I may have to wait in the car."

"Oh, there are lots of them sadder. Haven't you heard the expression about country and western music—'three chords and a broken heart'?"

We sat and watched the dancers and pronounced Annie and Justin the best-looking couple and best dancers on the floor. As my aunt used to say, "They're dancin' their shoe heels as round as apples." They didn't miss a song till almost 10:30. When they finally collapsed on their seats and Justin drank half a mug of Lone Star in one swallow, I said to Annie, "Before you get out there again, remember the tragic story of Tootsie Lines."

She laughed, but the other two looked puzzled, and Justin said, "Who's that?"

Annie said, "She's a girl from East Texas who danced twenty-seven sets at a square dance and then died of the sinus."

Liz and Justin said in unison, "The sinus?"

And Justin said, "You can't die of what you're calling *the sinus*. It's just 'sinus' and it's not usually fatal."

Annie took over, "Well, if I may quote Grandpa John, 'I tell the tale I heard told.'"

We wasted five minutes telling the saga of Tootsie Lines, five minutes that Justin and Annie could've spent "waltzing across Texas." When Blue cut down on a good rendition of Ernest Tubb's "Waltz Across Texas," I grabbed Liz and we threw ourselves into a madhouse of waltzers and pseudo-waltzers. We risked our feet and elbows as "old cross eyes" sang E. T.'s greatest song. A song Liz had never heard, needless to say. This girl needs a lesson or two in classic country music, I decided.

When the singer sang the line "When we dance together it's a fairytale ending come true," Liz started crying again. And so did I. I told Liz, "We're going to have to get hold of ourselves or our double-date partners may go off and leave us out here on South Lamar to walk back to the Driskill."

They didn't, and we made it back to the hotel just before midnight. The first order of business was to take showers to get the cigarette smell off. I called room service and asked someone to take our clothes to the valet for washing and deodorizing—I mean all our clothes. From the skin out. It's really good to be rich. I wondered how many Spokers had to go to bed smelling of stale smoke and beer. I hoped Annie and Justin had a laundromat nearby wherever they lived.

Then two old people (well, one old, one in the prime of her life), washed and dried and dressed for the night, fell into bed as exhausted as if they'd danced every dance that their young friends had. As I drifted off to sleep, I remembered how lonely it had been in my bed in Bodark Springs for so many years and how much better it was to drift into dreams holding a warm and wonderful woman. A woman I loved more than I could've imagined a month or two ago. Here was, by God, the love of my life. And then I felt like a traitor to Esther, long dead but still much loved. Those were my last thoughts as Morpheus took over.

By mid-morning with clothes cleaned, Buick un-valeted, and meager breakfasts eaten, we went east on Sixth Street to join Interstate 35 and set out for San Antonio. I stopped us in New Braunfels and did one of my boring lectures about its being one of the more famous German settlements. Prince Carl of Solms-Braunfeld named the town after his home region in Germany. That was in 1845 if I remember correctly. Prince Carl was leader of the *Adelsverein*, or nobility committee, that he hoped to establish as a New Germany in Texas. Until about 1957 New Braunfels still had a newspaper in German. I told her that the present-day paper was even given the half-German name of the *Herald-Zeitung*. We didn't explore Comal County the way we had Gillespie and Blanco, but I did bore her with the information that the county is named for the Comal River, the shortest river in Texas. By now I was boring me and told her we needed to find a New Balance store to buy walking shoes.

She looked down at her shoes. "Why?"

"Because we haven't had the exercise seniors need. We didn't get much last night when we only danced about four dances."

Liz took umbrage. "And whose fault was that? I would've been out on that floor as much as Annie and Justin if I'd had a partner."

"Yeah, and you'd probably be in Brackenridge Hospital this morning."

Liz was not sure what I was up to. "So tell me about all this exercise we're going to need tennis shoes for?"

"Walking shoes. Not tennis shoes. We're going make our visit to San Antonio all about walking. We'll traverse the River Walk, which you'll love. We'll go from the St. Anthony Hotel to the Alamo and back, and then there are the Hemisfair Grounds to explore, and—"

Puzzled at my recitation of San Antonio sights, she said, "The Hemisfair?"

"Well, in 1968, San Antonio staged a world's fair celebrating the 250th year since the city was founded in 1718. It may not have been as grand as the one we visited over and over in the summer of 1939, but it has a Tower of the Americas that rises into the sky as the fair's symbol, the way the Golden Gate was the emblem of the fair in San Francisco. Some psychic predicted—I think it was Jeanne Dixon or somebody— predicted that the tower would crash to earth and kill a lot of people.

But so far it's as steady as the Golden Gate Bridge. Remember 1939? It was the summer you gave me my walking papers. And I didn't even have any walking shoes then. I was sent off barefooted it seemed to me at the time."

Liz almost sobbed again. "Oh, John, I've suffered as much over 1939 as you have. 'If you'll forgive me, and I'll forgive you, and we'll be sweethearts again'—remember that one from the forties?"

"I could sing the whole song."

Liz made a wry face. "Yeah, but what tune would you shift to halfway through?"

"All right, you and Annie can make fun of my singing, which sounds good to me in the shower, but I'll find something that you two can't do someday."

We finally found a New Balance store on the outskirts of San Antonio and got ourselves sufficiently shod for the exercise I'd planned for us once we were settled in at the great old Saint Anthony, once one of the finest hotels in the country and still a great place to stay. Lyndon and Lady Bird honeymooned there, so maybe Liz and I could have what you might call a sort of platonic honeymoon while *we* stayed there.

Once we checked in, I decided I was tired of giving my half-baked lectures and bought Liz a guidebook to the Alamo City. She could read about the German influences and the Spanish air the city has today. She could learn about what Lon Tinkle called "the thirteen days to glory" that described the battle to the last man which allowed Sam Houston to escape east to get his army together to defeat Santa Anna, the self-styled Napoleon of the West. I could take her through the Alamo and the gift shop attached to it and tell her the story that my friend Luis Flores used to tell. He said when Alamo defenders Travis and Bowie and Crockett looked out over the Mexican army, one of them said, "Look at all them Meskins. I didn't know we're pouring concrete today."

Liz was not as impressed with the Alamo as Texans are supposed to be, but she loved the River Walk. We wandered it for the better part of two days. We ate at the Little Rhein Steakhouse, the Casa Rio, and several bad Mexican places along the river, but we dined in style at the St. Anthony's restaurant. Though she liked the River Walk, she found it strange that such a turgid and dirty little stream could be called the San

183

Antonio River. We loved our stay at the St. Anthony in what we called "our Semi-Honeymoon Suite."

I was tired of travel, and I suspected Liz was too, though she would've denied it out of courtesy to the old lecturer and half-assed travel guide. I was happy to point the Buick north on I-35 and head for Dallas. If we couldn't make it all the way to Bodark Springs, we could probably stay at the Adolphus, where I had not slept since escaping Arkansas in 1933.

As we passed through Austin, I found a phone booth and called Annie. I was lucky to find her at home and not on campus, and I told her Liz and I had "Pointed Them North." Since she was a history major she recognized old Teddy Blue Abbott's term for heading cattle to Kansas. I told her she could come back when it suited her and I would bend her tape recorder's ears with my drivel. She thought she'd be back within the week. Liz and I stopped in Salado to eat lunch at the Stagecoach Inn, which impressed Liz more than some of the places we had seen. She liked the waitresses reciting the various items on the menu and the prices for them. And the food was as good as we had had outside of a few fancy dining spots in Austin and San Antonio. She was especially impressed with the old shack of a building and the quaint atmosphere of Salado.

We got to Dallas before rush hour and decided to make it to Bodark before dark if possible. I had been in enough strange beds for awhile and longed for the queen-sized bed with its four posters that I'd spent half a lifetime in. I was ready for Liz to cuddle next to me in the house that had been in the Adams family for what seemed an eon. I didn't bother to garage the Buick. We just unloaded it in the circular drive and threw our bags on the floor of the foyer. We made for the parlor so Liz could find the most comfortable chair while I went to the refrigerator and uncorked a cold Hanzell chardonnay for her. I could barely wait to find Mr. John Walker—either red or black—and put my feet up. It suddenly hit me that I might be getting old after all. I hoped Liz wouldn't notice and decide to head back to San Francisco.

CHAPTER 16

I can't remember how the night ended, but the morning found us in my bed with her in my arms. Liz woke and said, "We're going to have to spend the rest of our lives together. That's all there is to it. Agreed?"

"Of course I agree. If I'd ever thought you might get away, I would've hog tied you like old Floyd Moore did Dulcie."

She hadn't heard that tale. "Who?"

"Oh, it's an old story I told Annie. You'll just have to wait till her book comes out. So we've settled the matter? We're gonna, as the song says, 'be together right or wrong, where you go I'll tag along, remember me, I'm the one who loves you.'"

Liz cringed. "Not if you keep singing like that, but, yeah, we're joined at the hip from now on. Or maybe not if you insist on quoting poetry and singing off key."

"I'll reform if it'll keep you around."

She was serious. "It's the 'around' that I want to talk about. I've heard how hot it gets in Texas in the summer. How would it be to spend the summers at my house and the rest of the year at yours?"

"I love it. Do you still have that wonderful house in the Mission District? I always liked being there back in those summers when I fled Texas for your house and bed. I'm ready to take up where we left off in 1939."

"No, I'm afraid the house you remember is now somebody else's. I married up, as they say, and I now live in the house that Herb and I had in Seacliff. You can see the Golden Gate Bridge, the ocean, and Marin County from my kitchen window. It's as grand as the Adams Mansion, and we can go to the Cliff House the way we used to when you were in San Francisco. Remember the Cliff House?"

"I do. I remember the view of the Pacific from the dining room. Oh, wait. It's coming to me. Wait! Father Barber and his family lived in Seacliff. I always listened to 'One Man's Family' on the radio. So you live close to the Barbers?"

Liz did remember the program. "No, silly, they're fictional, but I live in Seacliff all right."

"Will you leave it vacant for the months you spend here?"

She said, "No, not at all. I have a couple who live in, and that's what you need here when we're in San Francisco."

"Ha! I have no idea where I would find a couple, and if I had a woman living 'in,' as you call it, it might drive my neighbors to call the police on me. With you and Annie around and my possible 'live-in' I might be accused of having a harem."

Liz had a solution. "What about a houseboy like Kato in the old 'Green Hornet' show?"

"Right. Bodark Springs is full of Filipinos or Japanese or whatever Kato was."

Then she came up with what might work. "Then I guess you'll have to keep Rosie on as a twice-a-week housekeeper. That is unless she's so outraged by our sharing a bed that she'll turn you in to the sheriff for *fortification* with a woman not your wife. Okay, if we've settled the future living arrangements, why don't you get up and make the coffee while I lie here and try to recover some of the beauty I lost on our trip to the outback of Texas."

"I was hoping all the kitchen chores I've managed for years would pass to you now that we're what they call 'an item.'"

Liz liked the idea of an item, but she said, "Don't worry, when we're fully 'itemized' your sons will probably swear out some kind of restraining order on me and forbid me from ever coming east of El Paso."

"No, no, no. They'll welcome you with arms wide open. Eyes too.

Then they won't have to worry about me if I ever get old. Of course they'll all worry that you'll drive me to California in the LaSalle and it'll never be seen again."

Liz said, "Am I ever gonna see this famous LaSalle?"

"Maybe you will if you'll get up and make the coffee."

She didn't move, so I made the coffee and took it into the bedroom on a tray with cream and sugar and a daffodil I found outside the kitchen window. Then I stood looking at her. Not all women look good at first light, but Elizabeth Denney, with hair all ruffled and no makeup within a hundred feet of her, looked ravishing. I wished I was still young enough to do some ravishing as I stood looking at this beautiful seventy-year-old woman. What was it Holmes said to Brandeis? "Oh to be eighty again!"

I left Liz to think whatever thoughts she might have about life in general and an aged old roué in particular. I showered, shaved, and dressed neatly in case my sons and grandchildren and other heirs showed up to see if I'd survived a trip out of town with the person Charlie called "the new girl." As I combed my grizzled hair and adjusted the knot in my tie, I began worrying about the confession I had put in the safe deposit box. Confession, they say, is good for the soul, but did I really want my whole life anatomized for years after my demise? I would be dead so it wouldn't concern me, but there were many left behind to suffer the shame of a man thought in Arkansas to be a stone-cold killer. Maybe the document in the box should be torn up—no, burned—and the ashes distributed. Now that I think of it, possibly the fact that I wrote it down cleared it out of my soul. I just confessed it to myself, and the writing may have been enough. What would Liz think if she knew she had lain in bed for five summers with a man who'd devised and carried out what was thought of as a crime wave? Crime wave? That's how the *Arkansas Gazette* reported the killings and the arsons to the AP back in 1933. Some reporter had pieced the killings and the arsons together—even the car I burned in Texas—and there was probably a "John Doe" warrant somewhere in Arkansas still.

Worrying is not something I've spent a lot of my life doing, but now that Edward was voicing concerns about my father's and my uncle's murders and my missing year, I had put in some hours worrying. I wonder what Liz would think if I told her what I'd done? Or just told her that I had a dark secret that might land me in trouble? I knew Eddie would mount a strong defense. I guess I'd better destroy the document in the safe deposit box just in case I lose my wits and Eddie reads it when I'm declared incompetent and the box is opened. Hell, I might spend the rest of my days eating gruel in some prison's mental ward. See how worry works, I told myself.

When Liz was washed and dressed, she came out and looked up the staircase. She said, "The painting is gone. What happened? Maybe I'll miss it when we are living here part of the year."

"Oh, I had Boyd McGlothin, the painter, put it back in the storage it lived in through two wives. He painted the wall as you can probably tell."

She said, "I thought that was a really good portrait. Who painted it? Surely not Fra Pandolph."

"No, a portrait painter from Chicago came to spend a year at SMU back when Esther was working on a master's in art there. She did some modeling for him, and that's the fee for her hours of modeling—none of it nude studies, I hope."

Liz kept looking at the blank wall. "You could have left it up as far as I'm concerned."

"I suspected that, but I want to look up at that space and make a plan for a portrait of you hanging there. What do you think?"

She turned and looked at the blank space. "Not in a million years. First, I could never sit still long enough to have a portrait painted. And second, I'm afraid it would be like the picture of Dorian Gray and turn uglier and uglier."

"Maybe you read too much. I guess I'll go through our winters looking at a blank wall."

Our new double lives would require some logistics. Since money was not a problem for either of us, I could outfit myself at various men's shops in California, and she could raid Neiman-Marcus for fall, winter, and spring wear. We had a little time lapse since I was committed to a couple of weeks of Annie's taping, and if worse came to worst, I could always fly Annie out to San Francisco for any final tidying up of her manuscript. I didn't want Liz to go out alone and leave me here to drone on at the tape machine. I wanted us to go back to California together.

We could fly or drive. I would like the drive, and we could take a scenic route and not just jump on what used to be Route 66. I saw us spending a few days in Santa Fe. Maybe if we timed it right, we could spend a night or two at the Santa Fe Opera. Liz was sophisticated, and I could look at the night sky as the tenors sang about broken hearts. They would have more than three chords to signal their sad lost loves. After New Mexico, we could go to Denver and stay in the Brown Palace Hotel, a fine old establishment if I remember my two or three trips to Colorado. I would like to spend a night in Tahoe and wake in the morning to see the Golden State lying before me. I was making all these plans and Liz was probably intent on flying. Looks like I'll have to make adjustments if I'm no longer a solo operator. I hadn't been part of a pair since Barbara died. Yep, old Hoss, some adjustments may loom on the horizon, I thought.

While we waited for Annie to return and finish me off, I introduced Liz to the town. We ate at the Busy Bee, Powell's cafe, the new Italian place that had just opened on the edge of town, the Highway 82 Drive-In with the carhops on skates, a bad Mexican place that one of old Half-Moon Hinojosa's relatives had just opened, the Manhattan Cafe that served only hamburgers and hot dogs, and, of course, the Cotton Exchange Restaurant.

I took Liz all over town so the curious could meet the "Girl of the Golden West," to anglicise Puccini's "La Fancuilla del West." (I'm showing off here. I never saw the opera, but I was familiar with the Nelson Eddy/Jeanette MacDonald movie of a few years back.) We went to the hardware store so I could buy a 10-inch cast-iron skillet that I probably didn't need. At Safeway, I bought vegetables for making soup and introduced Liz to the produce manager and two of the checkers. At the City Meat Market, I bought a piece of sirloin that I could dice for the soup. Gus Bolas, the butcher, seemed pleased that I had found a woman whose looks suited him. They sure suited me. I never buy meat at Safeway or A&P because Gus's meat is up near prime—probably choice plus if there is such a grade. Liz and I bought some kitchen towels at Ben Franklin and some new kitchen curtains at H. Evans Department Store. By the end of the week, I had introduced Bodark Springs to Ms. Liz Denney from San Francisco in the great state of California. We held hands wherever we went and snuggled up close at the Pines Theatre for all to see.

You could tell, every time we went to the hotel, that Edward was pleased that Liz had come to town, though I wasn't sure how he would take the news that I planned to spend three or four months in San Francisco each year. My absence might cut down on his mystery visits to Bonham, though it was no secret that he was courting. I suspected that his children were pleased that their father and their grandfather had women on the string. Maybelline still looked askance at me when I came in holding hands with Liz. I'm sure she thought I was too old to have a live-in girlfriend. The whole town knew where Liz spent her nights and most people, a majority of whom had been my students, were pleased that old Prof could lure such a fine woman to his house—and possibly his bed.

Annie came back, and now I had two women to go around town with. Annie said she had pages and pages of oral history to work with and from here on would ask me questions on subjects that I hadn't filled in completely or some topics suggested by her faculty advisors at UT. Liz usually read when Annie and I taped, though sometimes she explored the town and visited with shopkeepers I had introduced her to. I think she made a few trips to Curl Up and Dye, Ruth Brasher's beauty shop, for her hair seemed to glow more auburn that it had a week or two ago. Once in awhile Liz would sit in as Annie and I taped. She even prompted me when she thought I hadn't made myself clear. When Annie started asking me questions about folk art in this part to Texas, Liz became interested. She had been, off and on, a docent at the DeYoung Museum in San Francisco and mostly knew about fine art, but she had read about folk art and once visited a collection of travelling folk art in Sacramento.

Annie said, "How does folk art differ from the kind of art that Liz has been talking about?"

"Liz can tell you, I'm sure, that a high artist seeks to be unique even when he or she is a member of the Hudson River School or perhaps is an Impressionist or an Expressionist, but the folk artist usually wants to produce the exact kind of art that he has seen and admired. If Mrs. Smith pieces double wedding ring quilts or Job's tears or one of a dozen popular patterns, then Mrs. Jones wants hers to be just like the ones she sees on Mrs. Smith's bed. Quilting is one of the more interesting arts in this part of Texas. Women gather scraps of material from clothes they've made or remnants from the fabric shop and piece the 'tops' in the patterns they hope to reproduce. They don't usually invent new designs. After the top is pieced, some have to have a large quilting frame suspended from the ceiling if there's a room big enough in the house. But most often, quilters get together in some church room or community center and have a large frame that they lower from the ceiling with a series of ropes. Then several quilters will add batting and a back and quilt Mrs. Jones's quilt or Mrs. Smith's or in some cases a communal top that several have worked on. Edna Lawrence, whose name has come up in our tapings before, once told me that once a year they sell chances and 'rassel off' a quilt and use the money for the church or school or to buy new frames."

Annie asked, "Aren't these communal sessions called 'quilting bees'?"

"Sometimes they are and sometimes they're called 'quilting parties.'"

Liz sang a line from a song she remembered,

> It was from Aunt Dinah's Quilting party
> That I was seeing Nellie home,
> Seeing Nellie home
> It was from Aunt Dinah's quilting party
> That I was seeing Nellie home.

I wish I could've said that Liz couldn't sing a lick, but she had a lovely voice, so I just applauded and didn't join in the song, even though I knew it all.

I told Annie that she could see several examples of quilts down at Jane's Fabric Shop since Jane Foley took quilts on consignment and had good stock on hand most of the time. I said, "Maybe I'll buy you a double wedding ring quilt for your wedding."

Now Annie had a remarkable idea. "You could buy two if you'd do the right thing and make an honest woman of Liz. Maybe we could have a double wedding and show off our two double wedding ring quilts at the reception."

"Liz wouldn't have me. At my age, I'll wind up needing a nurse in about twenty years, and I sure wouldn't put Liz through that ordeal. Did I ever tell you about old man Esau Fite?"

Annie said, "Was he a quilter?"

"No, he was an old coot who lived down past Eden and was a mean, tight-fisted old devil. He 'got down,' as they say in these parts, and had to have a nurse to take care of him. He hired Miss Ida Maxey, and then figured it would be cheaper to marry her than to keep payin' her. Well, she'd been an old maid for all of her sixty-five or seventy years, so she fell for it."

"And then?" Liz asked.

"Then nothing. Old man Fite died after a year or two, and I used to hear from his son Charles Clifford about the relationship between his pap and Miss Ida. Everybody called her *Miss* Ida Fite even after she married old Esau. Well, as C. C. told it, 'Miss Ida would get her a pan of warm water and a rag and start at the head and wash Poppa down as far as possible. Then she would throw the water out the back door and fill the pan again, get a clean rag, and start at the feet and wash Poppa up as far as possible. Then she'd throw out that water and get a fresh pan and a clean rag and wash 'possible.' "

Liz said, "You made that up. Nobody's that prudish."

"Well, you could ask Miss Ida. The old man died and left her without a dime, but she'd saved up two or three thousand dollars after a life of practical nursing and midwifing and cleaning houses. So she bought a little two-room house out near the drive-in movie. She must be as old as I am, but she's still alive and gets some kind of pension I hear. I see her in town once in awhile. So you can go and ask her if you don't believe me."

Annie said, "I'd be embarrassed to ask her about that."

Liz said, "Maybe I'll track her down and ask her since I've heard some of Johnny's tall tales about East Texas. He used to keep some of my friends in stitches when he was coming out to California and making me a dishonest woman years ago. I didn't believe all his lying ways back then—and now? Oh, and maybe I like not being what you call 'an honest woman.' It seems to be working wonders for my reputation here in Bodark. And Johnny is *pasha of the harem,* I hear. "

"All right, if you two will quit 'womanhandling' my life, I'll get back on the subject you're supposed to be grilling me about. It was not just quilts that were examples of folk art. Much was made of decoration. Did you ever see a bottle tree?"

"No, what is that?" Annie asked.

"You must've seen some when we drove around the county in the LaSalle the first time you were here. In lots of front yards somebody'll prune a dead tree—a small one—and then stick all kinds of bottles on the dozen or so limbs that are left. Or sometimes a person will take a two-by-four, sharpen the end and drive it in the ground. Then some smaller pieces will be nailed to the two-by-four and bottles stuck on the ends. You need colorful bottles, usually from some patent medicine or something to make it beautiful."

"That doesn't sound all that beautiful to me," Liz said.

"That's because you were ruint by all the time you spent in the De Young.

"Now, if you don't see the beauty of the bottle tree, think about the scalloped and painted tire. You must have noticed some when we drove around all day."

Annie made her "Yuck" sound. "You mean those awful pastel planters?"

"Exactly. What you do is take a worn-out tire. Not some modern steel radial or even a nylon tire, but one of those old rayon tires, preferably from a Model A or something with small tires—'casings' the old garage men called tires. You take the tire, take a good knife and notch it all around like you were scalloping the collar on a dress. With me so far?"

"No, but go on," Liz said.

"Okay, after the tire has been scalloped, you turn it inside out. That may take two strong men. Then it's ready to be painted, and the preferred colors are pastel pink and pastel blue. Then lay it on the ground, fill it with dirt, and you've got yourself a planter. Verbena is always good or moss roses."

Liz said, "Sounds like you're reciting a recipe."

"Well, I am. Sort of. I just thought Annie might move to the country after she and Justin have been made 'honest,' and it would do her good to know some country art forms."

Annie said, "I don't hate the idea of living in the country as long as it's in a bungalow or ranch-style house with all the mod cons."

"You probably won't be making your own clothes, but if you were, many of the same things you can learn about folk art would be helpful. Fashion was a foreign term to country women. They made dresses that looked like those of their friends, even though some differences in colors and patterns were tolerated. But if a country woman showed up in anything much different from others, she might be thought 'fast.'"

Liz said, "So I. Magnin would starve to death in Eastis County?"

"Probably. But things have changed a lot now that we've gone modern. You'll have noticed that Lucy, a farm wife, is not dressed in clothes from the Sears or Monkey Ward catalog. She buys her clothes at one of the two women's shops here in town or she goes into Dallas and shops at Sanger-Harris or Titche's. Though she has the money, she steers clear of Neiman's because high fashion is not appreciated by the ladies of the town. Now Liz is all right in her high-fashion rags because she is what the Germans of Fredericksburg would call an *auslander.*"

Liz wondered if that was why they looked at her funny in Safeway. "Are my clothes the reason?"

"No, they just wish they could rebel against the local customs and look as smart as you do. I'll bet some of them subscribe to *Glamour* and *Vanity Fair* and would love to break out of the Bodark mold. In a year or two, all the young girls who can afford to will kick over the traces and join the world of magazine fashion."

I was eager to end this recitation. "We're not getting very far with our folk art, so let me go on. Did you notice the mailboxes when we were driving in the LaSalle?"

Annie said, "I saw some very strange-looking ones, but you were driving too fast for me to see everything."

"You think twenty is too fast? Well, since you weren't observant, I'll tell some things you missed. Many old farmers—or probably their uppity wives—wanted the mailboxes on the rural routes to be decorated. Yes, I said decorated. So some people painted wheels on the bottoms of the boxes and then painted the boxes to look like covered wagons. Some guys who probably had welding equipment even made stylized horses pulling the wagon away from the road. It wouldn't do to have the ironwork pointed to the road because the mail carrier couldn't get at the box. I must've seen a hundred covered wagon boxes in my wanderings about the countryside. And then the poles to hold up the boxes are often decorated too. Instead of a common four-by-four, some are mounted on stone pillars or brick pillars, and some are poised on elaborately welded chains, chains as big as those used to anchor small ships. Where they came from I have no idea. I have seen a few where the mailbox is mounted on an old worn-out plow stock, with the handles pointing toward the road."

Liz asked, "What's a plow stock?"

"A plow stock is what they call the wooden part of a plow, the part the farmer holds onto as he tills the field. The iron or steel plow point is what digs into the ground as the horse or mule pulls the plow. Clear?"

Then Liz remembered. "Sort of. Oh, wait. I've seen the Winslow Homer painting of a farmer plowing with a horse. All right, clear. Oh, wait, I remember a little poem in my second grade reader that showed a farmer with his horse and plow. The poem stuck in my memory all these years. At the time I thought it was the most beautiful thing I'd ever heard:

> Warm soft ground,
> Birds that sing,
> Farmers plowing,
> That is spring."

She said, "I'll bet I sound like a really silly old woman to remember a little verse from second grade, but I can see the page in the book and the farmer and the poem as if it were still there. Damn, I must be getting soft in the head."

Annie said, "That's a wonderful little poem for children. I bet I'll remember that little poem of yours when I'm an old lady. Wait! I don't mean to say you are—oh shit—I mean I don't think of you as old."

I said, "What about me? Am I old?"

They said, "You're older than the dirt the farmer's working on, so don't try to plow the ground for compliments."

"Now, let's get back on the subject of folk art so we can get out of here before I starve. Let's dig into Liz's area of expertise: paintings and sculptures. Remember the famous 'paint-by-numbers' sets that came out a few years ago? They were all the rage among the folk hereabouts.

You could get scenes of country life and paints to make the houses glow in oleaginous glory. And here is where we get to folk art. There were only two or three different blanks that you could find selling in the Ben Franklin store downtown. The man that runs it told me he couldn't keep 'Happy Life on the Farm' blank canvases in stock. He had to return many of the others to the wholesalers because only about three different scenes were selling. These paint-by-numbers kits were a godsend to many frustrated women who had been using watercolors to copy magazine pictures or even tearing pictures they liked out of *Southern Agriculturist* or *Ladies Home Journal* and framing them. People are desperate for art, folk or high."

Liz said, "I wish you wouldn't make me out to be such a snob. When I move here for the—"

Annie bubbled over. "What? Are you moving in with Grandpa John? Are you two gettin' married? Wow! I mean Wow!"

"Wait a minute, young Annie, you know I hate 'wow' and as for gettin' married—"

Liz burst in, "We're gonna live in sin. Here in Texas in the cool parts of the year and out in San Francisco when it's unbearably hot in Texas."

Annie was elated. "Wow—oops, sorry. You mean Grandpa John's gonna be out there for months at a time?"

Liz said, "That's exactly what we mean, and since it's gonna be too hot for this California girl here in a few weeks, we're headin' west pretty soon. Right, Johnny?"

"It won't be long before we go, so you're gonna have to pick away at my brain fast or come to California and bring the tape machine."

Annie showed some real excitement. "You mean I can come visit? I've only seen the California around Bakersfield, and that seemed too much like Texas to be the California I've seen in the movies. I would love to see the real Golden Gate."

I said, "If I may interrupt this talk of marriage and where Liz and I are going to cohabit, let me suggest that you and Justin get married in California when Liz and I are living in sin and enjoying the cooling breezes off the Pacific. She tells me you can see the Golden Gate from her kitchen window."

Annie frowned. "I'd love that, but my mother'd have a cow if we married anywhere but Midland."

Liz said, "If you marry at the right time, you can always honeymoon in my house if Johnny and I are here scandalizing the citizenry of Eastis County."

"Now if you two ladies are through planning our lives, let me get in a few more words about folk art, a subject which I have been studying up on since early last week. About the sculptures. We're not talking Rodin or Michelangelo, but ladies hereabouts used to order these plaster of paris bas reliefs out of Sears or the J. C. Penney catalog. They depicted ladies in hoop skirts with a gentleman in a top hat bending over to kiss a hand. That was one design, and some were of floral arrangements or horses rearing. These little bought bas reliefs were chalk white, so a person had to buy paint to add the final touch, to personalize them or to make them exactly like the little figures Mrs. Smith had or Mrs. Jones."

"I hate to sound superior," Liz said, "but these things sound awful."

I said, "You're right, but they're no worse than another decorative item that swept the county a while back, back when I was still at JBH. Young women—and older women didn't go for this craze—would buy picture frames at the Ben Franklin and have boyfriends who had staple guns staple burlap to a board to use as a background for the art. The finished picture would often be made of a spray of plastic roses from the dime-store which seemed to grow out of plastic grapes. It looked as if pink roses grew out of clusters of red grapes. Now if you want tacky, there is some serious tacky. But I shouldn't be harsh. All they wanted was some beauty to lighten up drab homes and sometimes drab lives.

"Yard art like bottle trees and decorated mailboxes were just a few of the sculptures you could find in farm yards. I'll bet even San Francisco has a few pink flamingos decorating yards."

"Never," Liz said. "I've never seen one of those hideous things in San Francisco."

Annie said, "Oh, they're everywhere in Midland, and I saw lots of them when I visited my aunt in Bakersfield, so don't make California seem all that high toned."

I went on boringly, "Well, you'll see them out in the country here, and there are a few in the city limits. But they're not the only kind of yard art you'll find here. I know an old boy named Horace T. McGuffin who owns a welding shop over in Sherman, and he's filled yards all over Northeast Texas with art. When he's not occupied with serious welding for mechanics and farmers, he turns out hundreds of little oil derricks about three feet high. They can be seen everywhere in the county, though nobody in these parts ever struck oil. What is it Pope says? 'Hope springs eternal in the human breast.' "

Liz says "And I know the rest of that couplet: 'Man is always to be, but is never blessed.' "

Annie said, "Well, at the risk of sounding sappy, let me say that I am blessed to know the two of you. Maybe I'll just shuck Justin and move to California and get adopted by you two sinners."

"All right, if you two can get back on track, I'll try to finish my teaching.

"Another folk art form is the tattoo, but you see very few of those in Eastis County. There're some ex-servicemen who show tattoos on their arms in hot weather, and the inking is very much like the folk art we see in yards and houses. I mean it's not ever anything original or unique. You see 'MOM' circled by a garland of some sort. Or you see the ever-popular 'Death Before Dishonor,' with a bloody knife seeming to appear in a slash under the words. I saw one guy at the swimming hole in Bodark Creek years ago who had two tattoos on his breast. Over one nipple was the word 'sour,' and over the other 'sweet.' He also had a rooster tattooed on the top of each foot. He said they insured that he would never drown. One old merchant sailor who lived here in town years ago had a faded tattoo on the crook of his arm in the form of a hinge, and on the elbow he had a cobweb. One had his company and regiment and division numbers on his bicep, and one old ex-sailor had the names of the ships he had served on gracing his upper arm. He seemed to have been on the battleship *New Jersey*, the cruiser *Baltimore*, and the destroyer *Renshaw*."

Liz said, "You wouldn't believe the tattoos you can see around San Francisco. Even the women, usually barflies, have tattoos, and with so many sailors around, the tattoo parlors stay busy. Once when I was in Folsom where there's a prison, I saw some men on a road crew with what looked like homemade tattoos on their faces. I've heard that prisons are filled with self-taught tattoo artists covering the skins of their fellow inmates. Some of those are really vulgar tattoos, I've heard.

Some pachucos have blood teardrops on their cheeks signifying that they've killed somebody in a rival gang."

Annie was learning a new word, "What is a pach—what is it?"

"Pachuco. That's a Spanish word used to describe the street kids who wore zoot suits and sported tattoos. They were part of a Latino gangster culture, but some were just kids who liked to dress up and show off," Liz said.

I said, "I read about Pachucos once. They started calling themselves that name here in the Lone Star State if you can believe it. I read that the craze started in El Paso and really took hold in Los Angeles. That's where you see most of the zoot suits and long key chains that hang down to the ankle."

Annie asked me why I didn't have a tattoo since I was once in the service. "Or do you have one in some secret place. Have you seen one, Liz?"

"No I don't have one anywhere on my old carcass, and I never let Liz see me unless I am fully clothed. At my age, I don't want anyone to look on my tender naked flesh except my doctor, and I even hate that. No, I have no tattoos. Some men in my outfit got tattoos when we went through Havana on the way home, but I never got that drunk.

"Before we go to the Busy Bee for lunch, I'll give you my special lecture on folk architecture, what some books call 'vernacular architecture', a pretentious and silly term in my opinion. As you drive around the country, you'll note how so many houses look alike. Architects didn't design these houses, at least as they show up out here. Maybe somebody drew plans back east, but when people came out here, they simply constructed the kinds of houses they knew in the old states.

"If there was plenty of wood, they usually made log cabins, and those were just like the cabins they knew from Tennessee and Kentucky and back in the timbered Upper South. The simplest kind was the double log cabin with a dog trot. Don't bother to ask what a 'dog trot' is. That will all come clear. Now, where was I? All right, what they really did was build two little log rooms separated by six or eight feet but under one roof. The six or eight feet were open so that dogs—or chickens or sheep or people or raccoons or squirrels or even small cows—could walk or run through. One of the rooms was used for sleeping, and the other for living and cooking in, usually over the open fireplace in the living-kitchen room. If a fireplace was built on the bedroom wall too, they sometimes called these 'saddle houses.' The logs were chinked with mud, and the chimneys were made of river rock, what old Jimmy Lawrence, the mason, called 'nigger heads.' Don't look so disapproving. I didn't make up that racist name. You want me to be authentic, don't you? As time passed and prosperity increased—if it did—a lean-to room was added off the living room to serve as a kitchen, and then one could order a wood stove from Sears to cook on, which made the wife's work easier and the kinds of foods more various. They could then have biscuits and cornbread made in a proper oven. Sometimes a second lean-to was added to the bedroom to make a sleeping place as the family grew."

Annie said, "I guess this was the kind of cabin that Abe Lincoln was raised in?"

"I'm sure it was. They were all over the wooded parts of the South and West. Where trees ran out, people lived in dugouts with a plank and dirt ceiling that let dirt drift down on the food. Later, lumber would be brought out by wagon and later by train so frame houses could be built. They're the ones you see in the countryside here mostly. There are a few log cabins left way up north in the county. Not only were the houses 'vernacular,'—ugh—but the same went for the smokehouses, barns, corncribs, and outhouses. Remember the cartoons you've seen of outhouses with half-moons cut out in the doors? Those half-moons were real, not just for cartoons. They let light in, and made it possible to see in to learn if the facility was busy."

Liz said, "Oh, how awful! I can't tell you how glad I am that I was born in a little town in California after the advent of running water and electricity."

I said, "You should be. I lived on the farm down at Eden when we didn't have running water or electricity—and no 'facilities.' We had a frame house, and we lighted the evenings with coal-oil lamps and had to run to the outhouse in all weathers. I should get down on my knees and give thanks that I live in town and don't have to run to an outhouse. You know, a lot of this county had no electricity until after World War II. Rural electrification started under Franklin D. Roosevelt, may his name be praised, as the Mohammedans say."

Liz said, "I haven't heard the word 'Mohammedan' in years. What're they called now?"

"'Muslims or Moslems' is what we learn in school, but Grandpa John insists on the oldest possible terminology."

"Well what I insist on now is a trip down to the Busy Bee for lunch. I think it's fried chicken day."

We walked three abreast down Main to the Busy Bee. It only took forty minutes to make the ten-minute walk. Some people had to be introduced to one or the other of my companions, and some wanted to remark on the weather, and a few asked Liz how she tolerated a broken down old teacher. She thought they were joking, but I suspect they were serious.

When we entered, Harold rushed up to greet us with, "Well, Professor, I see you've added another lady to your entourage. Can I expect a third beauty next time you come in? I can use the business."

"Maybe so, Harold. Who taught you the word 'entourage'? If you can spell it, I may re-think the C- I gave you in American history. If I ask 'what's good' today, will I get the same smart-alec answer as always?"

"I sure hope so, Professor. I always like to have a snappy reply for my best customers. Anyway, I'm glad to see you have as good a taste in restaurants as you do in women. Welcome, welcome, ladies. And you too, Prof."

We drew Myrt Foster as our waitress today, and I could see she was in no humor for banter. The ladies ordered fried chicken, mashed potatoes with giblet gravy, baby lima beans, rolls and cornbread sticks, and iced tea. Before I could tell Myrt what I wanted, she said, "Before you ask, the soup ain't vegetable today. It's chicken and rice. I think the cook may be a Communist. I'll bring you some whether you eat it or not, and your usual salad and tea."

With that, she flounced away from the table muttering, probably about the Commie cook. Or maybe she was in the middle of a feud with Harold or that no-good husband of hers who worked at the waterworks. But the mood wasn't much different today than it always was. Liz said, "Is she always that surly?"

"Only since about 1956," I said.

Before the salads arrived to be slammed down on the table, as I knew they would be, Ruby Lathem came to the table. She greeted Annie as if they had been in a conspiracy since before the Korean War, and then turned to me and said, "Hello, Prof—I mean John Quincy—I'll never get used to that. Well, anyway, will you introduce me to the lady I've heard so much about?"

"I'll be delighted. Ms. Ruby Lathem, I'd like to introduce you to Ms. Elizabeth Denney of San Francisco, which is in California if you have forgotten your geography."

Ruby tossed her head and said, "Oh, you don't have to be so snide. I'm pleased to meet you, Ms. Denney."

Liz uttered some similar formula phrase and they nodded to each other.

I said, "Ms. Denney and I once lived in sin in San Francisco back when you were a baby, and now we plan to live in sin here in Bodark Springs unless your friends in the First Baptist Church of Bodark Springs decide to horsewhip me and send her back to California."

Ruby smirked. "Oh, you always make a joke of everything don't you Pro—John Q.? I'm sure your romance is not sinful and that Ms. Denney is as respectable as you've always been. Ms. Denney, I hope you can stand the constant joking that John Quincy Adams the Second is famous for here in Bodark Springs."

Liz went along with the plan. "Thank you, Ms. Lathem, but Johnny and I do plan to live in sin. He's deadly serious."

"Well, I never," she said and walked away.

Liz said, "She is probably right when she said, 'I never.'"

"Don't be too sure of that," I said as Myrt started banging the dishes around and sloshing my soup from bowl to saucer.

Annie was greatly amused by all that had gone on, but Liz seemed to be put out. She said, "I hate a surly waiter."

I said, "Okay, I'll only tip her twenty percent. That'll show her."

I marveled at the appetites of Liz and Annie. I was back to my abstemious regimen after eating my way across Central and South Texas. It would take me a week to get back to my accustomed diet of cereal, toast, soup, salad, and steamed vegetables. I wondered what I would eat when Liz and I were spending our summers in one of the great eating cities of the world. I had loved Chinatown and North Beach and the Fisherman's

Wharf restaurants, but I was younger then. I mused about food while I ate the soup that Myrt hadn't spilled into the saucer. Remembering Chinese food in San Francisco, I decided that Bodark Springs needed a Chinese place, maybe a small one, the kind Dashiell Hammett called "a Chink joint" in one of his San Francisco novels. I couldn't remember whether it was *The Maltese Falcon* or *The Dain Curse*.

Lunch over, Annie made her way back to the Cotton Exchange to Suite 307, which Edward had kept especially for her, and Liz and I strolled down Main Street to ruminate on our future life in sin. And, I fervently hoped, to take naps before we had to set out to Eden for the party Charlie and Lucy had laid on to welcome Liz to the family and to some of their and our friends.

Since we had hours before setting out for Eden, I suggested that we get in our pajamas and nap in bed rather than in our chairs. We always spun some of our best schemes while lying in bed. Maybe we could decide whether to set out for our Frisco summer—as she would never have called it—by car, or to fly out and hope we could get her 1956 Mercedes roadworthy after its sitting up in her garage since Herb's death. I really wanted us to drive so we could stop for a few days in Santa Fe to see *The Bartered Bride* and *Manon Lescaut* and then go up to Denver and stay at the Brown Palace for a couple of days' rest. After that we could go to Cheyenne and take I-80 through Salt Lake City, which Liz had never visited, and on across Utah and Nevada to Reno. I wanted to spend the night in Tahoe so I could wake early and go into the Golden State with dawn behind us and the whole world lying in wait for us at Seacliff near the Golden Gate. When we crossed the California line, I might risk contumely and burst into "California, Here I Come" in my melodious tenor.

As we lay holding hands and I laid out my scheme, Liz said, "I think we should fly. It won't take forever to get Herb's Mercedes in shape. It probably only needs new tires and battery, some fresh belts and hoses, a flushing of radiator and transmission, and a tune-up."

"Hey, were you a mechanic in your early life? How do you know all that auto stuff?"

Liz said, "I told you I grew up on a farm and once drove a taxi when I was in college. But the truth is, I had a mechanic look at the car and tell me what it needed just after Edward called me. I knew I could seduce you into coming back to San Francisco if I still had the feminine wiles I was famous for in the 1930s when I stole your heart. How does that sound to you?"

"It sounds like we're flying to California."

I thought about how I'd have to pack judiciously and then do some serious shopping at the men's stores that I remembered being down by Union Square.

"Now that you've settled our itinerary, we won't have to rush so in getting out of town. It will give Annie and me a few more sessions to get her all she needs for her report to Austin. All right, close your eyes—"

Wasted breath, since Liz was fast asleep. I should have guessed how our plans would lay out since I have been thrice married and remember what Mark Twain said—"A man who claims to be boss at home will lie about other stuff." I slept after a little worry about leaving home and hearth for such a long time and woke when the alarm I'd set for 5:00 went off. Liz, the perfect woman, was already up and dressed and sitting in my recliner. I washed and combed and dressed as neatly as the occasion demanded and told Liz I was ready to finally unleash the LaSalle to take her and Annie down to the farm.

I used my trusty dusting brush on the LaSalle, backed it out of the garage, and took it around to the circular drive to pick up Liz. When she came out I was standing beside the fine old GM product smiling and gesturing for her to climb in. She said, "You get in on that side. I'm driving."

Damn, I thought, maybe we got married when we were in San Antonio or New Braunfels and I didn't remember it. I got in and she expertly moved the LaSalle out into Main Street. She said, "I know how to get to the hotel, but you'll have to direct me to the farm."

"I thought maybe your intuition would guide you since you have taken firm hold of everything else."

Liz giggled. "Oh, Johnny, you know I'm fooling with you. We'll drive to California if you want to, and I'll get in the passenger seat when we get to the hotel. I just wanted to see how it was to drive a classic that you love so well. I'm pretty much putty in your hands."

"Ha! That'll be the day, as the Duke says in *The Searchers*."

Annie was waiting outside the Cotton Exchange as we drove up, and she was joined by Edward and a woman I had never seen before. I supposed this was the secret woman from Paris or Bonham or somewhere exotic. It looked as if the LaSalle would have to transport five to Eden, and before I could do anything positive, Annie got behind the wheel, Eddie got in the front, and I was in the back with Liz and Louise Foley, whose name I'd never heard. She was a most attractive woman of about fifty, I surmised. She was short but not plump, and she had done nothing to disguise the grey in her hair. She was dressed as modishly as Liz, but she spoke with the accent of Northeast Texas. I could see now why Eddie was off so often to Paris or Bonham or wherever she lived. It turned out she was from Honeygrove, where Eddie's mother was from. Small world, as they say. I don't know who "they" are and why they say it. But it fits for the first time in my life.

She said, "You don't remember me, do you?"

I mumbled something inappropriate and waited for her to clue me in.

She said, "You once taught me history when I was in the ninth grade. It was before my folks, who were separated, got back together and we moved back to Honeygrove where I lived except for that one half-year here. I've been there ever since except for when I went off to college at UT. I majored in history because you made me love it in that one semester I was in your class."

Here I was supposed to say something like "Oh, yes, of course, you're little Louise Something. Of course I remember you." But I didn't and I didn't even lie. I started feeling bad about that as the evening wore on and I discovered what a nice woman she is.

Annie drove expertly as I knew she would from our trip to Texarkana in her Impala. And Liz was promised she'd be allowed to drive the LaSalle back to town. Louise complimented me on the car, Liz on her clothes, and Annie on her beauty. Nobody remarked on my natty attire or Eddie's Hart Schaffner and Marx light gray chalk stripe. Maybe he and I are too old to rate compliments on our dress.

The party at Charlie's farm was quiet and pleasant. Up to a point. The food was good, and I managed to restrict myself to a clear soup, a nice green salad, and a small serving of tournedos of beef with asparagus on the side. The red wine was a nice malbec from Argentina and the white a David Bruce chardonnay. Annie chose white wine and Liz asked for water since she was to drive back in the dark; at least that's what I assumed.

Apart from the quintet who came in the LaSalle, plus Charlie and Lucy, there were their three children, Robert, Ann, and Margie and their spouses, whose names I've heard at least fifty times and can never keep straight. I think Margie and Ann are married to guys named Bob, but I don't know which is which. Robert Adams, also called Bob, helps to confuse me. His wife, I think, is named Betsy, probably short for Elizabeth, but who knows? The young generation seems nice and smart, but I can't testify to that since they're not around me much. Who'd want to hang out with a grandfather on the wrong side of ninety? They treat me as if I were made of Murano glassware and almost certainly incompetent. As I looked at these modern young folks, I wondered which of 'em could have tracked villains down in the wilds of Arkansas and killed 'em dead. Sometimes I'm not as tolerant of my off-offspring as a doting grandfather should be.

The conversations were just as they always are. After dinner, the women separated themselves and the men were left to talk about subjects that bored me. Some of the Bobs are hunters and fishers, and Eddie and Charlie have as much interest in wildlife as I do. So while the women were having their conversations, we were having two in the men's part of the house. This was turning out to be like an English dinner party where the women go away and the men smoke cigars and drink port. Fortunately, nobody smoked, and if there was port it was kept closeted. Finally, Charlie offered me a dram of Drambuie, which I gratefully accepted. It gave me something to do with my hands and a glass to stare into while the Bobs talked of fish and game. Eddie asked me if I was all right. Charlie asked me if I was all right. Then I asked me if I was all right. Maybe I should join the ladies so Liz, Annie, Lucy, Margie, and Ann could ask me in turn if I was all right. I was ready to go home and climb in bed with Liz, and it was only 9:15. When the men and women were back together, I started to explain that Liz and I were going to live in sin, but I didn't imagine that would shock anybody, so why bother?

The five of us drove back in companionable silence, and Liz and I made it to bed in time for some more talk of thee and me. I said, "Why didn't you marry me back in 1933, '34, '35, '36, '37, '38, and '39?"

She said, "At first, there seemed to be a cloud over you, and I couldn't figure out what it was. And then, since we were only together in summers, I decided that you still had something that kept you in Texas and kept you holding something back. I didn't *not* love you. I loved you from the start till this very day. I never got over you, but I didn't think you really wanted to marry me. Not really. I knew you loved me, but, oh, hell, Johnny, I guess I was some kind of fool. I should have said yes when I was asked the first time. I've run out of any excuses, haven't I? And now I'm too old."

"Old? Hell, I've got a pair of handmade boots older'n you. What if you knew I did something awful back in the 1930s and that's what made me seem to be drifting off when we were together? I don't think I drifted off much, but you're a better judge than I am."

She said, "I don't think I *could* ever care that you had some dark secret. If you were in on the McKinley assassination back at the turn of the century, I'd figure you had a good reason. You didn't shoot at Roosevelt that time in Miami back in the thirties did you? No, I think they caught him. And, Lord knows, you're too old to have been on 'the grassy knoll' when Kennedy was killed. So if you killed somebody, I'll bet my last dollar, my last million—you knew I had several, didn't you?—that if you did some horrible deed, you had a good reason."

"What if I told you that I killed two men just before I came to California in 1932?"

She was serious, I could see. "I wouldn't care, even if you claimed you did it out of meanness. I know you're not mean, and I defy anybody, including you, to call you mean."

"Well, I did kill two men and burned two houses and a car, and then I fled to California."

Liz took a deep breath. "I know you had a good reason. You can't make me quit loving you if that's what you're trying to do. Trying to make me go back to San Francisco and hate you. Wrong! Never happen. You don't have to tell me more. I'm on your side till death do us part. Damn, I sound like a wedding preacher. But I mean it."

"I know you do. Here's the short version. The long version is in a safe deposit box downtown. I'll get it tomorrow and you can read it. I wrote it to be read by Edward after I'm dead. These hillbillies named Scroggs murdered my uncle and my father, though Uncle Fred and Dad managed to take two or three of them down. The two who survived vowed to kill every Adams in Eastis County."

Liz gasped, "Oh, my God!"

"That meant me and my sons, so I went to Arkansas, established a couple of aliases, and set out to find 'em and kill 'em in cold blood. It didn't work out that way, though. I found 'em and waited in the woods for 'em to come away from their womenfolk, but they found me first and one shot me in the left shoulder and—"

Liz remembered. "That's the scar I saw when we first made love. Oh, my God! You said you fell off a hay bailer. Oh, my God!"

"I wasn't hurt bad. What western movies call 'a flesh wound,' so I managed to kill both those men. I went to get a shovel to bury them, but a bear got one and dragged him off into the woods. I buried his brother and got out of Arkansas. I burned the shacks I had rented and burned the clothes and the car and made my way to California and met you. The long version makes it clear that I acted in self-defense, but my intention was murder. No gettin' around that."

Liz was in tears again. "I admire that. I wish you'd told me then. I would've married you if you'd told me and got the burden off your shoulders. Oh, my God! I keep saying 'Oh, my God,' don't I?"

"There's a little more to the story. For the last few weeks somebody has been making phone calls and sending notes to me, to Lucy, to Annie, and who knows who else warning me to confess my sins. The note slipped under Annie's door mentioned that I had killed before. So I have been pretty upset of late. If worse comes to worst, I may have to flee to California and hide out again."

"Is somebody blackmailing you? How much do they want? I'll pay—"

"No, I don't think money is behind this. I think somebody wants me to confess to save my immortal soul. Of course if I do, the law is not going to think confession is good for my soul. They'll want me behind bars."

"So what should we do?"

I said, "We? I'm in this alone."

"Like hell you are. We'll face this together. Between Edward and the finest lawyers in San Francisco, we'll get the whole story of self-defense out."

"I wish I could have told you this when we fell in love back in California, but I was afraid you wouldn't believe this tangled story. I was sure the law was right behind me. Eddie suspects that something happened back in 1932, but I don't want to tell him and put a burden on him. I know he wouldn't tell, but I don't want him under pressure. I doubt that anybody is still looking, though there is a 'John Doe' warrant for whoever killed the Scroggs men. Now you can leave me and go home if my story's too strong for you."

Liz almost screamed. "You damned idiot! I plan to marry you if I have to hogtie you like old Somebody did to old Somebody in one of your stories to Annie."

"Floyd and Dulcie Moore, the hog-tie-er and the hog-tie-ee."

Liz sobbed. "Oh, Johnny, I wish we could make love the way we used to."

"We are, and this is better. Remember Keats: 'Heard melodies are sweet, but those unheard are sweeter.' Our heard melodies are our sweet memories and our present unheard melodies are even sweeter. How about a little Browning now that I'm stealing lines: 'Grow old along with me, the best is yet to be.' Now go to sleep—in my arms."

And we did.

After another blessed dreamless sleep, I woke to find Liz awake and looking at me. I thought of John Donne's lines: "And now good morrow to our waking souls/Which watch one another not out of fear." I knew by the way she smiled that my "Arkansas Event" had not changed anything. We looked for a full minute before she spoke. "All right, we'll drive to California. I'd walk if it meant we'd always be together."

Now I knew everything was all right and always would be. I said, "No, we'll fly. But first we have to make a trip to Dallas so I can buy some San Francisco clothes. I just figured it out. I can go to Neiman-Marcus and get suited up for our summers in California. They'll ship 'em, and all I'll need to take on the plane will be some Leddy shoes and one or two changes of clothes till my San Francisco duds arrive."

"Great idea. Then I can outfit myself for my long Texas falls and winters and leave those clothes here. Perfect solution. Is your wardrobe the reason you wanted to drive? We'd have to pull a trailer to get all your garments west."

I made the coffee and brought it to her bed with cream, sugar, and a whole bouquet of late daffodils I'd picked from the garden while the coffee was perking.

She said, "I don't deserve you."

"I know, but you can have your way while we're here, and then at your house I expect to be treated like the sheik of Araby."

She purred. "That'll be the day.'"

"Let's take Annie to Dallas with us. She can drive and help me select some ties or something."

She laughed, "I know what's on your mind. You think I need Annie to keep me from going to California. Oh, well, maybe she can. I guess I don't need somebody to westernize me since I already have the boots and western skirts from Leddy's, but Annie has that all-American, small-town-girl look. I can see right through you, Johnny. But, okay, let's drag Annie along to outfit me so I won't intimidate the locals with fashions from I. Magnin."

I thought this might be the last chance I'd get to see Annie since I'd told her everything I knew about the culture of Northeast Texas. Anything else she needed could be read in any number of books. Maybe Liz and I could gang up on her and persuade her to come to San Francisco to marry Justin. The thought of anybody being married in Midland just about gave me the fantods. If not San Francisco, maybe they'd marry in Austin, and then Liz and I could fly down and crash the wedding party.

Getting ready to make a trip to Dallas took a little doing. I made reservations for two rooms at the Adolphus, arranged for dinner at the French Room, and called Toby Rogers, the guy who always waited on me at N-M, and told him I'd need a whole new San Francisco wardrobe. You can imagine how that delighted him. The commission would be staggering. He put me onto a shirtmaker who could take my measurements and get two dozen shirts out to California in the same shipment as my other clothes.

Annie was eager to go with us to Dallas. The idea of being an advisor on clothes for Liz thrilled her. I told Liz I'd booked two rooms so she and

Annie could share one, and I'd take the other. Liz said, "You are plumb crazy, as they say in these parts, if you think I'm ever gonna sleep in any bed that you're not in. You're stuck with me till death etc., etc., etc."

I knew all along she'd balk at sharing a room with Annie, which I would never've let happen, but I was delighted at the other part of her refusal. I planned to spend all the nights I had left in the same bed with Liz. I may be getting sentimental, but what the hell, somebody has to do it.

We set out in the rain with Annie driving the Buick. I sat in the front seat because she had a bunch of questions for me about things she said I needed to clear up for her report. Liz read a copy of *Vanity Fair*, probably to get ideas for her new Texas wardrobe, as if anything in *VF* would aid her in clothes for Bodark Springs.

Annie wanted to know about folksongs. I told her my part of Texas was not a great spot for folksingers. I didn't know why, but I'd heard very few except for the play-party songs and lots of old fiddle tunes like "Soldier's Joy" and "WeevilyWheat" that were standards at square dances. I told her William Owens's *Texas Folk Songs* would tell her more than I ever could. She promised to find a copy and read it when she got back to Austin. "But before I read any more about folk music, maybe you can tell me the difference between a song and a ballad?"

"Ballads tell stories, mostly about love gone wrong or death and destruction. The most famous of all is probably 'Barbara Allen.' It tells the sad tale—a pretty stupid tale really—about Barbara and Sweet William. I could sing it for you."

Both Liz and Annie said, "No, no, a thousand times no!"

Annie said, "Just tell me why it's stupid if it's so famous."

"Okay, here goes. Sweet William is in a bar and mentions all the pretty young girls of the town but fails to mention Barbara. She scorns him and he takes to his deathbed, and Barbara comes to see him and says, 'Young man, I think you're a-dyin.' He does, and that kills her, and they're buried side by side. Out of his heart springs a red, red rose and out of hers a briar. These plants climb and they climb to the old church top and tie in a true lovers' knot. See?"

Annie asked, "So why is it famous? Is it really that bad when it's sung?"

"I offered to sing it, but you made fun of me. It's famous partly because a Harvard professor named Francis James Child collected what he considered the best of all the ballads sung in the British Isles. He died before he could explain why he'd chosen the four hundred or so he determined were the best. His daughter and another man, George Lyman Kittredge, published the book as *English and Scottish Popular Ballads* back in the 1890s. Each song is given a number—'Barbara Allen' is Child Number 84—and folklore collectors rush around the country trying to track down Child Ballads. If they find one, it's a triumph for them and it doesn't matter how sappy it is. I doubt that many of these Child Ballads are found in Texas, and I know of none in my part of the state. One of my favorites, one I used to hear in Arkansas, is 'Young Beichan,' called 'Lord Bateman' in America. It's Child 53. It doesn't end in tragedy. Lord Bateman goes to Turkey and falls in love with a Turk's beautiful daughter, but has to leave for some reason. Back home in England, he's about to marry, but 'The Turkish Lady,' as she's called in the song, comes on his wedding day, bangs on the door, and interrupts the proceedings. The servant who finds Lord Bateman tells him 'she has a ring on every finger and on one finger she has full three, and enough gay gold around her middle to buy Northumberland from thee.' So he sends the affianced bride away and marries the Turkish lady. He tells the mother of the spurned lady that she's not the loser because 'she came to me with a horse and saddle and she'll go home in coaches three.' Don't ask me why three coaches. I think it's for the rhyme."

Liz says, "I wish we'd let you sing. It couldn't have been worse than the telling of these tales."

Annie said, "So, let me ask again. How is a song different from a ballad?"

"Songs don't tell a story. They're just there for the fun of the singing. Here's one. No, I won't sing it, but I could. Here are some of the words:

> I'm as free a little bird as I can be,
> I sit on the hillside singing all alone,
> Just as free a little bird as I can be.
> I wish I was a little bird,
> I wouldn't build my nest on the ground,

I'd build my nest on some sweet girl's breast,
Where them bad boys couldn't tear it down.

Then the chorus again and

I wish I was a little bird,
I wouldn't build my nest in the air,
I'd build my nest on some sweet girl's breast
And roost in the locks of her hair.

"You should've let me sing. It's a catchy tune."

That was pretty much all I knew to tell her about songs and ballads, and by now I was as bored as they must've been. We rode in silence till Annie and Liz started talking about fashion. When we got to Greenville, we stopped for one of those lady restroom breaks, and I got in the back so Liz and Annie could go on and on about blouses and dresses and spring coats and undergarments. I drifted off and didn't awaken till we drove up in front of the Adolphus.

We had dinner in the French Room, and I worried that if I didn't get settled in one place—either at Liz's or back in Bodark—I might wind up 'diggin' my grave with my teeth,' as my dad used to say. A person can't restrict himself to soup and salad when confronted with all the comestibles on offer at the French Room. I managed a clear soup and a chopped salad, but I couldn't turn down the trout almondine with Brussels sprouts and roasted new potatoes. I drank two glasses of chardonnay and even managed to eat most of a strawberry mousse. Maybe I'd fast the next day. Ha!

After dinner, Liz and I went to our room on the fifth floor and Annie to hers two doors down the hall. I don't know how Annie spent the evening, probably calling Justin or her parents in Midland. I told her to go ahead and use the hotel phone for long distance. "You can call Austin or Midland, or, hell, even Hong Kong, China, if you know any-body over there. You're doing me a great favor coming on this excursion and helping Liz gear up for her times in Texas." Liz and I got in bed as soon as we could use the bathroom and dress in nightwear. Then we fell into bed and began talking about California.

Liz had talked to her brother-in-law in San Mateo and had arranged for a wrecker to take her 1956 Mercedes 300 sedan down to a mechanic in Redwood City that Herb swore by. It wouldn't be ready when we got to San Francisco, but that wouldn't matter, she said. "I belong to a car service since I never drive in the city. Actually, I've never driven the Mercedes. It's been in the garage at home since Herb died. I know the tires are flat and I'm sure all the fluids are congealed by now. But Sam, my brother-in-law, says it can be fixed as good as new. I think it has about ten thousand miles on it. We'll use it to roam all over California when it's back running."

"Do you think we'll go all the places we went back when I was in love with you?"

She snorted, "When I *was* in love with you? You still better be or I'll push you off the cliff at Seal Rocks when we get home."

"You know how I feel. I don't have to tell you all the time, do I?"

She said, "You damned well better. Every single day at least twelve times."

"Count on it. Now tell me about this car service. We used to ride the buses and the streetcars and the cable cars back when I was in love. You know way back when?"

She slapped me playfully, "Just keep on with this *was in love* talk! You do, and I won't let you get a wink of sleep. Anytime you doze, I'll punch you in the ribs."

"Okay, I'm behaving. Tell me about the car service. That's something new to me. We just have one old taxi in Bodark Springs."

She explained to the country bumpkin. "Well, I'm signed up with City Limousine Service. It costs a fortune even when I'm not using it regularly. But it works like this. I call and schedule a car and driver, and soon a large black Cadillac comes to the door, and a man in a neat uniform comes to the door and escorts me to the car. He waits as I shop or comes back for me when the opera is over or if I've been to a party. Having this service is one of my favorite luxuries. I've heard you say it several times—'It's great to be rich.' And even though I sometimes feel a little guilty having so much money, I'm not giving it to the IRS or some tax office in Sacramento."

At exactly nine the next morning, we met Annie in the hotel coffee shop so I could restrict myself to coffee and one small danish, while Liz and Annie ate as if the shopping day ahead would require untold calories. We were to lunch at the Zodiac Room at Neiman-Marcus, but I wondered if they would have any appetite after all this breakfast. I really didn't wonder that at all. I was sure that as I ate a lunch of soup and salad, my lady companions would make a serious dent in the N-M menu.

When we strolled down toward Neiman-Marcus, I was amazed to see how Dallas had changed since I rushed into town after my Arkansas adventure. Dallas now had almost a million people—800,000 plus—but back in 1932, the city's population was less than 250,000. Downtown was greatly different with stores I had never heard of and buildings that were reaching skyward. At N-M, Toby Rogers was delighted to see me. He was a great help in making selections when I told him I would spend my summers in San Francisco and not in the heat of Texas. He helped me select three suits, three sport coats, six pairs of slacks, and a light topcoat that we agreed would be needed for San Francisco nights. Most of our garments had to come from the deep inner reaches of the store since most of the clothes on the rack were for the summer season. Frank Lopez, the tailor who had measured me for years, came with tape measure and chalk and worked his magic. Both Toby and Frank assured me that clothes would be in San Francisco within two weeks. I left them and went to take a seat in Men's Haberdashery. I vaguely knew the woman who ran that section, and we got acquainted better as I ordered socks, ties, gloves, cashmere scarves, a few sissy pocket squares, handkerchiefs, and underwear. I decided not to do anything about hats or a proper cane till I got to San Francisco. Liz and I could shop some of the fine boutiques on Maiden Lane. As with the clothing section, the haberdashery lady—I never learned her name—had to go to the storeroom for some of the winter items.

I didn't want to bother the lady shoppers, so, all my choosing done, I wandered into the Fine Jewelry section and began looking at broaches and necklaces and other accessories for the well turned-out lady. I found a nice double string of pearls that I thought would go well with one of Annie's—what do they call them?—Oh, yes, twinsets. I found a broach that was perfect for Liz. It had a pair of diamonds on the base of a spray of golden daffodils in 18 carat gold. If the ladies needed to be spoiled, I was the man for the job. I had the jewelry packaged and decided to keep the packages until we were back in Bodark so they wouldn't go on and on about returning 'em to Fine Jewelry and getting my money back. I may not know much about women, but I know a little.

We had lunch in the Zodiac Room, and it was just as I knew it would be. I restrained myself, but the little bit of shopping they'd done made 'em eat like field hands. Well, maybe I exaggerate. The Zodiac Room doesn't have heavy field-hand food, but they did well with the mounds of chicken salad and the orange souffle, which is misnamed since it is really what church suppers call a congealed salad. N-M is famous for the rolls, which go by a fancy name I forget, and the desserts are moderately famous. It made me hungry just to see them eat, but I forebore. I can't outgrow my new San Francisco clothes before I get to California.

We went back to the Adolphus where Liz and I disrobed and climbed into bed to discuss the day so far. I should hasten to add that we didn't disrobe jointly since I am modest to excess, Liz says. We talked about the wonders of Stanley Marcus's great specialty store and drifted off into dreamland to wait for our dinner with Homer and Beth, who were coming over from Fort Worth so they could see what they could make of Ms. Elizabeth Denney now that we were going to live together. That wasn't the announced purpose, but it was probably the subtext.

Homer made reservations for dinner at the Pyramid Room of the new Fairmont Hotel. In my day, the Adolphus was Dallas's fine hotel, but I had heard that in the past two years, the Fairmont had become the place to stay and the Pyramid Room the place to eat. Since Liz and I had spent many hours dancing and dining at the San Francisco Fairmont, I was eager to try the one in Dallas. Homer and Beth were to pick us up in front of the Adolphus and drive us the short distance to the Fairmont. It was in walking distance of our hotel, but since the ladies would be in heels, we gladly accepted the ride.

The Fairmont was a beautiful hotel and the Pyramid Room as luxurious as any restaurant I'd ever seen. The room was a masterpiece, the chairs were padded and plush, and the service attentive. Everybody went wild on the menu, but I tried as hard as I could to get close to the regime that had seen me through many, many years. Homer ordered a bottle of Veuve Cliquot along with the appetizers, and I was so tempted by the items on the menu that I finally broke down and ordered the sea bass. But I barely sipped at the champagne and ate only a few bites of the Sweet Chili Brussels Sprouts that Beth ordered for an appetizer. Homer joined me in ordering the fish, but the ladies went for the filets and all the trimmings.

Finally, Homer got to the point. "So, what plans do you two have for the future?"

I said, "Is that your way of asking if our intentions are honorable?"

Beth said, "Oh, Homer, don't be rude. You know it's none of our business what Pop and Liz have in mind. Let's talk about Annie's wedding plans. Are you going to marry in your home town?"

Annie was relieved that Beth was taking the focus off the old people and their scheme for scandalous living. "Well, our plans are up in the air. My mother wants us to marry in Midland, but Justin—he's my fiancé— wants us to marry in Austin. Liz has some grand plan for us all to rush to San Francisco and be married in sight of the Golden Gate Bridge. Anybody have alternate plans?"

Homer said, "I'll suggest Fort Worth so Beth and I can be there. Maybe at the Stockyards—just to get the real western flavor."

Beth said, "Homer Adams, one more word out of you and I'll pour this glass of the 'Widow' Cliquot in your lap! You always have to make a joke."

I deputized myself as the peacemaker. "Everybody settle down. Don't waste good champagne on Homer's lap. Annie and Justin will decide where to tie their knot, and Liz and I'll tie a completely different kind of knot. I'm ready to answer Homer's original question—the one Beth tried to steer him away from. Liz and I plan to live in sin. We'll be sinners in Bodark Springs during the cool months in Texas and sinners in San Francisco during the hot Texas summers. How does that sound?"

Beth laughed heartily, "I love it. Maybe Homer and I can come to San Francisco for Pop's birthday in July. We can stay at the Mark Hopkins and pretend that *we* are living in sin."

Liz said, "No, no. Everybody stays at my house. I have five bedrooms. One for you and Homer, one for Annie and Justin—married or not—one for Charlie and Lucy, one for Johnny and me, and one for Eddie and whoever. There should be plenty of sin to go around."

Annie said, "I love it! I've always wanted to see San Francisco, and Grandpa John's birthday will be thrilling. It's not every Fourth of July that a person turns ninety-five."

Homer said, "Why do you call him Grandpa John? It wasn't a month ago that Eddie was warning me that you and my Pop were about to elope to Hugo, Oklahoma, and get married."

Annie explained. "I never knew either of my grandfathers, and since Johnny has been so good to me, I've adopted him. If I weren't engaged, and if Liz hadn't shown up, you might've had a wedding to go to in Hugo. Now he's my grandpa and Liz is my grandma. I hope she doesn't mind. She looks young enough to be an older sister. Oh, and while I'm on this monologue, I have a question: When Beth was threatening to pour champagne in Homer's lap, why did she call it a 'Widow'?"

Homer answered, "First, Annie, I would welcome you as a step-mother, and second I don't care that Pop and Liz plan to live in sin, and third, the champagne called Veuve Cliquot was once owned by a widow. The word *veuve* means *widow*, and people like Beth translate the word *veuve* to show off."

Beth said, "You're asking to meet the veuve in your lap."

The food came, and no questions about what Annie called wedding 'venues' were settled. Since the food was so delicious, we were for a time in silence, and then Annie spoke. She said, "Thanks for welcoming me into the Adams family—oops, I don't mean that creepy TV show. But I wonder if Grandpa John and Grandma Liz would like to make it a double wedding? If we did that, my mother wouldn't have a cow if we married in San Francisco. How about it?"

Now it was my turn. At long last. "Liz and I are not getting married. I begged her and begged her to marry me, but she wouldn't. Now she'll have to do some begging if she wants to make an honest man of me."

Everybody laughed, but Liz said, "If I didn't have this tight skirt on, I'd get down on my knees right here in the King Tut Room and propose."

Homer said, "It's the Pyramid Room, Liz, and if you're ready to get down on your knees, I'm ready to give the groom away."

Everybody had dessert but me. Then Homer drove us back to the

Adolphus so Annie could call Justin and Liz and I could continue our life of sin in each other's arms. Tomorrow would be another day, and Annie, Liz, and I could go back to Bodark Springs and begin plans of one kind or another. Beth could go to her clubs, and Homer could cut into a few thoracic cavities. And a good time would be had by all—well, maybe not by Homer's patients.

CHAPTER 17

On our way back to Bodark Springs, Liz drove and Annie and I sat in the back seat so she could unlimber her pencil and gather up any loose ends about the so-called culture of Northeast Texas. She'd asked very little about home remedies except for what little I'd told her about warts. And there were a few local customs that she wanted to go through before she went back to Austin and began writing her report on what her Grandpa Johnny had droned on and on about for several weeks.

I told her what little I knew about folk medicine. I suggested she get old Doctor Jarvis's *Folk Medicine*, published years ago. That old Vermont doctor certainly could tell her more than I knew about cures. Some of what he knew would apply, since remedies followed migration patterns as people moved about the country. Dr. Jarvis was a nut about apple cider vinegar and honey as a cure for lots of things, and he was probably right. But some of the cures you found in my part of the world were not only silly, but probably not of any use. A few might kill you. When I told her that the cure for hemorrhoids was to sit on a freshly sawed tree stump, Liz said, "Gag me with a spoon!"

I said, "Just stay in the front seat and pay attention to the road or we might need brown paper and vinegar to cure our busted heads."

Annie said, "Are there any remedies that are really helpful?"

"Maybe not. If you get stung by a scorpion, put some freshly chewed tobacco on the sting to assuage the pain. I doubt if that works any better than eating a bite of garlic every morning to ward off colds and flu. It might just ward off people who have the flu."

Annie said, "I could never eat a clove of garlic before breakfast."

Liz said, "Me either."

I agreed and fumbled my way through some of the most absurd folk cures, like keeping a potato in your pocket till it shrivels in order to cure rheumatism or that pumpkin tea kills tapeworms. I told my auditors that if you look at the eye of a person who has a sty, you'll get one too. Or that a child whose father dies before he is born can cure the thrash.

"The what?" they both asked.

"I don't know. I think it's some kind of throat infection. Now, see how silly all these cures are? You might be better off going to the doctor. I'm tired of this subject. Ask me something else or let's all just look for wildflowers along the way—all except you, Liz, you watch the road."

Liz drove well past McKinney, and I took the wheel to take us the rest of the way. The two ladies lay sprawled on the back seat. I said, "Did you two eat so much at the Cleopatra Room last night that you're sluggish today?"

Liz said, "It's the Pyramid Room, and we can't be responsible for a person like you who's on some kind of starvation diet. You haven't eaten enough at any meal to keep a poodle alive in all the years I've known you. When we get to California, I plan to put some real food in you so you'll get fat and jolly."

"Hey, I'm the jolliest guy you know. If I ate all I wanted, I wouldn't be on the verge of celebrating my ninety-fifth birthday. Speaking of which, I really do want all my brood, including Annie and Justin, to come to California to take full advantage of your hospitality. We'll see if you and your live-in cook can feed all those voracious eaters. I've seen the way some of you put food away."

Annie roused herself and asked, "Is there anything else you can tell me that will fill up my notebook?"

"I'm trying to navigate this car back to Bodark, so I need to keep my eyes on the road, but, hey, there is something I wanted to tell you about when we were off on marriage and courtship. It's called the 'Backwards Dinner.' Did either of you ever hear of that?"

Neither had, so I tried to remember what I knew of the old folk charm. "I think it worked like this. Several girls—maidens of course—would get together and do a supper backwards. They would dress backwards, cook the meal from behind their backs, walk backwards, sit back to front at the table, and eat dessert first. In short, do the whole meal in reverse. Then they'd walk backwards to bed and dream of the man they were to marry."

Liz, who taught English, reminded us of Keats's *Eve of Saint Agnes*. It was similar except that all the backwards stuff was left out. And it had to happen on a certain night, the night before St. Agnes Day. It was one of the many charms a girl could use to find the man she'd marry.

Annie said, "Liz, when we get back to Bodark, maybe we could have a Backwards Dinner. I already know the man I'm gonna marry, but maybe you could dream of your next husband. Grandpa Johnny doesn't seem to be on the list, right?"

I said, "Yeah, and maybe you'll dream of the man who's fixing up your Mercedes and marry him. Or some guy you've never met. Oh, Lord, don't dream of Eddie. I sure don't want you as a daughter-in-law."

Liz said, "I thought the girl had to be a maiden."

Then I remembered another. "You don't have to be a maiden for this one. You take a wet handkerchief and put it out in the evening so the moonlight will catch it. In the morning, you look at the wrinkles in the handkerchief and find the initials of the man you're to marry."

Liz said, "Oh, hell, I might just as well marry you."

I said, "I haven't heard any proposals. Your tight skirt kept you from falling to your knees in the Ramses the Second Room, so I guess I missed my chance."

Annie said, "For once and for all, it's the Pyramid Room. I may have to get a shotgun to get you two creeps to the altar."

I was out of charms and remedies, so I drove silently the twenty or so miles back to Bodark Springs. Since some of the clothes Liz had bought for her sojourn in Texas were in the trunk, I parked on the drive and we unloaded box after box from Neiman's. Another full wardrobe would have to be shipped up when they were altered or tailored or otherwise prepared. I wondered how she would manage to wear so many clothes in the months we were going to spend here. I thought my wardrobe being shipped to San Francisco was meager compared to hers. And Annie has accused me of being a clotheshorse.

Once we were safely inside, I poured some David Bruce chardonnay for the ladies and a healthy belt of Johnnie Walker Black for me, and we settled in the parlor for one more thing I wanted to do. I reached in my small suitcase and pulled out the two gifts I'd bought in the Fine Jewelry Department at Neiman-Marcus. (Notice the capital letters for Fine Jewelry. They are not to be missed, for N-M ain't giving those baubles away.) When I produced the carefully wrapped boxes, the usual gasps followed and the "*for mes*?" echoed in the room.

Annie couldn't believe the double string of pearls. She screamed and then broke into tears, "Oh, Johnny, I've never had pearls this fine. Look, Liz!"

Then the inevitable followed. "You'll have to take these back! I can't possibly accept such valuable pearls. I just can't! Let me look at 'em, and then we'll have to put 'em back in the box. I know Neiman's will take anything back. But first, I have to try 'em on! And then they have to go back!"

Liz hadn't opened her box. She just looked at Annie with the double strand around her neck and said, "Annie, just shut the hell up. This old bastard's rich enough to buy Sausalito."

Liz ripped into her box and saw what was in it and said, "Oh, my God!" Then she fell to her knees, ripping the tight skirt along the outside seam and said, "Goddammit, Johnny, are you gonna marry me or not?"

"I thought you'd never ask."

It was hard to tell who was happiest. Maybe Annie. She'd forgot about the pearls and was clapping her hands like a child. When she got control of herself, she said, "I believe it's 'ast.' 'I thought you'd never ast.'"

Liz frowned, "What do you mean 'ast'?"

I explained, "You remember Dulcie and Floyd. When Floyd told Dulcie he was gonna marry her whether she liked it or not, and she said, 'I thought you'd never ast.'"

Annie chimed in, "And they got married in the front seat of a Model A Ford. Maybe you and Liz can get married in the front seat of the LaSalle."

I said, "Annie, why do you seem so surprised that we're getting married? I knew it as soon as soon as she stepped off that plane at Love Field."

"You did? Oh, my God! Grandpa Johnny. You did?"

Liz said, "Of course he did. We know each other better than you think. I knew it when I got on American Airlines, and I knew Johnny would know it when he saw me. We may be old, but we're not dense. Now I've got to go and change skirts. Proposing is dangerous work."

Annie was all into logistics. Where and when and how. What would Liz wear? What would I wear? Who would get the LaSalle after all? Could we all do it in San Francisco? Maybe my birthday would be the time for it. I couldn't shut her up. When Liz came back, she took control.

She said, "Annie, don't ask Johnny anything. You and I'll handle all the details and Johnny and Justin'll have to go along. This is woman's work."

I said, "You two can do whatever you want. Me, I'm going down to the hotel and eat my supper as soon as I finish this Scotch."

Annie said, "While you finish your Scotch, can I go upstairs and run up your phone bill by calling Justin and my mother and tell 'em we're all getting married in San Francisco on Grandpa John's birthday? I wonder what the weather will be like and what I'll wear. I hope my mother doesn't just have a cow that I'm not getting married in Midland. Oh, my."

When she left the room, Liz said, "Is she always like this? Isn't this little girl getting a PhD in something? If she ever calms down, I'll tell her what to wear and where we're going to do the deed. Oh, and this is important: who gets the damned LaSalle?"

"You do. It can be your winter car here in Texas. I'll drive the wheels off your Mercedes in our California months. Fair enough?"

Liz started to cry. "Oh, Johnny, why did I have to be so damned old to finally come to my senses?"

"Oh, don't cry, Liz. Let's make up our minds to trust happiness at long last."

CHAPTER 18

When Annie came back, she was still in her happiness mode. "My mother is having a calf if not a cow about San Francisco. Justin loves the idea, and my father'll do what I want to. So let's take off for the Cotton Exchange so I can eat. I'm starving."

Liz said, "Me too."

I thought, Oh, God, it's eat, eat, eat all the time with these two.

When we got to the hotel, I sent them into the dining room while I went looking for Eddie. He was in his office, and I said, "If you've got a minute, I wonder if you have ever thought of being a best man at a wedding?"

He seemed puzzled, as I wanted him to be. "Why?"

"Well, if you did, do you think you could do it in San Francisco?"

Edward Jones Adams, an attorney who was trained never to be astonished, looked faint. "Are you telling me that you are about to marry Liz? Damn! I mean, uh, uh, San Francisco? I uh, uh—"

I laughed and said, "Well, we could always nip across the line and get hitched in Hugo, Oklahoma, if that'd work best for you. I don't want to put you out."

Eddie the lawyer got control of himself and said, "Well, I guess I should have said congratulations right away. But you always surprise me. You surprised me when I was a kid and have almost every year since. This is none of my business, but do you know what you're doing getting married at your age?"

"No. Probably not, but it may not be a federal crime to be an old fool in love, or do you know some statute about foolish old people getting married?"

Eddie was now embarrassed. He said, "I shouldn't have said what I did. Of course you know what you're doing. Always have. Well, maybe. Are you sure there's nothing you want to tell me about your years in California before you rush off to marry?"

"Eddie. We went over that not long ago, and the answer is no. When I die—probably from some excess of love—you can read the whole story in my safety deposit box. You'll also find three sets of rings for each of my wives and $100,000 in cash. Now just tell me if you'll be my best man in San Francisco on or about—as you lawyers say—July Fourth in the year of our Lord 1971."

He laughed. "Of course I will. Now that I'm over the shock, I want to apologize for doubting. I love San Francisco and may rent a whole floor of the Mark Hopkins or the Saint Francis for the rest of the family, all your heirs and assigns, as we lawyers say. Oh, Pop, I'm really glad you're getting married, and I hope you live to be a hundred and fifty."

Now it was my turn to laugh. "I plan to, but then Liz will be a hundred and twenty-five and I'll be stuck with an old woman. By the way, she and Annie are out in your restaurant eating everything in sight. Why don't you come out and try to talk Liz out of getting mixed up with the Adams clan. You never saw anybody eat like those two women. Now, are we okay about everything? I don't want to be crossways with you. With anybody for that matter."

Eddie was happy for once. "I'll go out and eat with 'em and you can drink soup and watch. Now that Annie is off your radar, maybe I'll see if she wants to join the Adams clan as Mrs. Eddie. Would I have to swap my horse and dog?"

We joined Annie and Liz, who were well past salads and were tucking into pork tenderloins and broccoli. It looked as if they might be eating sensibly for once. I ordered soup and a house salad, and Eddie opted for the same dish as the ladies—or women, as they preferred to be called.

Once the waiter had taken our orders, Eddie said, "Liz, I want to welcome you to the family. I'm very pleased that you're about to take the old man off my hands. I'll bet the two of you'll be happy jetting between here and San Francisco. I definitely will be at the wedding, and if Annie'll shuck that PhD fellow from Austin, we can make it a double."

Annie was tickled and said, "If I'd decided on an older man, you'd have been right in line behind your pop here. Thanks, but I don't want to break Justin's heart. He may not be as used to heartbreak as one Adams I could mention. Old Johnny has been carrying a torch bigger than Lady Liberty's for I don't know how long."

"1939," I said.

Now that we had the banter out of the way, I asked Eddie if he would pass the word to all those grandchildren and great-grandchildren that I couldn't possibly keep track of. "You handle the younger generation and I'll call Charlie in the morning and Homer when I get to it, but I think Homer saw it all happening in the Sphinx Room at the Fairmont."

Annie and Liz screeched, "It's the Pyramid Room, dammit."

Eddie was puzzled by all our hilarity and couldn't wait to find something to worry about. He fired off questions like "What will you do with the house when you're in San Francisco? Will you have all your mail forwarded? How often will you come back? How many months will you stay here and how many in California? When will you leave? This week or this month?"

I couldn't answer most of the things that worried him. Liz and I'd have to start thrashing out details once Annie was gone back to Austin and we had time to adjust to the life we should've lived all these years. I was worn out from being proposed to and couldn't wait to get back home and in bed with my new fiancée. I hoped Annie would stay here at the Cotton Exchange when we left. Her bubbling was wearing me out.

All the food consumed, the coffee drunk, the Grand Marnier savored, Liz and I strolled back down Main Street hand in hand. After a block of silence, Liz said, "How did Edward take the news?"

I said, "He was startled and then alarmed and then happy. I think. He's a lawyer and they're supposed to be hard to decipher. I think he's still worried about my missing years, but I told him that when I went to my reward, the answers would be in the safe deposit box with rings of my three wives, a letter, and $100,000 in cash."

Liz looked surprised at why I had so much cash hidden away. "Why so much money?"

I told her that I'd put it there in case I ever had to make a quick getaway, and she said, "Are you concerned that Arkansas will hunt you?"

I said, "No, not now. For a long time I feared that I'd look up some day and find the Arkansas State Police pounding on my door. But now I'm sure they've forgotten me. If they know what villains the Scroggs family were, they might've been glad they were no longer a menace on the landscape. No, I haven't worried about that in years."

I was lying because I may not have worried for most of the last forty years, but I had been sick with worry once the phone calls and the notes and letters started to appear.

Liz looked relieved and said, "Let's get in the house so I can start looking at the most beautiful broach I've ever seen. I wonder if Annie left the pearls at your house—our house soon—or if she put 'em in her purse and carried 'em to the restaurant? If she left 'em, maybe I'll try 'em on. I have some in San Francisco, but I'm not sure they are as lovely as those you got for Annie."

When we got inside, I was too tired even to visit Johnnie Black. All I wanted was to climb into bed with my lovely bride-to-be. We changed and fell into bed, happy to have something settled that had been unsettling for so many years. What an old fool I am. Why didn't I kidnap Liz forty years ago? While I was ruminating, Liz was sleeping soundly. Thus runs the world away!

The next morning I was the first one up by hours. I was sitting on my front porch drinking coffee and staving off worry by counting my blessings when Annie drove up on her way to Austin, I assumed. She bounded onto the porch and started up all over about those pearls. Some tears flowed, but not too many, since I threatened her if she didn't quit going on and on about a small token of my love and friendship and for playing the role of Liz for a few weeks till the real Liz showed up.

Annie was puzzled. "Is this what was going on after I came to town and got everybody stirred up?"

I said, "I think so. Once my sons saw me being in love with somebody young enough to be my great-granddaughter, they decided to take a hand. Charlie and Lucy and maybe Homer put Eddie up to tracking down Liz to save me from you. They didn't know that I wasn't in love with *you* you, but with the you that was the person you stood in for. They got Eddie to track Liz down, and here's the irony. Between the time Eddie summoned Liz and the time she got here, everybody in the Adams clan had figured out that you and I were not about to run off and do something silly. But then it was too late to call Liz off. The rest is, is—"

"History," Annie said.

"No, not history. Folklore maybe. Whatever it was—oh, wait—kismet or karma or just dumb luck. Whatever it was, it has made Liz happy, me happy, you happy, and I think my sons happy. I don't know about Rosie. She may be made of sterner stuff."

Annie said, "Is Liz up? I need to say goodbye to her before—"

"I'm up," Liz said, as she came on the porch still in her housecoat, the one she bought at Neiman's and which looked a lot better than the one of mine she wore when she first got here.

Annie said, "I just wanna say goodbye for now. I'm off to Austin to tell all my adventures to Justin, and then I'll go to Midland and pour oil on *those* troubled waters. And then we'll all go to Frisco and live happily ever after."

Liz said, "We hate it when people call it Frisco, but I can't wait for you and Justin and all your tribe to come to *San Francisco* and start a bunch of new lives. Be careful driving. You're too full of joy to watch the road I fear."

Annie drove away and I went inside and prepared a tray for Liz—coffee, cream, sugar, and one daffodil from outside the kitchen window. I came out, put the tray on the table between the two rockers, and sat sipping coffee with the love of my life and thinking I'm the luckiest sumbitch in Eastis County. I was having such wonderful daydreams that I didn't see my neighbor Estelle Stringer come snooping up the walk. She startled me when she said, in her unpleasant voice, "Good morning, Professor. Good morning, Miss Liz. I hear you two are gettin' married."

Liz said, "Oh, my God!"

I said, "How do you know that? She didn't propose till last night."

Estelle twittered, as she was wont to do, "She proposed! Oh, Professor, you always joke."

Liz said, "No, I proposed! And how did you learn early today what we didn't know till last night?"

I said, "Wait. I can answer that. Eddie told Maybelline, and Maybelline called the CIA of Bodark, and the phone lines buzzed from eight last night till four this morning. Get used to it, Liz. If you sneeze, Estelle here will know it before I do."

Estelle sniffed as I knew she would and turned on her heel and went back to report my rudeness to the entire county.

I said, "I hope the denizens of Seacliff don't have a spy network like the one here in this town."

Liz said, "They probably do, but I don't ever do anything gossip worthy there. When you come to town—soon I hope—we'll be the talk of El Camino Del Mar, my little street, especially if we live in sin till Independence Day. I can't wait."

"Nor can I. Now let's get cleaned up and go downtown and see how many people congratulate us."

We strolled downtown hand in hand and were greeted and congratulated and "best-wished" to death. My first order of business was to pop into the bank and rescue the engagement ring that had lain unused since 1939. And then in front of God, three tellers, a cashier, the bank president, and two old farmers from Cooks Springs, I dropped to one arthritic knee, slipped the ring on Liz's finger, and struggled to stand up straight so I could kiss her full on the lips. Then I discovered that Liz was still the best kisser in North America. After what seemed like three minutes, I turned her loose. Then she grabbed me in a bear hug and said, "John Quincy Adams the Second, you're an old fool."

And there in front of God and all the huddled masses, she began to cry. "But you're my old fool."

I heard one old farmer muttering to his friend from Cooks Springs, "That old fool got women all over'm. First, that redheaded girl and now this redheaded woman. It wadn't more'n a week ago, he'uz hanging around that young girl like a potlikker dog around a dead horse, and now he's puttin' rings on women's fingers and what not."

Then I heard the other one, "Them women are after him 'cause he's rich. Hell, he's got enough money to burn a wet mule."

I heard what those old cusses said, and I could tell Liz did too. I feared she might speak sharply to 'em, but she just groaned. I said, "I'll need to get a pencil and paper and write down those examples of 'folk say' so I can pass 'em on to Annie for her report."

Liz said, "I started to slap their old ugly faces."

Liz and I escaped the well-and ill-wishers and made for the Busy Bee. On the way, she said, "I don't see any papers in your hand. Did you decide to leave them for Eddie to find in—I hope and pray—about fifty years?"

"I did. I've confessed on paper and in person to you. I'm too happy right now to change a thing in my life."

Liz held on tight till we got inside the door, and then, damned if I could believe my eyes, all the customers stood up and cheered. Even Harold Higgins was clapping. Only Myrt the waitress looked disgusted and stalked off to confront the suspected Communist cook in the kitchen.

Finally, Myrt came with pad and pencil and was all smiles for once in her life. She looked us over and said, "Congratulations, Ms. Liz, and you too, Prof. I'm pretty happy to see y'all here this mornin'. I guess I know what you want, Professor, but what about you Miz Blushing Bride?"

Liz said, "I'm too excited to eat much—just some oatmeal, dry toast, orange juice, and coffee."

Myrt turned to leave, and I said, "Hold on, Myrt, I didn't order."

She said, "I know what you want. Just some—"

I interrupted. "I want two hen eggs over easy, three rashers of bacon, a sausage patty, biscuits, butter, and all the blackberry jam you can find."

Harold was dying laughing as Myrt dropped her pencil and joined in the hilarity. It never hurts to keep 'em loose.

After breakfast and a ton of congratulations, Liz and I made our way back to the house. I had a world of things to do if I was ever to get out of town. I either needed to get Eddie to find me a son or grandson to housesit, or I needed to fix it with Rosie to take over the house for four of five months a year, and I needed to get one of my banks in Dallas or Kilgore to transfer money to the Bank of America in San Francisco. I kept up my bank account there since I still had some of Uncle Fred's investments in California. Once I start to make any kind of change, I become a worrywart. Like now. Who could take care of my cars, pay insurance and taxes, keep the phone and the electricity paid? Hell, I decided I needed a business manager. Then it hit me. I'd call Lucy and see if she wanted to make some pin money and be my factotum for the months I was gone.

Lucy came up in the middle of the afternoon, and I saw immediately that I'd chosen the right person. She's smart and honest and capable of handling any emergency. I suspected that she did for the dairy what I was asking for here. And I'd pay a lot better than Charlie did. We settled on what had to be done and how much I'd pay her, which sort of stunned her when I suggested a figure.

With all that business behind me, I called Charlie and told him to meet us at the Cotton Exchange if he ever wanted to see his wife again. Then I called Eddie and asked him if he could come to dinner in his own restaurant, and I suggested he get Louise Foley to make up a sixth. He said she was in town and he was sure she'd like to get a look at the bride-to-be and see if a Girl of the Golden West could fit in with a bunch of Texas heathens. I could tell from the tone that Eddie had come around fully now.

Since I was much relieved at having got so much done, I suggested that Liz and I get into our pajamas and cuddle for the two hours before we had to stroll down to the restaurant. Cuddling was what Liz did best, and within fifteen minutes we were flossed and brushed and dressed in silks and lying in bed. We kissed and then I thought, Oh, to be seventy again and for Liz to be fifty, and . . .

I must've fallen asleep in mid-kiss, and the dreams I had were not suitable for an upright citizen and oldest member of AARP in Bodark Springs, Texas. When we roused ourselves, we decided to dress to make an impression. Liz got some of her California finery out, and I got a light gray Oxxford suit with a discreet blue stripe, a stark white shirt, and a maroon tie with diagonal white stripes. I could see as we set out that we—or certainly Ms. Liz Denney of San Francisco and Bodark Springs as she would soon appear in the local paper—would turn some heads all the way to the hotel and on into the restaurant.

232

And we did. Or she did. Everybody was used to me and hardly gave me a look.

The dinner was more than I could've hoped for. Liz and I were a "By God Couple" in everybody's eyes, and there was much talk of the wedding on July 4. I was never sure how so many people knew the date and even the time and place. I'd hardly taken all that in myself. But, as Liz and Annie said a day or two ago, "That's women's work." Charlie had already got things arranged so the dairy would run itself for a week so he and Lucy could come to San Francisco. Eddie didn't need much arranging since the hotel almost ran itself, and with Maybelline on duty in the summer when she was off from college, any intelligence the local CIA discovered could be passed on to the boss even if he was two thousand miles away. Sometime between the time I called Eddie and now, he had fixed it up with Louise to come west and join the festivities. I knew nothing about her, but I was sure Annie and Liz would suss it all out before the summer was over.

Somewhere in the middle of the meal it was all decided. Liz and I would fly out of Love Field in about three days, and Lucy, now my woman Friday, would drive us—in the LaSalle. I told her she had full use of it till I got back after the heat of the summer had abated. Imagine her delight! The food was wonderful, I hear. I had soup, salad, and a small order of baked and seasoned cauliflower. I knew I would have to fight myself when I got to one of the best eating cities in the world. There's my figure to think about. And my health. I didn't get this far eating hamburgers and french fries; in fact, I couldn't remember how hamburgers and french fries tasted. Or barbecue or chicken fried steak or chili or pork chops or mashed potatoes and gravy or puddin' pies. But I was in great health for a man breathing down a century's neck.

Two days later, Liz's Texas clothes arrived from Dallas, and she called her live-in couple and learned that my packages had arrived safely. While she was talking on the phone, I hear her call the housekeeper Sue, so when she hung up, I said, "Is she by any chance from Sioux City and does she have hair of red and eyes of blue?"

Liz got the reference and said, "No she's not from Iowaay, as the song says. She's from Burma, and her real name is much longer than Sue and harder to spell. I think it's something like—"

"Wait," I said, "it's Supiyawlet, I'll bet. Is her petticoat yaller and her little cap green?"

Liz nudged me in the ribs. "What? How do you know that? Have you been reading my mail all these years since I moved to Seacliff?"

Now I had her going, "No, no. It's Kipling. Didn't you teach English all those years?"

She bristled, "Yes, you know I did, and no, I never liked Kipling—all that Queen and Empire crap. What does he have to do with Sue's name?"

I loved this. "Okay, here goes:

'Er petticoat was yaller an' 'er little cap was green,
An' 'er name was Supiyawlit—just the same as Theebaw's Queen.
An' I seed her first a-smokin' of a whackin' white cheroot,
An' a-wastin' Christian kisses on a 'eathen idol's foot—
Bloomin' idol made of mud
What they called the Great God Budd.
Plucky lot she cared fer idols when I kissed 'er where she stud,
On the Road to Mandalay.

"Even if you don't know the wonderful poem, you must've heard the old Frank Sinatra song," I said.

She shrugged and said, "I've heard the song, but I don't think he did all that rigmarole about Supiyawlet. I saw the old Bing and Bob movie called *On the Road to Mandalay*, but I don't remember her name coming up and sure not all that doggerel you were spouting."

"Well," I said, "I didn't see that movie, but I saw *On the Road to Morocco* and *On the Road to Zanzibar*. And I don't call old Rudyard drivel. Maybe we can rent the *Mandalay* movie if we can ever get in gear and make it to California."

She said, "We'll never make it anywhere if you keep recitin' bad poetry at me. Please don't mention that poem to Sue when we get home. People from Burma probably hate Kipling."

I said, "I can do all of *Gunga Din* from memory. I hope her husband's name is not Gunga Din."

She clasped her hands as if begging. "*Please* don't recite any more Kipling. And her husband's name is Felipe. He's a Filipino."

I didn't get to do *Gunga Din*, though I began whispering it to myself, and we began packing for the trip. I'd called American Airlines for first-class tickets to San Francisco to be picked up at the counter at Love Field the day after tomorrow. We were on a deadline now. So I called Lucy and asked her to get us in the LaSalle, which she had been practicing on for three days. Then I called Eddie to give him Liz's phone number in California. He said, "You must know I already have it since I'm the one that got her here in the first place."

I forget little details sometimes, especially when I'm rushing to get out of town. Since I had him on the phone, I said, "Will you call Homer and tell him we have about six weeks till July 4, the fateful day? Tell him not to plan on cuttin' into anybody's innards for a couple of weeks. I assume you're making hotel arrangements unless all of you want to stay at Liz's mansion."

Eddie only thought for a second before he said, "No. Tell her I appreciate the offer, but I've thought about a place to stay. First, I thought about the Mark Hopkins, but then I decided the women would rather be close to the shopping, so I'm taking all the rooms we'll need at the St. Francis. I made an executive decision, and I'm sure Beth and Homer won't mind. And Charlie and Lucy are up for anything."

I said, "Since the Emperor of Japan stayed there, it should suit the Adamses. We're off day after tomorrow. I'll get back in touch once we're settled in at Liz's."

Eddie turned solemn. "Dad, you know I approve of everything you're doing, and I wish you and Liz the best and hope nothing bad comes of the other—"

"Leave it, Eddie. Nothing bad will happen. You can count on it. I've always taken care of everything. So let's hear no more about the dim and misty past."

Liz and I put together our traveling things and worried that two days would never be enough time to pack all we needed, even though we were taking mostly underwear, shoes, and toilet articles. Oh well. She called her brother-in-law, her late sister's husband, and learned that the

Mercedes would be ready tomorrow and that he'd meet us at the airport as soon as she gave him the flight information. She looked in her purse and found the flight number and told him we should get to SF International at 3:15 day after tomorrow. We would spend tomorrow worrying, and then the following day we'd rush around in a frenzy to be sure the stove was off and the doors were locked and Lucy had extra keys to the house, LaSalle, and Electra. And then we went to bed and dreamed of sugarplums and plane crashes.

We woke early on the day we were to leave, and decided to make it as normal a day as possible and not stew and sweat over what we might forget to take. We went to the Busy Bee for lunch and the Cotton Exchange for dinner. Maybelline was on the desk as we entered, and she suddenly was beside herself. "Married! Ooohweee! I wisht I was goin' to Frisco to get married to somebody rich and pretty like you fixin' to do. Yo soon-to-be Missis is sure some peach."

"No, Maybelline, peaches are from Georgia. Ms. Denney is a California Golden Poppy. If you're good and quit the dialect, maybe she and I will treat you to a trip to San Francisco. If you promise not to call it Frisco when she's around."

"I'm going to hold you to that promise. Maybe when I graduate and learn to speak properly. I've never been out of Texas, not even to Oklahoma. How about that English?"

"Perfect," I said. And then to Liz. "I just made another promise. If I keep on, I'll have everybody in Bodark out stayin' in your house."

Liz smiled at Maybelline, and then turned to me and said, "Our house."

CHAPTER 19

Lucy drove us to Love Field so we could begin our new life in the Golden State. The flight was smooth until we passed over the Rockies, and then it was bumpy until we cleared the air over Lake Tahoe. I looked down at the last of Nevada and said to Liz, "Maybe when we get to San Francisco, we could capture your Mercedes and drive it up to Reno and get married. Save all the fuss and bother of when all my family and Annie and hers get here."

Liz punched me on the shoulder, and I said, "If you keep hittin' on me, I'll be too bruised to get married. So you don't like my idea of an elopement."

"No," she said, "We're gonna do this right. San Francisco style. As soon as we get home, I'm calling the Legion of Honor to book a wedding for you and me and for Annie and Justin. It'll be small—no more than sixty people—but it'll be stylish. What do you think?"

I had forgotten how beautiful the California Palace of the Legion of Honor that Alma Spreckels, of the famous sugar refining family, had persuaded her husband to create here where the Pacific Ocean meets San Francisco Bay. She got the idea from the French pavilion at the 1915 Panama Pacific International Exposition. This setting, which is a replica of *Palais de la Legion d'Honneur*, the eighteenth-century Paris

237

landmark, is truly one of the most beautiful places in the whole state of California.

I said, "I liked the idea of eloping, but since the Legion of Honor is so beautiful and so close to Seacliff, I'll happily be wed there. Have you told Annie?"

Liz said, "Didn't Annie and I tell you not to get mixed up in all these plans? It's women's work."

I know when to keep my mouth shut. I never had a plan to elope, but I always like a chance to test the waters now and again. We sat in companionable silence till the wheels touched down at SFX or whatever the baggage handlers call the airport. When we emerged from the baggage claims area and made our way to the front door, I saw the most beautiful silver Mercedes I've ever seen. Standing next to the car was a man I took to be Sam. I'd never met her late sister or any of her relatives since our "California Idyll" was more or less conducted in secrecy from the Denneys back then. I assumed Liz had told Sam, the only member of her family left as far as I knew, what was going on in the world of 1971.

Sam Hawkins and I were introduced, and I decided he had no ill feelings about a renegade Texan marrying into the last of the Denneys. He was cordial, which was a relief to me, and he seemed to have a genuine affection for his sister-in-law. He drove us out of the airport and into what people out here call "The City." When we got to Liz's house in Seacliff, I was speechless—and that's new for me. The house was a beautiful white stucco with a red tile roof and enough lawn to play croquet on. I wondered if anybody played croquet anymore. The house made the Adams mansion look like something the live-in couple would be ashamed to set foot in. I almost said "Wow!" but then I caught myself.

When we went in Supiyawlet and Felipe were waiting at the front door ready to receive the lady of the manor. I had to remind myself that I'd better not slip when I talked to Sue. She probably hated Kipling too and had buried that Burmese name years ago. They seemed overjoyed that Liz was back, but I could sense a little wariness when they greeted me. Who could blame them, for I was an alien presence in an otherwise orderly household. I was glad when I learned that they lived in their separate quarters out back. I didn't want them to encounter me the way Rosie had when she saw Liz in my arms. I'd have to really work to accustom myself to the kind of staff that I feared Liz was used to. I didn't quite know what Felipe's role was. I doubted that he was a butler, and he sure as hell wouldn't be my valet. I'd seen too many English movies where the valet dressed the lord of the manor to be able to turn myself into the Earl of Seacliff. I couldn't wait for Liz to take me aside and tell me how to fit in here. But let me tell you, I wasn't about to jump ship even if I had to be dressed by Felipe.

Sue had tea for us since she knew when we'd be back. Sam had come here to get the Mercedes and to let her know about when to expect us. Sam left his car here because he wanted Liz to see the Mercedes in perfect running condition and for me to see the glorious product of German engineering. Apparently Liz had told him about the famous LaSalle, so Sam and I talked classic cars while he drank the Darjeeling Sue had prepared and consumed about eight finger sandwiches. Then he said he had to run. The Oakland Athletics were playing a night game and he didn't want to miss the first pitch. Sam seemed to be ready to accept me into Liz's world since I had an appreciation of fine engineering. Or maybe he knew better than to cross Liz.

When Sam was gone, I began my questioning about how the household operated. Liz laughed and said, "You were put off when you saw Felipe standing at attention when we came in, weren't you?"

"I was just a little worried that he might be my valet or something. We don't have such back in the Lone Star State."

She looked around to see that Sue and Felipe had disappeared into the vast caverns of the house. "I knew you'd worry when you saw him. I could have told you all about it before we got here, but I like to see old John Q. sweat a little. Relax. He doesn't work for me. He's an accountant with the City of San Francisco. When Herb hired Sue about fifteen years ago, she would only come if her husband could share the servants' quarters out back. By the way, it's never called that nowadays. It's the guesthouse. Felipe is a comfort to Sue because she always fears some intruder will break in and rob or rape us. I always felt better to have Felipe here after Herb died. There's not much crime in this part of town, but women alone are a temptation to some desperate thieves and robbers. And old Felipe was a captain in the Philippine Army and knows how to use the Sig Sauer that Herb bought for him years ago."

239

"So the only person I have to worry about catching us in bed together is Sue. I'm sure she won't be as startled as Rosie. I assume you told her we're on the verge of gettin' married."

Liz started to punch me, but held back. "Of course, silly, who do you think will stage manage the whole show at the Legion of Honor? I'll be too busy blushing and looking demure to manage a crowd. Oh, and I'm paying Felipe to help her keep order."

"Why? Do you think all my Texas gang will wreck the furniture or something? Or that Annie's mother'll have a calf when the vows are pronounced? By the way, who's pronouncing the vows? You're an Episcopalian, Annie's a Methodist, Justin's a Presbyterian, and I am what you call ecumenical or heathen or freethinker or all of the above."

Liz was fully in charge now. "Oh, Annie and her mother and I have that solved. We have the Reverend Spike Jacobs, a Unitarian. How about them apples?"

"Spike? Oh, come on Liz. Spike!"

Liz said, "I don't name 'em, I just hire 'em."

I took a long walk down to the facilities and was astounded at how luxurious this whole house was. Even the bathrooms would do honor to the White House. After I had washed my hands and made the long trek back to the living room—or parlor or drawing room or God knows what you called it in a house this grand—I found the tea things removed and Sue nowhere in sight.

"Well, we have more than a month till the fateful day. What are we going to do till then?"

Liz rose and began looking in a breakfront. "First we're gonna have something stronger than tea. I asked Sue to get Felipe to lay in some Johnnie Walker Black for you and some Hendrick's for me so I can have a martini. I'm sure it's five o'clock somewhere. Probably in Bodark Springs about now."

"Johnnie Walker. I thought you'd never ast."

Liz laughed out loud. "I can't believe you sometimes. Now, as to what we're gonna do for a month. Well, we're gonna exercise. You can't get married if you're not in fightin' trim. It's about a mile across the Golden Gate Bridge, so that's two miles there and back, and you'll find that there is a pretty good gym in the basement—treadmill, resistance machines, a few free weights from Herb's days here, and a dandy massage table. I always need a massage after my walks. Can you rub out the kinks?"

"I used to be able to when we lived on Hancock Street, and we didn't even have a dandy massage table. So, all we're gonna do is train for the Reverend Spike's ministrations day after day?"

"No, We're gonna run the wheels off that Mercedes. When we aren't trekking across the bridge and back, we're gonna dance at the Top of the Mark, drive the Mercedes up to Coit Tower to watch the submarine races the way we used to in Hawaii, ride the cable cars, go to all the plaques that mark where events in *The Maltese Falcon* took place, ride the ferry to Oakland, and then we'll go to all those places we used to drive to in your Fords. But this time we'll travel in style, in the most beautiful Mercedes you've ever seen. We'll go to Santa Cruz, Bodega Bay, Salinas, Modesto, Mount Shasta, Carmel, and Sacramento to see the Governor's Mansion that Ronald Reagan wouldn't live in because he says the street noise kept him awake. Ha! Where else did we go back then? Oh, I remember we would go up and down the Central Valley to see all the crops being harvested. You claimed to have an interest in agriculture back then. I didn't believe it, but if you want to see garlic and lettuce and radishes and celery springing from the earth, we can sure do it."

"I don't think radishes spring from the earth. But 'whither thou goest' etc., etc., etc."

There was no sign or sound of Sue, so we drank our drinks in perfect calm. She made her own martini, since I had no idea how much vermouth you put into what I considered a lady's drink. I knew how to pour Scotch, though, and I was generous with the JW Black. I suggested a nap after a while and hoped if we jumped into bed, Sue wouldn't come in screaming like Rosie or worse, Felipe waving his Sig around. We dozed off and then we slept. We awoke while it was still light, but evening shadows were crowding in. We dressed again and went into a kitchenette or butler's pantry or morning room or some space alien to me to find a table laid out with salads and cold cuts and San Francisco's famous sourdough bread. There was even a small Crock-Pot-like thing with delicious fish soup. I suppose Liz had spent time on the phone telling Sue about the abstemious old man she was moving into her Kingdom by the Sea.

We started the next day with the regime Liz had outlined. We spent the first week I was in San Francisco walking back and forth across the Golden Gate Bridge and testing the exercise machines in the basement. By the third day, I began to see why the bridge had such a high suicide rate: people making forced marches by sweethearts intent on whipping them into shape simply jumped. I did manage to hone my skills on the massage table in Liz's basement. Now not only were my legs suffering from the power walking, but my hands were sore from probing and kneading the muscles in Liz's back and legs. We did drive the Mercedes all over the peninsula, but we didn't make the long tips I had been promised. I hadn't seen a single redwood tree or a waterfall in Yosemite or a radish springing from the earth in the San Joaquin Valley.

I drove to various emporia and waited in the car as Liz did mysterious business inside. When I questioned the intention of the trips and long waits, Liz only repeated the Liz-Annie mantra: "This is women's work." I don't mean to say we had no fun in that week. We drove to Coit Tower to watch the submarine races. (I shouldn't be so cryptic in case my old friends from Bodark ever see these notes I'm making. There are no racing submarines in the Bay—or anywhere else; the phrase is one invented by people who go parking near bodies of water.) After a light workout one morning, we fired up the Mercedes, set out across the Bay Bridge through Oakland and then past the Gold Rush country and up through the Donner Pass to see Lake Tahoe. This was a sentimental journey because we'd made this trip in my 1934 Ford and had lunch in a quaint little log restaurant. It was a late lunch, and when we were almost finished, a small chip of pine fell from the ceiling into her snifter of Grand Marnier or Drambuie or Courvoisier or some cordial. We found the same restaurant and hoped a chip would fall to recapture the moment. None did, and we made our way around the lake and descended the mountain as the sun painted the western sky to prove that this was indeed the Golden State.

On Saturday Liz seemed to ease off on the activities, and then I knew something was up. We slept late, but Liz lay in bed after I got up, got dressed, and was on the porch eating my Raisin Bran and looking out toward the sea. When I went back inside, she was still lying in bed drinking the coffee Sue had brought her on a tray with cream and sugar but no daffodils. I saw I had to put my mind to the flower situation if I was to stay here four or five months of each year. A woman as beautiful as Liz needed to have flowers on her breakfast tray. If not daffodils, maybe petunias. No. Daffodils were required even if I had to plant some.

After an hour of wondering what she was hiding from me, I looked up as she came out on the porch and said, "Is the car all gassed up?"

I said, "I doubt it. We drove a lot the last few days and that Mercedes is not easy on the petrol."

She said, "While I pretty myself up some more, would you be a dear and take it to the Shell station and get it filled—oh, and the oil checked?"

"You know that much of my wealth is in Texaco stock, don't you? But if you want to make the Dutch Royal Family richer, I'll go to your place."

She laughed, "Take it where you will, but don't start driving all around. We have to make a little trip this afternoon."

"Great. I'm eager to get on the road. Where are we going today?"

She looked mysterious and said, "You'll see. Just get the car ready. Oh, and would it be too much trouble to get it washed while you're out?"

I agreed that the beautiful Mercedes needed a wash, so I set out on my appointed rounds. I was as impressed with this 1956 Mercedes as I was with my LaSalle. Well, almost. One thing, besides its beauty, was that it was the first Mercedes with automatic transmission, and that made it perfect for going up and down these hills in "The City." With standard transmissions, you had to manage to hold the clutch pedal and the brake down when you had to stop at every cross street, and you had to be quick to release the brake and let out the clutch and feed the gas before the car had a chance to roll backward into the damned Bay. I mastered the technique when I had those Fords out here in the thirties, but I was glad I didn't have to wrestle with a stick shift. This automatic tranny was perfect for the hills.

After I brought the clean—and filled—car back, my mysterious sweetheart said, "All right, let's go."

"Where?"

She smiled her sweet smile and said, "Just start driving down the peninsula like you're going to Redwood City."

"What's in Redwood City that's such an attraction as to make you dress up in such San Francisco-style finery?"

"Just drive."

I drove as instructed, and when we got to the entrance to the airport, she told me to turn in and take her to Gate 7. I was through asking questions to which I knew I wouldn't get answers, so I kept quiet and maneuvered the car onto the airport grounds. She then said, "When we get to the gate, let me out and drive around in the parking lot for ten minutes and then pick me up. If I'm not there, take another turn and I'll be there."

On the third trip around, I saw her with enough luggage to fill two trunks, and then standing behind one of the piles was Annie. Justin came out the automatic doors with a third bag. I could see why Liz was so mysterious: she wanted to see my surprise when the young folks came for the wedding two weeks early. I saw it all now: the four of us would see the redwoods and the sea from Bodega Bay and the Saroyan country around Fresno and the Steinbeck country around Liz's home town of Salinas and the Jack London country up north. Not to mention the wine country around Napa and Russian River. This would be more vacation and less grueling exercise, and maybe I wouldn't be tempted to throw myself off the Golden Gate Bridge unless Liz meant for Justin and Annie to pound the steel across the bridge with us every single day.

I got out of the car and was hugged by Annie and then by Justin, who seemed to have taken me on as a grandpa too. I knew Justin was an orphan, so Annie must have sold me to him as an ancient ancestor. When we got the suitcases stowed in the trunk and two on the back seat where I was now sitting with Justin, Annie said, "I can't believe I'm here. I've never flown first class before. I can't wait to see your house. I can't—"

No telling how long she would've gone on if I hadn't said, "Liz and I have decided that we should all elope and get married in Reno. Save all that bustle with the Legion of Honor."

Annie squealed, "Grandpa John, you wanna kill my poor mother? She's been reading up on this Legion place and has ideas about—"

Liz interrupted. "Pay him no mind. We're gonna have a double wedding that'll make your mother proud. She may have a cow, as you say, when she sees the place you're going to be married in."

I wanted to know about the trip out and when her parents would arrive and whether Justin and I would have to endure some dreadful bachelor party and whether we had to hide out from the brides on the wedding day. Suddenly I found myself as giddy as Annie was. Since I knew nothing about Annie and Justin's sudden arrival, I didn't know what the plan was. I had been told to mind my business since all this was "women's work," but I was a little bit curious to know who was where and what was what in all this melee. It turned out that Justin and Annie were staying with us and that her parents were determined to be on Nob Hill, either at the Fairmont or the Mark Hopkins. They wouldn't be here till two days before the wedding. That was about the same time that all my tribe checked in at the St. Francis. And, no, Justin and I wouldn't have to avoid seeing the brides till the wedding actually took place. And no, I wouldn't have to wear something borrowed and something blue—that was "women's work." I feared, though, that Justin and I would fall into the hands of my sons for some awful bachelor party. Oh well. I'm not sure all this folderol was better than gettin' married in the front seat of a Model A. Dulcie and Floyd stayed married for fifty years or so. And I hoped for that long for me and Liz—and even more for Annie and Justin.

You can imagine how Annie took on when we drove into the city of San Francisco. She marveled at the Bay and the bridges and Alcatraz off to the right. She couldn't believe how San Francisco was made up of hill after hill. After all, this girl came from Midland, which is flat and dry and awful (my opinion). Her eyes grew wide as she saw Liz's house. Here was a woman of twenty-five or so turning into a fourteen-year-old girl. She loved Seacliff and the view of the Golden Gate Bridge. Once inside, she couldn't believe the luxuriousness of the furnishings. She wore me out and probably embarrassed Justin with all her enthusiasm. Liz took it as I knew she would. She was once Annie, but that was a long time ago.

We did all the things I knew Liz had planned. We spent a week in and out of town. Up to Napa for a day, down to Carmel to look at the ocean, over to Sacramento to see the capitol, up north so Annie could see the famous tree with the tunnel cut into it so cars could pass through. Annie drove carefully through it so as not to scratch Liz's beautiful car, which Annie pronounced the equal of the LaSalle. Hurt my feelings, too, or so

I said. I never drove an inch during this week. Liz too got a rest since Annie and Justin couldn't wait to pilot the Mercedes.

One afternoon before all the wedding people got to town, Liz, Annie, Justin, and I strolled over to the Cliff House for dinner, but we were early and stopped at Seal Rocks to see what Browning calls "the dropping of the daylight in the west." It was almost sundown, and the clouds were gathering as the sun began its descent. Justin and I walked ahead of Liz and Annie right up to the edge of the cliffs so he could get a good view of the Seal Rocks and the sunset, which was red and gold and blue all at once. The sunset was at its glorious best, and Justin said, "I can see why this is called the Golden State. Look at the golden sun coloring those clouds."

I said, "Maybe you're looking in the wrong direction if you really want to see why this state is golden."

He was puzzled by an old man's obvious confusion, so he said, "I don't get it, Grandpa John."

I said, "Don't spend all your time looking at the beauty out toward the west. Turn around and look to the east at those two beautiful women who came out here to watch the sunset with us. They are what make this the Golden State. Those two 'Girls of the Golden West.'"

He looked. Then he smiled. He didn't need any help in seeing what I had known for a long, long time.

CHAPTER 20

W hen all the outsiders hit town, things got really busy. One night the ladies all gathered at the Mark Hopkins and the men at the St. Francis for the dreaded bachelors' evening. Homer had brought a pair of limited edition Johnnie Walkers. The two bottles must have set him back four hundred bucks. Edward bought twenty-five-year-old Balvenie for the single malt crowd. I had never seen such an outlay for Scotch in one place.

Eddie said, "I have some information to impart. First, I found out who was making the threatening calls and slipping notes under doors. It was Helen Wilson, who has worked as a waitress in the hotel for several months."

Charlie said, "So she sent that note to Lucy about Pop? How did you find her?"

Eddie said, "She was slipping a note under my door when Maybelline saw her and told me 'that new girl was runnin' somethin' under your door.' When I found the note, it said, 'Tell your poppa to get right with God before it's too late.' When I confronted Helen Wilson, I told her that the sheriff could send her to prison. Of course the sheriff can't just send anybody to prison, but she didn't know that. She started crying and saying she was doing what her grandma told her to do.

I said, 'I don't think your grandma knows the penalty for blackmail. How much money did she ask for?'

"Helen said, 'She don't want no money. All she wants is for your daddy to confess his sins and get right with the Lord.'"

It turns out that her grandmother was a Scroggs and knew that somebody named Adams had been in some kind of feud with the Scroggses from back in the early thirties. She told Helen to go to Texas and find out who had killed Estes and Jeremy back in Polk County. It had to be an Adams, and all she had to do was find the right one and bring him to Jesus. She said there was never any question about money. They wanted justice and to save the soul of the man who carried on the feud.

"And," Eddie added, "they figured that you were their man." All three sons stood silent for a moment, looking at their daddy.

I said, "I remember that girl that was waiting on tables for the last month or so. I thought there was something strange about the way she looked at me, but I put it down to country-girl shyness. Well, Eddie, does that end it all? No more notes or calls? And what about the John Doe warrant I heard about years ago. They were looking for the man who killed the Scroggs boys."

Eddie said, "That's all settled too. There is no warrant for John Doe or person or persons unknown in Polk County."

Homer said, "How did you manage that trick?"

Eddie told how his investigator, an ex-FBI man named Miles McAdoo who did a lot of work for him, went to Polk County and searched the records. It turns out that about twenty-five or more years after the shoot-out, an old man named Mitchell Cogburn from out in the Shady settlement had his daughter read him the *Mena Star* one day—old man Cogburn can't read—and she read that the local law was looking to find who was involved in killing the Scroggs boy back in the thirties. Old man Cogburn got his son John Earl to drive him into town and told the county judge that he had seen the shooting and that the Scroggs boys tried to kill "some man with a dark beard. Wounded him the shoulder, but the man managed to kill the Scroggs boys. I was still huntin' at the time and seen it all."

"So about twenty-five or more years ago," Eddie concluded, "the case was closed. The judge believed old man Cogburn and said the stranger, whoever he was, had obviously acted in self-defense. End of story."

Homer asked, "Then why was Dad getting all those notes suggesting that he was somehow mixed up in this? Wait—wasn't it somebody named Scroggs who killed Uncle Fred and Grandpa Adams? Is that what this Helen person was off on?"

What the hell. I might as well clear everything up. "I was the man with the dark beard, and I shot and killed the Scroggs boys because they threatened to kill every Adams in East Texas. I meant to go up there and hunt 'em down and kill 'em before they got to us. But they shot first. This fellow Cogburn has it right."

You could have heard a pin drop.

Damn, I hate that cliché. But you could have.

Homer said, "You had a beard? Damn!"

I said, "It itched like hell, and I was glad to get rid of it after I had killed those men."

Charlie said, "I'm a son of a bitch! You went in the woods and killed somebody? I mean, I mean, I mean . . . here you were a mild-mannered school teacher, and you shot up—"

Eddie interrupted "So you didn't go to California—"

I said, "Enough! Hell, yes, I went to California. How do you think I met Liz? I went to Arkansas. And then I went to California. You can read my whole confession when you get back to Bodark."

Homer said, "You wrote out a confession—"

I interrupted. "Eddie, what about Helen? Are you gonna fire her? I mean it seems to me that her intentions weren't criminal or even mean. How is she taking this?"

Eddie said, "I told her the whole story and showed her the report from McAdoo. She was satisfied, though she still wants Pop to get right with God. She and her folks belong to some kind of Holiness Church that hates the idea of revenge. So all they wanted was to save a sinner's soul."

Charlie asked Eddie, "Did you have to pay her off? I'll help out if you were out a lot of money

"Me too," Homer said.

"No," Eddie said, "I paid her tuition to beauty school in Sherman. That was her aim in life, she said—to learn to fix hair."

I turned to Homer and said, "Well, now that all this is out, I wrote the whole story and put it in a safety deposit box back at the Eastis County State Bank. Then, before we left, I took it out of the box and put it in the top left-hand drawer of my desk. The key is in the middle drawer. Get it and read it. I wrote it up for Eddie to find once I am in my grave in about twenty years, but I decided since whoever was causing the ruckus wouldn't stop till I made a move, I took it out and put it in my desk and thought I might send it to the *Dallas Morning News*."

Charlie said, "Really? You were gonna put this in the paper? Pop, what were you thinking?"

"No, Charlie, I was not gonna put it in the paper! I just decided to let Edward read it after I'm married and living happily ever after out here in San Francisco. But now the heat is off, the cat is out of the bag, and you can all rush home and read it."

Eddie said, "Does Liz know all this?"

"She does and she still wants to marry me. Killer and all. So tomorrow let's go and make honest men out of Justin and me."

Then they performed as sons are wont to do.

Eddie asked me if I was sure. He didn't say about what.

Then Charlie got me aside and asked me if I was sure. He didn't either.

Then Homer, as we were leaving, didn't ask me if I was sure. He said, "You're making the best damn move of your life."

I was sure.

The wedding day was a blur. Justin and I dressed in normal suits—no morning coats or top hats, no spats or striped pants. The ladies were dressed in some of the finest clothes that I. Magnin can provide. Liz had outfitted Annie for the occasion and had spared no expense. It was becoming embarrassing to Justin and Annie that Liz had popped for first-class airfare for them—both ways—and a proper costume for the ceremony. She had offered her house for the honeymoon as soon as we were out of there. Annie asked, "Where will you and Grandpa John honeymoon?"

I said, "The Royal Hawaiian on Waikiki Beach."